D0974878

WRITING AS CINNAMON BURKE, NEW YORK *TIMES* BESTSELLING AUTHOR PHOEBE CONN DELIGHTS READERS WITH HER MOST SENSUAL AND CAPTIVATING ROMANCES YET!

Rapture's Mist "is sure to ignite a spark of passion and warm your heart."
　　　　　　　　　　　　　　　　　—*Romantic Times*

"Ms. Conn...excels as a gifted storyteller!"
　　　　　　　　　　　　　　　　　—*Rendezvous*

"Ms. Conn proves that the blazing fires of romance burn even more fiercely in the far reaches of outer space....Ms. Conn writes with a sweeping grandeur and an unerring touch for sizzling passion!"
　　　　　　　　　　　　　　　　　—*Romantic Times*

A PERFECT MATCH

"I doubt anyone actually believes the games are honest at The Diamond Mine, but when they're as blatantly crooked as yours, a man's got a right to become surly."

"Be careful," Ivory retorted. "Or you might win an opportunity for a burial in space."

Ivory's photograph hadn't really done her justice, for when she was mad, her fair coloring took on a rosy glow that was utterly captivating. That a pirate's daughter could blush, even in anger, amused Chase. "I am a pilot. Nothing else would be appropriate, but I certainly hope you'd grant me my last request."

"Don't count on it."

Playing his part to the hilt, Chase moved behind her, put his hands on her shoulders, and turned her around to face him. As he tilted her head, the side of his thumb fit the cleft in her chin perfectly, and when he bent down to kiss her, he was surprised to find their lips were an even better match.

CINNAMON BURKE

LADY ROGUE

LEISURE BOOKS **NEW YORK CITY**

A LEISURE BOOK®

January 1994

Published by

Dorchester Publishing Co., Inc.
276 Fifth Avenue
New York, NY 10001

Printed in the United States of America.

Lady Rogue is dedicated to the memory of the incomparable blues singer Janis Joplin, whose soul-searing music still soars.

Prologue

December 13, 2259

Drew Jordan stood in the icy mist, silently watching a sheer veil of fog float through the cedar forest ringing Horseshoe Bay. The dancing vapor rippled through the dark green boughs with an effervescent caress teasing his senses with poignant memories of his youth. Born and raised in Vancouver, he loved the rain and sea with a passion no woman had ever inspired. Drenched to the skin and shivering, he felt at peace with himself as he did nowhere else in the universe.

When violent earthquakes had devastated California in the twenty-first century, Vancouver had become the principal Pacific port. Soon after, British Columbia had followed Quebec's example and seceded from Canada, but rather than become an independent nation, its citizens had chosen to join the United States. Drew's bond with the beautiful land went far deeper than mere national ties, however, for he was part Haida Indian, and the spirits that whispered across the vast forests of the Northwest Coast sang in his veins.

A descendant of Haida chiefs, Drew's grandfather had filled rainy days with the magic of legend, and as Drew closed his eyes briefly, he heard echoes of the dear old man's voice. Drew had loved the tale of how Raven, lonely after the great flood, had been walking on the beach, found mankind huddled inside a giant clamshell, and had enticed the frightened beings out to play. How he envied those first men their sense of wonder as they explored their new world, for at thirty-six, he had lived through so many harrowing adventures he no longer found anything intriguing or unique.

At Drew's elbow, Control glowered impatiently and, seeing no trace of beauty in the wretched day, spoke in a caustic whine. "You're already overdue at the base, and while they will hold the shuttle indefinitely, I think you'd have some consideration for the crew even if you have none for me."

Six feet four, Drew glared down at his diminutive superior. "I'll be away for months, possibly years. What difference does a few more minutes make?"

Exasperated, Control glanced up toward the heavens and was rewarded with an eyeful of stinging rain. He sputtered and coughed. "This operation has been coordinated to the last second.

If you're not at Spider Diamond's outpost when Yale Lincoln arrives to start the brawl, you'll not be able to infiltrate Spider's operation."

Not intimidated, Drew discounted Control's warning. "Yale's far too bright a man to start the brawl without me."

"That may very well be true, but he's already en route and we can't change his orders without sending a message Spider might intercept and decode. That would endanger your life as well as Yale's. Must I remind you that you volunteered for this mission? Spider is supplying arms to colonies that were chartered for the peaceful settlement of the universe. All it will take is for one fanatic to begin seizing territory by force, and the whole concept of peaceful development of new territories will fail. War is a plague more virulent than any disease, and with Spider encouraging the acquisition of arms, it's only a matter of time before a colonial chief makes the mistake of using them. He must be stopped now, Drew, and I'm confident you can do it. Now let's get out of this accursed rain and begin."

"That was a most inspiring speech. You've missed your calling. You ought to have been a politician, or an evangelist."

Disgusted by his protégé's sarcasm, Control turned and gingerly tiptoed around the pools of rainwater dotting the sand to reach the sleek hovercraft lying in wait at the shore. Emblazoned with Alado's double triangle and lightning bolt crest, the ship served as Control's personal vehicle on the rare occasions he deigned to leave Alado's glass-walled headquarters in downtown Vancouver. To the casual observer, the impressive office building was the center from which a multiplicity of the vast Alado Corporation's operations were directed, but that it also housed the firm's highly trained intelligence unit was a secret known only to its own elite corps, and Alado's board of directors.

To the others who worked in the building, Control was merely head of an obscure research team whose annual reports made for such dull reading they were seldom opened, let alone studied. A spymaster of extraordinary skill, Control basked in his carefully cultivated anonymity, but at times like this, when one of his operatives behaved with the very same independence that was crucial in the field, he was thoroughly annoyed. Once inside the hovercraft, he shook off his heavy black overcoat, tossed his bedraggled hat aside, and sat down in the main cabin to sip a steaming cup of hot chocolate while he waited for Drew to join him. Meditation was a practice he frequently recommended, but he had never relied upon it himself and was far from calm by the time Drew finally appeared.

Control waited for him to cast off his wet coat, and towel the rain from his thick, black hair, then handed him a mug of hot chocolate and a packet of photographs. "Spider Diamond's an elusive bastard, but easily recognized. He comes from Viking stock, as does Stokes, his second in command, and Vik, who relishes distasteful assignments, apparently the more revolting the better. The Asian woman is Summer Moon, Spider's lover; the other, his daughter, Ivory.

"Be careful of her. Spider has raised her as

a son, and she's undoubtedly even more ruthless than he. Ghastly bunch of pirates is all they are, and once you have enough information to close down their entire enterprise, they'll live out the rest of their lives in the deservedly wretched hopelessness of a maximum security prison."

Drew would have much preferred something stronger than cocoa, but Control did not imbibe spirits of any kind, nor did he provide them to his operatives. In winter he urged hot chocolate on everyone, and in summer, delicate herbal teas. He was rumored to have a wife, but neither Drew nor anyone he knew had ever met her. Drew could not help but wonder if when Control and his wife got in a wildly passionate mood, they might not smear each other with the foamy whipped cream that Control heaped atop his cocoa.

Erasing that inappropriate image, Drew set his hot chocolate aside on the low table between their comfortably padded seats. "Aren't you forgetting they'll have to be tried first?"

"No, certainly not. If we didn't need evidence for a trial, we'd send in assassins rather than you. Alado won't stoop to murder, however, no matter how just our cause."

Drew opened the packet and began to shuffle through the candid photographs taken at The Diamond Mine, Spider Diamond's frontier outpost, by another of Control's minions. While the pictures were of excellent quality, the poses left a great deal to be desired. Spider had been standing at an angle, looking down, and other than unshaven cheeks and a thatch of blond hair, Drew couldn't make out much.

"Who took these?" he asked.

"Nelson, a wiry little fellow who runs with one of the Corkscrew gangs. He's a nearly invisible sort who can come and go without attracting any notice wherever he's sent. It's a valuable quality you'd do well to cultivate."

Drew scoffed at that ridiculous bit of advice. "You aren't paying me to be invisible, Control, but to match wits with the galaxy's master criminals, and survive."

Control conceded the point with a faint nod. "Nelson has his place, however. After all, you could scarcely pass as a Corkscrew at Spider's outpost."

"I wouldn't even try."

Corkscrews were youthful bands who amused themselves by boarding private starships and briefly terrorizing the owners. They diverted the craft for joyrides, but were pranksters who soon released their captives and went on their way, unlike the far more evil and ambitious pirates who seized starships and made slaves of their owners and crews. It was pirates' careers that Drew was sent out to end, and like the once famous Canadian Mounties, he always got his man, or woman as was sometimes the case.

The second photograph was of Stokes. He wore his dark blond hair long, but carefully combed off his face. Nelson had caught him in the midst of an argument, clean-shaven and intense, his mouth open, the tendons in his neck taut. Next came Vik, whose once handsome features had been thickened by years of brutal brawling. Drew flipped to the fourth photograph and found that Summer Moon was a lovely little thing, her long black hair braided in a single plait. He thought it a pity she had such miserable taste in men.

Even among a gang of pirates, the last photograph proved shocking. Ivory Diamond was a slender, blue-eyed beauty with a wild, tawny mane. Nelson had caught her in the midst of a fluid, undulating stride, but rather than her extraordinary grace, it was the deadly laser pistol clutched in her left hand that brought a gasp to Drew's lips. Dubbed the Celestial Cannon, it was an experimental prototype Drew had seen in drawings, but had never fired.

"How did Spider get a Cannon? I didn't realize they had even gone into production."

"They haven't."

"Then what's she holding?"

"It's a Celestial Cannon, all right, but one Spider manufactured himself. We've found the leak in the weapons division and ended it, but there's a possibility the Cannon isn't the only prototype Spider has. That's one of the reasons this mission is so urgent. Armed colonists are dangerous, but armed with Celestial Cannons and God knows what else, they will be invincible. As you know, the weapon was developed with the sole intention of use in the unlikely event of an invasion of Earth by savage aliens. Because none has ever even been found to exist, let alone threatened invasion, the Cannon would have been stockpiled and never fired. Or at least that was Alado's intention. It obviously isn't Spider Diamond's."

Drew studied Ivory's clear blue eyes, framed by a thick fringe of long, dark lashes. She had a remarkable beauty even in a time when cosmetic surgery was commonplace. The static quality of a still photograph didn't disguise the smoothness of her gait. She might have been a talented dancer rather than a pirate's daughter, but to hear Control tell it, she was more dangerous than her father. Hers was the best photograph of the lot, and Drew could easily imagine Nelson eyeing her with a lascivious gaze while he drank a volcano, the fuming brew illegal in colonies but favored by the lawless drifters who frequented the outposts on the frontier.

Transported by a vivid imagination, Drew let his mind wander freely and it soon carried him into the photograph he held. He heard the riotous clang of the games lining the walls of the crowded tavern. Smoke from a dozen different banned substances stung his eyes and blended with the pungent smell of grease and sweat-soaked leather.

Ivory was no longer looking toward a hidden camera, but right at him. She was easily six feet tall, but had to look up to meet his gaze. She had a slight cleft in her chin, and, unable to resist the impulse, he reached out to tip her face toward his. Without bothering to introduce himself, he kissed her long and hard, his mouth dominating hers with a lazy insistence he didn't end until he was completely satisfied she understood he intended to have a great deal more from her than a single soul-searing kiss.

He smiled at her then, with a wicked self-satisfied grin that froze on his lips as she leveled the Celestial Cannon at his chest. He raised his hands, but before he could utter the first word of an apology, she fired, and he felt his chest explode in a haze of bloody bits that sprayed over her but didn't touch her defiant stare.

Drew owed much of his success to an innate ability to imagine his adventures before he lived them, and his vivid daydreams were usually enjoyable, but dying, even in his imagination, wasn't. He winced, and swore under his breath.

"I agree," Control said. "They're a disgusting lot, but no worse than some of the others you've dealt with successfully. You'll introduce yourself as Chase Duncan, a commercial pilot who's lost not only his license for carrying contraband, but all sense of honor." Control handed over a closely spaced printout. "Memorize the background information and destroy it. Should Spider wish to access Alado's computer files, he'll find ready documentation of Chase Duncan's shady past. You've fled Earth to avoid prosecution, and can't visit any of our colonies for fear of arrest."

"That's plausible, if not very exciting."

"If your story were any more exciting, then others would be expected to know it. You needn't worry you'll run into anyone who ever knew Chase. He's one of my creations, so there's no one who can contradict your tale, providing you adhere to what's in the file. Don't embroider it. That will only make Spider suspicious."

"I understand the rules." A veteran operative who had assumed more than a dozen identities, Drew was well acquainted with Control's procedures. In his opinion, many of those procedures lacked imagination, but he couldn't argue with their effectiveness.

Meticulous about his appearance, Control squirmed unhappily in his damp clothes. His sharp, ratlike features had a bluish cast, and despite the warmth of the hovercraft's cabin, he was still cold. "As has happened when you've gone undercover in the past, Spider Diamond will probably demand you prove your loyalty by successfully completing a challenge. Whatever it is, do it. As always, you'll enjoy complete immunity from prosecution once the operation ends with Spider's arrest."

Drew re-sorted the photographs, this time placing Ivory's on top. Control had already warned him about her, but he sensed she was even more dangerous than his superior believed. Beauty and evil were a lethal mix, and he knew this mission might easily prove to be his most difficult. He just hoped it would not also be his last.

"If anything goes wrong, send my insurance money to my parents."

"There's still no woman in your life?"

Drew's laugh was his first of the day. "There are plenty of women in my life, but none I'd care to reward with that kind of money."

Control raised his mug. "To the success of your mission," he proposed. "And to Chase Duncan."

Drew was happy to drink to that. He just wished he had something far stronger to swallow.

PART ONE

Chapter One

The Diamond Mine

Ivory Diamond's glittering silver gown was slit up the side to display more than she thought necessary of her sparkling hose. She had refrained from insulting her father by saying so, however. Whenever he returned from a trip with an expensive present, she thanked him profusely and wore the garment a time or two before relegating it to the back of her closet. She sat down on her bed to pull on a pair of soft silver boots, then stood and bent over to brush out her hair with half a dozen languid strokes. When she straightened up, she gave her head a shake and the honey blond curls spilling over her shoulders danced into place.

A single glance in her bedroom mirror was sufficient to satisfy her that the studied elegance of her appearance was the same that night as all others, but inside, she lacked even a hint of the glowing serenity of her reflection. Restless, she picked through her jewelry, and after a lengthy search through the priceless gems, donned a shimmering pair of star-shaped diamond earrings. Wishing her outlook were as bright, she left her cabin for the tavern where she expected to do nothing more entertaining than deal in a few of the high-stakes card games.

Located on an asteroid that Spider had claimed without opposition twenty years prior, the outpost consisted of a seven-level compound. The family living quarters were at the top, four levels above the profitable haven for the galaxy's malcontents and felons known as The Diamond Mine. As was her custom, Ivory rode the elevator down only three floors, debarking on the outpost's security floor and using a hidden viewing port to observe the crowd gathered in the tavern on the level below. Along with excellent maintenance facilities for spacecraft, her father's outpost supplied whatever vice a traveler might crave, and as she scanned the latest group of arrivals, she wondered about the darkness of their tastes. Her job was to encourage gamblers, which was scarcely a challenge when the fever to wager and lose was in their blood, but tonight, as she had begun to do with increasing frequency, she longed to find something, or someone, who might excite her.

Midweek, there was the usual assortment of regulars, plus an occasional face she only dimly recalled from a previous visit. Discounting them, she continued to peruse the crowd until her glance fell upon a broad-shouldered man seated at the bar. His black hair curled over the collar of his gray pilot's jacket, but with his head slightly bowed as he sipped a volcano, she couldn't make out his features in the smoky mirror behind the bar. That was a small problem, however, for a spiral staircase to her right led to a hidden passageway behind the bar.

She made her way down it with light, dancing steps, and then standing behind the two-way mirror, observed the dark-haired stranger. His features proved to be even more appealing than she had expected, and knowing she would have remembered him had they ever met, she wondered who he might be. That he had come to The Diamond Mine meant he had business on the frontier. It couldn't possibly be legitimate business either, but, never having known a man who earned his living honestly, she wasn't discouraged by that fact.

She liked his looks. He had nice eyes: dark brown, shadowed by thick lashes, and framed with expressive brows. Unlike many of their regular patrons, his nose hadn't been broken so many times it had been pounded flat. When he turned to look over his shoulder, his profile was as handsome as those on ancient gold coins. His ebony hair looked as soft as silk, and aching to slide her fingers through it, she curled her hands into tightly clenched fists at her sides. She kept watching him, waiting for him to speak to the bartender, and when he exchanged a joke with the man, she was pleased by the brightness of his smile.

"What are you doing back here?" Stokes asked as he walked up beside her. "Aren't you supposed to be at your table?" He leaned against the wall and crossed his arms over his chest. A mocking smile tugged at the corner of his mouth, giving him the predatory look he so richly deserved.

Ivory hadn't heard Stokes approach, but shrugged rather than admit she had found a customer to her liking. Eager to avoid him, she took a step to the side. "What's the hurry? Nobody's going anywhere. I was just looking over the crowd."

Intrigued, Stokes surveyed the bar, and spotting Chase, quickly guessed who Ivory had been observing. As far as he was concerned, she was his girl, even if he had yet to convince her of that, and, growing jealous, he straightened up. "The man on the end got caught running contraband on routine flights for the Alado Corporation. He's no one you'd want to know."

"What sort of contraband? Drugs?"

"How should I know? He was stupid enough to get caught, and that's all that matters." He lowered his voice to what he thought was a seductive level. "I'd much rather talk about you. That gown fits you better than a snake's skin. Why don't you rub against me later, and shed it."

Stokes never missed an opportunity to whisper the sickening suggestions he mistook for flattery, but she was as disgusted as always. "Why don't you try that line on one of Summer Moon's girls? We pay them to be gullible." Right then and there Ivory decided if Stokes didn't channel his misdirected affections elsewhere, and soon, she was going to complain to her father. That prospect filled her with hope, and hurrying away, she left Stokes without a backward glance.

* * *

Chase had braced himself as he entered The Diamond Mine, but it had been devoid of the garish lights and hideously mismatched decor he had anticipated in an establishment that catered to the underbelly of the galaxy. There were no naked women dancing atop the tables, nor drunken musicians playing loudly off key. There was no raucous laughter, nor stinging ring of shouted insults. Here, there was only an oasis of elegance and calm delicately laced with the sound of a gently plucked harp.

The walls and furnishings were covered in deep midnight blue, the floor was glossy blue-black marble tile, and the lighting was provided by tiny twinkling bulbs recessed in the dark blue ceiling. The effect was as spectacular as it was unexpected, and like all the outpost's visitors, Chase felt as though he had just stepped outside on a warm summer night on Earth. He had to remind himself that he had not come to relax, however, but to destroy Spider Diamond's empire.

He had sat down at the bar, and assumed that the dark mirror behind it screened anyone who wished to observe the activity in the tavern without being seen. He had been there for nearly an hour before he felt the uncomfortable sensation of being watched. He had docked his ship, and paid the rental fee for two nights without causing so much as a raised brow, but someone must have noticed him, and he hoped it was Spider Diamond himself. Over the years, he had come to trust his instincts, and not wanting to make the unseen pirate's task an easy one, decided to move.

Cinnamon Burke

He finished the last of his volcano, a vile drink in his opinion, but one that went with the reckless image he was being paid to project. Sliding the empty beaker back across the ebony bar, he rose and after leaving a generous tip for the bartender, began to explore. He soon discovered that the tavern had several more rooms and offered diversions ranging from gambling to girls. While he wasn't interested in the type of woman who could be expected to ply her trade there, he did want to see everything else.

The adjoining room was decorated in a warm blue-gray with red accents and featured individual booths in which for a reasonable fee patrons could choose to play a number of simulation games on their own individual screen. He chose Banshee Quest, a game consisting of an aerial battle between two warring spaceships, and because he played with both daring and skill, he soon drew an audience of Corkscrews who greeted each of his victories with ecstatic whoops.

He nodded and smiled as though impressing them was exactly what he had set out to do. Sporting a variety of outlandish hairstyles that in several instances made it difficult to discern whether they were male or female, they were all dressed in black leather, and dangling from their belts like obscene fringe were collections of the grotesquely shaped keys for which the Corkscrews were named. Used to start spacecraft not much larger than a motorcycle, the shiny metal keys constantly clanged together, creating the piercing howl of a demon's tuning fork. Annoyed by that jangling distraction, Chase quickly lost interest in the usually absorbing game and relinquished the booth to the next player.

The third room held a casino, and like the first, had a lush, deep blue decor. The patrons here were older than those in the game room, and thinking Spider might be among them, Chase began to stroll around the perimeter. He recognized only a few of the games; others were frontier favorites not played elsewhere, but from the heaps of chips stacked on the tables, it was plain that a fortune could be won, or lost, there in a night.

He had circled half the room before he noticed Ivory Diamond seated at a table not twenty feet away, and he was annoyed with himself for not seeing her much sooner. She was shuffling a deck of cards with the careless ease of a practiced gambler. Not caring what game the three men already occupying her table were playing, Chase quickly crossed the room and joined them. When she looked toward him, he felt a sudden jolt of recognition, but attributed the feeling to the fact he knew her quite well from her photograph.

"If you're starting a new game, deal me in," he asked.

Through the smoky mirror, Ivory hadn't been able to appreciate the golden bronze of the stranger's skin, and when he smiled at her, the contrasting whiteness of his teeth was dazzling. He had an actor's deeply resonant voice, and she hoped he would prove talkative. Then she felt foolish for wanting more than the few words they would exchange during the game. Handsome men came and went through the outpost with such frequency that while she thought him more attractive than most, she doubted he would remain long enough for it to matter.

"We're playing poker with The Diamond Mine rules." She slid him a neatly printed list. "Most men like to watch a couple of hands before they join a game."

Chase read the bizarre set of rules and, though completely confused, shook his head. "No, deal me in." The table was covered in midnight blue felt, and the matching deep blue cards would have been invisible on it had they not borne a sparkling spray of shooting stars. Drew picked up his cards and sat back to consider his first move.

The men seated with him quickly placed their bets, and then glared at him to make his. One was a Corkscrew barely out of his teens, while the other two were in their thirties. Their shaved heads and small beady eyes made them look like unfinished androids, but Chase hadn't expected any better class of humanity from The Diamond Mine's patrons and was unconcerned about making them wait.

Because he supposedly dealt in contraband, Chase had been given sufficient cash to gamble for several days even if he lost consistently. When he actually won the first round, he was even more surprised than his three companions. He then lost what he had won in the second, but did well in the third and fourth. It wasn't until Ivory began to deal the cards for the fifth that he caught her dealing off the bottom of the deck. He was positive of what he had seen, but calling her on it didn't serve his purpose and he pretended not to have noticed while the heaviest of his bald companions lumbered to his feet.

"Spider's rich enough without his dealers cheating," the man rasped in a hoarse croak. "Give me back what I've lost, or you'll share my bed till I've been repaid."

Yale Lincoln wasn't due to arrive for another day, but Chase saw no reason to wait for a staged brawl when he could so easily prompt one now. "Sit down and shut up," he ordered. "No one's trying to cheat you."

"You calling me a liar?" the bald man bellowed.

Chase threw his cards on the table and rose with a weary stretch. "No, I'm calling you stupid and ugly."

A fiery hatred leapt to life in the belligerent man's tiny eyes, and lowering his head to serve as a battering ram, he started toward Chase, who at the last second stepped out of his way. Careening on, the bald bully plowed into a Corkscrew who had made the mistake of crossing the aisle at the wrong moment. Both men went down, slamming into the floor with a bone-jarring thud, but as he came up, the more agile Corkscrew got in a savage punch to the heavier man's nose.

A frantic swarm of Corkscrews came running to their friend's aid, while an equal number of burly pirates came to the bald man's defense. The fight began in earnest as the two sides met, and not caring who won, Chase circled the table, took Ivory's hand, and pulled her to his side. "Show me the way out," he shouted above the noise of the melee.

Ivory had seen too many fights to care how this one came out and led Chase off the casino floor out onto an observation platform where, surrounded by glittering stars, she leaned back against the rail and drew in a deep breath. "I can take care of myself," she argued. "I don't need to be rescued by well-meaning strangers."

Chase had grabbed up his winnings in his free hand, and now shoved the chips into his jacket pocket. "That's difficult to believe when you're one of the sloppiest dealers I've ever seen. You're awfully pretty, but that doesn't mean men are going to be too distracted to notice you don't play by The Diamond Mine's own rules."

Insulted, Ivory turned her back on him. She was disappointed to discover he was as obnoxious as all the other men she knew, but even more disgusted with herself for hoping for something better. Men were men, she thought sadly, and none of them were any good. "Why did you call Wayne stupid if you agreed with him?"

"Wayne? Slug would be a better name. Let's just say I enjoy rescuing women, even if they don't have the good manners to thank me."

Ivory shot him a malevolent glance. "Had Wayne raised a hand to me, he would have been dead before his palm brushed my cheek."

Chase leaned back against the rail and folded his arms over his chest. "That's a bold threat for such a careless dealer. You wouldn't need protection if you practiced your moves, or turned honest. I doubt anyone actually believes the games are honest at The Diamond Mine, but when they're as blatantly crooked as yours, a man's got a right to become surly."

"Be careful," Ivory retorted, "or you might win an opportunity for a burial in space."

Ivory's photograph hadn't really done her justice, for when she was mad, her fair coloring took on a rosy glow that was utterly captivating. That a pirate's daughter could blush, even in anger, amused Chase. "I'm a pilot. Nothing else would be appropriate, but I certainly hope you'd grant my last request."

"Don't count on it."

Playing his part to the hilt, Chase moved behind her, put his hands on her shoulders, and turned her around to face him. As he tilted her head, the side of his thumb fit the cleft in her chin perfectly, and when he bent down to kiss her, he was surprised to find their lips were an even better match. He had meant to silence her taunts in a way that would surely inspire more, but she tasted so sweet he forgot what his original intention had been. Then a searing pain tore through the side of his head, his knees buckled, and going limp, he fell and lay sprawled over the toes of Ivory's silver boots.

Grinning widely, Stokes slipped the small, perfectly weighted metal club he had used to subdue Chase under his belt, and drew back his foot, but Ivory blocked his kick.

"There's no reason for that when he won't even feel it," she cautioned.

"He'll feel a few broken ribs when he wakes, if Spider allows him to waken. If not, he won't be the first we've tossed out the airlock this week, and how battered he is won't matter."

Ivory was well aware of her father's policies, for while he welcomed all travelers to The Diamond Mine, he was the one who decided when they left, and by what means. She raised her hand to her mouth, but rather than wiping away the arrogant stranger's kiss, she caressed the deliciously warm memory of his lips. He may have kissed her without her consent, but he had been tender rather than rough, and that had been a delightful surprise.

"I don't want him beaten," she ordered firmly. "Just take him down to the tank, but keep him in a separate cage. I want my father to see him before we decide what's to be done with him."

Stokes bent down to search the unconscious man's pockets. "Won quite a bit, didn't he?" He quickly confiscated the chips, plus the cash he found, but kept rummaging through the zippered pouches on Chase's flight suit until he found his identification. He studied the laminated card, then rolled Chase over and compared the photograph to his face.

"Chase Duncan's the same name he gave when he docked. We know he's wanted, but there might be a bounty on him. I could use a little spare cash, and I'll be glad to split it with you."

"You start turning in men for bounties and you'll empty the casino. Don't do anything more than lock him up." Ivory went to the door and glanced out. Screaming Corkscrews and wild-eyed pirates were still attempting to tear off each other's limbs, and she let out a weary sigh. "Another night in paradise."

"Yeah, but it's your paradise, and owning it has got to be quite a consolation."

Ivory turned back for a final glimpse of Chase Duncan. She made no attempt to explain how little her father's money meant to her when Stokes would never understand, but at that moment, a loving kiss from a stranger meant far more to her. That was such a pathetic thought that she went up to the security floor, where the sterile surroundings didn't promise something so precious she didn't even know its name.

Having completed his search, Stokes got a firm grip on Chase and half-dragged, half-carried him to the elevator and took him down to the lower level where Spider Diamond kept the patrons who broke his rules. Dimly lit and purposely cooled so that the air always held a damp chill, he took his prisoner to a closely barred cell and stripped off his clothes. When he found Raven tattooed across Chase's back, he mistook it for a stylized eagle, and because the bird of prey was popular among pilots he dismissed it as unimportant, and delivered the savage kick that Ivory was no longer there to prevent.

Chase didn't awaken until morning, but Stokes had taken his watch and he had no way of knowing the hour. His head was throbbing with a torturous rhythm, but as he struggled to sit up, his cracked ribs complained with a wrenching pain that brought a swirling wave of nausea. He closed his eyes in an effort to subdue it, then, remembering where he was, he opened them gradually. The ache in his ribs was a familiar one, for a man in his line of work often suffered broken bones. The secret was not to move too quickly, or to take deep breaths.

Feeling that he now had control of himself, if of nothing else, he eased himself carefully into a sitting position. Then he began to look around. Bare walls were all that faced three sides of the cage, but on the fourth he found Spider Diamond observing him with the coldest glance he had ever seen. The man's eyes weren't blue but the dark gray of steel, and Chase found it difficult to be glad he had finally found him. Being naked and in pain put him at a distinct disadvantage, but he tried not to let it show.

"Who are you?" he asked.

"I'm Spider Diamond, and I already know you're Chase Duncan so don't bother with an alias. The Alado Corporation is eager to have you back. Give me a reason not to hand you over to them."

Adjusting his position with care, Chase raked his hair out of his eyes. "You've got a dealer who's absolutely worthless," he began. "When Wayne caught her cheating, I tried to defend her, but it sure doesn't look like she was grateful."

Spider hooked the leg of a stool with his foot and after kicking it into place sat down. "That's my daughter, and yes, she's prone to playing pranks. It's a fault I consider endearing. There's a rumor I toss anyone who approaches her out the airlock. It's completely untrue, but unfortunately most men believe it and avoid her. She said you kissed her, though. What makes you so brave?"

Intending to be believed, Chase started to take a deep breath, but the agony in his chest stopped him cold. "I don't know if I'd call kissing her brave, because I had no idea who she was."

Spider tilted his head to better observe Chase through the bars. "How'd you get caught?"

"I don't know. Someone hit me from behind."

"No, I'm not talking about kissing Ivory. I mean running contraband."

Chase wasn't too cold and uncomfortable to remember his cover story. "A bitter ex-girlfriend turned me in to the authorities. After what I'd spent on the bitch, I deserved more loyalty."

"Is loyalty important to you?"

"Certainly," Chase swore convincingly. "I'd never turn in a friend."

"How about an enemy?"

"There's no reason to show any loyalty to an enemy, or at least none that I can see when he'd be likely to betray me at his first opportunity. I didn't even realize I had an enemy until I was arrested. Women," he muttered, as though that word alone told his story.

Spider was dressed in an impressive navy blue flight suit with matching boots, but as in Nelson's candid photograph, he had several days' growth of beard, and his fair hair, while not overlong, was so wildly disarranged he appeared to have styled it in a wind tunnel. Amused by his captive, he probed for more information.

"What sort of contraband were you carrying?"

Chase responded with a sheepish shrug. "Well now, I called it art, but the men who arrested me swore it was pornography. As I see it, there aren't nearly enough women in the colonies, and if a man can satisfy his needs for companionship with photographs of beautiful women, I don't see how anyone can call it a crime."

Spider nodded in agreement, and continued to study his prisoner closely. After a moment, he stood, and walked around the cage observing him from all angles. Apparently pleased with what he saw, he came to a decision and returned to the stool. "I have a proposition for you."

"Good. Could we discuss it somewhere warm?"

"No, I find cool temperatures invigorating. Now, while you're obviously unaware of it, my daughter's taken a liking to you."

Chase gave his head a rueful shake, and instantly regretted it when his headache worsened. He gripped the sides of his head in a futile attempt to ease his pain. "I hope you'll forgive me for saying this, but she has an odd way of showing it."

"Perhaps, but she's inexperienced where men are concerned."

Chase had found himself in a number of peculiar situations during his career, but he could not recall one to equal this. He had expected Spider Diamond to be the usual brand of despicable cutthroat, and perhaps he was, but he had never imagined the man might want to have a heart-to-heart talk about his daughter. His teeth began to chatter.

"Just what do you mean by 'inexperienced'?"

"She's a virgin, and likely to stay that way unless she meets a man she can regard as an equal. I think you might be that man."

Control had warned him to expect a challenge, but Chase doubted that his boss had considered this bizarre a twist. He raised his hand. "Wait a minute, I'm starting to get confused. Just what is it you want me to do?"

Spider rose and kicked the stool out of his way. "I want you to marry my daughter and be an exemplary husband. You'll have to make her fall in love with you first, of course, and that won't be all that easy to do. If you need time to consider my offer, you may have it. Just tell the man who brings your food you've come to a decision and I'll come see you again."

Already at risk of hypothermia, Chase grabbed

hold of the bars and drew himself to his feet. He was shaky but remained standing. "I'll give you my answer right now, sir. I'll be proud to marry your daughter."

Spider's gaze traveled down Chase's well-muscled frame before coming to rest on his face. "Ivory must never suspect this conversation has taken place. If you ever even hint to her that it has, it will be the last words you speak."

"I understand. She'll never suspect a thing. You have my word on it, but what if after my best effort she fails to fall in love with me?"

Spider laughed as he again turned away. "Then I'll toss you out of the airlock, and your troubles will be over instantly."

Sickened by that threat, Chase remained standing while he waited for his clothes, but try as he might, he couldn't think of any way to use Yale Lincoln to get him out of this mess.

Chapter Two

Spider handed Chase a ceramic cup. Glazed an iridescent blue-green, dappled with yellow ochre, it was shaped like an iguana. The head, complete with finely detailed mouth, nostrils, and eyes, jutted from one side. The hollow body held a generous amount of wine, while the tail curled out and back over the side to form the handle. It was the strangest drinking vessel Chase had ever used and it proved to be so heavy he needed both hands to guide it to his lips. His thumb and index finger found the shallow indentations in the beast's jowls, and after the first couple of tentative sips, the fanciful mug felt as comfortable in his grasp as the finest silver goblet. As for Spider's wine, it was delicious, without being too sweet.

Chase's clothes had been returned to him within minutes of his conversation with Spider by a taciturn fellow he recognized as one of the dealers from the casino. The chips he had won and his extra cash had been in the pockets, if not the same pockets in which he had originally stowed them. Once he was dressed, his escort had shown him to a medical unit as fine as any the Alado Corporation maintained for its employees, and a few minutes beneath a healing light had ended the agony in his head and ribs.

Now he was sharing a meal with Spider at an octagonal table in his private quarters. Unlike the dark hues of The Diamond Mine, the colors here were bright, shimmering golds and rusts. Murals of scenes from classical Greek mythology were painted on the walls in such delicate shades they appeared to be meticulously restored frescoes. The light coming from the recessed fixtures in the ceiling provided the warmth and heat of natural sunlight. It was a charming room, but Chase knew better than to allow himself to grow comfortable. There was a vast difference between infiltrating a pirate's operation and actually becoming a pirate, and he never lost sight of that vital distinction.

He played with a heaping plate of steamed vegetables topped with shredded cheese, but no amount of rearranging disguised the fact he had eaten only two bites. Finally he gave up the effort and pushed away his plate. Like the wonderful iguana cup, it had been hand-thrown on a wheel, but while it matched the cup in color, it was simply a circle without any resemblance to a living creature.

"You're not fond of vegetarian fare?" Spider asked.

"Like many men from Earth, I prefer the traditional meals, but I know how costly it is to store fresh meat in space, while vegetables can easily be grown to continually replenish the food supply."

"While that's generally true, I have a meat locker to rival any on Earth and I'll see you're given something more to your liking for dinner. What do you think of my daughter's ceramics?" Spider raised his own iguana cup to his lips with one hand.

"Ivory made these extraordinary cups?"

"Yes, and the plates. She likes to keep busy." He gestured toward the beautifully decorated walls. "She painted the murals as well. She's a remarkable young woman in all respects. Ask her to sing for you sometime and you'll have an additional reason to understand why I'm so proud of her talents. I must warn you, however, that if you caught her cheating at cards last night, then it was precisely what she wanted. She's never careless, nor does she do anything without reason. But as I explained, she likes you. I have no idea why, but when have men and women ever required logical explanations to be attracted to one another?"

Before Chase could reply, Ivory joined them. She was dressed in a silver flight suit that hugged her curves as beautifully as the gown she had worn when he had last seen her. "Good morning," he greeted her warmly.

"It's afternoon," Ivory corrected. As soon as she had taken her place across from him, the same slender young man who had served Chase brought her an identical serving of vegetables and cheese. While Chase had not found the nutritious dish to his liking, she obviously did and began eating with gusto, pausing only to wind an occasional thick thread of cheese around the tines of her golden fork. She also handled her iguana cup with one hand and didn't look up until she had swallowed the last piece of succulent squash on her plate.

Spider noted the rapt attention with which Chase had watched Ivory eat and could not help but laugh. "As must be readily apparent, my daughter's manners have suffered from a lack of suitable female companionship. I find her uninhibited nature charming, however."

Propping her elbows on the edge of the table, Ivory took hold of her iguana cup with both hands and looked over it at her father. "Aren't you forgetting the delightful residents of Summer Moon's brothel? I've learned a great deal from them, but nothing I'd care to display during a meal."

"That's enough, Ivory," Spider cautioned sharply. He poured Chase more wine. "My daughter disapproves of Summer and misses no opportunity to express it. Like every family, we have our disagreements."

Chase feigned ignorance of the subject of the conversation. "Summer Moon is a person?"

"Yes, she's my woman, and manages our most intimate forms of entertainment. You'll meet her when you get back," Spider promised.

"Back from where?" Chase asked.

"I want you to accompany Ivory on the day's run to our bank."

Ivory slammed her iguana cup down on the table. "You don't even know this man."

"I don't need to know him, my pet, when he knows me and how vicious I can become should he disappoint me. Would you rather go with Stokes, or Vik?"

"No, of course not. I'd rather go alone as I usually do."

"Indulge me," Spider coaxed. "Chase came here looking for work, and I have plenty. He'll be your bodyguard today. Be back in time to dress for dinner; you know how annoyed everyone becomes when you come in late and interrupt the discussion."

Ivory looked over at Chase, her gaze so darkly menacing he had to remind himself that Spider must have some reason to believe she liked him. He forced himself to smile. "I won't get in your way."

"No more than once," she predicted flippantly. "Well, come on. We've already wasted more than enough time."

She was out of her chair and halfway across the room before Chase could rise. As he started after her, he looked back at Spider and winked, and the pirate acknowledged his gesture with a nod. Catching up with Ivory at the door, Chase did his best to make amends.

"If I insulted you last night, I'm sincerely sorry. Like your father said, I need a job more than trouble, and I don't want to make an enemy of you."

"It's a little late to decide that, isn't it?"

Chase waited until they had entered the elevator and then backed Ivory into a corner. Her eyes widened, but perceiving her reaction as surprise rather than fear, he refused to step back. "I think you enjoyed that kiss last night just as much as I did. More in fact, because you didn't get knocked out because of it."

Ivory turned her head, but Chase was standing so close she could feel the warmth of his breath against her cheek. She had thought of little but him since they had parted, but refused to admit how much his kiss had meant to her. She shared her feelings with no one, and ducked under Chase's arm and darted from the elevator as soon as the doors slid open.

They were on the level housing the docking bays and maintenance facilities. She felt much safer here where the lights were bright, and crews performing routine maintenance kept up a lively banter that filled the air with teasing jests and raucous laughter. Corkscrews, who did their own maintenance on their small ships, kept to themselves, but were a colorful addition in the bays. The stench of rocket fuel and grease hung in the air, but every few minutes huge fans supplied a thunderous burst of oxygen and gave the mechanics a chance to fill their lungs with fresh air.

Most of the ships being serviced were PJC Tomahawks, the huge transports favored by pirates, but Chase made no attempt to memorize their serial numbers to report them. "Busy place," he said.

"Don't worry, there's a crew that services my ship every morning."

Chase hadn't been concerned about flying in an unsafe ship, but when Ivory led him into a private bay, he was relieved that they'd be traveling in a relatively new shuttle. It was unmarked, but the anonymous nature of the craft simply called attention to it. Each of the corporations chartered for the exploration of space had its own insignia, as did all private craft. That Ivory's bore no colorful crest or bold lettering made it unique, and also illegal. That Spider Diamond had failed to register the ship didn't surprise Chase, but he thought the man could have at least faked the appropriate identification.

Once on board, he found that the seats in the main cabin had been removed to make room for seven tightly sealed aluminum crates. Approximately square, with handles on each side, they were small enough to be carried by a single person if their contents weren't too heavy. They were scuffed and dented from use, suggesting that Ivory made frequent runs to a bank of some sort.

There was a real danger in Chase's asking too many questions, as it would make Ivory suspicious about his motives, but a total lack of curiosity would also strike the lovely young woman as odd. Chase attempted to strike a happy medium. "Because Spider said we were going to the bank, I'm assuming those crates are full of money. How have you handled them by yourself in the past? Aren't they too heavy for you to carry?"

"Obviously not. Now come on up to the cockpit. I want to see if you can really fly."

Control never supplied a background story an operative couldn't convincingly fake, and Chase was in fact a skilled pilot. Before joining Alado's intelligence branch, he had been one of the corporation's top-ranked pilots and had flown missions all over the galaxy. He slid into the pilot's seat, buckled his seat belt, and activated the ship's navigational computer.

"Is the ship already programmed with the bank's coordinates?"

"Of course." Ivory took the co-pilot's seat and punched a coded message into the computer.

"Good afternoon, Ivory," the computer replied in a mellow male voice. "Flight time to the bank is forty-seven minutes."

"Thank you, Rex." Ivory sat back and made herself comfortable.

"You've named your computer Rex? That's a dog's name."

Ivory drummed her fingers on the padded arms of her seat. "It's actually Tyrannosaurus Rex. I have a great fondness for dinosaurs and reptiles, not dogs."

"To give a computer a dinosaur's name is still inappropriate," Chase argued. "They've been extinct for millions of years and your ship's technology is quite modern."

"Are you always such an insufferable idiot?"

Chase didn't recall another woman ever referring to him in such derogatory terms, but then most women tried to impress him favorably. It was plain that Ivory didn't share their goal. "Well, I suppose that's all in your point of view," he argued, "but I tend to look for a logical explanation for things."

"Which saps the life right out of them," Ivory countered. She leaned forward to punch in another code, and the lights at the end of the private docking bay began to flash a bright red. A siren's shrill blast signaled the opening of the metal door at the end. "Let's see if you can get us out of here without careening into the walls."

Accepting her challenge, Chase flew the ship out the bay and banked sharply over Spider Diamond's outpost to get another view of it from the air. It had been built with a standard modular design and there was nothing on the exterior

47

to indicate what a remarkable place it was. It could have been the headquarters of a mining colony, or one of the many outposts which provided maintenance facilities and provisions for travelers. Leveling out, Chase took his hands off the controls.

"Rex can take over now," he suggested.

Ivory gave Rex a voice command and the computer assumed control of the shuttle. She then turned toward Chase. "I can't remember the last time my father hired a pilot, or any man for that matter, who'd just showed up looking for work without one of our regulars to vouch for him. What's so special about you?"

"Other than my extraordinary good looks?"

Ivory brushed aside his jest without so much as a smile. "I want the truth, Chase, and if we're ever to get along, you'll have to start telling it now."

Considering his mission, that was an impossible demand, but Chase shrugged slightly, as though he weren't completely baffled by her request. "I've no family," he lied with the understated delivery in which he had been well tutored, "and no career prospects once Alado discovered I was doing a brisk business in what I still insist was art rather than pornography. Serving time certainly didn't appeal to me. Hiding out in some obscure mining colony for the rest of my life would have been an equally wretched existence I didn't deserve."

He paused and looked Ivory straight in the eye. "I don't feel I did anything wrong, other than trusting the wrong woman with information she was quick to use against me when we parted company. I can't go back to Earth, nor to any of the major colonies, so I came to the frontier where an ambitious man can still do well, and I intend to stay.

"I'd like to do even better than just getting along with you, but I'll be patient and wait until we've had a chance to get to know each other. Now I have a question for you. Who hit me last night?"

Weighing the consequences, Ivory paused a long moment before replying. "I'll tell you only because he'll brag about it at his first opportunity. It was Stokes; he's one of my father's human guard dogs. Vik's the other one. Watch out for them both."

"Thanks for the warning. Will they be at dinner?"

"No. Neither is welcome in our private quarters, which infuriates them no end. My father enjoys more stimulating conversation than either of them can provide. He prefers to have a few poets and philosophers around as guests."

Spider Diamond was proving to be a far more complex individual than Control had led him to believe, but rather than express surprise, Chase made no comment on how unlikely it was for a pirate and poet to be friends. "What about you?" he asked. "If you haven't any suitable women friends at the outpost, do you have some special male friends?"

"That all depends on what you mean by 'special.'"

Chase leaned toward her. "Close, caring, intimate. The kind who kiss you the way I do." When Ivory instantly looked away, he had his answer. From what Spider said, she had never had a lover, but she behaved as though she had been jilted and still nursed a broken heart.

49

Cinnamon Burke

She might attempt to hide behind a pugnacious attitude, but it didn't completely cover her vulnerability. He had spent enough time alone to recognize loneliness when he saw it, and he knew just how badly such an awful emptiness hurt. His objectivity blurred by feelings he had never expected to have for a pirate's daughter, he reached out to lace his fingers in hers.

Her hands were as beautifully proportioned as the rest of her, strong, yet delicate. Her fair skin contrasted sharply with his darkness, but he thought it a very handsome clash. "You're a beautiful, talented, bright young woman and I wanted you from the moment I saw you dealing cards in the casino. Now I realize you must hear those same compliments from other men so often you no longer listen, but when you know me better, I hope you'll believe I'm sincere."

Chase's hand was as warm as his words, and Ivory fought away the tears she feared he would consider pathetic. She pulled her hand from his. "I need to check the cargo." She released her seat belt and left the cockpit, but all she did in the main cabin was sit down on one of the crates and try not to let a handsome stranger play havoc with her emotions.

She could barely remember her mother. She had been told how closely she resembled her, but her memories weren't clear. She had a bottle of her mother's perfume, and its fragrance brought an almost unbearable longing for the love she still missed, but she couldn't recall a single incident they had shared. For the most part, Spider had raised her alone, with an assortment of tutors and mistresses, some of whom had actually been caring.

Now Chase Duncan had swaggered into her life, and all her instincts told her she ought not to trust him, while her heart wanted so badly to believe in his kindness. She never forgot she was Spider Diamond's daughter, however, and he had always warned her to be wary of men who made extravagant promises. He swore they always offered more than they ever gave, and he didn't want to see her hurt as so many women were. While he might not have said a man's only interest in her would be in his fortune, she had understood it without being told.

They were nearing the underground fortress where her father stockpiled all manner of stolen goods as well as the enormous amounts of cash taken in at the casino, and setting aside her conflicting hopes and fears about love, Ivory returned to the cockpit. She used Rex, in addition to her own intuition, to locate the cleverly camouflaged complex. At her signal, a docking bay built into the side of a crater slid open, and dipping low, she sailed her ship inside a wide concrete corridor and brought it down as gently as a wind-borne feather.

"This is what we call the bank," she explained. "Because we're the sole depositors, it lacks the amenities of a commercial bank, but it has the advantage of being impenetrable. Don't even fantasize about breaking into it."

"The thought hadn't crossed my mind," Chase assured her with a teasing grin. He noted the sadness in her eyes, and wondered what had occupied her mind and doubted it had been the cargo.

As soon as Ivory had closed the docking bay and repressurized the corridor, she left the ship and Chase followed her. Their footsteps echoed with an eerie ring as they approached the first door. She fed a code into the numbered panel beside the door and it slid open to reveal a small chamber in which five gleaming metal robots stood at attention.

They were human in form, and so beautifully crafted they would have passed for live beings at a distance. As close as Chase was, however, they were obviously a scientist's creation rather than God's. Their bodies were silver, and their features, which had been modeled on Spider's, were handsomely accented with gold. Fully articulated, they had taken a step forward as soon as the door had opened. Rather than the choppy movements so common in animated machines, their motions were as smooth as a living organism's.

"Come on, boys," Ivory called to them. "Time to get to work."

They were at least seven feet tall, and Chase took care to move out of their way as they marched from their chamber and, after executing a sharp left turn, continued in single file down the corridor. When they reached the shuttle, they swiftly unloaded the crates and carried the first five to the corridor's second door, where they waited for Ivory to press the appropriate code. As they carried the crates inside, Chase could so easily imagine a warehouse filled to the ceiling with stacks of neatly wrapped bills that he didn't even try to peek inside.

"What model are they?" he asked. "I've not seen anything like them."

"No, and you're unlikely to for several years. They're a prototype that's still being tested elsewhere. My father likes to keep abreast of the latest technology, and because he's the only one involved in decisions, it's easy for him to beat the corporate bureaucracies into production."

She made no mention of the industrial espionage which accounted for Spider's acquisition of revolutionary designs from laboratories in the vanguard of technological development, and Chase could not help but wonder if she knew that her father had probably stolen the plans for the remarkable robots just as he had the Celestial Cannon. "He must have not only the best engineers and technicians in the galaxy, but the finest laboratories as well if he's capable of producing mechanical men of such high caliber."

Ivory dismissed Chase's praise with a careless shrug. "They're merely drones we use for their strength. They have no special mental capacity. Rex is infinitely more complicated."

Chase watched two of the robots return to the ship for the last two containers. "Obviously they can count. Only two of them went back for the last of the crates."

"Two-year-olds can count."

That Ivory was stubbornly refusing to consider the elegant robots more valuable than a forklift annoyed Chase. "That may be true, but your robots can not only count, they can do heavy manual labor, and don't have to be fed or paid. After an initial investment, mines could run far more cheaply with robots than human miners. Has Spider considered going into mass production?"

"The mines already use a great deal of robotic equipment."

"Yes, along with human miners. What if you were to render the human component unnecessary?"

Ivory looked in the doorway and noted how far the robots had gotten with counting and stacking the previous day's receipts. Satisfied they were working at optimum efficiency, she returned her attention to Chase. "When you were a child, did you ever hear the fairy tale about the goose that laid the golden egg?"

"Yes, I remember it, why?"

Ivory shook her head as though he were incredibly dense. "In addition to the minerals shipped from the mining colonies, a great deal of cargo goes into them. Occasionally some of it is diverted, and large profits are made. Much of that profit ends up in our casino. Take away the human miners, and the amount of supplies needed to keep a mine running would decrease dramatically, as would our profits. Now, we could manufacture robots, or simply run The Diamond Mine and bring a fortune out here every day. Which strikes you as the most cost-effective operation?"

"You might make money in the short term with that philosophy," Chase agreed, "but eventually someone else is going to begin producing a similar robot, and then the question will be moot. The robots will be in the mines, and you'll be out of business."

"Fortunately, my father has no shortage of interests, Chase, and The Diamond Mine is only one of them."

"That's why I'm here. It's where the opportunities lie."

"Then speak to my father about heading up a new robotic division. I'd rather spend my time on other things."

Chase hoped she wasn't involved in the illegal production of the Celestial Cannon, but because he had seen a photograph of her holding one, he thought it likely that she was. He would leave that subject for later, when he knew her better. "Are you talking about art? I think your iguana cups are splendid, as are your murals. If you have a studio, I'd like to see it when we get back to the outpost."

"Are you serious?"

"Yes, of course, why wouldn't I be? I've been in several artists' studios and I've always found them to be fascinating places."

"Oh yes, I'd forgotten. You're into pornography."

"No, I'm not. I was selling art. I wish I had some of my samples to show you. I handled work by several artists and photographers who regarded the female body with an awe bordering on adoration. I wasn't selling filth."

"So you say."

The robots had completed their task, returned the now empty cases to the shuttle, and marched back into their chamber with the same smooth precision as they had left it. Unlike human workers, they were content to remain at attention until next called into use. Ivory said no more about them, but Chase was still certain he had seen something extraordinary.

As they reboarded Ivory's ship, Chase glanced

over his shoulder. The corridor might have run a mile back under the surface of the asteroid and he could make out the recessed openings of more than a dozen doors. Could this be where Spider stored the weapons he was reputedly selling to colonists? he wondered. That was one of the things he had been sent to discover, but for now he took the pilot's seat and pretended to have no interest other than impressing the maddeningly distant Ivory Diamond.

When they reached the outpost, Ivory reluctantly consented to show Chase her studio, but as they approached the elevator that served her family's private quarters, two men moved out into the corridor to block their path. Chase recognized them as Stokes and Vik from the photographs that Control had shown him. Chase was amazed when Ivory took a protective step in front of him, but, confident he could take care of himself, he elbowed his way around her. He smiled at Stokes, as though he weren't eager to twist his head right off his neck.

Just in time, he stopped himself from letting on that he recognized Stokes. It was an amateurish error, but his usual professionalism was difficult to maintain around this woman. Pulling himself together, he greeted the two men as though they were strangers. "If you have business with Ms. Diamond," he began, "make an appointment with her social secretary. She's busy with me now."

Stokes took another step closer. He hooked his thumbs in his belt, and then spoke in a surly tone that matched his pose. "The last time I saw you, you were lying naked in a cage. I don't know why

Spider let you out, but I don't take orders from anyone but him and Ivory."

Chase turned to Ivory. "Is this Stokes?"

Ivory nodded, and provided introductions that consisted of no more than a brief announcement of names. Having satisfied Chase's curiosity, she spoke to Stokes. "You've overstepped your bounds so many times you've obviously forgotten them. Chase is with me, and that's reason enough for you to show him some respect. Now, we've business upstairs, and you two ought to be screening the early arrivals at the casino."

Ivory hit the call button for the elevator, and it slid open immediately. She took Chase's elbow to draw him in, and the door closed before Stokes or Vik could utter more than a frustrated hiss. "Stay away from them," she warned. "They're no smarter than our robots, and that makes them dangerous to be around."

"I've already learned that," Chase argued, "but I've lived without your protection for thirty-six years, so I'd appreciate it if you let me handle Stokes and Vik on my own."

"I'll do what I damn well please," Ivory countered. "Besides, if you were so good at taking care of yourself, you'd still be working for Alado rather than hiding out on the frontier."

"You may have a point there." Looking decidedly sheepish, Chase shoved his hands into his jacket pockets.

"Perhaps you'd rather see my studio another time."

"No, lead the way."

A man who obviously enjoyed living well, Spider had living quarters as large as The Diamond

Mine. Ivory led Chase to the wing she described as her suite, then opened the door to a spacious, brightly lit room whose high ceiling made it perfectly suited for an artist's studio. At one end were two wide tables, a potter's wheel, and a kiln, along with a bank of cupboards containing her clay, tools, and glazes.

A mirror lined the far wall, and the oak flooring served as rehearsal space for dancing. Off to one side stood an easel, and another set of tables loaded with painting supplies. Clearly the studio was used for a variety of artistic endeavors. Curious as to what Ivory might be painting, Chase walked over to the easel.

An angel was the last thing he would have expected, but Ivory had begun to paint one of such spectacular beauty he was stunned. As in the murals he had seen earlier, she had used muted shades of rust and gold. The ethereal being radiated light, and yet seemed achingly human. Her arms outstretched, her gaze cast heavenward, she seemed suspended between an earthly world and the divine. Serenely beautiful and lithe, the angel resembled Ivory, but had glorious masses of red curls that were gently blown against her wings.

"This is magnificent," he said. "Is it a self-portrait?"

"Thank you, but no. I meant it to be my mother."

Chase had been given no information about Ivory's mother. "Tell me about her," he coaxed.

"There's nothing to tell. She died when I was small, and I can't really remember her."

"What does your father say about her?"

Ivory moved to a table and absently stirred the

brushes soaking in a jar of turpentine. "Nothing really. By the time I was old enough to ask, I could see that my questions caused him unbearable pain. I don't think he really loved any of the other women who shared his life."

"Not even Summer Squash?"

"It's Summer Moon!" Greatly amused by his jest, Ivory began to laugh with a pure, sparkling giggle.

Chase stared as Ivory's usually serious demeanor slipped away, revealing a young woman who clearly loved to laugh and did not have nearly enough opportunity for fun. Charmed, he pulled her into his arms and kissed her, lightly at first, but with increasing insistence until she opened her mouth to accept a deeper tribute. He wound his fingers in her hair, holding her close until he felt her arms encircle his neck and knew she had no desire to get away.

As before, she tasted sweet, and filled his embrace so comfortably he soon eased his hands down to her narrow waist, and then to her hips. He pulled her against him, blatantly proving how strongly she affected him. From the instant he touched her, it took no effort at all, no conscious thought that he was merely part of a well-constructed plot to catch a criminal. No indeed, he was merely a man who hungered for the same bliss as the vibrant beauty in his arms, and he was sorry the well-equipped studio had no bed.

When at last Ivory pulled away, he noted her flushed cheeks and breathless gasp, and knew they shared the same delicious dizziness. "Hey, come back here." He reached for her hand, but she eluded him again, and he remained still rather than pursue her. There was not simply the risk of rejection, but Spider's wrath to deal with as well, and he did not want her complaining about him to her father.

"I suppose you're right," he admitted. "If we get any more distracted, we won't have to worry about arriving late for dinner. We won't get there at all."

Ivory took another trembling step backward. "How do you do that?"

"Do what?"

Fear guiding her words, Ivory just shook her head. She did not want him to think her as inexperienced as she was, and surely admitting that his kisses affected her so strongly would merely amuse him. She could not bear the thought that he might laugh at her for enjoying his kisses, and quickly took herself in hand. "Find André; he's the man who served our lunch. He'll show you to a guest room, and provide formal clothes for dinner."

She left the studio before Chase could beg her to stay, but he was in no hurry to leave. He remained to study her painting, and this time had the insight that the red-haired subject was not sublimely floating to heaven but desperately seeking to leave Earth. Was this what Ivory wanted too? he wondered. Did she wish to escape a pirate's world and explore the galaxy beyond?

She was not what he had been led to expect, and if he could turn her against Spider, then he could destroy the Diamond empire from within. It wasn't the plan he had been given, but that did not mean it wouldn't work. One of the reasons he had been so effective in his undercover assignments had been his ability to turn every event to his own advantage. His instincts told him that Ivory held the key to Spider's demise.

He checked his watch. If he was quick about it, there would be time to find Yale before dinner; if not, he would be forced to find a way to slip away later and meet him in The Diamond Mine. Thinking that the next time he kissed Ivory, he did not want to have to stop for any reason, he set out to find Yale now. After sending Yale away, he would devote himself to following Spider's orders and do his best to give Ivory a night she would always remember.

Chapter Three

Even in the afternoon the ambience in The Diamond Mine was one of seductive serenity. Chase scanned the room, searching the dark corners for Yale Lincoln, and finally spotted him seated at the bar. They had worked on numerous assignments together, but their association had always been one of aggressive rivalry rather than friendly competition. It wasn't because they were too different to appreciate each other either; it was because they were much too similar in style and taste.

Also in his mid-thirties, Yale was another of Alado's pilots who had been recruited by Control to work in the intelligence division. At six feet two inches tall and 190 pounds, he was only slightly smaller than Chase. His dark brown hair was just as thick, but his eyes were crystal green rather than brown, lending his stare a chill that Chase's warm dark eyes couldn't match. Yale was handsome, but in a sharper, more predatory way.

Chase took a stool three stools away from Yale. He caught Yale's eye in the mirror, and tapped the bar with what appeared to the bartender, and any other casual observer, to be a careless rhythm. It was one of a half-dozen signals which could be used to cancel a mission. Yale ran his fingers through his hair, an equally innocuous motion, but one that acknowledged that Chase's message had been received.

Chase turned away from Yale, ordered a volcano, and sipped it while silently observing the tavern's other patrons. He noted a couple of big men with shaved heads, but neither was the pirate that Chase had taken such delight in insulting in the casino. He chuckled to himself at how predictably that encounter had gone, even if nothing in the aftermath had. Volcanoes were stong, and wanting a clear head for the evening, Chase left most of the drink in the triangular beaker and left to go look for André.

Yale Lincoln was dead tired. He had just finished an assignment in which he single-handedly captured half a dozen smugglers and had expected to be put on leave for an extended vacation rather than coming to The Diamond Mine to back up Drew Jordan. Thoroughly disgusted that Drew had waved him off, he ordered a second volcano and didn't wait for the hazy blue vapor to drift away before he began to drink it. Volcanoes had a kick, but by God he needed it.

Even if his services weren't required, he decided to remain at The Diamond Mine a few days and observe. He reasoned that it couldn't hurt to provide Control with his impressions of Drew's progress, as well as a separate description of the Mine's clientele. He had heard that Spider employed the most beautiful prostitutes in the galaxy, and it would enhance Yale's cover if he met a few. Having come this far, he deserved some exotic recreation and he left the tavern to revel in it.

The private living quarters were on the top floor, and as Chase stepped out of the elevator, André came from behind his desk to meet him. He was dressed in the same navy blue tunic and slacks worn by the employees in The Diamond Mine. "Please come with me and I'll show you to your room. I had been told to expect you earlier, and was beginning to worry you might have become lost."

Like many of Spider's staff, André was fair-haired and blue-eyed, but that was the only similarity. Rather than a brawny brute, he was slim, with a dancer's grace that lent his gestures a butterfly's soft flutterings. Chase was at first amazed that Spider would employ such an effeminate individual on his private staff, but swiftly realized it must have been a deliberate choice to shield Ivory from a more aggressive male. Chase made a mental note of it, for it showed how closely Spider guarded his daughter's virtue.

"How could anyone become lost here?" Chase asked with a good-natured grin. "This isn't that large an installation, and isn't the security accurate enough to track everyone's whereabouts at all times?"

Amused by Chase's question, André also broke into a smile showing off sharply pointed eyeteeth.

"Our technical equipment is way beyond my meager capacity to understand, but there's more than one way to become lost here."

Readily understanding André's meaning, Chase nodded. "For others maybe, but Summer Moon's girls don't interest me."

André grew positively coy. The thick midnight blue carpeting muffled the sound of their steps, but his were so light he was nearly dancing as he guided the way down the corridor. "Is that true only of her girls, or women in general?"

Chase didn't wait for André to offer the male companionship he appeared about to extend. "Sorry, André, I definitely like women, but the only one who interests me here is Ivory."

After passing by the elegant frescoed dining room where Chase had eaten earlier, and a spacious lounge, the corridor branched off to the right and left. Making a quick count, Chase noted eight doors along the hallway before he was shown to the last room on the left. André keyed in the code to open the door and then handed Chase a card bearing the sequence of numbers to permit him to enter on his own.

"Your odds of succeeding are better in the casino," André advised slyly.

Chase laughed. "We'll soon see." He entered the room first, and was pleased to find it had clear acrylic walls on two sides providing a spectacular view of the star-filled universe. The carpet was again deep blue, as were the cover on the bunk and the towels in the adjoining bath. The furnishings were the same wire-brushed chrome found in any outpost, but of superior design. In addition to the bunk, there was a comfortable recliner in which to relax, a desk, and above it a viewing screen from which a large bank of entertainment files could be accessed. But Chase doubted he would do anything more in the room than shower and sleep.

André slid open the closet. "Your luggage is here, and I took the liberty of providing your clothes for the evening. When you're ready, please join the others in the lounge."

Chase yawned and stretched. "Do I have time for a nap?"

"Yes, of course. Dinner won't be served until nineteen hundred. Should you need anything, use the call button here by the door. Is there something else you require before I go?"

André looked desperately eager to perform some personal service, but Chase just shook his head and closed the door after him. He was tired, but rather than stretch out on the bunk, he first conducted a quick search for surveillance equipment. Not surprisingly, he found a camera cleverly hidden in the viewing screen's control panel. The location of the microphone was equally well disguised, but neither presented a man of his talents with much of a challenge to discover. An intensive search of the bathroom showed it to be clear, and, relieved he wouldn't be watched all the time, Chase set the alarm on his watch for an hour, lay down on the bunk, and went to sleep.

He awoke on the first ping of the alarm, showered, shaved, wrapped a towel around his waist, and then checked the closet for what he assumed would be evening clothes. What he found was a dark green military uniform adorned with gold braid and a lieutenant general's three stars. It was his size, but he couldn't believe that Spider had really intended him to wear it. He pressed the call button, and André appeared almost instantly.

"You've made a mistake; I've got the wrong clothes," Chase complained.

André first admired Chase's well-muscled torso with an appreciative glance, then pulled a neatly folded list from his pocket and quickly consulted it. "No, Spider requested that uniform. The mistake is mine for not informing you he prefers costumes to formal dress. It makes the evening so much more festive if everyone has another identity to assume. There's quite a range of costumes available, but Spider likes to surprise his guests by making the selection himself rather than letting them choose."

"Does he now?" Under any other circumstance, Chase would have handed André the uniform and worn his own conservative attire, but he dared not assert his own individuality now when he was supposed to be actively following Spider's orders to court Ivory. "Well, I've never had any interest in serving in the military, but I guess I can be a general for one night."

"Yes, that's the idea. It's merely Spider's manner of play."

That a pirate apparently intent upon arming the formerly peaceful elements of the galaxy liked to dress up in costumes struck Chase as totally absurd, but he dismissed André and donned the handsomely tailored uniform. It was surprisingly comfortable, but he could not help but wonder who had been the last man to wear it. Not certain he really wanted to know, he dimmed the lights and walked down to the lounge. As he entered, he tried to hide his disappointment at not finding Ivory there.

A small white-haired man dressed as Napoleon Bonaparte set his drink aside and greeted him. "Good evening. I'm Avery Berger, and knowing Spider's taste in guests, I'm positive I ought to recognize you, but I'm afraid I don't."

"*The* Avery Berger?" Chase asked, startled to meet a Nobel Prize-winning poet.

"Well, yes, of course," the poet laureate replied, "but you didn't answer my question, general. Who might you be?"

Even before Avery's genius had been recognized by the Nobel committee, his exquisitely beautiful poetry had been praised by critics and was enormously popular with the public. Chase did not embarrass Avery by reciting some of the verses he had memorized, but he was nonetheless awed to meet his favorite poet. "I'm honored to meet you," he began, "but I'm merely a pilot and of no particular consequence to anyone but myself." His smile widened as Ivory joined them.

"Don't let him mislead you, Avery," Ivory warned as she looped her arm through his. "Chase Duncan must possess extraordinary talents, or my father would never have hired him."

Ivory was dressed in fringed buckskins, mocassins, and a beaded headband. Chase stared at her a long moment. On one hand he was afraid that Spider had discovered who he was and had dressed Ivory as an Indian maiden to taunt him, and on the other, he desperately wanted to believe it was merely a stunning coincidence. "You make a lovely Indian," he finally had the presence of mind to say. "Are you supposed to be anyone in particular?"

Chase looked so completely at ease in the general's uniform, Ivory was positive he could successfully command any army. That he had played havoc with her senses that afternoon probably meant very little to him, but she was still shaken. She held out her skirt to swing the fringe. "My father likes to call this our Pocahontas outfit, but I prefer to think of myself as Maria Wise Chief, the first President of the United States of American Indian ancestry. She had a much more exciting life."

Chase had thought that Ivory's silver sheath and flight suit set off her blond beauty to perfection, but the honey-gold of the buckskin dress blended so beautifully with the peach tones of her skin he changed his mind. "Yes, that's a more intriguing choice. You ought to always wear gold rather than silver. It's very becoming."

Enormously pleased by his compliment, Ivory nevertheless felt foolish and had to swallow hard before she was able to reply. "Thank you. May, have you met Chase Duncan?" she asked as a plump, red-haired woman dressed in a maroon Victorian gown joined them.

Chase was astounded to discover this was May McKesson, another renowned poet. While Avery wrote melodious lyric verse, her work was strident and politically charged. Chase greeted her warmly. "I'm sorry, but your costume is too subtle for me. Who are you supposed to be?"

"Spider insists I'm to be Marie Curie, but personally I prefer Emily Dickinson."

Avery scoffed at her choice. "You know Spider

refuses to allow us to be anyone in our own field. You'll have to be Marie Curie and that's all there is to it."

A tall, gaunt man dressed as Abraham Lincoln entered the room and came forward to hug Ivory. "My darling, it has been much too long since my last visit."

Chase frowned, for the newcomer looked to be in his fifties, which in his opinion was much too old for Ivory. When he was introduced as Nathan Rowe, a respected philosopher, Chase tried not to allow his annoyance to show. "I've read some of your work," he remarked.

"Really?" Nathan did not appear to be particularly impressed by that compliment and continued to concentrate his attention on Ivory. He ran his hand up and down her back as he leaned down to whisper in her ear, and then toyed with the fringe at her shoulders.

Rather than watch Ivory being pawed, Chase turned away, only to find Spider Diamond observing him from the doorway. Spider was clad in a flowing purple wizard's cloak. He was clean-shaven, but his tangled hair was barely tamed by his tall, star-sprinkled hat. Summer Moon, dressed in a red satin sheath embroidered with a gold dragon, was at his side. Chase walked over to them.

"I didn't realize you'd be entertaining celebrities tonight."

Spider introduced Summer Moon before responding. "Is that because you didn't think I'd know any, or because you believed they'd be afraid to come here?"

Summer Moon was several years younger than

Chase had estimated from her photograph, but she was hanging on to Spider's arm and gazing up at him with an abject adoration that was absolutely nauseating. Clearly she was devoted to the man, but Chase recalled Ivory's doubt that her father had ever loved anyone other than her mother. Perhaps Summer Moon regarded Spider as a challenge, but Chase simply felt sorry for her.

Hating to admit how greatly he had underestimated Spider's popularity, Chase conceded his point with a slight nod. "I feel badly out of place in such illustrious company."

"You better get used to it tonight," Spider suggested with a menacing grin, "if you hope to stay."

"I'll do my best." Chase turned back toward Ivory. She had been looking his way, but quickly spoke to Nathan Rowe as though her attention had not wandered. That she found him more appealing than Nathan wasn't surprising; but Chase wondered what it would take to inspire her to admit her preference and praise him to Spider. "Am I supposed to be a particular general?" he asked suddenly. "There's no identification badge on my uniform."

Spider shrugged. "You'd be surprised by how many men have unfulfilled military ambitions. The uniform was designed to fit any such fantasy."

That he had been assigned no particular identity was too close to the truth of Chase's actual existence to please him. He simply nodded, however, and smiled politely as an Oriental gentleman wearing a silver flight suit joined them. His name tag identified him as Captain James Kirkwood, the leader of the first Mars expedition, and Chase would have much rather played him than an anonymous general. Spider introduced him as Ming Wong, a Chinese philosopher who exerted considerable influence on Earth. Again amazed to find Spider entertaining a man of Ming's caliber, Chase made no attempt to converse with him.

The last guest was Caldwell Cornell, a handsome dark-haired man in his forties who had been dressed in a baggy white shirt and pants, given a paintbrush to carry, and told he was Pablo Picasso. He was also a philosopher, but with views which contrasted sharply with those of Nathan Rowe and Ming Wong. At last understanding that Spider's purpose was to assemble people likely to argue rather than spend a harmonious evening together, Chase doubted he would taste a bite on his plate.

Finally escaping Nathan Rowe, Ivory moved among the guests encouraging them to sample the appetizers and replenish their drinks. Ming Wong needed a refill of the pale green melon cider he always brought with him, and she gestured for André to bring him more. She had tasted it once and found it too insipidly sweet for her taste, but her father had trained her to be a gracious hostess and she kept her thoughts on Ming's passion for the vile liquid to herself.

She felt someone move up behind her, recognized Chase by his sheer size, and taking a deep breath, turned to face him. "You've nothing to drink," she noted. "André can supply whatever you'd like."

Chase bent down to whisper, "He's already

offered, but I told him you were the one I wanted."

Ivory could feel the heat of a vivid blush flood her cheeks, but she pretended an indifference she did not feel. "Is such a direct approach effective with most women?"

"I don't approach most women, directly or otherwise." Chase could see he was moving much too fast for Ivory, and it wasn't only Spider's insistence that he impress her that had caused him to set such an inappropriate pace.

Chase's smile was charming but held more than a hint of the passion they had shared that afternoon. Ivory had felt the same rakish energy emanating from other men, but rather than the squeamish dread she usually experienced, she found Chase's unsettling admiration unaccountably appealing. Before meeting him she had not even suspected she could have such an appalling weakness for any man. That he obviously knew precisely what he was doing, while she did not, was more than she could calmly bear.

"I wish you'd tell me what your true purpose is here," she countered. "None of our other employees is ever included in our private parties, so clearly your relationship with my father is unique."

Chase barely mouthed his response. "Not nearly as unique as the one I'm going to have with you."

That seductive promise warmed Ivory clear to her toes, but, untutored in verbal sparring, she chose not to compete with him. "Excuse me," she uttered softly and, escaping his taunting gaze, she joined May and Caldwell huddled around Avery. They were a witty trio and laughed easily at each other's jokes, but she was so acutely conscious of Chase's presence in the room she heard little of their sparkling banter.

A woodwind trio began to play in the dining room, providing an elegant call to supper, and at Spider's urging the guests made their way across the hall. He had arranged the place cards on the dining table, and when Ivory found that Chase was to be seated at her right, she caught her father's eye with a questioning glance. He nodded, clearly pleased by the seating arrangements, and she slid into her chair without voicing the objection that rang so clearly in her heart. With several of the most brilliant minds in the galaxy sharing their table, why had the place of honor at her side gone to an undistinguished pilot? she asked herself.

Summer Moon was watching her, and, knowing how much it upset her to see Spider's daughter seated in the hostess's place rather than her, Ivory smiled and Summer Moon turned away, but not before Ivory had seen the evil light in her glance. Summer Moon meant nothing to Ivory. She was merely another of her father's numerous mistresses, and he had never expressed any feelings for the woman in her presence, so she doubted that he had any. When Chase nudged her knee with his, she jumped.

"I beg your pardon," Chase said. "One of the disadvantages of being tall is never having enough room, but I didn't mean to disturb you."

Ivory smiled sweetly as she responded in a voice only he could hear. "That is a damn lie and we

74

both know it. You're deliberately disturbing me every chance you get."

"I'm so relieved you've noticed."

Thinking him absolutely impossible, Ivory turned to Ming Wong who was seated on her left. "How is your work progressing since last we met?" she asked.

Ming leaned back slightly as André began to serve a delicately scented broth in a transparent porcelain bowl. "My progress has been quite good, thank you, but I'm seeking to transcend traditional views of justice with a more sublime interpretation."

That remark was enough to set Nathan Rowe on a loud discourse on the value of the traditional views he accused Ming of continually trying to circumvent rather than transcend. Caldwell joined in what soon became a shouting match despite the elevated nature of the subject. Spider sat back and enjoyed every hostile word. Summer Moon watched only him, while Avery and May consumed the savory broth with silent sips.

Chase had studied philosophy in college, and was delighted to hear noted philosophers argue over which was the supreme value, justice, liberty, or equality. Like the poets, he chose to remain silent, but unlike them he listened with rapt attention. He glanced toward Ivory, who had taken only a single spoonful of her soup before pushing her bowl away.

He was uncertain whether it was the erudite argument raging at the table, or merely a dislike for the broth he had found a bit too salty for his taste that had caused her to withdraw, but he felt it safe to assume that she never took part in

her father's guests' discussions. He watched her
tap her fingers in time with the musicians' soft
classical serenade. "Which do you believe to be
the greatest good?" he asked her.

Appearing surprised that he would inquire,
Ivory hesitated a moment and then replied in as
hushed a voice as he had used, "Equality means
most to me."

Chase had expected her to choose liberty, for
what pirate does not love freedom? Certain she
had good reason for her choice, he nodded and
hoped they might have an opportunity to discuss her views at another time. As the meal prog-
ressed, Spider steered the conversation toward
poetry, and just as Chase had expected, Avery and
May had opposing views on the very nature of
the art. Avery insisted it consisted of imagery and
metaphor, while May was equally adamant that
a memorable, and preferably stirring, message
was the most essential element. When Nathan,
Caldwell, and Ming chose sides, the conversation
grew as loud and animated as when the subject
had been philosophy.

Chase began to admire the musicians, who continued to play the clarinet, oboe, and bassoon
as though they had the most attentive of audi-
ences. As he again scanned the frescoes, he could
not help but think this one of the most unusual
evenings he had ever spent. The artistic setting,
eminent guests, elaborate costumes, and philo-
sophical nature of the conversation set it apart,
to say nothing of the extremely dangerous man
who was hosting the affair.

Then there was the delicious Ivory Diamond,
who had captivated him at first sight. Cautioning

himself to recall this was an assignment, not strictly a pursuit of pleasure, he began to observe Summer Moon. While she frequently reached out to touch Spider's sleeve, and smiled at him constantly, he gave little indication he was even aware of her presence. Chase then realized he had not seen Spider touch Ivory either. That was also an important point to remember, for a young woman raised without affection would shy away from it, making Chase's task doubly difficult.

The lively discussion at the table was scarcely slowed as they all enjoyed a crisp salad. The others were then served thin rice noodles with a curry coconut sauce heaped with steamed squash, carrots, and peppers as the main course, but as promised, Chase was given a superbly broiled steak. He sliced off a bite and, savoring it, chewed slowly. Then he noticed Ivory's horrified expression.

"I'm sorry, does watching me eat meat offend you?" he asked.

"I was raised on vegetables grown in our hydroponic gardens and the thought of consuming flesh of any kind is utterly revolting, but please, don't allow my views to diminish your pleasure."

"I won't," Chase promised, and he ate every last bite of the steak. He had also been given steamed vegetables, but ate only a couple of carrots before pushing them aside. He supposed they were good, as vegetables went, but he could have lived a very long while without them. Dessert was an unbelievably rich chocolate cake layered with chocolate mousse and topped with chocolate fudge, whipped cream, and fresh raspberries. Never fond of sweets, Chase barely sampled it, while Ivory consumed every delectable morsel.

There was something about watching her lips close over the cream-covered raspberries that Chase found incredibly arousing. Finally having to look away, he found Summer Moon staring at Ivory with a gaze of such open contempt he was appalled. Was she jealous? he wondered. Perhaps Spider's fondness for his only child annoyed her, but Ivory continued to eat, apparently unaware of Summer Moon's darkly menacing stare. None of the others at the table seemed to notice Summer Moon's unveiled hostility, but Chase was deeply disturbed by it.

After dinner, Spider announced a return to the lounge, but when Ivory turned toward the elevator rather than joining the others, Chase did not bother to get Spider's permission before following her. She entered the elevator and was looking down, selecting a button to push, when he slipped through the doors just before they slid shut. "I can't take any more of that spectacular company either. I hope you don't mind if I join you."

Remembering how easily Chase had backed her into a corner on a previous elevator ride, Ivory braced herself to resist, but this time he kept his distance. Still, she dared not relax around him. "You know without asking that I do."

The doors opened on the sixth level and Ivory left the elevator without a backward glance. She might have thought her lack of interest would discourage Chase, but he overtook her as she entered the hydroponic gardens she had mentioned earlier. This was where the fresh produce was grown for the installation. At that hour, the technicians were off duty and the lighting was a pale blue that mimicked moonlight. Still, Chase could make out row upon row of nutrient-filled tanks which gurgled softly, nurturing the edible plants they contained.

The atmosphere in the huge agricultural wing was humid, but not uncomfortably so, and while the scent hanging heavily in the air was that of chemicals rather than fertile soil, it wasn't unpleasant. As his eyes adjusted to the dimness, Chase followed Ivory through the maze of aisles until she came to a small garden filled with orchids. Backed by an acrylic wall that provided as spectacular a view as in his room, the exotic garden was both eerie and serene. Even knowing he had invaded one of Ivory's favorite spots, Chase was not even tempted to allow her the solitude she appeared to crave.

"That was the strangest dinner party I've ever attended," he began, hoping to put her at ease. "It was all staged, wasn't it? There wasn't a moment that your father hadn't planned. Does he manipulate your life as easily as he does his guests?"

Ivory moved to the rail along the clear wall. "No."

"Then you've traveled extensively, seen something of Earth and the colonies?"

"No, it's far too dangerous for me to leave. Besides, I have all I need right here to be content."

Chase moved up beside her. "You don't appear to be any more content than Summer Moon. Did you realize she despises you?"

Ivory continued to gaze out at the heavens. "Yes, of course. She can't abide the fact my father

79

loves me, and not her. I don't take it personally. It's a common failing among his mistresses."

"How can you remain so detached? Aren't you afraid she might try to harm you?"

"In what way? She has no power over me, and nothing she could say or do would destroy my father's love."

Seeing he was not making any progress using Summer Moon as a wedge, Chase returned to his original focus. "Your father provides amusing guests, although he appeared to be far more entertained than you. How does he lure such respected people to his lair?"

Ivory observed Chase's reaction with a subtle sidelong glance. "Powerful men have an almost hypnotic appeal. Our guests wish to see how close they can get to him without being caught up in the danger that surrounds him. He's also wonderfully generous. He supports the work of most of the guests here tonight with endowments made through prestigious foundations."

"Are they aware of that?"

"Yes, of course, but they come to enjoy my father's company, not out of gratitude. He is truly free, you see, as few people ever are. That's what fascinates philosophers and poets."

"But he says it's too dangerous for you to leave? He's made a prisoner of you," Chase argued. "Can't you see that?"

"You misunderstand," Ivory murmured. "He excludes those who might harm me, but I'm never locked in my room."

Chase reached out to stroke her hair. The soft strands curled around his fingers like living coils. "You're an artist and ought to be allowed to appreciate the beauty of Earth, but you've never seen it. Even if you're not locked in a cell, what kind of freedom is that?"

Ivory turned toward him. "The perfect freedom, for it allows me to journey inward and find the beauty in myself. It's the solitude that fuels my art, and art is my passion."

Chase framed her face with his hands. "You have another passion now," he promised before his lips brushed hers. He felt her tremble, and deepening his kiss, he dropped his hands to her waist to pull her close. She smelled so sweet, and tasted better than the dessert he had watched her finish with such tantalizing bites. The warmth of the gardens fueled a primal desire, and a dozen kisses didn't satisfy him.

"I've never met anyone like you," he whispered against her ear. "This is the magic Avery describes, but even his talent with words barely captures what you do to me."

With his hips pressed against hers, Ivory could feel exactly what she was doing to him, but a far deeper awareness of what he was doing to her singed her soul. "No," she exhaled against his chest. "My father would kill you if he found us here like this."

Ivory had no way of knowing that Chase had been threatened with death if he weren't with her, and that was not a secret he would ever confide. Instead, he tilted her chin so she had to meet his gaze. "He likes me, Ivory. I wouldn't have been at the party tonight if he didn't."

Ivory frowned slightly, for what Chase said was true. Still, she was as afraid of her body's ago-nizingly sweet response to him as she was of

Cinnamon Burke

provoking her father. She gripped his arms, feeling his strength, even as she summoned her own. "No, you must leave me alone. I beg you."

She tore herself from Chase's embrace before he could catch her and left him to find his own way out of the gardens, but that was scarcely a challenge compared with mastering the puzzling labyrinth of her heart.

Chapter Four

Chase went down to the The Diamond Mine, took a corner booth this time, and ordered his favorite Martian ale. It was warm and thick, exactly the way he liked it, but did little to cool the heat that Ivory had aroused within him. He wished there had been time for him to pass a message to Control through Yale Lincoln, but, not knowing how he could possibly describe his current predicament in the terse code Control required, he thought he was probably better off that there had been no such opportunity.

How could he have explained that Spider Diamond had indeed presented the challenge Control had anticipated, but with a bizarre twist no one could have foreseen? He felt like the hero of some mythic quest, for he had been presented with a nearly impossible task for a mere mortal. Mythological heroes always survived their adventures to claim the prize, but when a few fevered kisses sent Ivory into a panic, he didn't know how he was ever going to win her consent for marriage.

The fact that Ivory was so difficult a woman was only part of his problem, however. Chase was a superbly trained operative, but seduction was not one of the skills in which he had been tutored. He had no difficulty in spinning all manner of fanciful yet convincing tales to win a pirate's trust, but to use the same artfully conceived subterfuge on Ivory filled him with remorse. It was not a feeling he was used to, and that added another uncomfortable burden. He might live by a code that permitted him to lie to criminals, but he was scrupulously honest with all other men and, before now, women as well.

Sipping Martian ale to soothe his aching conscience, he lost track of time and didn't return to his room until after midnight. When he came through his door and found Spider stretched out on his bunk, he knew this was the wrong time to be so deliciously drunk. Not wanting to risk an angry confrontation in such a confused state, or confined space, he left his door open.

Spider had discarded his wizard's cloak for his customary dark blue flight suit and was again his usual menacing self. "I thought you'd left the party to be with Ivory," he stated accusingly as he rolled off the bunk. "I wasn't at all pleased to learn she spent the evening alone in her studio. If you're not going to take our agreement seriously, then I'll cancel it immediately, and you along with it."

Chase had no difficulty in understanding Spider's threat, but raised his hands in a conciliatory gesture. "Believe me, I am taking our bargain seriously. Ivory's the one you ought to be lecturing, not me. She's scared to death you'll kill me if you find us together. The more she comes to care for me, the more terrified she'll become, which is going to get me nowhere."

Chase began to unbutton his jacket. He had drawn several odd glances down in the tavern and only now realized that his splendid uniform must have been the cause. "Your daughter is so starved for affection she trembles when I touch her. How was she raised, by a cyborg nanny?"

Insulted, Spider Diamond came close, his face a mask of fury. "I don't tolerate that kind of surly insolence from anyone else," he confided darkly, "and I won't accept it from you. How I choose to raise Ivory is no concern of yours; marrying her is. Don't expect me to play cupid for you. If you're not man enough to make her love you, then just say so and I'll find someone who is."

Since such an admission would be tantamount to suicide, Chase did not even consider it. Besides, he was confident he was more than enough man for any woman, and that definitely included Ivory. "Ivory is already fond of me," he swore. "It's only her fear of you that's keeping us apart."

Out of patience, Spider thumped Chase's chest hard enough to push him back a step. "I'm going to take care of that problem by sending you two on a trip together. See that Ivory's well on her way to becoming your wife by the time you return, or you'll make an amusing dummy for Stokes and Vik to use for target practice. Don't try running, either. You may have escaped Alado's security patrols, but there isn't a hole in the galaxy dark enough to hide you if I want you dead."

Chase didn't have to pretend the anxiety he so justly felt. He moved in front of the door to block Spider's way. "Ivory must already have feelings for me or she wouldn't be so terribly worried about my safety. It's cruel of you to cause her that torment, but apparently she has good reason to be afraid for me. How many men have paid with their lives for loving her?"

Spider frowned slightly, then glanced away to run a quick mental tally. When he looked back toward Chase his gaze was taunting. "You'll make it an even dozen if you fail."

"I've no intention of failing," Chase assured him, "but you shouldn't make Ivory suffer for wanting me."

"Must I repeat that how I treat Ivory is not your concern? Join us for breakfast, and I'll present your assignment. Appear reluctant at first; then Ivory won't be as suspicious of your motives."

Chase didn't know why he was surprised that Spider took such a vicious delight in manipulating his daughter's emotions when clearly it was a practice he undertook often, but it sickened him thoroughly. He stepped aside and Spider left, but he couldn't shake the revulsion their conversation had caused for a long while. After a sleepless night, he entered the dining room expecting to see some of the guests from the previous night's party, but Spider and Ivory were alone.

"Good morning," Chase greeted them. They were eating an almond and grain cereal, and as soon as he sat down, André brought him a bowl. "Well, now, doesn't this look good," he said without enthusiasm.

Ivory took a sip from her iguana cup rather than respond, but Spider was eager to talk. "Ivory and I have just been discussing an assignment. She is not merely my daughter, but also a trusted partner in every enterprise I undertake. Because she understands me so well, I believe she'll make a superb emissary."

"Emissary?" Chase asked. He continued studying Ivory's expression, but she wouldn't look at him directly. Annoyance and anger added a sharpness to his words. "Are you going away?"

Misinterpreting his emotion, Ivory believed him to be sincerely pained by that possibility and, unused to either travel or solicitous concern, she simply shrugged. "There's no great distance involved, so I won't be gone long."

"Still, you'll be away," Chase pointed out.

Fearing that Chase had revealed too much, Ivory sent an apprehensive glance Spider's way. She expected him to give Chase the same impatient dismissal she had seen so often in the past, but he surprised her. Instead of commanding that her travel arrangements were not a subject for discussion, Spider was actually smiling. It wasn't his usual knowing smile that preceded some damning announcement either, but a teasing grin that thoroughly confused her.

"I have a ship," Spider explained. "It's not quite as fine as Alado's Starcruisers, but it's adequate for the voyage you're about to make. I'm sending you along with Ivory, to serve both as her pilot and bodyguard."

Shocked by what he was suggesting, Ivory gasped. "I really don't think that's wise."

"Of course it's wise," Spider contradicted. "You

know the capabilities of our weapons as well as I do, but ignorant men like Mordecai Black can't be trusted to show you the proper respect without a strong man by your side."

Ivory finally glanced toward Chase and found him observing her with sly amusement. He looked far too pleased with the assignment he had been given. Feeling trapped, she rebelled. "We might have made it to the bank and back together, but that's scarcely proof of his worth. This mission is too vital to trust to amateurs."

Spider's eyes narrowed as he questioned his daughter. "Do you know what Stokes would give to go with you?"

"Yes," Ivory replied with obvious distaste, "anything you'd name, but I'd much rather take a few of the silver boys than him or Chase."

"Yes, they'd make impressive escorts, but I want them to remain a secret for a while longer, so parading them through the Eagle's Nest doesn't fit into my plan. Just take Duncan. I'm positive he won't disappoint you, will you, Duncan?"

Chase squared his shoulders. "No, of course not, but who are the 'silver boys'?"

"The robots you saw at the bank," Ivory replied, "and I still think they would make better company than you."

Chase much preferred that show of temper to her earlier reserve and laughed heartily. "Believe me, I can find far more creative ways to keep you entertained than they ever could."

"It's not entertainment I require," Ivory cautioned. She leaned forward, her breakfast forgotten. "I'll be conducting business in my father's name. All I care about is doing it well."

The set of her jaw convinced Chase of that, but he had business of an entirely different sort. "I work for you," he reminded her in a softer tone. "Just tell me what it is you want done."

Before Ivory could provide a list of his duties, Spider supplied one. "You'll pilot the ship to the Eagle's Nest. It's located on an asteroid not nearly as inviting as mine, but caters to miners and does a tremendous business. Once there, you'll protect Ivory's life with your own. She'll handle the negotiations for arms, but I want you always at her side. Should anyone be so foolish as to attempt to take her hostage, it would bring instant retaliation of the worst imaginable sort. Other men in my line of business are well aware of the dangers of crossing me, but there's always the chance you'll encounter some hot-blooded fool who wishes to make his own reputation at the expense of mine. I expect you to prevent any such unfortunate occurrence."

"You have my word on it," Chase swore with an ease that surprised him. "I won't let anything happen to Ivory, not ever."

Embarrassed to be discussed as though she weren't present, Ivory left the table. "Apparently I'm to have no say in this, so I'm going to pack. Meet me in docking bay three in thirty minutes. We'll check out the ship together, and then go."

"I'll be there," Chase promised. Grateful for an excuse not to finish the cereal, Chase set his spoon aside. He watched Ivory leave the room with her usual elegant stride. Her soft silver flight suit sculpted her curves beautifully, but he would still have preferred to see her dressed in gold.

He turned to Spider. "I'm sorry, but Ivory had

so little interest in having me along, I had no chance to appear reluctant as you'd asked. Putting us together for a mission was clever, but I still say you've got to tell Ivory that neither of us will have to face dire consequences should she want more than a bodyguard."

Spider ran his fingertip around the rim of his iguana cup. His gesture was lazy, careless, but his mood was not. "I had my reasons for selecting you for her husband, Duncan. Be grateful for that extraordinary piece of luck and stop complaining."

Feeling as though he had been asked to dance on a stage with a concealed trapdoor, Chase couldn't agree. "Love and fear don't mix," he warned. "I came here knowing exactly what you were, so I've no reason to complain if you want to send me out to negotiate arms deals, but when you demand a more personal service, then the least you can do is remove the obstacles in my way."

Spider's laugh was a dry, rasping howl. "I own you, Duncan, body and soul. Now stop wasting your breath and my time and get ready to leave."

As he rose to his feet, Chase slammed his chair into the table hard enough to jar Spider's bowl, but he was so disgusted with the way his mission was turning out, he couldn't remain with the heartless rogue another second. He had little to pack, but he welcomed the excuse to leave the room. He had heard of the Eagle's Nest, and though it was one of the wildest saloons on the frontier, that morning it held a definite appeal.

Not nearly so uninterested in his daughter's welfare as Chase supposed, Spider immediately went to her room. "I'm sending Chase Duncan along with you for a reason I didn't care to share with him," he explained. "There may come a day when we'll be presented with an opportunity we'll want to seize without risking either of our lives in the bargaining. This is merely the first test in many I've designed for Duncan. If he passes, he'll proceed and be given more responsibility, if not, well . . ." Spider paused a moment. "I've seen the way you look at him, and if you like, you may keep him for a pet."

Ivory was perplexed by that remark and had no idea how to take it. She swung her flight bag off the bed and asked, "What are you saying?"

Spider walked with her to the door. "It's high time you had a lover, and Duncan is obviously eager to please you. Let him try."

Ivory stared at him. She knew all his expressions as well as her own and detected no sign of treachery in his face. Still, what he suggested frightened her badly. "You've always kept men away from me. Why is Chase Duncan any different from the rest? We both know it's not me he wants, but a share of your power."

"Yes, that's undoubtedly true, but if he gives you pleasure, he'll deserve a reward and you can be sure I'll give him one."

Ivory felt the painful tightness in her chest she'd come to associate with Chase. "No, you've taught me too well. I don't want him."

Finally gaining an appreciation for the difficulty of Chase's task, Spider nodded. "Think of it as an experiment then. You're an artist. You must live life fully in order to express yourself more completely in your art."

Ivory scoffed at his advice. "That sounds like one of the flattering lies you told me never to believe."

"Perhaps, but in this case it's the truth. Besides, you might one day want children, and having a husband would be an advantage then." When Ivory shook her head, Spider kissed her forehead. "It was merely a suggestion. As always, do as you please."

"If I were allowed to do as I please, I wouldn't be taking Chase Duncan with me."

Spider took her elbow and walked with her to the elevator. "Trust in my judgment," he begged, "as you always have."

Ivory boarded the elevator without replying. She felt torn between the cynical caution her father had advised, and the thrill she felt in Chase Duncan's arms.

Chase was too preoccupied to care what sort of a ship he was expected to fly until he entered docking bay three and found a Peregrin Blaster. The Peregrin Corporation was Alado's chief rival in the lucrative exploration of space, and to become the first of Alado's pilots to fly the pride of Peregrin's fleet was a joy he couldn't disguise.

Rather than Peregrin's stylized falcon, this Blaster bore an abstract insignia featuring a white spider silhouetted against a gleaming black diamond. It was a striking image, vaguely reminiscent of a skull-and-crossbones. The sight gave Chase chills, and he assumed that that must have been the designer's intention. In the next instant he realized that Ivory had probably devised the

symbol for her father. She had certainly captured
the darker elements of his personality.

The mechanics who had fueled the sleek triangular Blaster were expecting Chase, so he
climbed the ramp and went on board without
waiting for Ivory. Comparable in size to the Alado
Starcruiser, the Blaster had a luxurious cabin with
deeply padded seats which could be folded down
into comfortable bunks. In the aft were a galley
fully stocked with prepackaged provisions and
compactly designed lavatory facilities. He went on
up to the cockpit, dropped into the pilot's seat, and
began to inventory the controls. Enjoying himself
immensely, he failed to notice Ivory's arrival.

Ivory watched Chase gleefully scanning the
dials and hoped the ship would keep him fascinated for the whole journey. She leaned over
and tapped his shoulder to get his attention. "The
ship's been cleared for flight. If you're ready, I'll
close the hatch."

Startled, Chase was embarrassed that she had
caught him so engrossed in the ship. "Show me
how to access the computer first. I'd hate to call
him Rex if that wasn't his name."

"*Her* name," Ivory took a particular delight in
pointing out, "is Rainbow." She had to take her
seat and lean across Chase to activate the computer. "Good morning, Rainbow. I've a new pilot
for you. His name is Chase Duncan and he'll need
your maximum level of attention."

"The hell I will," Chase argued.

"Good morning, Chase Duncan," Rainbow replied. Her voice was low and surprisingly sultry
for a navigational computer. "Please give me an
additional sentence for a more accurate tracing

and your voice pattern will become a permanent part of my files."

"Good morning, Rainbow. I'm Chase Duncan and I'm fully qualified to fly any ship ever built. I'll have absolutely no problem with this Blaster."

Rainbow replied with a sensuous hum. "Hmm, that is so comforting to hear."

Astonished, Chase reached out to grab Ivory's arm as she started to rise. "Wait a minute. Is this your father's idea of a joke? Rainbow sounds more like the receptionist for Summer Moon's girls than a Blaster's computer."

"How she sounds is irrelevant," Ivory assured him calmly. "Her programming is excellent, her performance outstanding, and even if you're annoyed with her voice, it's not going to affect the flight. Now let go of me and I'll close the hatch."

Chase released her, but he couldn't shake the uneasy feeling that something wasn't right with Rainbow. Of course, he wasn't what he seemed either, but believing he would be safe with Ivory on board, he kept his misgivings to himself. When Ivory rejoined him, his first question was the most obvious one.

"How did Spider get this ship? I realize it can't have been honestly, but I'm curious nonetheless."

Ivory buckled her seat belt and sat back to get comfortable. "I'm sorry to disappoint you, but Peregrin found itself with more ships than it required and auctioned off a couple. We bought them. The sale wasn't widely advertised, so it's no wonder you failed to hear of it."

That was either the truth, or a clever lie. It had been told with such a relaxed delivery that Chase couldn't tell which. He knew exactly what Ivory and her father were, so expecting the truth about anything was absurd. Still, he hoped, without any valid reason, that they would not choose to lie to him.

The mechanics had left the bay, and after running through the preflight checklist with Rainbow, Chase started the sequence to open the wide doors at the end. Red lights began to flash and a siren whooped an alarm as they prepared to launch. Rainbow began a countdown in a sexy whisper.

"Last night you told me it was too dangerous for you to travel, and today you're coming with me to the Eagle's Nest. That's a rather sudden change in your routine, isn't it?"

Ivory released her exasperation in a sibilant sigh. "Let's get one thing straight right now, Chase. I'm not going with you; you're coming with me. When you asked if I'd been to Earth, I said no, but that doesn't mean I don't sometimes fly for business rather than pleasure."

"Who usually flies with you?"

"My father. He's a skilled pilot and taught me how to fly. I could have easily made this trip alone if he hadn't insisted that you accompany me."

Her displeasure was so plain in her voice and expression that Chase made no attempt to soften her view for the time being. The bay doors were fully open now, and he took the controls to ease the magnificent ship out into the perpetual darkness of space. As he had done with the shuttle, he banked to fly over The Diamond Mine, and then eased back and let Rainbow chart their course for the Eagle's Nest.

"What's our time, Rainbow?"

"Thirty-five hours, twenty-three minutes," the computer replied in a lazy drawl.

"Thank you." Still intrigued by the ship, Chase continued to observe the design of the controls. "That's going to bring us into the Eagle's Nest close to midnight tomorrow. I don't know about you, but that strikes me as a particularly poor time to negotiate an arms deal. Wouldn't you rather that we arrived the next morning?"

Ivory was sorry she had not asked the same question earlier. "Yes, I would. Frankly, my father was so anxious to have us gone, I forgot to take our arrival time into consideration. We'll orbit the asteroid tomorrow night, and land the next morning." She pursed her lips thoughtfully, then turned toward Chase. "Do you have instincts you can trust?"

"Usually."

"What do you mean, 'usually'? Either you do or you don't."

"Not in my case. I have a sixth sense that keeps me out of most trouble, but it's worthless where beautiful women are concerned." He winked at her. "Of course, you already knew that."

An artist's keenly discriminating eye wasn't required to appreciate Chase's dark good looks, but Ivory longed to peel away the layers of superficial charm and view what truly lay in his heart. She doubted that this voyage would be long enough to even begin such a difficult endeavor, however. "I suffer from no such handicap where men are concerned," she boasted, "and I have a wretched feeling this flight will be plagued by problems. I don't need additional trouble from you. I'm afraid my father is setting you up to fail. Entertaining himself at another's expense is one of his favorite pastimes, so be careful not to make any mistakes. They may cost you dearly later."

The irony of Ivory's warning wasn't lost on Chase, but he pretended not to share her concern. "I'm not only an excellent pilot, Ivory, I'm cautious as well. I don't take foolish chances, and I don't make stupid mistakes."

"Really? I seem to recall a reference to trusting the wrong woman."

Chase winced. "Yeah, you're right. I made a gigantic mistake there, but I thought we were discussing technical expertise."

Ivory shook her head, and her tawny curls brushed her cheeks. "No, there are any number of ways for you to fail on this mission. A single careless word to Mordecai Black might be enough to spoil the deal." She caught his eye. "Don't risk it."

"I'm just tagging along as your bodyguard, Ms. Diamond, and bodyguards never have a say in anything."

"I'm glad to hear you understand your role." Ivory unbuckled her seat belt and stood. "I'm going back to the cabin to work. You needn't stay here if you don't want to, but I insist that you keep yourself amused without bothering me."

She looked as if she meant what she said, and again Chase chose not to argue with her. "What kind of work do you mean? Are there still details to work out with the arms deal?"

"No, but I have some sketches I want to make for possible ceramic projects. I'm an artist, remember, and that's my primary interest."

Cinnamon Burke

Finally satisfied that the siren-voiced computer could handle the ship, Chase followed Ivory into the main cabin. "Wait a minute. Shouldn't you be making plans for the meeting you'll have with Mordecai Black? I realize Spider must have sent along some sort of instructions, but what if Mordecai won't pay your price?"

Ivory opened her flight bag and removed a sketchbook and pencil. "There's no need for me to rehearse when we operate with a few simple rules. We offer whatever it is we wish to sell at the price we expect to receive. We negotiate amounts of merchandise, delivery dates, terms of payment, but price isn't something open to debate. Either we receive precisely what we initially demand, or there's no deal."

Ivory's gaze was steady, conveying the clear impression that she agreed with her father's principles. Sickened by that possibility, Chase sat down on the arm of a seat and stretched his legs out into the aisle. The interiors of Starcruisers were decorated in subtle grays that made for a restful journey. This Blaster's interior was stark white and black. Reminded of prison stripes, he tried to smile rather than gag.

"All right, you obviously know how to conduct business, but I think we ought to have a pre-arranged signal in case you want to call off the negotiations and leave. Let's say Mordecai won't agree to your terms, and turns surly. What will you do?"

Ivory rolled her eyes. "I'll stand up and say, 'Come on, Duncan, we're leaving.' Is that clear enough for you?"

"Perfectly, but that doesn't mean Black might

not have some muscle there to stop us."

Ivory laid her art materials aside and again reached into her flight bag. This time she pulled out a Celestial Cannon. "Does this give you an idea of how easily I'm able to put across my point?"

Fighting a sickening wave of déjà vu, Chase waited to make certain she wasn't about to level the weapon at his chest before he nodded. "My God, what is that?"

"It's a Celestial Cannon, or rather my father's interpretation of Alado's design for one. I won't arm it until we're ready to leave the ship. Here, do you want to take a look at it?"

Chase took hold of the laser pistol with both hands in a reverent grasp. He checked first to make certain it truly wasn't armed, and then closed his fingers around the handle. It was much lighter than any pistol he had ever fired, and he already knew it was far more deadly.

"Is this what you'll be selling Mordecai Black?"

"Yes. There's a ready market for the cannon. We can sell them as fast as they're manufactured."

Chase knew it was pointless to argue the ethical aspects of arms sales with a pirate's daughter, but he certainly wished he could convince her she needn't follow Spider's path. "That must be some operation," he mused thoughtfully. "I'd like to see it. Is it there at The Diamond Mine?"

Ivory's glance narrowed slightly. "Do you really expect me to provide that information?"

Chase pretended not to understand her question. "Yes, why not?"

Ivory took the cannon back and, with almost careless indifference rather than the awe Chase had shown, shoved it down into the bottom of her bag. "I was against taking you to the bank, if you'll recall. There's no way I'll ever give you a tour of any of our factories."

"You've got more than one?"

"Give it up, Chase. You may have convinced my father that you're worthy of a particle of his trust, but that doesn't mean you've impressed me. I told you, I have instincts that don't fail me, and for a man to show up out of nowhere, be hired as a pilot, be invited to a private party, and be sent on an arms mission all in a matter of days is too unusual for me not to wonder if there isn't something damn odd about you."

Chase had moved close while examining the Celestial Cannon and hadn't stepped back. He took advantage of their proximity now. "Don't forget the best part," he advised softly. "There was an incredibly exciting moment in an elevator, another in your studio, and last night, if only you hadn't left me, we might have made the orchids blush in another minute or two."

Ivory stared at him coldly. "You're on this flight to perform a specific job. Attempting to flatter me with ridiculous descriptions of a few hasty kisses isn't part of it. The controls for the games are in the armrests. Use earphones so you don't bother me. If games don't appeal to you, access the story files, or film library, but I don't want to hear another word from you until it's time for lunch."

Chase responded with a slight bow. "Would you care to place your order now, Ms. Diamond? If I can't keep you entertained, I can at least keep you well fed."

Another man might have been insulted by the

order that Ivory had given, but she could tell from the bright sparkle in his eyes that he was merely amused. She couldn't shake her earlier apprehension, however, and did not even smile. "Just toss together a couple of the rice and vegetable packets. That will be all I'll need."

"Fine. We should do all we can to avoid the dangerous isolation of space, though, and eat together even if I have to sit at your feet."

"You try sitting at my feet and I'll kick you clear up to the cockpit. Now find something to do and leave me alone."

"It will be a pleasure," Chase assured her, and he turned away before she could see the smile that hinted at his intention to make her beg him for something far more gratifying than solitude.

Chapter Five

Accustomed to warfare on an intimate scale, Chase had little interest in the wild target games most pilots played in their off-duty hours. He knew he would never be able to concentrate on a written tale, but found that the Blaster's film library offered a wealth of comedies in addition to involving dramas. Needing a laugh, he chose a comedy and thoroughly enjoyed it until lunchtime. He got up from his seat and, taking care not to disturb Ivory as he walked by, went back to the galley.

He didn't like to eat much in flight and preferred the nourishing protein drinks that Alado's ships carried. Assuming there would be an equivalent on board, he began to sort through the stores. The first bin contained juices, and the next dried fruits. The third held grains and pastas, and the fourth all manner of vegetables and sauces. There were utensils and containers stowed in another cabinet, but nowhere did he find the delicious protein drinks he craved.

Thinking he should have made his request before they'd left The Diamond Mine, Chase blamed only himself for his disappointment with the cuisine, but on the off-chance he had missed what he was looking for, made another inventory. This time he sorted the packages from each bin in neat stacks on the counter, but no matter how they were arranged, what he wanted for lunch just wasn't there. Doubting he would have an opportunity to buy the rich protein shakes at the Eagle's Nest, he began to toss the packages back into their bins and couldn't stifle the impulse to slam the lids shut.

When Ivory first heard Chase opening and closing the bins, she had thought he was merely perusing their supplies before preparing lunch. The noise he was making grew in intensity, however, until it appeared he was ransacking the galley rather than preparing to cook. Too hungry to wait for him to stop playing with the food, she closed her sketchbook and entered the galley. One look at Chase's dark expression convinced her he wasn't pleased with what he had found.

"What's wrong? We buy our flight food from the same firm that supplies Alado. Can't you find anything you like?"

After the way Ivory had banished him earlier, Chase was surprised to find her showing any interest in his comfort, but both her expression and tone implied such a concern. That made him feel even worse. "No, I didn't. There's plenty of the rice and vegetables you wanted, but none of the protein drinks I like."

Ivory grimaced. "Vampire floats? You actually like those?"

"There's an enormous difference between drinking liquid protein and blood, Ivory," Chase shot back, and then, knowing how pompous he had sounded, he began to laugh. "I'm sorry. Yes, I like vampire floats, but I thought that was a term only Alado's pilots used. How did you hear it?"

Unwilling to reveal her source, Ivory simply shrugged. "We hear all kinds of slang at The Diamond Mine, and that includes Alado's inside jokes. Now isn't there something here you can eat?"

"Sure, I can eat all of it. I just don't want to."

Thinking he sounded like a petulant child, Ivory began to lose sympathy. "That's a shame, but you're going to have to eat something. You'll make a pitiful excuse for a bodyguard if you're faint from hunger."

Chase nodded. "I know." He took out the rice and vegetables she had requested, then began again to rummage through the bins for something for himself. Ivory waited at his elbow, and made him so self-conscious he quickly chose a packet of noodle soup from the pasta bin. "This will have to do."

"Go ahead and heat it," she urged. "Then I'll fix mine."

"No, I volunteered to be the chef on this voyage and that means I do all the cooking. Go back and sit down. I'll bring your lunch when it's ready." Ivory looked unconvinced, and he shooed her away with a hasty gesture. "Go on, you need privacy to work, and I need it to run the galley."

"Fine," Ivory called over her shoulder, and returned to the main cabin.

The directions were printed on each packet, and all Chase had to do was pour the contents into a bowl, add water, pop it into the oven, and wait a few seconds for the dish to cook. Despite his boast, he had little experience with cooking and misread the time required on the soup. Rather than warming it to a pleasing temperature, he boiled it. He removed the steaming bowl from the oven and set it aside to cool while he heated Ivory's meal. This time he was more careful and had better results.

Grabbing a fork and napkin, he carried the plate in to her. "I'm a poor waiter it seems. I forgot to take a beverage order."

"Any of the juices will do. Thank you." Ivory took the plate and set it on the tray she had been using to work. "Well, aren't you going to join me? After your earlier warning, I don't want either of us to risk arriving at the Eagle's Nest too deranged from loneliness to carry out our mission."

Inordinately pleased that she wanted his company, Chase broke into a wide grin. "Right. I'll get your juice and my soup." The soup was at least cool enough to carry, but Chase brought along a juice for himself and sipped it until he could swallow the soup without fear of leaving the roof of his mouth in shreds. "How did your sketching go this morning?" he asked between spoonfuls.

Ivory leaned over to pick up her sketchbook and showed him. "I'm working on candlesticks to match the iguana cups. It's just a question of

Cinnamon Burke

how ambitious I want to be."

The drawings were far more detailed than Chase had expected and ranged from one lizard curled around a candle to groupings of several entwined to form the most grotesque candelabra he had ever seen. He just couldn't imagine anyone enjoying a meal with such a monstrosity staring him in the face, but he didn't dare say so. It bothered him that Ivory appeared to have a fondness for the ugly little reptiles, when he would have much preferred to see her drawing gossamer winged angels.

"How are you planning to do the big one, with separate pieces or as one big sculpture?"

Believing he was intrigued by her designs, Ivory was pleased and readily explained. "I'm thinking of making several pieces which can be put together in a variety of configurations to be used for anything from a large dinner party like the one we had last night, or for just a few guests."

Chase searched his mind for something, anything intelligent to say about the hideous little scaly beasts of which she was so fond. "You've certainly captured the essence of an iguana. Do you have one for a pet?"

Ivory set her sketchbook aside and jabbed her fork into another bite of squash. "No, I've never seen one live, but I have a good film featuring them in my science files."

The woman continually surprised him. "You maintain science files?"

"Of course." Ivory played with her rice, pushing it into a pyramid on the side of her plate and then lopping off the peak with her fork. "The first of my tutors began a set of educational files, and I've

106

kept adding to them over the years."

Ivory was eating her lunch with the same undisciplined enthusiasm about which Spider had complained the first time the three of them had eaten together. That a gorgeous woman would have such a childlike nature was indeed enchanting, but Chase had not forgotten how easily she had handled the Celestial Cannon and dared not make the mistake of underestimating her. "Did you have only tutors, rather than going away to school?"

Ivory laughed between bites. "Do you honestly believe I'd have been accepted by one of Alado's academies if I'd had the audacity to apply?"

"No, probably not, but that doesn't mean you couldn't have attended one of the prestigious art schools on Earth. The sketches you made this morning are impressive enough to gain entrance to any of them."

Ivory paused in midbite. "Do you serve on the admissions committee of an art school in your spare time?"

"No, of course not, but I know excellent work when I see it."

Ivory looked skeptical, and then nodded. "Oh yes, of course, I keep forgetting you used to sell pornography."

Chase had to be careful not to spill his soup into his lap as he shouted his reply. "I did not sell pornography! How many times do I have to say that the photos I sold were art? Very elegant art they were too."

Ivory didn't respond to his outburst. She simply took a sip of juice and continued eating her lunch. Several uncomfortable minutes passed before she spoke. "All right, let's say I believe you," she finally offered. "Wouldn't figure studies be better samples of my work than a tortured heap of iguanas grasping candles?"

Chase would not have described her work quite so bluntly, but that was precisely what she had drawn. "Yes, I suppose so. Do you ever work from live models?"

Thinking she had finally found a way to discourage Chase from ever wanting to travel with her again, Ivory began to smile. It was a beautiful smile that lit her eyes with a dancing light. "Usually I don't. When you finish your soup, why don't you strip and I'll practice with you?"

She had made the suggestion in the same offhand fashion as she had discussed the Celestial Cannon, but Chase was no piece of exotic weaponry. "You can't mean that," he replied.

"Why not? You keep telling me you're an art lover. I thought you'd be eager to pose for me."

She had him there, but Chase just couldn't agree. "I'll be happy to take off my clothes if you're curious about how I look, but with you around there's no way I could sit calmly enough for you to make sketches. Besides, if you really want to explore my body, there are far more pleasurable ways to do it than with your eyes."

None of Chase's frequent sexual innuendos was lost on Ivory, but she pretended a cool detachment and regarded him with a level stare. "You've obviously forgotten something."

"I can't imagine what. Rainbow's flying the ship and we've plenty of time to kill before we reach the Eagle's Nest. As far as I can see, there's nothing to prevent us from exploring each other by delicious inches."

Not even tempted by Chase's teasing invitation, Ivory finished the last bite of her lunch and handed him the empty plate to return to the galley. "Do you recall waking up naked in a cage?"

Chase remembered it vividly, but it had never occurred to him that Spider hadn't been the only one to observe him in his natural state. "You were down there?" he asked, praying that she hadn't been.

Ivory had not thought it was possible to embarrass Chase Duncan, but clearly he was mortified by the possibility that she might have witnessed him in such a humiliating circumstance. She had expected to gain a triumphant satisfaction by putting him in his place, but all she felt was a gritty disappointment with herself for stooping to the level of her father's tricks. "You needn't be ashamed. You've a magnificent body, and I thought your tattoo was one of the handsomest I'd ever seen. It's a design from the Indians of America's Northwest Coast, isn't it?"

On more than one occasion Control had strongly advised Chase to have Raven removed because it was far too distinctive a tattoo and one by which he could easily be identified. Apparently Spider had not known what it was, but any artist with a minimal knowledge of aboriginal art would. Now far more worried about the risk of discovery than the embarrassment of, nudity, he just shook his head.

"Yes, it's Raven as the Haida drew him. But the next time you find me without my clothes, I hope

I'll be awake to appreciate it."

"Well, if you're not going to pose for me, then there'll be no next time. Excuse me, but I want to make certain Rainbow hasn't come across any problems. I still have a vague sense that something's amiss, and unlike Alado, we've no repair crews I can call."

She rose and started toward the cockpit, and Chase carried their dishes back to the galley, jammed them into the washing unit, and then joined her. He had had his own doubts about Rainbow's capabilities, but he was afraid that Ivory was picking up a sense of his masquerade rather than any incipient technical difficulties. Intuition was merely heightened awareness, and surely an artist with her eye for detail would have strong intuitive powers. If she was keying in on his deception, then he was going to have to do a whole lot better at distracting her. She had taken the pilot's seat, so he dropped into the co-pilot's.

"How does it look?"

"I'm running a check of all systems now, but everything looks fine. Still, it never hurts to be cautious."

Chase reached over to squeeze her knee. "I agree, but if you carry it too far, all you'll get is the dullest of routines rather than high adventure."

Ivory swatted his hand away. "Is that why you want to work for my father? Do you think he'll provide the adventure you seek?"

Chase laced his fingers together and extended his arms in a lazy stretch. He was an excellent pilot, but he had never enjoyed long flights. That was the main reason he had gone to work for the intelligence unit. His work was usually on the ground rather than in the air. He shifted in his seat, and finally got comfortable.

"I already told you I didn't have a lot of options once Alado found out I was dealing art on the side. Your father runs a large operation. I figured he would have a job for me, and he did. It was a matter of simple economics, really. I hate being broke."

"You're lying, Chase."

That she had called him on what was the most believable part of his story was startling, but Chase didn't let his discomfort show. He returned her steady gaze with a relaxed smile. "Considering where you were raised, I'm not surprised you doubt everything you hear. A healthy skepticism might be wise, but there has to be a point at which you'll begin to trust me. I hope we get there soon, because I'm too attracted to you to pretend an indifference I don't feel."

There was an unmistakable ring of sincerity to that vow, but Ivory was still wary. "My father suggested I make a pet of you, but I'd really rather have an iguana."

That Spider had encouraged her to use him, if not love him, was at least a step in the right direction. Chase was relieved the man had not ignored his pleas for help in impressing her. "You told me equality was important to you," he reminded her. "It is to me too, and I won't be any woman's pet. That would make me her slave rather than her equal."

Impressed by his remark, Ivory relaxed slightly. "I agree with those who say love can only exist between equals, but equality can take so many forms I fear it's merely an illusion."

"Yes, I suppose in any pair one is always brighter, or more attractive, or more industrious, and the imbalance will surely cause friction."

"Don't forget power," Ivory cautioned. "When one has the power to end the other's life, fear will always outweigh love."

Chase reached for her hand, raised it to his mouth, and kissed each of her fingertips. "Don't you forget there are men who thrive on danger. They'd find such a powerful woman endlessly exciting."

As he bent his head to place a kiss in her palm, Ivory longed to run her fingers through the inky blackness of his hair, but, uncertain where their conversation was leading, or where she truly wished it to go, she didn't dare touch him. "I have the distinct impression you're repeating phrases you've found effective in seducing other women. I do wish you'd find a more original approach."

Her criticism was so accurate that Chase couldn't help but laugh. "Forgive me," he begged. "You're a remarkable woman and you definitely deserve a more creative approach. Unfortunately, we may be back at The Diamond Mine before I find one."

"Would that be such a tragedy?"

"For me it would be," Chase replied, but he was unwilling to explain that his life depended on it.

For a brief instant, Ivory wondered if it weren't simply Chase's dark coloring that made him so different from everyone she knew. She swiftly discarded that notion, however, deciding it was the cockiness of his attitude that set him apart. Stokes shared that trait, but Chase was clearly the more intelligent of the two, and that gave him a decided, and perhaps lethal, edge.

"Don't torture yourself composing poetry," she replied as she pulled her hand from his. "You've just admitted you're attracted to danger rather than me, and after that damning confession, no approach, no matter how imaginative, will succeed. Now go find something to occupy your time until supper. I'd like to be alone."

Feeling as though she had cleverly led him into a verbal trap, Chase realized too late that he had indeed made the error she described. "All I said was that there were men who were attracted to danger. I didn't say I was one of them."

"Oh, please," Ivory moaned. "You're only making it worse. Just get out of here."

Reluctantly Chase bowed to her command and went back to the passenger cabin. Doubting he could find any amusement on board to compare with Ivory's taunting fire, he paced the aisle for several minutes before his gaze fell upon her sketchbook. Certain she would not be joining him any time soon, he sat down and began to leaf through it. As he had earlier witnessed, Ivory had a knack for capturing the uniqueness of any object and he was fascinated by her drawings.

The first pages in the sketchbook were devoted to still lifes but bore no resemblance to traditional assemblages of fruit or objects because she had combined knobby vegetables with an assortment of mechanical parts. The contrast in textures between the living and inanimate things was rendered so beautifully that Chase could not resist the urge to run his fingers across the pages. He traced the lines, marveling at Ivory's extraordinary talent.

Eager to see more, he went through page after page of careful sketches depicting everything from a colorful group of patrons slouched over the bar in The Diamond Mine's tavern to fabric in a wild abstract pattern draped over a pair of men's boots. Expecting more unusual combinations, Chase drew in a sharp breath when he found that Ivory had not merely seen him in that damn cage, but had taken the time to draw him from every imaginable angle.

His outrage wasn't dulled by the magnificence of the drawings of him, either. Perhaps he had been nothing more than an artistic challenge. Spider had said that Ivory liked him. Now Chase feared it was because he had provided an interesting new subject for her artwork.

Thoroughly disgusted, he struggled to his feet, carried the sketchbook up to the cockpit, and waved one of the nude sketches at her. "Did you find drawing me amusing? I could have frozen to death it was so damn cold down there, but my comfort, or lack of it, didn't enter your mind, did it? I must not have meant anything more to you than the iguanas in your science files, just some poor human being lying in a tortured heap. You're your father's daughter all right. You may have a keen eye, and the dexterity to draw whatever you please, but you haven't an ounce of soul and you'll never be a great artist."

Chase flung the sketchbook at her and returned to the passenger cabin.

Startled, but not surprised that Chase had snooped through her drawings, Ivory grabbed the incriminating book and followed on his heels. "How dare you look through my work?" she

Lady Rogue

shouted. "Everything I own, every single thing, is private, and if you ever make the mistake of snooping through my work, or anything else connected to me, you'll beg me to kill you to end your misery!"

Chase, too angry to think clearly, saw only an incredibly desirable woman, not one whose aggravation matched his own. Rather than respond with equally vivid threats, he reached out to pull her into his arms and kissed her with a demanding passion. Her frantic efforts to break free of his confining hold only intensified his need to punish her with devouring kisses. He twisted his body to imprison her in the aisle and then pulled her down across his lap in the nearest seat.

Her curls tumbled across his face, blinding him like a golden curtain. Lost in that sensuous caress, he was beyond caring that he was jeopardizing his mission. His only need was to subdue the lithe goddess in his arms. She was breathing in ragged gasps, but he refused to set her free until he could be certain she would willingly return to his arms. Striving to make her want him, he gradually softened his forceful kisses to a deliciously tempting lightness, but as the minutes passed, Ivory showed only a smoldering defiance.

Finally realizing that she had been raised by a man who would scorn any show of tenderness as evidence of weakness, Chase shifted his weight to force the seat into a reclining position and pinned her firmly beneath him. It sickened him to have to resort to such a barbaric technique, but clasping her wrists, he nuzzled her ear. "I'd make a very dangerous pet unless you took the time to tame me."

115

Cinnamon Burke

"I'd sooner coax scorpions to sing."

Chase raised himself up slightly. "That comment was as strange as some of your drawings. I'm too late, it seems. Loneliness has already driven you mad."

"Are you so conceited you can't conceive of a sane woman rejecting your crude pawings?"

Taking a firm hold of her wrists with one hand, Chase slid his other hand down over the sweet fullness of her breast. Even through her flight suit he could feel her nipple become a taut bud. He massaged it with a lazy delight. "You don't feel revolted by my touch."

Ivory's stare darkened. "Revolted, nauseated, disgusted—"

Chase again seized her lips to silence the string of insults he was positive she did not mean. He forced her legs apart with his knee and slid his hand lower. She arched her back, inadvertently dipping toward him, and he grabbed her thigh to still her writhing, then moved his hand up until the heel rested against her mound. He used only light but insistent pressure in the surest means he knew to teach her why women wanted to be with men.

Inspired by the increased warmth he could feel, he continued to torment her with a smooth, seductive touch. Making love to Ivory Diamond was as great a challenge as teaching scorpions to sing, but he was willing to take the risk. She had ignited something deep within him that he had to arouse in her. He didn't quit until he sensed what was surely a thrilling tremor of ecstasy rather than revulsion course through her. He released her hands then; dazed by the pleasure

116

he had bestowed, she made no immediate move to escape him. Instead, she lay still, her eyes closed, her breathing rapid, and her expression one of pure contentment.

Before Chase could congratulate himself, Ivory's mood changed to one of such wild indignation he had to scramble to his feet. He raised his hands as he backed away. "I was merely providing a lesson I thought must be missing from your science files. A simple thank you will do."

"You touch me again and I'll cut off your hand and make you eat it."

Chase didn't doubt her intention but merely laughed lightly. He was positive he had discovered how to reach her, and he refused to appear in the least intimidated. "You'd never cut off my hands when you know how good they can make you feel."

Ivory's whole body ached for more of Chase's caresses, but she was far too proud a young woman to admit it. "There will be whores at the Eagle's Nest. Satisfy yourself with them while I'm talking to Mordecai Black. Otherwise, I'll take you back to The Diamond Mine in chains."

Chase winked. "I've no interest in other women when we're so good together."

"You're as good as dead."

"So what? Life isn't worth living without risk, and you are definitely worth the risk."

Ivory couldn't help but admire Chase's courage. Thinking perhaps her father had seen and appreciated the same quality, she did not want to engage in any lengthy battle of wills in an attempt to break his spirit. Neither did she want a repeat of their last, and most physical, encounter.

"If you imagine I enjoyed being pinned to the seat like some butterfly in an exotic collection, you are sadly mistaken. There may no longer be a death penalty in the rest of the galaxy, but at The Diamond Mine, it is still the punishment for rape."

Chase rested his elbow on the adjacent seat with practiced nonchalance. "As well it should be, but what just happened between us doesn't come close to the definition of rape, and you know it. I happen to think we make a great team on any number of levels, but I've the experience to recognize the magic we make together for what it is, and in time you will too. I'll try to be more patient."

That he would taunt her for being innocent where men were concerned was more than Ivory could abide. "Yes, do that," she encouraged, "or I might be tempted to demonstrate the Celestial Cannon's accuracy, with you as the target. That would not only impress Black, but end your annoying presence as well."

"Perhaps, but it would also leave you without a bodyguard, and we both know that wouldn't be wise. The Eagle's Nest will be filled with all manner of vermin, most with two legs."

"Your relatives?"

While he admired Ivory's wit, Chase decided she was a deeply angry person, harboring a furious rage that erupted all too easily. He was determined to find the cause of her anger and permanently defuse it. Rather than react to her barb in kind, he changed the subject.

"Is there anything in particular you'd like me to prepare for supper? It will be a long afternoon

118

and I'd like to have some useful task to keep myself occupied while you seethe over whatever it is that bothers you so."

Ivory raked her fingers through her tangled curls. "You're the only thing bothering me."

"You bother me too," Chase revealed in a hoarse whisper.

Why her father had encouraged her to take such an obnoxious man as a lover still perplexed Ivory. She saw the same raw desire in his gaze that often brightened Stokes's eyes. Despite her father's wishes, she feared that exploring Chase's passions would be the worst mistake of her life.

Ignoring his husky comment, Ivory replied to his previous question. "I doubt I'll want anything to eat later, but if I do, I'll fix it myself." She plucked her sketchbook from the aisle where it had fallen and brushed by Chase on her way back to the cockpit. She was much too anxious to draw, and sat staring blindly at the navigational computer.

Rainbow had completed her check and was reporting optimum function of all systems. Ivory was relieved that at least the technology of the ship was running smoothly, even if she felt far from well. She sat back and tried not to think how much she hated Chase Duncan for dismissing the bliss he had shown her as no more than a science lesson. She would repay him for that insult, and soon.

Chapter 6

Ivory remained in the cockpit until Chase summoned her for supper. Even though she had told him she would fix her own meal, he had prepared a delicate pasta smothered in a savory wine sauce, and the aroma was so tempting she decided against refusing the dish just to spite him. She wasn't interested in conversation, but his first question surprised her so greatly she answered without thinking.

"I expected to see some of the guests at breakfast this morning. Were they all sleeping late?"

Ivory wound the slippery strands of pasta around her fork. "No, they'd already gone. The Diamond Mine will be an unlisted detour on their itineraries. None will admit they've ever been there if they're asked, which they won't be. We're popular, but only as long as our notoriety doesn't tarnish our respectable guests' fame."

"Don't you find that insulting?"

Ivory looked up, and was instantly sorry. Just meeting Chase's gaze brought on a cresting wave of desire. The fact that she had never found another man nearly so appealing puzzled her. She had become adept at ignoring men's stares, but Chase's heated glance traveled over her with the sensuous grace of a caress and was impossible to deny.

She whipped the pasta around her plate in a futile effort to distract herself, then took too large a bite and nearly choked. When she was finally able to swallow, she gave an impertinent reply. "No, not at all. Our guests receive the exquisite thrill of consorting with a dangerous criminal element, while we enjoy the benefit of their sparkling intellects. It's a fair trade. I thought you were enjoying yourself last night."

"I was. I never expected to meet any of those people, and certainly not at The Diamond Mine."

"We average several such groups a month. You'll find working for my father provides a great many advantages over Alado."

Chase quickly agreed. "Yes, I'm already enjoying what has to be the greatest advantage right now, and that's being here with you."

When Stokes made similar remarks, Ivory was merely disgusted. Chase had far more polish, but she wished his interest in her did not have such a narrow focus.

Ivory pushed her empty plate away. Her tone was firm but not harsh as she spoke. "You're making me extremely uncomfortable. From now on, keep your thoughts about me to yourself."

Chase waited for the dire threat that Ivory

usually coupled to her demands, but this time there was none. She was looking down at her hands, and at that moment she seemed not merely uncomfortable but vulnerable as well. Perhaps it was the careless toss of her head to sweep her curls off her face, but she had never been more alluring.

"I'm not sure that I can," he confided honestly.

Ivory did not want to hear any more. "You must. We discussed postponing our arrival, but I can't take spending two nights on board with you. Let's go ahead and land at midnight tomorrow. If you give me the slightest bit of trouble tonight, I'll leave you at the Eagle's Nest. Mordecai Black might be able to use a man with your talents, but I won't put myself through another hour of your company if it's going to be objectionable."

Chase nodded thoughtfully. "I knew you could come up with a threat if you just put your mind to it. Stranding me at the Eagle's Nest is way below your usual standard, though. You're the most creative person I've ever met. Surely you can come up with something more gruesome."

Insulted by his sarcasm, Ivory found it easy to douse the flames of desire. She eyed him coldly. "Don't laugh at me, Chase. It's the worst mistake you could ever make."

For a fraction of a second, Chase saw the same dangerous light glowing in Ivory's eyes that lit her father's, and he couldn't suppress a chilling shudder. "All right, you needn't be hostile. I promise to behave myself. It's much too early to go to sleep. Would you like to play a game, or watch a film together?"

Ivory had never been asked out on a date. There

was nowhere for either of them to go, so Chase's offer could not really be considered as such, but she was still embarrassed by his polite request for her company. She would be too exquisitely aware of him to concentrate on a film, or remember the rules of a game. "No, thank you, I'd rather be alone. It's what I'm used to."

Chase continued his verbal pursuit. "Who did you play with as a child?" He was also finished eating and set both their plates aside. He leaned back to get more comfortable, and hoped he could keep Ivory talking for hours. She had a marvelous voice, low and soft when she was describing her artwork or making casual comments, but it took on a biting edge when she was peeved with him, which was far too often. Either way, her voice was as unique as the rest of her, and he enjoyed just listening to her.

Ivory hesitated, then decided she had no objection to satisfying his curiosity on such a small point. "We had employees with children in those days, and the room that serves as my studio was our school and playroom. Everyone's grown up and gone now and there are no children at our outpost."

Chase could easily imagine Ivory as a cute little girl with a paint smudge on her cheek. He wished he could have known her then and watched her grow into the beautiful woman she was now. Surprised by the sentimental turn of his thoughts, he said, "You must miss your friends."

Ivory refused to admit how long it had been since she had been surrounded by the happy children who had been her only true friends. She had missed them terribly at first, but now she had been alone so long that solitude was as natural to her as the blue of her eyes. That was a pitiful secret she would never share. "Do you miss yours at Alado?"

"Yes, of course, but the good times we shared are over. I hope to make new friends, though." His smile invited her friendship, but just as he had expected, she failed to respond in kind. Instead she glanced away. "You're the most serious individual I've ever met," he mused softly. "I think I've only heard you laugh once, and you have such a pretty laugh, I miss it."

Ivory recalled the incident clearly. "It's not every day that someone makes a joke about Summer Moon. Now I'll think of a squash every time I look at her."

"It must be difficult to be around her."

"No, we avoid each other quite well. That prevents problems before they arise. Summer has been around longer than most of my father's mistresses, but that's no guarantee she'll be there forever, and I will."

Chase couldn't bear to think of Ivory never leaving The Diamond Mine. It was too easy to imagine her as a radiant princess imprisoned in a tower fortress. He was certainly no knight sent to rescue her, but that did not mean he would not try. "I still think you ought to attend an art school on Earth. How is anyone ever going to appreciate how beautiful your work is if you never have an opportunity to show it?"

Embarrassed by his praise, Ivory steepled her fingers, then laced them together. "I don't have to sell my work to survive, so there's really no need to show it. I do it simply to please myself.

It's my own private source of joy."

Chase forced himself to sit very still so as not to frighten her away. "You are like one of the lovely orchids in your gardens: shy, reclusive, a spectacular bloom few ever see. Hiding you away might be your father's greatest crime."

"I'm not hidden," Ivory argued. "I deal for one of the poker games nearly every night in the casino. That's as public an appearance as anyone could ever make."

A slow grin spread across Chase's lips. "Do you always deal off the bottom of the deck when there's a man at your table you'd like to meet?"

His question inspired another rare laugh from Ivory, but it was derisive rather than musical. "It must be wonderfully comforting to believe you're irresistible to women, but don't you find it a terrible burden? After all, how can you find time for them all?"

Again turning serious, Chase leaned forward slightly. "There's no one else, Ivory. I've plenty of time to be with you."

Ivory hadn't forgotten her father's encouragement to take Chase for a lover, but despite his obvious willingness, she knew it would not be right. She did not make paintings devoid of meaning, or sculptures that were mere blobs of clay, and she could not perform the physical act of lovemaking without giving it significance. "I believe in love," she whispered, "and I don't want a man who means less to me than my art. My father uses people; I don't."

Chase had never had such an intense desire to be used, but Ivory's pensive manner made any flippant response absurd. His training told him he had just found the key to reaching her, for clearly she wanted the same stirring honesty from a man that she demonstrated in her art. Complete honesty was impossible in his case, but he would give her all he could.

"I understand," he assured her, "but I've never been in love, and if I had waited for something which never came, I would have missed a great deal of tender affection, and that's very nice too. Life doesn't always provide everything we want, but that doesn't mean we can't appreciate what we do have."

"Live for the moment? Is that what you mean?"

"No, it's more like live *in* the moment. Don't you feel especially alive when you paint or sculpt?"

Ivory nodded. "Yes. Is that how you feel when you fly?"

"Yes, but not everything needs to be a heart-stopping thrill. Pleasure of a much more leisurely sort is also very, very good."

Ivory's glance swept Chase slowly. She noted his relaxed pose, his casual gesture, and finally his teasing smile. Her heart ached to reach out to him, but fearing she would never be anything but a pretty prize he would use to impress her father, she shoved her tray aside and rose. Her knees were shaky, but she leaned back against her seat to cover her lack of grace.

"I prefer to sleep in the cockpit, and I don't want to be disturbed. I'll see you in the morning."

Chase had to grab for their plates before he could stand. Feeling clumsy as well as hopelessly frustrated, he watched Ivory walk away without being able to think of a single thing to say to make her stay. He had had a long string of passionate, if brief, affairs with female pilots whose lives were as uncluttered and unfettered as his own. No one had ever gotten hurt when the romances had come to their inevitable end, but when Ivory wasn't angry with him, which wasn't often, he glimpsed a sorrow so profound he knew no man could walk away from her without feeling he had torn her heart from her chest, or lost his own.

He carried their plates and utensils back to the galley, then stripped off his clothes to shower. The water was too warm to cool his ardor, however, and once dry, he felt not in the least bit refreshed. He dressed in clean clothing, then sat back down again in the passenger cabin and selected another humorous film. The characters were amusing, their plight ludicrous, and while he knew he should be entertained by the silliness on the screen, he couldn't seem to follow the story.

He kept recalling the photograph of Ivory holding the Celestial Cannon. He had known right then that this would be an assignment like no other. Until now, he had never felt sympathy for the criminals he had been sent to apprehend. He had no trouble at all maintaining a professional detachment with Spider, but with Ivory he was lost. He longed to simply hold her until she had shed what he feared was a lifetime of tears. Then she might be able to trust him enough to love him, but loving him would destroy her.

At the same time, he knew that not loving her would destroy him.

The following day passed more easily than the first because Chase respected Ivory's preference for solitude. That did not stop him from longing to be with her, but he now knew enough about her to keep not only his distance, but his amorous thoughts to himself. That wasn't easy in a Blaster, but while Ivory passed her time sketching in the cockpit, he played exercise tapes and worked out in the passenger cabin.

Later they contacted the Eagle's Nest, and were cleared for docking. Chase waited until Ivory had showered and dressed to discuss their final plans. He paced up and down the aisle flexing his muscles and trying to assume what he hoped was a bodyguard's bearlike demeanor. He was used to using his brains rather than brawn, but he knew the negotiations were Ivory's show and he had promised himself not to interfere unless she needed protection. Then he looked up and realized she was definitely going to need protection— from him.

Ivory left the lavatory dressed in a shimmering silver suit that caressed the lush swells of her slender figure with erotic abandon. The sight played havoc with Chase's carefully cultivated self-control. Although the fabric wasn't transparent, it might as well have been. A long moment passed before he glanced up from her breasts and was jarred anew by her startling wig of metallic curls. They were copper and gold, not silver, but the total effect was uncomfortably close to the silver boys who guarded Spider's bank.

"My God," Chase moaned, "what are you trying to do to Mordecai, and to me?"

Ivory shook her head, sending her springy curls into bouncing waves. "The object is to distract him so thoroughly he will lose all interest in arguing for better terms."

"Well, you have definitely achieved your goal. That looks like a Rocketball suit. Do you play the game?"

"It is a Rocketball suit, all right, but no, we don't have a court. The game's too frantic to stage at The Diamond Mine, so we don't compete with the mining colonies running tournaments."

"Frantic is an understatement," Chase murmured, still awed by her outfit. Rocketball was a modern derivation of jai alai. It had been popularized in the twenty-first century and continued to be avidly followed by millions on Earth as well as throughout the colonies. Racquets were used rather than the original wicker baskets strapped to the wrist, but the game was every bit as fast and deadly as jai alai had ever been.

"You don't know how relieved I am to hear you say that. I've never been able to watch the female Rocketball teams. They just scare me to death."

Surprised by that admission, Ivory cocked her head and regarded him with an appraising stare. "Occasionally a player breaks an arm or leg, but fatalities are few. The danger is something the players readily accept as part of the game, but the actual risk isn't nearly as high as spectators are made to assume. That's merely the promoters' propaganda to make the games seem even more daring than they already are. The public craves excitement, and apparently the specter of death provides it in abundance."

Chase was amazed by her cool analysis of the fast-paced game. "You sound as though you've made a study of the statistics."

"Rocketball involves gambling, and that quite naturally excites my father's interest. I've learned about the sport from him. Most of the teams are honest, but there's a player now and then who needs cash and can be bribed to throw a game."

While Ivory was calmly discussing bribing athletes, and Chase could think of little else than how gorgeous she looked, he knew enough not to register his disgust that no aspect of criminal activity escaped Spider Diamond's notice. "Only an occasional player?" he asked skeptically. "I'm surprised Spider doesn't control entire teams."

"No, we'd lose the element of surprise then. Fans would soon learn which teams were controlled and we wouldn't have the amount of wagering we'd get otherwise. Now that's enough about Rocketball. Let's go over our plan a final time."

Chase could follow the gentle curve of her ribs through the silver suit and doubted he could discuss anything of a serious nature with her dressed in such a seductive fashion. "Do you wear that costume when you travel with your father?"

"Of course." Ivory gestured broadly but with a grace that made Chase wish she would wrap her slender arms around him. "This is not only a distracting garment, but a clever disguise. Just look how long it took your gaze to reach my face."

"I'm sorry," Chase insisted. "I didn't mean to leer. I'd still like to see you dressed in gold, though. Can you get a gold suit?"

"I can get whatever I want," Ivory replied confidently, "and tonight what I want is for you to follow me and keep your eyes open. Let Mordecai and his men gape like the witless lechers they undoubtedly are. You just stand watch so we don't get attacked from behind."

Ivory picked up a soft silver cape and slung it around her shoulders. She pulled the Celestial Cannon from her bag and hid it easily in the flowing garment's deep folds. "This has to be all business, Chase. Wipe your mouth and stop drooling, or take along a sponge to mop up after yourself."

"You love to talk tough, don't you?"

"I'm not just talking; I am tough. Now you're along to dock the ship, so take care of that, and then we'll be ready for Mordecai Black."

Apparently unworried about the upcoming meeting, Ivory took a seat and leaned back, but Chase knew she was merely giving a performance. She might be a fine actress, but she wasn't tough. It was all a pose, and, determined to see that she got away with it, he saluted before heading up the aisle for the cockpit. "Yes, boss, whatever you say."

Chase had never visited the Eagle's Nest, but as he started their descent, he got a very bad feeling. He quickly checked the Blaster's instruments, but there was no problem there. As he began his final approach, the doors of the docking bay he had been assigned rolled open, revealing an interior so poorly illuminated it presented an extreme danger rather than a safe harbor. He pulled the ship up and sent a foul-tempered message to the docking tower requesting a change of assignment.

He then hit the intercom button and spoke to Ivory. "I'm not landing in a bay I can't see clearly.

There's too great a chance of an explosion and I won't risk your life or mine just to sell a few cannons."

Ivory came forward immediately and took the co-pilot's seat. "What's wrong?"

"They either have no maintenance or the sloppiest crews in the galaxy, and I won't land any ship in the dark."

From their present position the docking bays weren't visible, and Ivory hesitated to take Chase's word for their condition. "Is this just an attempt to keep me on board tonight as you originally suggested?"

Astonished that she could imagine he would pull such a stupid stunt, Chase glared at her. "That's beneath you."

"Perhaps, but not you."

"I meant the accusation, not the lie!" Chase found it difficult to look at Ivory when her outlandish costume made her resemble a dancer in some obscene review. She was all long slender legs, full breasts, and big eyes, and the last thing he needed was a distraction. Rather than argue, he made another pass by the docking bays so Ivory could see precisely why he was complaining.

What she saw was a bay lit by so few lights the interior was heavily shadowed. It was impossible to accurately judge the bay's dimensions, and that was one of the primary requirements for a safe landing. "I'm sorry. I wouldn't land here either. Put the Blaster in orbit."

Chase did so. "Do you think it's a trap?"

"If so, it was pitiful and deserved to fail." Ivory rested her head against the seat and drummed her fingers on the armrests.

"If you want to go home, I'll back you up. It's your call."

"It always has been."

Chase let out a weary sigh. "True, but it always helps to have a witness confirm your story. In that regard, I'm better than your silver boys."

"There's a recorder taping the flight. It would have supplied all the proof I'd need, but believe me, my word is sufficient for my father."

"I can appreciate that. It's good to be trusted."

Knowing he was referring to them rather than to her and her father, Ivory ignored his comment and spoke with the docking tower herself. "You were notified of our arrival time two days ago. That your facilities are so ill-prepared to receive us is inexcusable. You have one hour to correct the problem, or we will be forced to refuse to dock. Inform Mordecai Black of the situation immediately."

Ivory shut off the transmission before receiving a response, but nothing the docking officer could have said would have pleased her. She turned toward Chase. "That's it. If we're unable to dock in an hour, then we're going home. Not having the docking bay ready for us shows a lack of respect my father would never tolerate. He would already be on his way home by now, but because I have a far more generous nature, I'm giving Mordecai a chance to rectify his mistake."

There was no resemblance to the sad, waiflike creature who had shared dinner with him the previous evening, and though Chase was convinced that the vulnerable girl was the real Ivory Diamond, he could not help but admire the resolve she displayed now. "Mordecai Black must want the cannons badly enough to replace the lights in the docking bay himself. You're going to make him pay for this delay though, aren't you?"

"Damn right I am. I'm adding a twenty-five-percent surcharge to the price of the cannons."

Chase reached over to slap her knee. "You're my kind of woman, Ivory."

As usual, Ivory brushed his hand away. "Calm down. You haven't seen anything yet. Once the silver boys go into production, Mordecai will want a whole regiment and they're going to cost him double."

"A regiment?" Chase's breath caught in his throat, and for a terrible instant he knew he had betrayed his true feelings. He covered the slip with a cough and prayed Ivory had not noticed. "You said you'd not sell them to mines, but you mean to sell them to colonists to be used as soldiers?"

Ivory nodded. "Conflicts between corporations over the acquisition of new territory are common, but their boards are unwilling to wage full-scale war. Colonists, however, engage in border skirmishes constantly. Mordecai Black will sell a few the Celestial Cannon, which will put them ahead until the opposition gets the new arms too. The silver boys will bring another round of fevered buying, but war is as old as mankind, and the loss of a robot, even an extremely expensive one, can't compare to the loss of a human life."

The prospect of a regiment of silver boys marching down a road carrying Celestial Cannons was terrifying. Because robots could be programmed to kill anything that moved, Chase was sickened by the bloodshed they would surely cause. A human soldier would hesitate before shooting a woman or child, but not a robot. A robot would take aim and fire, then march on to seek its next target.

He had to swallow hard before he could speak. "Is that Spider's theory, or yours?" he asked.

"We share many of the same opinions, except for Summer Moon's value, of course. We'll never agree about her. The next time we have a group of philosophers for dinner, I'll try to remember to ask them if they believe man's nature is essentially warlike."

"Yes, please do, I'd like to hear their opinions."

"We have nearly an hour," Ivory reminded him. "Tell me yours."

The Alado Corporation was so firmly committed to peaceful exploration that Chase needed a moment to shift his thinking in line with hers. "Well, I say we can't argue with the lessons of history, and people have never gotten along well. Most couples can't stay together, so it's no wonder that countries encounter so much strife, or that the Earth colonies have followed the same pattern. Peace is a beautiful dream, but only that, a dream."

"Do you place love in the same category? After all, if you've never been in love, you can't really say whether it exists or not, can you?"

Chase opened his mouth to respond, and then realized how cleverly she had redirected the conversation. "What are you doing? Have you switched topics on me just because I agreed with you? You warned me your father liked arguments. Do you like them too?"

Ivory scooted down in her seat, an elegantly clad woman who seemed totally unaware of her beauty. "No, not at all. I like to be left alone so I can work without being distracted."

Chase slid his finger down her cheek. "Do you find me distracting?"

"Terribly."

"Good."

"No, it isn't good at all."

Ivory had such marvelously expressive features that her despair was touching. Chase wasn't certain how they had gone from discussing warrior robots to love, but he was grateful for the chance to talk about anything other than widespread destruction. "It's all a matter of focus," he confided softly. "There's a time to seriously devote ourselves to work, and another time to savor the joy of love. Those needs don't have to conflict with each other, and you and I don't necessarily have to fight."

Ivory glanced toward him, then back at the instrument panel. Rainbow was running the ship with a comforting hum, but she longed for the solitude of her studio. "If we're able to complete this assignment, my father will give you more responsibility. He'll eventually send you out to make deals on your own. Then I can stay home and paint, or sculpt iguanas all day. I'm looking forward to that, so please don't disappoint either of us tonight."

Chase studied her profile and wished he had the artistic talent to paint her from a hundred different angles, because she would be superb from every one. "I'll look forward to that time. Then maybe you'll be happy to see me when I come home."

"Don't count on it."

Chase chuckled at her defiant retort, then leaned over and kissed her. She did not immediately shove him away, so he kissed her again, and again. He knew he had to prevent Spider from selling even one of the silver boys, let alone a regiment of soldier robots, but that did not keep him from wanting Ivory so badly that he refused to consider her part of her father's underworld empire. He touched her metallic curls and wished it were her own silken hair.

Chase's first kiss had caught Ivory by surprise, but by the third she was enjoying them too much to object. She wasn't about to take things any further, but kissing him was so nice, she wished that she could spend the night in his arms. She might have, had the docking officer at the Eagle's Nest not contacted them. Chase sat back with a frustrated groan, but she responded as though she had been eagerly waiting for permission to dock.

"We've been assigned to bay four. If it looks good, take us in."

Chase knew several sayings about the value of good timing, but this wasn't an example of any of them. Angry at being interrupted before he had even begun to show Ivory how much he cared about her, he straightened up and again assumed control of the Blaster. The bay awaiting them was as well lit as the day it had been built, and he landed the ship smoothly.

"How long do you want to stay?" he asked. "I think it would help to limit the negotiations if you set a time to leave now."

"No, let's be open-minded and see how the situation feels."

That Chase was more concerned with arms

Cinnamon Burke

sales than with what they had just shared confirmed Ivory's suspicions that whatever feelings he had for her were definitely in the lust category. That she was so hurt told her far more about herself, though. Believing she was pathetically eager for love, she pushed herself out of her seat and went back to the passenger cabin to get her cape and the Celestial Cannon. For now she would concentrate on Mordecai Black. She would deal with Chase Duncan later.

Chapter Seven

Chase had never worked as a bodyguard, but being naturally protective of Ivory he easily projected the appropriate menacing toughness as he led the way down the Blaster's ramp. He paused at the bottom, and only after making certain the three unarmed men sent as their escorts presented no danger did he wave for her to follow. He was surprised that Mordecai Black had not met them personally, and knew Ivory would interpret the oversight as an insult, but the trio of escorts were so excruciatingly polite he was relieved when she did not vent her anger on them.

Dressed in gray uniforms, with closely cropped hair, they resembled senior cadets at a military academy rather than a colonial leader's personal guard. They walked with as purposeful a stride

139

as Spider's silver boys, and stood at attention in the elevator. Looking at them, Chase got the distinct impression that Mordecai ran his colony in a strict military style.

When the doors opened at a tavern every bit as loud and lewd as Chase had expected The Diamond Mine to be, he wasn't shocked as much as disappointed. Not only was the music blaring at an ear-piercing level, an obviously drunken clientele was enthusiastically cheering the nude women dancing on a stage that ran the entire length of the crowded room. Along the other three walls, rear-screen projection supplied images of couples and groups engaged in a wide range of sexual activities.

Revolted, Chase immediately hit the button to close the elevator doors. Considering the revealing way Ivory was dressed beneath her cape, he knew his demand would sound ridiculous, but he did not care. "Ms. Diamond is not about to walk through a tavern where women are being exploited in such a vulgar manner. If there's no other way to reach Mordecai's office, then he'll have to come to our ship while we're preparing to leave."

Drilled in obedience rather than initiative, and panicked by Chase's demand, the escorts searched each other's faces for an appropriate response. Their dismay was almost painful to observe. Finally, one supplied a halting answer. "There is a back way to the office, but Mordecai has never authorized its use for guests."

Impressed by Chase's attitude, Ivory backed up his demand by raising the Celestial Cannon and pointing it at their perplexed escorts. "You may tell Mordecai that I authorized the private approach. Now let's go."

In a rush to back away, the three young men collided with each other and slammed into the side of the elevator. With anguished gasps, they raised their hands and looked ready to drop to their knees. "Whatever you say, Ms. Diamond," the spokesman assured her. He leaned around Chase to press the button for the next level, and this time when the elevator doors opened, it was on an empty hallway.

Chase stepped out, looked around, and was relieved there were no boisterous crowds on this floor. Here the only sound was the gentle whir of the ventilation system, and the highly polished floor was unscuffed by the constant passage of booted feet. Satisfied as to their safety, he nodded to invite Ivory and their escorts to join him in the hall.

"It's just down this corridor," the most composed of the escorts directed. He hurried ahead to open a door that led to a narrow stairway. "Mordecai's in the office at the bottom."

Ivory waved him on with the cannon. "Announce us, please."

The young man did not look eager to do so, but nodded. "Yes, Ms. Diamond. I'll be proud to."

Chase would have blocked Ivory's way, but she made no attempt to move past him. She waited at his side until they heard a startled Mordecai Black swear, and start up the stairs. Also dressed in gray, he was a powerfully built man whose wide shoulders brushed the sides of the narrow stairway. His shaved head gave him an unmistakable resemblance to a bullet, but just as Ivory had predicted, his concentration faltered when his gaze reached her delectable breasts. He missed the top step and nearly fell.

Catching himself, he frowned in an attempt to recapture his dignity. He was under six feet tall, forcing him to look up to greet Ivory. "Apparently my men misunderstood my directions," he apologized immediately. "I never intended for them to bring you through the tavern. I'm merely one of many investors here rather than the sole owner, and that must have caused their confusion."

Mordecai Black was an intense man, and worry had etched deep lines between his eyes and around his overly large mouth. Framed by bushy brows, his dark eyes were devoid of even a faint spark of humanity. Knowing him to be a perfectionist who was obsessed with detail, Ivory did not believe his explanation.

"I can't imagine how," she said. "If you're unable to give clear directions on how to escort guests from the docking bay to your office, then you ought to see to the task yourself."

Chase had to bite the inside of his cheek to keep from laughing, but he knew Ivory well enough to know she was enjoying herself. Her boots added a couple of inches to her height, as did her curly wig, making her appear nearly his equal in stature. She was staring down at Mordecai, her expression as menacing a mask as any Spider had ever worn. She was a woman with an astonishing range of abilities, but Chase had the presence of mind to keep his attention focused on Mordecai and his quivering men rather than her.

Mordecai had dismissed the man who had alerted him to Ivory's presence, and now turned a fierce gaze on the two men who remained in the hallway. Blaming them for creating such an inauspicious beginning to his meeting with her, he dismissed them as well. "I'll speak with you later," he hissed through clenched teeth. He turned back to Ivory, his lips forming the slight curve that passed for his smile. "Yes, you're absolutely right," he agreed. "Please accept my apologies."

Ivory's manner didn't soften. "Must we do business here in the hallway?"

"No, certainly not," Mordecai assured her. "Please, the office is at the bottom of the stairs."

Again Ivory gestured with the cannon. "After you."

Mordecai's eyes widened at the sight of the gleaming weapon. When he finally managed to wrench his gaze from the laser pistol, and noted Ivory's increasing impatience, he hurried down the steep flight of steps. Opening a door, he turned to issue another welcome.

The office contained a long ebony desk and matching chair. Three battered metal chairs were placed opposite the desk, but otherwise the brightly lit, white-walled room was bare. If the manager of the Eagle's Nest ever worked there, then he or she was remarkably neat, or so completely disorganized he did not even keep the employees' schedules posted. Chase went to the far door, opened it, and glanced down a smoke-filled corridor that led to the tavern.

Everything appeared as it should be, but although Ivory took the center chair, Chase preferred to stand. He had not actually seen her arm the Celestial Cannon, but a glowing red light atop the pistol proved she had. It was an evil-looking weapon, and doubly so in a graceful, feminine hand.

Mordecai offered refreshments before taking his place behind the desk, but Ivory refused them. "I came here to do business, not to be entertained. The price has increased twenty-five percent since last we spoke. If you can't cover the extra cost, then I'll adjust the number of cannons you've ordered."

Angered by such an unexpected demand, Mordecai puffed out his cheeks with a muffled gasp. "But I thought everything had been settled. How can the price have changed?"

"How can the owners of the Eagle's Nest abide incompetent maintenance crews?"

Confused by the seemingly irrelevant question, Mordecai opened the top drawer of the desk and yanked out a price list. Chase was standing where he could see the man's every move, and noted there was nothing to identify the single sheet of paper with Spider Diamond. It was merely an anonymous transmission and could not be used in court to prove Spider's involvement in arms dealing.

Ivory sat back in her chair. "I came for the cash, Mr. Black. Do you have it or not?"

"I have it, but I want the original one hundred cannons I ordered, not seventy-five."

Mordecai Black had used the same abrasive manner to intimidate a great many men, but Ivory was immune to blustering bullies. "Fine, you may purchase as many as you like, but at the new price."

Nearly strangling on his rage, Mordecai sat back and glared. He looked ready to explode. Clearly he was not used to being crossed, and to find Ivory such an intractable individual was galling. "This just isn't right," he announced. "I'm going to contact Spider."

Again unfazed, Ivory merely shrugged. Her cape slid from her shoulders revealing a relaxed pose that was both taunting and seductive. "Go ahead, but hurry. My schedule will not permit a lengthy delay. A great many people want the Celestial Cannon, and if you're going to quibble over price, then I'll sell the weapon elsewhere."

"Satellite transmissions require time."

Ivory yawned. "Yes, they do, and it's already quite late." She rose with a lazy stretch. "Let's go to the communications center. I too would like to send a message to my father."

Mordecai's gaze slid over Ivory's slender figure with an insulting languor. Even knowing she was deliberately being provocative, Chase didn't appreciate Mordecai's response. It wasn't merely lust he saw in the bald man's eyes, but an almost anguished desire, as though he had a wife or mistress who never satisfied his needs. What he was imagining was all too clear, and Chase stepped in front of him to block his view.

"After you," he prompted.

Forced to redirect his thoughts, Mordecai lurched to his feet and led the way back up the private stairs. The communications center was down the hall from the elevators, and at that hour was staffed by two sleepy technicians. They leapt to their feet and stood at attention.

"Take a break," Mordecai ordered. "I've a private message to send."

Grateful to be excused, the pair left before he

could change his mind. Mordecai sat down at the central communications console and typed in the code for The Diamond Mine. He then sent Spider a terse complaint about the new price on merchandise he carefully did not describe. He swung around to face Ivory.

"Do you wish to add your message to mine?"

"No, I'll wait for my father's reply and respond then."

Mordecai nodded, and sent the transmission along a prescribed series of satellites. Too nervous to remain seated, he stood and began to pace with a short, choppy stride. Ivory chose a technician's stool and, leaning back, showed off her supple figure in all its exquisite detail. Each time Mordecai turned in his pacing, he looked her way and continued to fondle her with his eyes.

Chase used his time to study the center's equipment. It was of the latest design. Clearly, the owners of the Eagle's Nest made a huge profit. The room was cool to accommodate the computers, and he was glad to have a jacket, but Ivory appeared equally comfortable dressed in little more than her skin. He leaned back against the counter, folded his arms across his chest, and continued to play the part of the strong, silent type.

The wait had grown uncomfortably long before Spider's response appeared on the screen. " 'The new price stands,' " Ivory read over Mordecai's shoulder. "Did you really expect him to countermand my change?"

"If he valued me as a customer, he would have," Mordecai replied.

"Finding customers is not a problem for us,"

Ivory explained, "which proves the ancient law of supply and demand. Now which is it to be, one hundred Celestial Cannons at the new price, or seventy-five at the old one?"

Beaten, Mordecai gave in, but not without making his displeasure plain. "I'll pay your new price, but the next time we do business I want your father's word there will be no last-minute changes."

"Rather than renege on promises, we won't make any," Ivory informed him. "I won't need to send a message after all. I'd like to be gone within the hour. Have the money loaded on board my ship by then."

Mordecai clenched his fists at his sides. "I have the original sum ready to load. I'll need time to gather the rest."

"One hour."

"You bitch."

Chase had heard enough, and again moved between them. "You owe Ms. Diamond an apology. Make it quick."

"Get out of my way," Mordecai shouted. He put his hands against Chase's chest and, using his greater bulk, tried to shove him aside, but Chase did not budge.

"Now you owe me an apology too," Chase warned. "I'd be quick about it, or Ms. Diamond will pierce your ears with the cannon. I think you'd be real cute sporting a pair of Corkscrew keys as earrings, but when she's angry her aim isn't all that good, and you might end up with a ventilated cranium instead. It's your choice. Make it quickly."

Chase then stepped aside, and, just as he had

known she would, Ivory aimed the Celestial Cannon at Mordecai's left earlobe. "Well," Chase urged, "make up your mind."

Mordecai could feel the heat of the target beam and had no difficulty in making his choice. "I'm sincerely sorry," he muttered.

"Louder," Chase ordered.

"I said I was sorry!"

"No, no," Chase coached. "That was much too loud. Try to act like a gentleman, and then you'll be excused to pack up the money."

Mordecai's face was bright red now and he sputtered as he spoke. "I am sorry," he repeated in a softer tone.

"Thank you," Ivory replied, but she did not lower her weapon. "We'll meet you in docking bay four in one hour. Don't be late, or we'll cancel your order and leave."

Mordecai clearly wanted to argue, but having learned he could not win, he responded with a curt nod and strode out of the room. Chase raised his finger to his lips to warn Ivory to be still until he was certain the man had gone. "Is this the way your typical negotiations go when Spider handles them?"

"He has a certain finesse that I'm afraid I lack, but yes, confrontations, and sometimes bloody ones, usually do occur. We always get our way, though: the money first, and then the arms are delivered. Come on, let's go down to the tavern. Do you suppose the films repeat all evening? I'd like to see what happens with the woman and the two men holding the snake."

Ivory started for the door, but Chase hurried to catch her. He had hoped he had managed to close the elevator doors before she had caught a glimpse of the rowdy tavern, and he was disappointed to learn he had failed. "You can't want to go down there."

Ivory sent him a questioning glance. "Oh, but I do. It's a form of research, really. I want to see how our competition operates, and I never miss a chance to learn something which isn't in my science files."

Chase knew he deserved that barb, but refused to give in. "Look, if I tell you what happens on that particular tape, will you go back to the ship with me?"

"No, I really don't trust you to provide all the delicious details. Let's go."

Chase followed her into a waiting elevator, but it was plain he wasn't pleased. "There aren't many women on the frontier, so let me find us seats in the back where you won't be disturbed by men who probably have never seen anyone who looked as good as you their whole lives."

Ivory rather enjoyed Chase's worried frown. "I thought I just proved that I know how to handle men. As for you, the bit about piercing his ears was inspired."

"Yeah? Well I knew you'd aim lower, but that was enough to frighten him into behaving as he should."

When the elevator opened, Chase took her free arm. Entering the tavern with his head down, he escorted her around the wall farthest from the stage where five nude women were performing an elaborate tumbling routine. They were remarkably agile, but he doubted that any of the men present had noticed anything other than their breasts bouncing this way and that as they bounded across the stage. Fortunately there was a vacant table in the corner. He directed Ivory into the seat against the wall and sat at her right.

"A waiter probably comes by every hour or so," he shouted to be heard above the raucous music. "I hope you didn't want anything to eat or drink."

The table was sticky, and Ivory decided she would be better off not sampling the Eagle's Nest's fare. She shook her head, then turned her chair slightly to get a better view of the screen where the snake charmers were still performing with the woman. While their motions were certainly suggestive, nothing particularly exciting was going on. On the next wall, two men held a woman sandwiched between them, but she looked bored rather than ecstatic to be the recipient of so much attention.

The final wall was filled floor to ceiling with flickering images of two nubile young women pleasuring each other. Ivory turned back to the trio with the snake. One of the men was now unwrapping his turban and using the trailing fabric to tie up the woman. Ivory leaned over to Chase. "Do you recognize any of the actresses?" she asked. "Did any pose for your photos?"

Chase didn't even want to look, but had to make a show of trying to identify one of the models who had supposedly posed for the "artwork" he had claimed to sell. He gave the huge images projected on the walls a cursory glance, and shook his head. He spotted a Corkscrew making his way toward them through the scattered maze of empty chairs and straightened up. Ivory had the

Celestial Cannon in her lap, but seemed unconcerned as she watched the man approach.

When he reached them, the Corkscrew resorted to mime rather than shouting to be heard. He laid his hands over his heart and blew Ivory a kiss. He then jerked his head toward Chase and waved good-bye, silently requesting that she get rid of him.

Ivory shook her head and pointed to the chair beside her. When the Corkscrew was seated, she leaned toward Chase. "He's one of our regulars," she mouthed. "Let him stay."

The Corkscrew smiled as though he had just gotten away with something wicked, and cupped his hands around his mouth and leaned close to speak with her. Apparently able to hear his comment over the din, Ivory laughed. Chase doubted he would want to hear anything being said, but continued to keep a close watch on Ivory.

The Corkscrew was a wiry little fellow with frizzled red hair, pale skin, and eyes of translucent blue. He looked harmless enough, but Chase remained alert, ready to pluck him out of his seat and send him flying should Ivory appear to be in the least displeased with his company. He preferred watching the Corkscrew to the obscene entertainment encircling them. He could understand other men's craving, after the silence of space, for the wild lights and noise of taverns like the Eagle's Nest, but he did not share it.

All he wanted was to take Ivory back to the Blaster and get her away as fast as he could. Even if she was a pirate's daughter, Chase hated to see her surrounded by such a disgusting array of lewd perversions. Fortunately, the Corkscrew's

151

animated conversation seemed to be distracting her from the pornographic films. He checked his watch and moaned inwardly. They still had plenty of time to kill.

Ivory nodded as the Corkscrew recounted his trip there, but she was not actually paying attention to him. She was far more intrigued by the fact that Chase, who supposedly sold pornography, showed no interest in either the naked acrobats or the lewd films filling the walls. Instead he was watching her, as though she were the most fascinating entertainment in the room. She reminded herself he was probably just intent upon doing his job well.

So was she. She patted the Corkscrew's arm, and gestured for Chase to rise as she left her seat. Hiding the Celestial Cannon in the folds of her cape, she walked with him out to the elevators. "My ears couldn't take any more of that cacophony," she complained. "I don't know how Nelson and his friends stand it."

Chase immediately recognized the Corkscrew's name. Nelson worked for Control. Now Chase could understand how he had been given such a good photograph of Ivory. She considered Nelson a regular, and therefore a friend. "Nelson? Don't most Corkscrews have names like Slash and Slicer?"

Ivory waited until Chase joined her in the elevator to reply. "Yes, I suppose they do. Nelson's name probably isn't Nelson either. He and his friends spend a great deal of time and money at The Diamond Mine, so I didn't want to be rude to him."

As they reached the level housing the docking

bays, Chase took Ivory's arm. "How did he recognize you in that superb disguise? That certainly isn't the way you look at the Mine."

For an instant, Ivory's gaze filled with confusion, and then she relaxed and smiled. "He saw me dressed like this once before. I don't recall where my father and I had been, but Nelson was on the docking level when we returned and, thinking I was a new entertainer, he rushed up to meet me. When he got close, he saw it was me and laughed about his mistake. I should have remembered that, and worn something else. I didn't expect to see him here, but I should have been better prepared for the unexpected, shouldn't I?"

"Corkscrews are harmless," Chase assured her, even though he knew full well that Nelson's working for Control made him very dangerous to Ivory indeed. "Let's check the ship again. I want to make certain no one tampered with anything while we were away."

Ivory preceded him up the ramp. "There would be no point in sabotaging our ship while we're carrying their money," she argued. "After we'd delivered the Celestial Cannons, perhaps, but not now."

"Are we coming back with the cannons?"

"No. My father and I handle only the cash, never the arms."

"I understand. Ferrying large sums of money around is no crime, but carrying arms is."

Ivory tossed her cape over a seat in the passenger cabin and went on up to the cockpit. "I'm pleased you have such a ready grasp of the obvious, Chase. Look, Rainbow reports no boardings of any kind while we were away."

153

That Ivory had set a silent security system before leaving the ship didn't surprise Chase, but he was annoyed with himself for not thinking of it. "You don't miss a thing, do you?"

"No, I don't, which is why I didn't need you along, but your cooking has been good, and that's a plus in your favor."

Chase cocked a brow. "Only my cooking?"

Before Ivory could think of a clever reply, she sighted Mordecai Black walking toward the ship with several men bringing the same size crates she used to transport The Diamond Mine's cash. "See that the money is stowed, and I'll deal with Mordecai."

"Don't you want to count it?"

"That would take days. I'll let the silver boys do it when we get home. Mordecai won't cheat us, not when we still have the cannons he's so eager to buy."

Chase shook his head sadly. "As always, you have an answer for everything."

Not where he was concerned, Ivory thought, but she would never admit that. She just shrugged and went to greet Mordecai. Chase remained on the ramp until the men were ready to load the crates. He opened the doors to the cargo hold, and watched them work with what he hoped would pass for complete boredom.

As he had expected, they soon forgot him and began talking about what they hoped to accomplish once the Celestial Cannons were delivered. Clearly defense wasn't what they had in mind, but instead an aggressive assault on a neighboring colony. Chase knew that Spider wouldn't care what Mordecai did with the weapons, but Chase

154

did. Nelson would report sighting him there, and Control would take it for progress on Chase's part. Now all he had to do was discover where the cannons were being made so the operation could be shut down permanently.

Ivory bid Mordecai a hasty good-bye as the last crate was loaded. As soon as Chase had sealed the cargo hold and the main hatch, she yanked off her wig, shook out her hair, and followed him up to the cockpit. "Get us out of here," she ordered, "and fast."

"I feel like taking a shower first."

"So do I, but it will have to wait." Ivory slipped into the co-pilot's seat and buckled the seat belt. She covered a wide yawn, settled in to get comfortable, and closed her eyes.

Chase contacted the docking tower and announced they were ready to depart. Bay four had to be cleared before the doors were opened, and while Ivory was relaxed now that they had completed their mission, Chase couldn't sit still. "I don't know how Spider can send you to such a revolting place. I'm glad we don't have to return with the arms."

Ivory opened an eye and peered at him. Anger gave his dark eyes a fiery glow and she smiled slyly. "Business is business; what does it matter where I conduct it? I certainly don't have to worry about my reputation being sullied."

"Nor do I!" Chase exclaimed. "I just wish I weren't wanted so that I could take you to one of the resorts for colonists on our way home. I bet you've never seen any of them, have you?"

"Resorts? Are they any different from The Diamond Mine?"

"Yes, they're not simply casinos and taverns, but feature whole environments: beaches with beautiful sunlit lagoons, ski lodges, hiking trails, luxurious bedrooms with satin sheets. Whatever you want, they have, but with Alado after me, I'd be arrested the instant we docked."

The bay's warning lights were beginning to flash, and Ivory watched as Chase worked his way through the preflight checklist. Suddenly, returning home was not nearly as appealing as it had been a few seconds earlier. "We've the equipment on board to provide you with new identification," she offered softly. "If you had a new name, and identification badge to prove it, would anyone at any of the resorts you mentioned recognize you as Chase Duncan?"

"No one," Chase assured her. "Do you want to go?"

"Where's the closest resort?"

Chase asked Rainbow to make a search, and she promptly displayed a name and coordinates on the navigational screen. "Paradise Retreat is one of the newest and best," Chase remarked. "We can be there by the time you've had a nice nap, and thanks to Mordecai Black, we've got plenty of cash to cover our expenses. Just say the word and I'll set our course."

"I've never seen an ocean. Oh, I realize it wouldn't be a real ocean at the Paradise either, but still—"

"Still, it's worth seeing," Chase coaxed. He doubted he would have any better luck with Ivory at the Paradise Retreat than at The Diamond Mine, or on board the Blaster, but he knew an exotic locale couldn't hurt his chances either.

"Have you ever had a vacation?"

"No. I love my work, so there's really no need to leave it."

"You can't have loved meeting Mordecai Black."

"Well, no, he won't make my list of favorite people, but—"

"Stop arguing, Ivory. Let's just do it. You got twenty-five percent more than Spider expected for the cannons. You deserve a reward."

Ivory responded with a deep, throaty laugh. "Can going to the Paradise Retreat with you be described as a reward?"

The bay doors rolled open. Chase gunned the Blaster's engines and guided them out into space. "Believe me, going anywhere with me would be nice, but it will be especially nice at the Paradise. Let's think of a new name for me, and please don't pick one of another man who's on Alado's wanted list."

"I hadn't thought of that," Ivory mused. "What a fiendish idea—to offer a man a new identity, and then provide him with one that will cause him even more trouble than his original name."

"You wouldn't." Chase shot her an anxious glance, and saw by her mischievous smile that she definitely would. "All right, that's a damn good idea, but save it for another man. Please."

"The Diamond Mine operates by a very strict code. We don't cooperate with any authorities on anything, so you can trust me not to get you in any more trouble than you're already in. Set our course for the Paradise Retreat, and wake me when we get there."

Cinnamon Burke

Elated by the romantic possibilities the Paradise would present, Chase couldn't help grinning. It wasn't until he had given Rainbow their new course that he realized his excitement had nothing to do with the thought of successfully completing his assignment.

Chapter Eight

The Paradise Retreat was located on a huge rotating space station. One of an ambitious chain of frontier resorts, its purpose was to provide recreation for the personnel laboring to spread civilization across the galaxy. The resort featured entertainment ranging from live performances by popular musicians and opera, ballet, and theatrical companies to an occasional Rocketball tournament. There were also spectacular amusement parks with thrilling rides for children, and a zoo with exotic animals.

For guests who sought only relaxation, there were a variety of lush Earth environments as well as enchanting fantasy worlds. Whether guests remained for a few hours or several weeks, all had such a marvelous time they were eager to return. As a pilot, Chase had been through several such resorts, but this would be his first visit to

159

the Paradise. He woke Ivory in plenty of time to make certain before they docked that she could actually produce the new identification she had promised.

A light sleeper, Ivory awoke as Chase's fingertips brushed her sleeve. She gave a lazy stretch, brushed her hair out of her eyes, and sat up. "You need the new I.D., right?"

"Right, but you'll have to help me come up with a name."

"That's no problem. I have a list from which to choose. Rainbow, give me the male alias file, thirties age range, please." As a column of names scrolled down the computer screen, she waited patiently for something appealing. "See anything you like?"

"Who are these men? Not that I really think you'd give me a name that would cause me grief, but I'm still curious as to where you got them."

Ivory regarded him with a skeptical glance. "The usual source is obituary columns. Surely you know that."

"Sorry, but I've never had a reason to use an alias before, so I don't know any of the finer points."

Uncertain how much she ought to divulge, Ivory turned back toward the screen. As before, she was uncertain just how far to trust Chase, but this was such a small matter she decided to risk it. "The corporations are always behind in maintaining their personnel files, so an employee can be dead several months if not years before his name is transferred from the active list. That's what makes obituary notices a good source. Still, there's always a risk in using a dead man's name, so we prefer to rely on fictional beings."

"Fictional beings?"

"Yes, it's what the corporations use for their undercover operatives. They simply create an identity for their agents, rather than letting them assume one that someone has already lived. That's what we do too. These names belong to men who were never born, but their histories are so deeply embedded in the corporation files that it would take years of diligent searching to prove they're not real."

Chase didn't realize he was holding his breath until the pain in his chest grew acute. He forced himself to breathe deeply while hoping that Ivory had not the slightest suspicion she had just described Chase Duncan's origins. "The corporations brag about their security," he said. "I didn't realize anyone could access their files and add to them without their knowing."

Chase sounded amazed rather than curious, but Ivory decided she had already told him enough. "Either you pick a name or I'll have to because I need some time to make your new card."

"There, how about that one, Carl Drake? At least my initials will be the same and I'll be able to remember it."

"Fine, Carl Drake it is." Ivory held out her hand. "Give me your old I.D. card. I'll give it back later, but I'll need to copy the photo."

Chase searched through his pockets and finally produced it. "Unfortunately, that photograph isn't all that flattering. Maybe you can take a better one when we get back to the Mine. After all, if I'm going to assume a new identity, I ought to do it in style."

Ivory studied the photograph on Chase's card and thought it remarkably handsome. He had such classic features she doubted he ever took a bad photograph, but he was already so conceited she did not dare tell him so. "This one will do. How much time do we have?"

"Rainbow says thirty-seven minutes."

"Fine. I'll see you in thirty-five."

Ivory left the cockpit. Chase would have liked to have watched her make the new I.D. card, but he did not want to appear too keen to see how things were done. That Spider Diamond was creating fictitious identities and scattering them through the major corporations' files was a stunning piece of information. Chase could not help wondering what else the man might have managed to accomplish.

Chase had infiltrated several criminal organizations, but none had been nearly as ambitious as Spider Diamond's was proving to be. Closing his eyes for a moment, he tried to imagine what Spider would take on next, and the most logical step would be to produce transport vehicles for the silver boys.

When Ivory returned, she was dressed in her usual silver flight suit. Her hair was damp and caressed her neck with springy curls. "Here's your card. You're with a branch of the Alado Corporation that constructs modular furniture for spacecraft."

"I've never even heard of it," Chase responded truthfully. "Am I any good at my job?"

"Yes, you're an excellent employee. That's why you've won a vacation."

"All right. I hope it's for two weeks at the very least."

"Sorry, we can't stay more than a day. We should have sent my father a message before we came within range of the Paradise. I don't want him thinking we're missing."

Ivory looked sincerely worried, and Chase reached out to pat her hand. "I sent one while you were asleep. Rainbow, show Ivory a copy of the last transmission, please."

It flashed on the screen, and when Ivory saw that her father had acknowledged the message with the instruction that they were to enjoy themselves, she knew exactly what he meant. "I just want to see the Paradise," she cautioned Chase, "and that doesn't mean that I want, or expect, anything even remotely exciting to happen between us."

She was lovely, and fresh from the shower she radiated a virginal sweetness. He knew she was frightened of him, and he did not want her to be afraid. "I realize that fleeing to avoid prosecution on a pornography charge doesn't make me sound like much of a gentleman, but I know how to behave myself. I'll ask for separate quarters, and I promise you now that I'll stay in mine. Of course, if you'd like to visit me, you'll be most welcome."

Ivory shook her head, but Chase couldn't tell if she was refusing his hospitality or attempting to discipline herself. "Sometimes resorts have art galleries," he remembered. "I hope the Paradise has one so you can see how much better your work is than the competition."

Relieved by his change of subject, Ivory buckled her seat belt and got ready for the approach to the space station. "Maybe I will go to Earth someday," she murmured more to herself than to Chase. "It would be nice to see the real thing, rather than simulations."

"Yes, it would, but I promise you won't be disappointed here. If you only want to stay for a day, we'll just try to see as much as possible. Maybe on another visit we can stay longer."

Ivory was tempted to scold him for being presumptuous, but it was so nice to hear him talk of her future as though he really intended to be a part of it.

The Paradise Retreat offered guests a great many attractive options in lodgings, but Ivory immediately selected one of the tropical island environment's thatched cottages. Chase asked for the adjoining bungalow, and carried their flight bags to the elevator. When they reached their level and the doors opened on a sunlit beach, he couldn't help but be amused by Ivory's delighted surprise.

"You see, I told you you'd not be disappointed."

The sandy beach came right up to the elevator. There were families with small children frolicking in the surf, and couples lying on colorful beach towels tanning themselves beneath the artificial sun which lent the whole scene a bright golden glow. The azure water beckoned invitingly, and in the distance, sailboats could be seen drifting by.

A magnificent fuchsia bougainvillea grew over a sign pointing the way to the cottages, and Chase started in that direction. "Come on, let's get rid of this stuff and then we can stay out on the beach the rest of the day."

"Everything looks so real," Ivory called as she followed along behind him. "Is the salty scent in the air the way the sea really smells?"

It was the scent of home to Chase, and he turned back to assure her that it was. "See the birds dipping down over the water? Those are sea gulls. It must take them a while to discover they can't fly past the clouds, but I'll bet they're well fed and content."

"Please, don't spoil the illusion," Ivory scolded. "I don't want to be reminded there's a ceiling above the clouds, or a false bottom to the lagoon. Let's just pretend this is a real island."

"It is real," Chase assured her. "The flowers are actually blooming, live birds are flying, and I'll bet we could even catch fish and eat them for dinner if we wanted to. Look, there's a parrot."

Ivory scanned the palm trees shading the path and saw the colorful bird. She called to the parrot, which flew away in a streak of yellow and green. "Do you suppose I could buy a parrot here and take him home?"

"Probably not, but we can ask. Would you like to teach one to talk?"

"It might be fun."

"Birds are messy," Chase warned. "They scatter seeds all over the floor, never talk on cue, and then squawk just when you want them to be quiet. I wouldn't recommend one for a pet."

"Then I'll buy a whole cageful!"

"That's the problem right there. Birds belong in the wild, not cooped up in cages as pets."

His comment reminded Ivory of how angry he

had been when he found her drawings of him while caged. There had been times when she thought it might have been a mistake to let him out, but now as she followed in his shadow, she knew he would never be content as any woman's pet. "How much farther is it?"

"Not far. Are you tired? Shall I go on ahead and then come back and carry you?"

"No, I'm fine." Ivory stopped to watch some children playing with a beach ball and then had to hurry to catch up with him. "I've never run on sand," she said in a breathless rush. "It isn't easy, is it?"

"No, but it's fun to play in. I'll show you how to build a sand castle."

"I've seen those in books. We'll need a bucket and shovels, won't we?"

"Yes, but I'm sure we'll find some."

Just as Chase had predicted, when they reached their cottages they found a heap of sandy pails, an assortment of child-sized shovels, and a big basket of toys to float in the water. Ivory was delighted at first, and then began to worry. "This looks as if it's all meant for children. Don't adults like to play in the sand?"

"Yes, of course they do." Chase was surprised such an independent young woman would be concerned about what the other guests might think of her. That she had the confidence to order Mordecai Black around but feared that strangers might laugh at her was a touching contradiction. He carried her bag through the door.

The cottage consisted of a single room with a bed covered in a bright tropical print, a bamboo table and chairs, and an adjoining bath. There were splendid yellow-green orchids in a glass vase on the table, and paintings in vivid hues decorated the walls. Grass mats covered the floor to complete the artfully assembled lodging.

Chase opened the closet. "There are plenty of clothes in your size. Put on one of the bathing suits and meet me down by the water."

Wanting to make the most of their stay, Ivory quickly sorted through the stunning array of swimsuits. There was no place to swim at The Diamond Mine, and she had never even tried on a bathing suit. Discarding those she considered too scanty, she chose a blue and white print with a softly draped skirt. It fit nicely, but as Ivory studied her reflection in the mirror on the closet door, she feared it made her legs look much too long.

"Are you ready?" Chase called through the screen door.

Reluctantly Ivory decided she would look no better in any of the other suits, so there was no point in changing. "I'm afraid I look like a crane," she complained as she joined him on the porch. "Too much of me is legs."

While the Rocketball suit had shown off the elegance of her proportions to perfection, the bathing suit allowed the luscious peach tones of her skin to show, and Chase could not see anything to criticize. "You have very beautiful legs, Ivory. Not even an ornithologist would compare you to a crane. Now stop worrying about how you look and let's build a sand castle."

Chase had yanked on the first pair of trunks in the closet and not given a thought to how he looked. He grabbed a couple of plastic pails and handed Ivory the child-sized shovels. "I wonder if the tide comes in here. It's always exciting to watch the water slowly creep up to the castle, and finally wash it away."

"You're an expert on sand castles?"

"Please, I'm too modest to claim to be an expert on anything. Haven't you discovered that?"

Dressed in a pair of bright red trunks, Chase looked every bit as good as Ivory had remembered, and she was glad he had thought of something for them to do that would be sufficiently distracting to keep her from simply staring at him all day. When he started walking toward the water, she again admired the depiction of Raven tattooed across his back. The wings spread across his shoulders in a powerful symbol that suited him somehow. An ancient motif, the stylized bird nevertheless was as modern and alive as he was.

She kicked the fine white sand with her bare toes as they moved along. "I've never been away from the Mine without something specific to accomplish. I'm not sure I can take a whole day of playing in the sand. I hope you won't mind if I want to leave early."

"No, whenever you get bored we'll go exploring. There's lots to see here."

"No, I meant I might want to leave for home." There was a fragrant breeze blowing, and Ivory raised her hand to sweep a stray curl out of her eyes. Chase had chosen a secluded stretch of beach, but she could hear the happy children laughing in the distance. "I'm not used to just having fun," she apologized.

Chase dropped the pails, reached for her hand, and led her down to the water. The frothy waves had an inviting warmth and lapped up over their ankles. "I don't think it's your science files that need updating. You just need a chance to experience life. You don't have to work at having fun. Just relax and let it happen."

The sailboats on the horizon looked real, but Ivory was sure they were merely part of the setting. "How can I experience life surrounded by such a pretty illusion? Isn't that a contradiction?"

Afraid she was right, Chase couldn't argue. Instead, he drew her close and kissed her cheek lightly. "Come on, let's build that castle. There will be just enough time before lunch."

"I want a moat."

"Of course, every sand castle has a moat. Now hand me one of the shovels and we'll get started."

Ivory knelt beside him in the sand, and she was soon so absorbed in their task that she forgot all about leaving the Paradise Retreat early. Chase didn't just build a sand castle, he created an enchanting architectural marvel with towers at the corners and notched parapets. He kept building it higher and higher until they had to stand to smooth out the walls. Children began to gather, and helped carry pails of water to fill the moat. By the time Chase finally announced it was finished, it was after two o'clock.

"Aren't you hungry?" he asked.

Ivory reached up to brush a spot of sand off his chin. "Yes, I suppose I am, but I'd like to make a sketch of the castle before we eat. Do you mind waiting?"

As they backed away, the children began to dance around the castle in a boisterous circle. Ivory could only dimly recall being that lighthearted. She frowned slightly as a faint image of a woman, perhaps her mother, tugged at her memory, but it faded before Ivory recognized her.

Misinterpreting her expression, and thinking she was apprehensive about his response, Chase encouraged her. "No, not at all, make all the sketches you like." He took her hand as they walked up to her cottage to get her things. "I'll go and find us something to eat and we can have a picnic on the beach when you're finished."

"You really don't mind?"

"No, not at all. Why would I?"

Ivory knew he had built the castle to please her, and she thought he ought to have a chance to have a good time too. "Artists are often criticized for being self-absorbed, and I don't want you to feel neglected."

Although flattered that she had begun to consider his feelings, Chase took care not to gloat. He had had such a good time building the castle with her, and he was pleased by how much she had enjoyed the project. "I won't. You take care of the artwork and I'll provide lunch." He gave her hand a squeeze and started off down the beach. When he looked back, Ivory had already picked up her sketchpad and pencils and was running back toward the castle. She was such a gorgeous creature he stopped to stare, then had to prod himself to move on.

He had every intention of finding something for lunch, but first he located the communications center for that level and sent a coded message to Control. Maintaining contact was high on Control's list of priorities, and Chase knew he was going to need all the points he could possibly score on this mission. In his brief message he relayed the fact that he was making good progress with Spider, but he omitted the information that he was trying even harder to make progress with Ivory.

When he returned to the beach carrying a picnic basket and a couple of striped beach towels, Ivory was drawing portraits of the children. The sketches, in which the children were posed against the castle, were beautiful examples of her work. Three of the children were holding their own portraits, while the final pair, a brother and sister, were trying to sit still for theirs. Chase set the basket aside and watched as Ivory added the last of the delicate shading to her drawing.

"Your parents are going to treasure these sketches," he assured the children when Ivory finished. "Carry them very carefully so they don't get wrinkled on your way to your folks."

Beaming with pride, the children walked away holding the sketches out in front of them as though they understood how precious they were. "They're cute little kids," Chase remarked, "but I don't know if I could stand having them underfoot all the time."

Ivory had made a detailed sketch of the sand castle before beginning the portraits. She dated the drawing, closed her sketchpad, and set it aside. "I hope you'd be sufficiently attached to your own children to tolerate their company for extended periods of time."

Chase had never really given having children any serious thought, but as he looked at Ivory, the children dancing in his mind's eye were blond

Cinnamon Burke

and blue-eyed like her. He glanced toward the
sand castle to dispel the image rather than reveal
where his thoughts had strayed. He unfurled the
towels to sit on while they ate.

"I hope you like tuna sandwiches. They seemed
appropriate for the beach. You do eat fish, don't
you?"

Ivory watched him sort through the picnic basket. He had a pitcher of punch, mangoes, papa-
yas, and a bag of coconut cookies in addition
to the sandwiches. "No, I don't usually eat fish,
but you're right, we're at the shore, and it seems
appropriate." She sat down on a towel, reached
for a sandwich, unwrapped it, and took a bite.
"Hmm, this is good."

"If you like seafood, there are several excellent
restaurants on this level, or we could find something else if you'd prefer. I know you must want
a change from my cooking."

"Let's finish lunch before we start worrying
about dinner."

That had sounded like the old Ivory rather than
the delightful young woman who had helped him
build the sand castle. Chase wondered what he
had done wrong. "Do you like to swim? We'll
have to wait awhile after eating, but the water's
so warm it would be fun."

Ivory took another bite of sandwich. The bread
was freshly baked, the tuna prepared with delicate seasonings, and she savored it for a long
moment before replying. "I don't know how to
swim, and we won't be here long enough for me
to learn."

"A woman ought to know how to swim," Chase
advised. "Spider said we were to enjoy ourselves.

If you want to stay here until you're a proficient swimmer, I doubt he'd mind."

"We don't have a pool at The Diamond Mine, so what would be the point?"

Chase reached out to pinch her knee. "The Diamond Mine isn't the whole galaxy. There are millions of places to swim, and you might visit every one."

"You've been on a business trip with me. There wasn't time for a playful dip in Mordecai's pool, if the Eagle's Nest had one, which I doubt. No, I don't need to know how to swim for my work."

Ivory Diamond was the most exciting woman Chase had ever met, and also the most stubborn. "Consider it an experience for your science files," he teased. "You ought to go swimming at least once, and it's much easier to float in salt water than fresh."

"Really? I had no idea." Ivory finished her sandwich, drank two glasses of punch, and ate half a papaya and two cookies before Chase yawned, leaned back on his elbows, and announced it was time for a nap. Neither of them had gotten much sleep the previous night, and a nap was appealing to Ivory too. She walked down to the water to wash her hands, and then smoothed out her towel and lay down beside him.

The sea gulls' constant calls took a bit of getting used to, but as a sleepy haze settled over Ivory they sounded less strident. Cradled in the warm, soft sand, Ivory relaxed completely. She sifted the silvery sand through her fingers, and wondered what it would be like to live in such an idyllic spot year-round. She was envisioning a real island, though, not a spectacular illusion like the one they were enjoying. She turned to ask Chase if he had ever been on a real island, but he had already fallen asleep.

There was a faint shadow of beard along his cheeks, but it scarcely detracted from his appearance. Ivory leaned on her elbow and studied him as she had when he had been her father's captive. She would not draw him **again**, but just watching him sleep was very pleasant. At least asleep he did not pay the teasing compliments or issue the taunting challenges she had come to expect from him.

She supposed they would produce remarkably handsome children together. They would be dark, with slender builds, and she was certain they would have her serious demeanor rather than his arrogant attitude. Then again, they might be tall, swaggering blonds she would not even recognize as her own.

She lay down again and turned her face away from him. She would probably never have children, and if she did, it would not be with Chase Duncan. It would have to be with a poet or a painter who came to The Diamond Mine as a casual guest and never left. Only a man who lived by his own talent could ever truly love her. Chase couldn't. Chase would always be her father's man, never hers, she mused as she drifted off to sleep.

Chase awoke before Ivory and sat with his arms propped on his knees watching the gulls fly in lazy circles overhead. The sailboats looked real, but he soon discovered they followed a predictable pattern, and he doubted they were any more substantial than projected silhouettes. The water, however, would be genuinely refreshing. It looked

so inviting he decided not to wait for her and
waded out far enough to swim. He moved parallel
to shore, his strokes long and lazy, but he checked
often to make certain Ivory wasn't awake and
lonely.

Not that she would ever admit to missing him,
but he was anxious for her to wake and join him
in the water. Finally he got too impatient to wait
and left the water. He walked up to Ivory, leaned
over, and shook out his hair, sending a rain of
salty sprinkles across her shoulders. Before she
could sit up, he moved back and attempted to
look contrite.

"I'm sorry. I didn't mean to wake you."

Ivory brushed off the water. "What were you
trying to do then?"

"Nothing much, but now that you're already
wet, you might as well come in the water with
me."

"Didn't we discuss this earlier?" Ivory felt at a
disadvantage on the sand and rose to her feet. "I
can't swim."

"You don't have to be able to swim here. The
lagoon's an illusion, remember? I swam way out
and it never gets deep. I'll bet you could walk
all the way to the end without getting your hair
wet."

Attentive to every detail, the designers of the
lagoon had programmed the lighting to reflect
the day's passing, and now it cast long shadows
across the sand castle. They had not created tides,
however, and the fanciful structure was in no
danger of being washed away. Ivory could readily
appreciate the beauty of the lagoon, but she was
still wary. "The water really isn't deep?"

Chase extended his hand, and she took it reluctantly. "We'll go real slow," he promised. "I won't rush you."

"You're talking about the water, I assume?"

"Of course," Chase assured her, but he gave her a sly wink. He kept his word, and waded out into the lagoon at such a relaxed pace Ivory soon pulled in front of him. He let her go, but stayed close. "It's easy to float. Just stretch out on your back and go limp. The water will hold you as tenderly as a lover."

"What you mean is that I'll sink like a rock."

"No! You'll float as blissfully as the clouds. Try it." Chase leaned back and gave her a demonstration. He used his hands to stir the water gently, but otherwise was perfectly relaxed. "I could stay this way all day."

Despite his height, Chase made floating look easy, but Ivory wasn't brave enough to try. She just watched him. Finally he stood, swept his hair out of his eyes, and again offered his hand. Water was trickling down his chest in tiny rivers that caressed his bronze skin with seductive trails. Distracted, for a moment Ivory forgot what it was they were trying to do.

Embarrassed, she tried to hide her inattention. "You won't drop me?"

"Of course not." Chase moved close and scooped her up into his arms. "Now I'm going to put you down very gently, and the water will hold you just as well."

Ivory quickly wrapped her arms around his neck. "I don't think so."

"All right," Chase agreed. "This is so nice, I'll be happy to hold you for an hour or two."

With their noses a mere inch apart, Ivory glared at him. His skin was all slippery and wet, but warm and inviting to the touch. She believed him, and knew the lagoon was probably no more dangerous than a big bathtub, but still, she didn't feel safe. "Didn't you say something about hiking trails?"

Amused, Chase kissed her. She tried to draw away but couldn't, and what began as a teasing exchange grew increasingly passionate. He felt her arms tighten around his neck with what he hoped was desire rather than fright, but before he could tell which, they were surrounded by the five children who had helped them build the castle. They were laughing, diving, splashing, and calling them all manner of imaginative names.

"I seem to have picked the wrong place for a public display of affection," Chase whispered in Ivory's ear. He set her down on her feet but kept hold of her hand.

The oldest boy tugged at Ivory's other hand. "Mother wants to know if you'll come make a drawing of the baby. She says she'll be happy to pay you for it."

Ivory did not need an excuse to get away from Chase. All she needed to do was walk off, but her feet felt stuck in the sand. Determined not to display the weakness that swept through her each time she was in his arms, she willed her defiant legs to move. "I'd love to make a sketch of the baby," she replied with a charming smile. "Come on, let's get my paper and pencils and we'll go."

As Ivory left the water with her youthful escort, Chase slammed the heel of his hand across the water to create a towering spray. "Damn!" he swore under his breath, but before Ivory started off down the beach, she turned to look back at him and he was elated by what he was certain were tears of regret brightening her gaze.

Chapter Nine

When Ivory returned to her cottage, she found that Chase had already showered, shaved, and dressed for dinner. He was sitting on the porch of his bungalow, watching the artificial sky fill with a rosy glow. She gazed out at the water. It was all shimmering silver now, sparkling as she supposed it must every evening.

"Do they ever have a storm here?" she asked.

"What do you mean, a charming rain squall or a wildly exciting and destructive hurricane?"

"Either, just the kind of natural phenomenon one might expect to strike a real island."

She looked sad, and Chase rose and went to her. "No. All the resorts guarantee perfect weather whether you want to enjoy the beach or snow ski. The desert hiking trails are always warm, the rain forests always humid and damp. The beauty of artificial worlds is their perfection."

Cinnamon Burke

Chase typified perfection of another sort, but Ivory realized she knew very little about him other than how good he looked, and how quickly he had moved to protect her when Mordecai Black had turned belligerent. A faithful guard dog would do the same, and she wanted so much more from him.

"I didn't mean to complain. Thank you for bringing me here. It's convinced me I really should do some exploring. I want to visit Earth, or Mars's colonies, clear across the galaxy, anywhere that's real. This is like trying to live in a theatrical set, and I feel as though everyone knows his lines but me."

Chase slid his fingertip along her jaw. No one would get sunburned on this beach, but after being outside all day her fair skin had gained a pretty golden glow. "You and I are real. That's all that truly matters, and we don't need anyone to hand us a script," he promised softly. He longed to kiss her, but forced himself to wait.

"I wish you'd brought the silver gown you were wearing when we met in the casino, but I don't suppose you packed it. Let's find something else in the closet and go to dinner. If you liked the tuna, you'll love lobster. Then we can explore this whole resort if you like."

Despite the sweetness of his touch, he was offering a pleasant evening rather than a romantic one, and Ivory didn't know whether she was pleased or disappointed. She just nodded, and took her sketchpad and pencils inside her cottage. She had been looking for a bathing suit the first time she had perused the contents of her closet; now she was surprised to find a much wider selection of clothes than she had first noticed. The silver gown Chase had admired was not one of her favorites, and she did not wish to duplicate it, but she found a long-sleeved gold sheath that was attractive without being provocative.

She showered, washed her hair, and coiled it atop her head. When she stepped out on the porch in the gold dress, Chase gaped, and she looked down expecting to find something amiss. She turned slowly. "I'm sorry. Is there something wrong with this? You've suggested several times that I wear gold, and I thought you'd like it."

"Believe me, I do," Chase assured her. The spectacular dress had deceptively simple lines. The high neckline tickled her throat while the rest hugged her figure with a graceful elegance that was incredibly appealing. Short, it showed off her legs as beautifully as her swimsuit had, and the matching gold boots completed the outfit perfectly.

"All the clothes in your closet are new. If you want to take that dress home, and I hope you will, you may."

"I'll think about it." Chase was wearing his Alado flight jacket and slacks, and while she knew how fond pilots were of their uniforms, she was disappointed that he had not wanted to wear something special too. "What about you?" she asked. "Didn't you find anything more interesting in your closet than what you have with you?"

"There are some nice black silk pajamas, but I thought they were too informal for dinner. I'll try them on for you later, if you like."

"You needn't bother."

"Good, I prefer to sleep nude."

Chase was eyeing her with such an appreciative glance, Ivory began to regret her choice of attire. "I think I should have borrowed the black pajamas," she told him. "Then maybe you wouldn't be looking at me as though I were going to be on the menu."

Chase straightened his shoulders and tried to adopt a more serious expression. He was only partly successful because she definitely looked good enough to eat. "Sorry. I promised to be on my best behavior, didn't I? Let's go."

He took her hand before she could object, and they went down the path toward the elevator. The walkway had been swept clean of sand here, so they could move along at a brisk pace. Most people had left the beach now, and even the gulls had grown quiet. There were hotels to their right with spectacular views of the lagoon, but Ivory was still glad she had chosen a small cottage right on the sand.

A ten-minute walk brought them to a fishing village clustered around a pier. "The best restaurant is at the end," Chase told her. "I made reservations while I was getting our lunch."

Ivory didn't know if it was because of the salty scent of the breeze, or simply the busy day, but she was desperately hungry. "If we find something we especially like, my father can arrange to have it brought in regularly. I'm just so used to an abundance of vegetables, I don't think about eating anything else."

"It's a healthful diet," Chase agreed with a smile, but he was glad to escape the heaps of produce Spider served. "Every colony has its own fare, but the resorts tend to feature delicacies from Earth.

Even those not born there seem to crave them."

History had not been Ivory's favorite subject, but she knew it was the migration to the space colonies that had saved Earth from the catastrophe of overpopulation and enabled environmentalists to make it the paradise it was today. She had never had the slightest interest in visiting Earth until Chase had arrived at The Diamond Mine. She blushed as she considered some of the other thoughts he had inspired.

They started toward the restaurant, but Chase soon drew Ivory to a jewelry shop window. The jewels on display were scattered about on a sand-filled tray. There were delicate gold charms featuring marine motifs, necklaces, bracelets, and earrings designed in clusters of golden shells. "Do you like the earrings?" Chase asked.

Thinking the cascade of spiral shells exquisite, Ivory nodded. "The craftsmanship appears superb. All the work is very fine."

"Come on, let's go in. The store won't still be open when we're finished eating dinner."

As they came through the door, the young man behind the counter greeted them warmly. "I saw you admiring the shell earrings," he said. "They would be perfect with your dress."

"This isn't really my dress, but thank you." Ivory glanced through the glass-topped counters at the man's other work. It was all lovely.

"Would you show us the earrings, please?" Chase asked.

The designer quickly removed the pair from the window for Chase to examine more closely. When he held one up, it rang with the sweet sound of a cluster of bells. There were shells, starfish, and sea horses; each charm was an exact copy of the thing that had inspired it.

"Try them on," Chase urged.

"They're very beautiful, but—"

"Surely the expense can't bother you," Chase teased. "Don't worry. I'm well paid."

Ivory didn't know what to say. A man had never bought her an expensive present, and she could not help but think that accepting it would create a troublesome obligation. "No, really—"

Chase grew more insistent. "Please, try them on."

Had they not been so pretty, Ivory would have resisted more strongly. She owned many pieces of diamond jewelry, but nothing so delicate as these charming gold earrings. She tried them on, and then studied her reflection in the mirror the designer provided.

"They'll make the perfect souvenir," Chase exclaimed. "We'll take them."

"I want to pay for them," Ivory argued.

"I didn't think you'd brought any money with you," Chase said.

Ivory had forgotten that point. "I'll go back to the cottage and get some."

"No, I want them to be a gift from me."

Ivory tried to argue, but the jeweler and Chase completed the transaction before she had made the slightest impression on her determined escort. He then took her elbow and led her out the door. "Thank you, but I really can't allow you to spend your money on me. I'll repay what these cost."

The earrings caught the light from the lanterns strung along the pier and shone with an enchanting glow. "You will not. They're a gift. Now come on, I'm too hungry to argue."

Ivory did not feel like arguing either. She would just tell her father to provide Chase with a bonus which would cover the cost of the exquisite earrings, plus a little more. That would free her of any sense of obligation. Relieved at the solution to her problem, she smiled. "All right," she agreed. "I won't mention it again."

Something in Ivory's smile made Chase doubt he had heard the last about the earrings, but he chose not to press the issue. He had never bought anything more extravagant than dinner for a woman, but it had felt so good to give Ivory a present that he vowed to provide them whenever he could. He pulled open the heavy door of the restaurant, then taking Ivory's hand led the way into what the management claimed was a perfect re-creation of a seventeenth-century pirate's den.

Ivory paused to read the sign describing the restaurant's decor. "A pirate's den? How appropriate."

"Yes, I thought you'd like it, but I chose the place because of the food, not because you'd feel at home here." In truth, the restaurant was nothing like The Diamond Mine. It was all highly polished teak accented with brass lamps and nautical gear. The waiters, dressed in striped shirts and bell-bottom pants, frequently gathered in clusters to serenade the patrons with rousing sea chanties.

"Come on," Chase coaxed. "The second floor is far more private."

The room at the top of the stairs was all glass and provided a superb view of the bay and the city skyline beyond. Dozens of skyscrapers were silhouetted against the setting sun, and as the lights came on in the buildings, the whole scene took on a breathtaking sparkle. Charmed, Ivory wondered aloud, "Is that a depiction of a real city or just an imaginative interpretation of one?"

That Ivory continually saw through the fantasy surrounding them was disconcerting, but Chase quickly recovered. "Let's not ask. Let's just choose a place we'd like to be, and call it that."

"My geography isn't what it ought to be," Ivory confided. "You pick the place."

Chase waited until they had been shown to a window table. "Alado's Earth headquarters is in Vancouver. The Pacific Northwest is very beautiful; so for tonight, we're in Vancouver."

"You're sorry about leaving Alado, aren't you?"

Chase reached across the table to take her hand. "I'm sorry about the way I left, the way I was forced to leave, actually. But I'm not a bit sorry for what's happened since. There's no point in wasting time on regrets when, as I see it, the future is bright."

The waiters on the second floor were dressed in dark tunics and pants, and were paid to be discreet. Chase released Ivory's hand with a fond squeeze as one approached. "How's the lobster tonight?" he asked.

"Superb, as it is on all nights," the waiter assured him. "We have the finest cuisine at the Paradise." He related a lengthy list of specials, and then withdrew to allow them time to make their selections.

Chase made his choice quickly, but Ivory pored over the menu so long he began to worry. "If you don't see anything you like, we can go elsewhere.

Lady Rogue

I just chose this place because it's the best on this level."

Ivory remained absorbed in her menu and didn't look up. "I just didn't expect so many choices."

"This menu isn't all that extensive. Where do you usually go?" As soon as he asked the question, Chase knew: Ivory had never been in a restaurant. She had never been anywhere except The Diamond Mine and on dangerous expeditions like the one to the Eagle's Nest where fine dining wasn't part of the mission.

"I'm sorry," he apologized quickly. "You haven't had many opportunities to visit restaurants, have you? Go right ahead and study the menu for as long as you like. I'll just enjoy the view. It reminds me of home."

That was another slip, Chase realized a moment too late. Chase Duncan wasn't from Vancouver, he was from . . . Chase drew a complete blank. He had read and memorized Chase Duncan's bio and destroyed it as ordered, but he couldn't recall any of it other than the supposed pornography charge at the end. He had never had such an alarming memory lapse, and it was terrifying.

Ivory closed her menu, and immediately noted Chase's pained expression. "Chase, what's wrong? Are you sick?"

Chase wiped his hand across his eyes. "No, I think I'm just hungry. I felt sort of faint there for a moment." He forced a smile. "I'm fine now. I don't mean to rush you. Take all the time you need."

"I'm too hungry to take any more time." When she glanced toward their waiter, he returned to their table. "I'd like a stuffed artichoke, a shrimp cocktail, the spinach fettucini, the lobster, and a green salad, please."

While the waiter looked a bit startled by Ivory's lengthy order, Chase had had ample opportunity to appreciate her hearty appetite and wasn't at all surprised. "That sounds so good, bring me the same, and I'm sure we'll want some dessert later."

"We have an excellent selection of colonial wines," the waiter suggested.

Ivory shook her head, so Chase requested water. The restaurant was dimly lit to take advantage of the cityscape in the distance, and to provide a wonderfully romantic atmosphere. A quick glance assured Chase the other diners were all too lost in each other to notice what was happening at their table. He kept his voice low to force Ivory to be attentive, then was ashamed of himself for manipulating her so shamelessly.

"I don't mean to assume things," he began. "If something here is new to you, or seems strange, I'll do my best to identify it and explain. I won't laugh at your curiosity."

Rather than being reassured as Chase had intended, Ivory was insulted. "I've seen restaurants in films, read about them in books. I'm not ignorant, Chase, far from it." Having made her point, she looked out at the lights. A shuttle was taking off from the top of one of the skyscrapers. Lights flashing, it circled and disappeared into the mist beyond. She wondered where it was bound, then remembered it was only part of the animated scenery.

Exasperated by her petulant response, Chase

forgot about speaking softly. "I didn't say you were. At least give me credit for being thoughtful, even if I did it poorly."

"Don't worry. I'll tell my father you did your job in an exemplary fashion," Ivory assured him flippantly.

"Spider has nothing to do with this!" Chase hissed.

Startled by his outburst, Ivory glanced sharply at him. His brows were knit in a fierce line, and the depth of his anger surprised her. "Please, you needn't take offense. We both know my father has everything to do with us being together tonight."

For a horrible instant, Chase feared that Spider might have told her that his real assignment was to marry her. He was too well trained an operative to volunteer such damning information on his own, however. He grabbed her hand, and this time rather than a fond clasp, held it tightly.

"I might work for your father, but that's all it is—a job. What happens between you and me is private, and as far as I'm concerned, precious."

The waiter arrived with their artichokes, and when Ivory tried to pull free, Chase refused to release her hand. Embarrassed, she pleaded with him, "Please, let me go."

"No, not until I'm certain you understand me."

His manner was far too insistent for Ivory to mistake his meaning. "Yes, I understand."

As her eyes locked with his, Chase saw an entire kaleidoscope of emotions reflected in their azure depths. She was afraid, and yet beneath the fear he saw a childlike wonder that longed for acceptance and love. There was a fine line an operative was forbidden to cross, and Chase knew he was not merely coming close but jumping right over it by offering Ivory the love he had no right to give.

I have every right! he shouted silently. His feelings for her were real, not the shadows of reality that surrounded them at the Paradise Retreat. Spider was the enemy, not his exquisite daughter with the tragic gaze. "Good," he encouraged gently, and he released her hand so the waiter could serve their appetizers.

Neither of them glanced at the waiter and he quickly backed away. Chase watched Ivory skim off the fleshy part of an artichoke leaf with her teeth and could barely stifle a moan of delight. She was merely eating, not flirting with a coy glance, but it was deliciously erotic all the same. Determined to keep his desires under control, he began eating his artichoke with the concentration he would give to defusing a bomb. In the far corner, a harpist had begun to pluck a poignant melody.

Ivory didn't know quite what to make of Chase's surprising declaration. She tried to recall his specific words, and failed, but she was inordinately relieved to learn he did not regard being with her as work. It was frightening too, to think he might be sincerely interested in her, as that required an equally sincere response.

She could feel the tickle of the shell earrings each time she turned her head. As comforting as Chase's touch, the gentle caress made her feel special, and she found her mind wandering so much, she knew she was doing a poor job of holding up her side of the dinner conversation. She looked out at the lights, and wondered what the mythical people did in all those imaginary buildings.

Unlike the fanciful scene, the artichoke was real, and she licked the delicately flavored garlic butter sauce off her fingers. "This is awfully good," she said sincerely.

Chase had never thought artichokes were worth the trouble to eat, but that night he welcomed the time-consuming routine required to eat the peculiar vegetable. He dared not look up at Ivory until she finished hers, but when he saw her wiping her hands on her napkin, he took the risk. "I feel better already. How about you?"

"Yes, I feel better too." She smiled and laughed with him. There was nothing humorous really, just the sudden realization of how nice it was to be together. Ivory relaxed then, and Chase became the most charming of dinner companions. He told her about a deep-sea fishing expedition he had made during which the boat had begun to leak and the effort to stay afloat had become the real adventure.

"I much prefer space travel," he told her. "There's always the possibility of rescue, and never a danger of drowning."

His eyes glowed with a mischievous sparkle that was far more engaging than the beautifully lit backdrop. Ivory found the shrimp marvelous and the lobster divine. She made a mental note to ask her father to order both with their next shipment of provisions. Feeling an inner warmth as delicious as the meal, she slowed her usual hasty pace to make the evening last as long as possible.

After the sumptuous meal, she still had room for

dessert and had a dish of strawberries smothered in coconut-flavored whipped cream. She chose cinnamon tea rather than coffee. Feeling too content to move, she felt as if she did not ever want to leave the charming restaurant, or her even more appealing escort. When Chase finally reminded her of his promise to explore the whole Paradise Retreat, she confessed she wasn't certain she could move.

"You won't have to," Chase promised. "There's a tram stop at the end of the pier. We'll just take a seat and ride until you've seen everything."

After debating the invitation for a long moment, Ivory rose with a graceful stretch. She had never ridden on a tram, but she was willing to give it a try. She looped her arm through Chase's as they left the restaurant.

"Thank you again for the exquisite earrings." She raised her free hand to set them ringing. "I've never used any sea motifs in my work. It could lead me in a whole new direction."

"I knew stopping here would inspire all sorts of good things. You see, experiencing life more fully does contribute to your art."

His voice was low, seductive, and Ivory instantly grasped his meaning. Earlier in the day, she had refused even to consider having an affair with him, but now she knew she was thinking about far more than an affair.

They had to wait only a few minutes at the tram stop, and when it arrived, they were the only people to board the car. Another couple was seated in the front, and Chase chose a seat in the rear where they couldn't be overheard. Moving slowly, the tram curved around the miniature city they had admired while dining, and then gathered speed.

"It almost looks real, doesn't it?" Ivory asked.

Chase kissed her to silence her doubts. "Just pretend everything is as real as I am, and you'll enjoy it so much more."

Ivory relaxed in his arms and looked out at the passing scene. The city lights faded and she felt the tram begin to climb. "What's on the next level?"

Chase pointed to a poster overhead. "Looks like the rain forest. We'll have to take this same ride in the daytime to fully appreciate it." He nuzzled her neck with teasing nibbles. "Of course, the tram will probably be a lot more crowded and we might not have nearly as much fun as we will tonight."

Ivory raised her hand to touch his cheek. "I thought you wanted me to enjoy the view?"

"I do; keep watching."

She laced her fingers in his. "Stop distracting me, or the only idea I'll have will be to draw you again, and you've already refused to pose in the nude."

"I could be persuaded to reconsider," he whispered against her ear.

Ivory doubted she could make sketches of him now that she knew him so well. Whatever artistic detachment she had once had was gone. She turned so her back was against his chest, and he cradled her in his arms. Ivory gasped in delighted surprise as the tram entered the enchanted world of the rain forest.

She could feel the increase in temperature, and yet the heat wasn't unpleasant. Short palms, coiling ferns, and broad-leafed philodendron covered the forest floor. Vivid red orchids clung to the trees, providing a burst of color in an otherwise verdant world. Vines filled the top of the towering trees covering the primal world with a lacy canopy that would filter out most of the sunlight even at noon.

"There must be jaguars prowling the forest, and sloths hanging from the thick branches, but I'm afraid we can't see them tonight. Oh yes, there are probably rainbows of butterflies. We'll really have to come back tomorrow."

Ivory could so easily imagine the wildlife that dwelled in the rain forest that she did not really need to make a second trip. She knew what Chase was attempting to do, however—to provide an excuse to keep her there at the Paradise for more than a day. She was tempted, for returning home would simply plunge her into an all too familiar routine, while staying at the Paradise offered a whole array of delicious new possibilities. She was glad she had refused the wine at dinner, for Chase's company was intoxicating enough.

"I remember the night you came to The Diamond Mine," she mused softly. "There's a two-way mirror behind the bar, and when I saw you, I wondered if you'd have a nice smile. You laughed at something the bartender said, and I saw that you did."

"Ivory Diamond, I'm surprised at you," Chase marveled with a rumbling chuckle. He did not admit he had felt her watching him, but he was delighted to learn she had been curious enough about him to observe him for a while. "I thought

I was the only one who liked what I saw that night."

"I didn't say I liked you all that much. I just wondered about your smile."

The tram slid to a stop at the hotel in the rain forest, but no one got on or off and it swiftly pulled out of the station. The couple in front were paying no more attention to the scenery than Chase, and he was surprised there weren't more amorous couples on board the romantic ride. He was grateful there weren't, however.

"You're never going to make things easy for me, are you?" Chase asked.

"No, of course not. Besides, you're the type who relishes a challenge. I'd soon bore you if I were a slave to your desires."

Chase plucked the pins from her hair, spilling it down over her shoulders. Dry now, it curled softly against her nape. "There are men who will pursue a woman until they catch her, and women with the same failing as well. The chase is what excites them, not the object of their fleeting affections. I'm not like that, Ivory. You would fascinate me regardless of how you behaved. Just be yourself with me."

Ivory turned slightly to look up at him. His request was a simple one, but she played a variety of roles. Her favorite was as a thoughtful artist, but she was also a clever dealer in the casino, a gracious hostess for her father, and upon occasion, a defiant and demanding woman who did business in his name. It was very dangerous business, and she shivered slightly as she recalled the evil light in Mordecai Black's eyes.

"I don't have one self," she apologized. "I can

be so many things, even more than I've had the opportunity to try as yet."

Chase brushed her hair away from her cheek and kissed her. "You can be whatever you wish, but you'll always be the same wonderfully unique Ivory inside."

Touched by his insight, Ivory swallowed hard. "You do understand me, don't you?"

"Better than you could ever imagine," Chase swore, "and we've only just begun to get acquainted. Stay here with me, Ivory. Stay until we can find all that we can be together."

As his lips brushed hers, Ivory thought only of him, and the love that flavored his kiss. She knew they could spend only a few precious days in the magical world of the Paradise Retreat, but she longed to remain with him forever. She ran her fingers through his hair, encouraging him to deepen his kiss. Lost in the sweetness of his affection, she prayed it wasn't just another magical illusion.

Chapter Ten

The tram followed its spiral route, curving around the perimeter of the Paradise Resort's exotic environments without either Chase or Ivory noticing they had left the rain forest. Another couple got on, the first couple left, and finally the sleek tram returned to the station at the end of the pier. As the doors slid open, the familiar tangy scent of the sea invaded Chase's befuddled senses. Looking up, he discovered they had returned to the lagoon.

"We can get off here, or stay on all night if you like," he offered. Just holding Ivory in his arms and kissing her until they were both breathless had been so delightful, he would have been content to indulge any whim she might have.

Knowing the tram would soon continue along its route, Ivory slipped from Chase's embrace. She felt dizzy as she stood and had to grab for the back of the adjacent seat for support. "No, I think we ought to stop now, while we can."

Intrigued by that ambiguous response, Chase pulled himself upright. He took her hand, then draped his arm around her shoulders when they reached the platform. The beach was silent, and tiny lights strung along the path illuminated their way. The temperature was cool but not unpleasant, and they strolled along, enjoying the night breeze.

Ivory knew Chase must have been with lots of women, all more sophisticated than she. She wondered what such a woman would say under these circumstances. Would she entice him in with seductive promises? Or perhaps use affection to lure him over the threshold and into her bed. When simply kissing Chase was so wonderful, she knew that making love would feel incredibly good, but what would happen then? Would he treat her as sweetly tomorrow as he had tonight, or would he boast that he had taken her innocence and expect her to give up her independence as well?

Chase could actually feel Ivory closing him out of her heart and mind. He didn't want the evening to end with them estranged. When they neared their cottages, he coaxed her out on the sand. "Come on, let's take a towel and sit out on the beach for a while. It's such a pretty night, and I'm not sleepy. Are you?"

The other cottages dotting the shore were dark, their residents still out or asleep, but Ivory was too excited to close her eyes. "No, not at all," she replied. She waited while he fetched a big beach towel off his porch and then walked beside him out on the sand. There were stars overhead, but a gentle mist obscured all but the brightest. She pulled off her boots and, sitting down on the edge of the towel, slid her feet through the sand, which still held the day's comforting heat.

Ivory had become so withdrawn that Chase was almost afraid to touch her now. He sat and waited, silently hoping his presence would provide the reassurance she seemed to need. When he could no longer bear her silence, he raised his hand to her nape, and then slowly moved his fingers down her spine. She pressed against his touch rather than shying away, so he began to rub her back in gentle circles and gradually he felt her relax.

He longed to reassure her, but it would be pointless if she did not want him as desperately as he wanted her. Even if she did want him, he was afraid that words would frighten her away. He could only massage her back, and pray she would not sit there until dawn and then just walk away. It took a long while for him to realize that the small tremors he felt beneath his fingertips were caused by her silent sobs.

Leaning forward, he placed his hands on her shoulders and turned her toward him. She looked away, but even in the dim starlight, the trails of her tears were plain. In a gentle sweep, he pulled her down on the towel and dried her tears with eager kisses. "I can't bear to see you so sad," he whispered. "So often, you seem as though you have a lifetime of sorrow buried inside you. I would give anything to make you happy."

His sincerity was unmistakable, and Ivory raised her arms to encircle his neck. His first kiss was light, the next devouring. The blissful warmth she had found in his arms earlier returned with an even greater heat. She still had many unanswered questions, but they seemed unimportant now. Chase made her feel safe, loved. Even if it wasn't more than desire on his part, would she be wrong to take what he offered when she needed it so badly? Ashamed to think he might consider her pathetically needy, she kept all her doubts and fears inside, but with each kiss she wanted him more.

Chase couldn't force himself to think. Instead he ran his hand up Ivory's slender thigh. Her skin was soft, smooth, but her flesh firm, the muscles tightening in response to his touch. She had a dancer's supple body, and he explored it slowly, savoring each swell and dip with a lingering caress. He wanted to take his time with her, all night if need be. He wanted to show her how glorious making love could be. At the same time, he wanted her so badly he could scarcely breathe. Clinging to her, he buried his face in the curve of her shoulder and simply held on as he tried to bring his passion for her under control.

Unaware of his torment, Ivory arched up against him, drawing him back down under her spell. His mouth returned to hers, and she rolled her tongue over his, making the kiss her own, but the next was his. She clung to his shoulders, then grabbed handfuls of his hair, for the need he had created within her brought a sweet pain she could not endure alone. She ground her hips against his, and muffled his anguished moan with her lips.

Even lost in the moment, Chase knew exactly who he was, who Ivory was, and what lunacy it was to make love to her on a deserted beach. None of those concerns mattered in the slightest, and he shrugged off his clothes before peeling away hers. Once freed of her lingerie, her lithe figure glowed beneath the stars, and he lowered his head to her breasts, flicking the pale pink nipples with his tongue and then drawing one into his mouth. Her flesh was as delicious as her kiss but didn't come close to satisfying his raging hunger for her.

Ivory ran her hands across his broad shoulders. His muscles rippled at her touch, and it was as though Raven's tattooed wings were curling around her. Breathless, delirious with desire, she felt herself merging with the magnificent bird. Borne afloat, she soared on the salt-scented breeze until Chase caught her in a fiery embrace. He bore her down into the sand, and with a searing lunge made her his own.

She gasped, crying out in surprise more than pain for it was such sweet agony. She felt whole rather than torn, complete for the first time in her life. It was as though she had always belonged to the man in her arms, and had at last come home. She did not want the delicious closeness ever to end.

She returned Chase's fevered kisses with grateful abandon. She felt his passion surging through him and into her. The ancient rhythm of life was echoed in the fierce beating of their hearts, and she had never been so exquisitely alive. When Chase's climax shuddered through him, she held him more tightly and knew she would never love another man.

As soon as he had caught his breath, Chase covered Ivory's face with tender kisses. "I'm so sorry. I meant to be gentle, to be—"

Ivory's kiss hushed his apology. "You were

yourself. That's all you need ever be with me."

Chase sighed softly and smoothed her hair off her face. "I've waited a lifetime to find you, and I don't want to ever lose you. Marry me, Ivory. There must be facilities here for weddings. I want to take you home as my wife."

"And present my father with a *fait accompli?*"

The mention of Spider cleared Chase's head instantly, but he fought back his anger. "I want you because I love you, not because you're Spider Diamond's daughter. How can I prove that to you?" Still lying within her, he felt himself again growing hard and moved slowly to explore her heated depths.

"You feel so good," he whispered against her cheek, "so tight and hot."

Ivory savored the luscious warmth of his skin, the strength of his whole body pressed so firmly against her own. His scent mingled with that of the sea, and she longed to believe him. "You told me you'd never been in love."

"I lied," Chase admitted, "for I loved you even then." He kissed her, slowly, deeply, as he continued to move with the gentle rhythm he had meant to use the first time. He slid forward, changing his position slightly to bring her the pleasure he wanted them always to share, and as her breathing quickened, he knew he was succeeding. She was a remarkably responsive woman, and he felt her muscles contracting around him, again coaxing forth the ecstasy he fought to hold back until he no longer could. He joined her then in a heated rush toward another stunning climax that rocked him clear to his soul.

He withdrew this time and, rolling onto his

back, held Ivory cradled in his arms. He combed her tangled curls with his fingertips and waited until he again had the courage to speak. "A proposal demands a response, Ivory. You can't simply ignore the fact I've offered marriage."

Ivory responded with a lazy stretch, then clung to him more tightly. "I've never met another man I wanted for a husband."

"Is that a yes?"

Ivory trailed her fingers down his chest. Chase caught her hand and moved it lower. Her nude drawings of him had been explicitly detailed, but it had not been like touching him. She followed his urging and caressed him with a sure and loving touch.

"It's a qualified yes," she whispered.

"Well, can I at least consider us engaged?"

"Anything else would be too tentative, wouldn't it?"

Chase hugged her. "Good. I'll try to be satisfied for the time being, but I hope you don't believe in long engagements."

"Just long enough to be certain you aren't too good to be true."

That poignant response pierced Chase's heart with a sharp stab of guilt, for while his affection for her was most definitely real, Chase Duncan was not. He was as phony as the shallow lagoon beside them. Unable to bear the thought of how hurt Ivory would be when she learned his true identity, he urged her to sit up. "Let's go inside, shower, split the pair of silk pajamas, and get some sleep where we won't have to worry about waking up in the morning with a bunch of cute kids dancing around us."

Laughing at the excruciating embarrassment of that possibility, Ivory failed to note Chase's change of mood. She gathered up her clothes while he found his, and arm in arm they walked up to his cottage. It was identical to hers, but reversed. Feeling no embarrassment at being nude, she laid her clothes over the back of a chair, removed the beautiful new earrings, and went in to shower first. She had just turned on the soapy spray when Chase joined her.

"The water is recycled here, but we ought to conserve," he teased playfully.

His magnificent body glistened with the supposedly precious water, and Ivory doubted that conservation was his goal. It certainly wasn't hers as she reached up to kiss him. His eager response thrilled her clear through. The tenderness of his touch was mirrored in his glance, and each kiss offered the assurance she needed so desperately that he loved her for herself and nothing more. By the time she fell asleep in his arms in the bed, she almost believed it was true.

Chase waited until noon to wake Ivory. He hated to do it even then, but he was too lonely to let her sleep the whole day away. "Here's a cup of cinnamon tea. I have something else for you, but drink your tea first."

Ivory gave a lazy stretch as she sat up, then pushed up the sleeves on the silk pajama top. She was surprised to find Chase already dressed, and yawned sleepily before accepting the cup of tea. "What time is it?"

"Time for lunch. Are you hungry?"

Ivory took a sip of tea. It was warm and sweet, exactly like Chase, she thought to herself. He sat down on the edge of the bed and watched her. His sly smile made her curious. "What else do you have? Something to eat?"

"No. I thought we'd try another of the resort's restaurants when you're up and dressed."

He still looked far too pleased with himself, and Ivory was afraid she knew why. "I don't recall agreeing to stay here another day. Did you just take it upon yourself to extend our reservation?"

"You could say that. I'm sorry if it was presumptuous of me, but you weren't awake to help make plans."

"So you were forced to make the decision yourself?"

Chase squeezed her knee. "Exactly."

Ivory looked around for her flight bag, and then remembered they were in his bungalow. The Celestial Cannon had been safely stowed on board the Blaster, not that she would have used it on him to remind him who was in charge, but she did not want to lose track of her belongings. She leaned back against the bamboo headboard and continued to sip her tea.

"Well, does whatever this other thing is have anything to do with what you'd like to do today? I doubt I could learn to ski in a day, any more than I could learn to swim."

"No, it's not a pair of skis."

"Good. Having been raised in a controlled environment I'd probably be too sensitive to the cold to stand being in snow."

Ivory looked far too gorgeous in a bathing suit

for Chase to want to see her bundled up for snow. "Like everything else here, the temperature on the mountain level is maintained for the comfort of the guests. It isn't too cold, even with plenty of snow."

"If it isn't something to eat, or something I would find useful today, then what is it?"

"Just finish your tea and I'll show you." Chase leaned close to kiss her. After their late shower, her hair had still been damp when she had gone to sleep, and rather than falling in graceful waves, it stuck out straight from her head like a shattered halo. The pajama top was much too large, but even in borrowed clothes, and with her hair in frightful disarray, she looked beautiful. He was prejudiced, he knew, but surely a passing stranger would praise her too.

"I had no idea you had so little patience," he said.

"You're just teasing me," Ivory scolded. "Besides, the lovely earrings you gave me last night are all I'll need to remember the Paradise Retreat."

Chase dropped his voice to a husky purr. "I hope you'll have another reason to recall our stay here."

"I might," Ivory replied, proving to be as adept at word games as he.

"Only might?" Chase exclaimed, but Ivory continued to calmly sip her tea without reacting. "You are a terrible tease, Ivory."

"I'm not the one claiming to be holding some mysterious gift."

Chase had to concede that point. "That's true."

He reached out to take the cup of tea, and left the bed briefly to place it on the table. He then pulled a small box from one of his jacket pockets and handed it to her. "I went back to the man who made the earrings. I hope you like it."

"Oh, please, Chase, you shouldn't have bought anything else for me." Ashamed she had nothing for him, Ivory left the box lying in her lap. "It's not that I don't appreciate it. I do, but—"

Having no need of apologies, Chase opened the box himself and took out the diamond solitaire. "I'm sure you haven't forgotten that we're engaged, and I want you to have a ring."

The ring was stunning, with a delicate gold setting that perfectly complemented the magnificent stone. Overwhelmed that he would buy her such a beautiful ring, Ivory began to cry. "I didn't expect anything like this," she sobbed. "I didn't expect anything at all."

Chase had expected excited squeals, not huge tears. He pulled her into his arms and hugged her tight. He was about to ask if she had changed her mind when he realized she had already told him why she was crying. That she had not expected a ring, or love, he supposed, was heartbreaking. He leaned back and framed her face between his hands. "You have every right to expect whatever it is you need from me, Ivory. I don't want you to feel alone or afraid ever again. I love you, and I want to be with you always."

After placing a kiss in his palm, Ivory dried her tears on the hem of her pajama top. "I'm sorry. I feel very foolish. It's just that I'm not used to getting attention from men. No, that's

Cinnamon Burke

not exactly true. I am used to receiving attention, but none of it was welcome before I met
you."

Chase touched the dimple in her chin to tilt
her lips to his and kissed her lightly. "I understand. Now here, try on the ring and see if it's
the right size."

Ivory handed it to him. "No, you put it on,
please."

Chase's hand was trembling as much as hers as
he slipped the sparkling ring on her finger. It fit
perfectly. "Do you like it? If not, we can go back
to the shop and you can choose another."

"No, I want the one you chose." Ivory threw her
arms around his neck and gave him an ecstatic
hug. "Thank you." As soon as she sat back, she
climbed out of bed. "How am I going to get next
door to get my clothes?"

"Just wear a towel. If anyone is nearby they'll
assume you've just slipped out of your bathing
suit."

"Oh, good."

Chase grabbed a beach towel off the porch and
came back inside. He held it for her, and when
she tossed the pajama top aside, he wrapped her
up with a flourish. He would much rather have
kept her in bed all day, but he wanted her to
understand that it was her charming company he
loved, not just her luscious body. He gave her bottom a playful swat as she went out the door, and
went out on the porch to wait for her to return.

Their sand castle had crumbled during the night
and all that remained was a heap of sparkling
white sand. He was determined, however, that

208

he and Ivory were going to build a lasting love. He had absolutely no idea how he was going to convince her to stay with him once she discovered who he was, but he had never wanted anything more.

"Do you suppose they might have an iguana?" Ivory asked before licking the last bits of a gooey cinnamon roll off her fingertips.

Chase drained the final sip of coffee from his cup and shoved his crumb-cluttered plate aside. They had eaten brunch in a magnificent tree-house restaurant overlooking the rain forest and were now planning the rest of their day. "We can check the information directory at the tram stop, but most zoos have a reptile house and it wouldn't be complete without an iguana or two."

Ivory responded with a delighted grin that lit her eyes with a radiant glow, and Chase was thrilled by how frequent her smiles had become. Gone was the fearful waif who had cried over receiving an engagement ring. In her place was the confident young woman he had first encountered in The Diamond Mine's casino, but the tough layer of cynicism had been peeled away to reveal the enchanting nymph beneath. He had never really seen her smile before, and it was simply dazzling. She had chosen to wear her own flight suit, but in his eyes it was every bit as flattering as the gold sheath.

"You're a very beautiful woman," he told her. She blushed at his praise. "I'll check the directory for an art gallery too."

Ivory looked down over the rain forest. They

had seen the rainbows of butterflies he had promised, and the shrill calls of a hundred different birds echoed in the air. Perfectly content, she could have done nothing more exciting than watch for sloths all afternoon, but she sensed he wished to be on their way. "I'll be happy to visit any place you choose."

Chase leaned close so she would be sure to hear his whispered reply. "You must know what I want to do, but let's see more of the Paradise first."

Ivory pretended to be shocked, then shook her head. "Yes, I think we better do some more exploring. I don't want you to grow bored with me."

Chase could not imagine such an unlikely eventuality. "I won't live that long."

Ivory's bright gaze clouded instantly and her lashes shadowed her cheeks as she looked down. "Please, don't talk like that. Let's hope to live forever. I couldn't bear to lose you too."

He had not meant to remind her of her mother's death while they were sharing such a happy moment. It was a valuable insight, however. She had told him she could not remember her mother, but clearly she felt the pain of her loss to this day. "Are you finished? Come on, let's go."

As soon as they had left the restaurant, he pulled her into his arms for a joyous hug. "There's only now, this precious moment, Ivory. Let's glory in it."

Ivory clung to him until they heard someone coming up the overgrown path. "Iguanas," she reminded him. "We wanted to see some real live iguanas."

"Right." Chase took her hand and they walked

across the suspension bridge that connected the tree-house restaurant to the tram stop. As on their arrival, Ivory showed not the slightest hesitation traversing the swaying bridge that spanned a steep gorge, and as always, he admired her courage. A quick review of the resort's directory revealed there were indeed iguanas in the zoo, but no art gallery on any level. Chase was disappointed by the omission, but Ivory seemed not to care.

Chase had expected Ivory to want to observe the iguanas briefly, tour the rest of the zoo, and then possibly explore another environment, but she insisted upon bringing along her sketchpad and pencils, which slowed their progress considerably. Comprising one whole level, the zoo featured extensive native habitats, and, not wanting to miss a single beast, Ivory stopped at each and every viewing port. It took them nearly two hours to reach the reptile house.

Snakes had never held much appeal for Chase, and he hurriedly guided Ivory to the corridor featuring lizards. At last they turned a corner and came face-to-face with an iguana closely observing the afternoon's visitors, or at least he appeared to be. Ivory pressed close and looked him right in the eye. Turning shy, the iguana slowly climbed a convenient branch to avoid her.

"I'm surprised," she confessed. "I thought a live iguana would have more personality."

Chase pointed to the second iguana curled up near the water container. "Don't feel insulted. Perhaps they save their best for each other, the way we do."

Ivory looked skeptical, but was sufficiently intrigued to make a detailed sketch of the iguana hugging the branch, while Chase enjoyed himself studying her. "Do you suppose they are passionate creatures?" she asked.

Chase nodded. "Wildly, but they contain themselves during the day when the zoo is open so as not to frighten children."

"How thoughtful of them."

"Oh yes, anyone can see they're wonderfully considerate lizards just by looking at them. You see how they respect each other's privacy? We saw lions lounging in a graceful heap, but not iguanas. They like their own space and don't crowd each other."

Ivory glanced up from her sketch. "Should I be listening closely to what you're saying?"

"Always." Chase had to back up out of the way to allow room for a family with boisterous twin boys to observe the iguanas, but their curiosity was swiftly satisfied, and they moved on. "I think you're incredibly talented. You need time to pursue that talent, and I intend to give it to you."

"Give?" Ivory repeated with arched brows. "The freedom to pursue my own interests is my right, Chase. It's not a gift from you."

"You're absolutely right, of course," Chase quickly amended. "All I'm saying is that you won't find me making unrealistic demands on your time."

Ivory did not want to leave fingerprints on the glass, but she raised her hand to bid the pair of iguanas farewell. Then she turned toward Chase, her expression a teasing grin. "Good, but what are you going to do about the fact that I intend to make inordinate demands on yours?"

Chase laughed, caught her in a hug, and lifted her clear off her feet. "Go right ahead. I'll never complain. Now come on, let's go back to the lagoon."

Ivory knew precisely why he wanted to return to his cottage and she was as eager as he to renew the bond that making love had created between them. She closed her sketchpad, pocketed her pencils, and took his hand. "It's a shame they've not found any new species on any of the planets we've colonized, isn't it? I keep expecting to hear of furry elephants, or tiny orange and blue zebras, or something wonderfully strange."

"I'm just thankful we haven't discovered any new life forms," Chase confided, "because they would be just as likely to be nasty creatures who developed a passion for human flesh."

"What a ghastly thought. Of course, even the most vicious beast could be stopped with a single blast from a Celestial Cannon."

"True." Chase didn't want to think about weapons now, though, and as they made their way toward the closest tram stop, he guided the conversation to less dangerous topics. That his beloved dealt deadly arms as easily as she dealt cards was not something upon which he wished to dwell.

Chase waited on the porch while Ivory dropped off her art materials, but then he pulled her into his bungalow. "We ought to have music," he murmured between kisses, but the only sounds were of the surf and in the distance the faint laughter of children.

213

Cinnamon Burke

"Incense would be nice," Ivory added, "or scented candles."

"Sparkling wine," Chase suggested as he unzipped her flight suit.

"Chocolates," Ivory breathed against his ear.

Chase ended the list with a series of ever deepening kisses that left them too weak to stand. They sprawled across the bed and lost themselves in the newness of love without giving another thought to things they really did not need to enjoy the magic of being together. Their clothes ended up scattered about the floor in rumpled heaps, and it wasn't until Chase was nude that he noticed he had left the door standing open. He slid off the bed to close it, then quickly returned to Ivory.

"Sorry. I didn't mean to be so careless. I'll do better at safeguarding your reputation."

Ivory welcomed him back into her arms, but thought his vow absurd. "I have no reputation to guard, Chase, and neither do you. I treasure that really, because it means I can do as I please without having anything to lose."

Chase was well aware of how the criminal mind functioned, and Ivory had been tutored from birth by a master. Selling arms was merely a business transaction without any moral connotation to her. Harboring felons, and she believed he was one, brought not the slightest sense of guilt. A stubborn refusal to cooperate with any authorities was as close as she came to having ethics. Her whole life was damning, but as his lips found hers, nothing she had ever done or thought mattered to him.

The afternoon light lent the room a pale golden glow, and he traced the lush fullness of her breasts

214

with his fingertips before laving·the pale crests with his tongue. He moved his thumb down her ribs and spread his fingers over the hollow of her stomach. Her skin felt so alive that caressing her was an endless thrill.

He did not want to shock or frighten her by the way he chose to make love to her, but then he remembered a chance remark she had made about what she had learned from Summer Moon's girls, and he decided she probably knew more than he did about giving pleasure. All she lacked was practical experience, and he had every intention of giving her plenty of opportunities to hone her craft. He slid down over her, tracing an eager trail with tender kisses, teasing, pleasing, delving into her lithe body's secrets until he was drunk with her taste.

He felt her hands at his shoulders, then clutching his hair, guiding him, silently begging him for still more, and he had so much more to give. He was so lost in loving her that her pleasure was his, and her sweet shudders of joy throbbed through him as well. He moved to join her then, bringing their bodies together as one, and he buried himself deep within her glorious heat. She was his, truly his, and the beat of his heart called her name.

Rolling on waves of rapture, Ivory writhed beneath him. She saw him in her mind, ablaze with a searing light. His heated touch burned her flesh with the permanence of a brand, and left her marked for life. She felt her own power to give him pleasure too, and, elated by the joy they shared, she held him ever more tightly, until a blissful release left them both too relaxed to cling.

Sprawled atop the bed, they slept in each other's arms. Unaware of what the future would bring, Ivory's dreams were sweet, but Chase awoke filled with dread and with Spider Diamond's name on his lips.

Chapter Eleven

His conscience aching badly, Chase held Ivory in his arms and gradually her sweet warmth lulled him back to sleep. This time she appeared in his dreams surrounded by swirling images, bits and pieces of the drawings she had made at the zoo. The animals were rendered in crisp black lines slowly fading to gray, leaving only the honeyed tones of Ivory's hair and skin and the haunting beauty of her smile. Even in his dreams he reached for her, and longed to make her his wife.

The next time he awoke, Ivory was standing over him dressed in a long, low-cut, scarlet dress. Her hair was piled atop her head in a crown of curls, and the delicate cascades of golden shells danced at her ears. She possessed a remarkable talent for transforming herself at will, but he definitely liked what he saw and sat up.

"Am I late for dinner?" he asked.

Cinnamon Burke

"Not yet, but you soon will be."

"Just give me a minute." Chase rolled off the bed and went into the bathroom to shower. It wasn't nearly as enjoyable without Ivory to share it, and he was out and dressed in less than ten minutes. Ivory was waiting for him at the open doorway, silhouetted against another of the lagoon's perfect sunsets. He had never seen her wear red, but it was a glorious complement to her fair coloring. He walked up behind her and nuzzled her nape.

"Take this dress home too, please. Whoever stocked your closet must have had you in mind."

Ivory turned slowly in his arms, her motion as relaxed as her mood. "I've never had much interest in clothes, or in men, until now."

That sultry comment was enough to prompt Chase to take her elbow and guide her out the door. "If we stop to discuss your recently acquired interests, we'll not reach a restaurant before breakfast."

"Would that be so tragic?"

"Yes. I'm trying to behave like the fine man you deserve rather than a love-starved iguana."

Ivory's red sandals made a soft scraping sound on the sandy path. "Now that's an intriguing image, but there's absolutely no comparison between you and an amorous iguana, assuming they're capable of love."

"Try me."

"I thought you wanted dinner," Ivory responded with a throaty laugh.

"Yes, I do." Chase hurried her along the path. "Good nutrition is vital for stamina."

"I didn't realize I'd pushed you to your limits."

218

While Ivory's comments were provocative, it was the seductive way she was making them that moved Chase. He had never wanted her so badly, and yet he was positive that dinner was what they needed most, at least for the present. "Don't worry, you haven't. Would you like to go up to the mountain level and try one of their restaurants? We can watch the snow fall from a comfortable room warmed by a cozy fire."

"A real fire?" She looked amazed.

"Yes. People relied on fireplaces for centuries to heat their homes. Even if you haven't one at The Diamond Mine, trust me, they create a marvelously romantic atmosphere."

"Snow and an open fire," Ivory mused. "How quaint. You've done it before, haven't you? You've cuddled with some sweet little . . . what, another pilot?"

"Do you want me to lie?"

"No, I simply want you to be more original. Let's go somewhere that's different from any place you've ever been with another woman."

They were nearing the tram stop, but Chase pulled her to a halt. "You needn't be jealous, Ivory. There's an enormous difference between playful affection and making love."

Ivory regarded him with a level stare. "I'm not jealous. I just want our memories to be separate from all your others."

"You're so wonderfully unique, there's no danger of my memories becoming blurred. Nothing I've done with any other woman compares to being with you, so whatever we do together will be new. I won't force you to enjoy a leisurely meal in front of a fire if you'd rather try something else, though. Let's look through the directory and find something more to your liking."

"How about a picnic on the lip of a volcano?"

As always, Chase had to admire her creativity. "Tempting, but I don't believe that's among the choices here."

As they viewed the possibilities on the screen, Chase waited patiently for Ivory to select one, but he was disturbed by how quickly she had gone from a playfully seductive to a melancholy mood. He longed to see her smiling again as she had at the zoo. Her upswept hairstyle showed off her proud posture and elegant neck so beautifully he had a difficult time even thinking of food, let alone being hungry for anything other than her.

"What do you think of the menu at the Toucan's Nest?" Ivory asked. "It's in the rain forest and certainly looks colorful."

"Perfect, let's go."

"Don't you want to know what they serve?"

Chase laced her fingers in his and led her on board the tram. The car was crowded with people going to dinner, so he had an excuse to lean close and whisper in her ear. "No. Your company's all that matters," he assured her with a teasing wink.

Ivory chose not to argue when his company meant as much to her. She glanced at the others on board. There were young colonists with children, handsome couples of almost every age, and a few people seated by themselves. She hoped they were on their way to meet someone, rather than vacationing at the Paradise alone. She smiled at Chase and squeezed his hand. He was easily the best-looking man on board, and she was proud to be with him.

The Toucan's Nest proved to be not merely colorful but almost garish. Live musicians in bright costumes provided jungle rhythms liberally accented with birdcalls, and the waitresses were clad in flowered sarongs and wore gardenias in their hair. Chase hesitated at the door, but Ivory was delighted and pulled him inside. They were shown to a table that looked out over an aviary filled with brightly plumed parrots and cockatoos. Ivory was clearly thrilled, so Chase did not complain that the evening was not going to be anything like the quiet, romantic one in front of a fire that he had envisioned.

"Why don't we order different things tonight, and then we can trade?" Ivory suggested.

The first thing Chase saw on the menu was duck. "Do you believe they serve duck here?" he asked. "I don't think I could take a bite of duck with all those parrots watching us."

"Hmm, yes, that does seem a bit insensitive on the chef's part, doesn't it?"

"At the very least." Chase looked down the menu. "I'll take the rice-paper-wrapped catfish. What about you?"

When their waitress arrived, Ivory ordered the curried chicken salad and the sweet and spicy peanut prawns with scallops and snow peas, and then consulted Chase for an appetizer. "What do you think, the artichoke hearts with melted cheese, or the lobster ravioli?"

Chase couldn't face another artichoke, even if it was only the heart. "The ravioli, please. Tonight let's sample one of the wines." He chose one he had enjoyed before and urged Ivory to have at least a sip when the waitress brought it to their table. "This tastes very much like strawberries," he said. "I think you'll like it."

Intrigued, Ivory took a sip, but it didn't taste anything like strawberries to her. She frowned slightly and tried to identify the hint of fruit in the delicate wine. The first colonists had become adept at making fine wines from every possible source, but she had never cared for any of them. "No, this is very good, but it reminds me of lemons."

"Lemons?" Chase took another sip. "No, it's strawberries."

Ivory was amused by his insistent tone. "There's no way to prove that everyone tastes the same thing in exactly the same way, Chase. When we look at the parrots here, you might notice the red ones first and I the blue. Neither of us is right or wrong in our choice. It's just a different way of looking at things."

"Being an artist, you may know that people observe things differently, but we're talking about taste here, and this wine is definitely flavored with strawberries."

Ivory arched her brows slightly. "Must we agree on absolutely everything?"

Her question was asked with casual nonchalance, but Chase could sense that his answer was important to her. At least she hadn't bristled with indignation the way she once did when he had said something she did not like. She was turning her wineglass with both hands, and seeing his ring on her finger made him too happy to argue over such a ridiculous point.

"If the wine tastes like lemons, persimmons, or

blueberries to you, fine. As for being in agreement, I'll always respect your opinions, and we'll make important decisions together. I want us to be a team, not rivals who are constantly vying for power."

"So do I, but it's going to be difficult. I'm my father's only heir, Chase. That's one of the reasons Summer Moon despises me, because he won't make her his wife and give her a child who will share my inheritance."

"Spider's a relatively young man. You're a long way from receiving an inheritance."

"If years were the only consideration, I'd agree, but in my father's line of work, few men die of old age. Most of the men he knew when he first developed the idea for The Diamond Mine are gone."

"Or in prison?" Chase guessed aloud.

Ivory shook her head. "No, they're all dead, and my father would surely choose death over imprisonment."

"How did we get on such a dreary topic?" The Toucan's Nest throbbed with a zest for life, and Chase was suddenly grateful they had come there. He added more wine to her glass and raised his for a toast. "To us."

Ivory touched her glass to his and took a sip. Lemons, she thought again, definitely lemons. "There are so many things we need to discuss, Chase. If not here at the Paradise, then before we return to the Mine. We're not like most couples, and we shouldn't pretend that we are."

Ivory was correct, but Chase dared not reveal just how different they truly were as yet. "I'm usually the practical sort," he confided, "but I know this in my heart: If we truly love each other,

we can solve any problem life hands us. I don't
want to get caught up in the politics of running
The Diamond Mine. It belongs to your father, and
I'll be happy to work for him, but you're what's
most important to me, Ivory, and it will always
be you, not money, nor power, nor anything else
you can name. It will always be you."

Ivory was still silently studying Chase's expression when the waitress returned with their ravioli.
She trusted her feelings for him, but still, way
back in the far reaches of her mind a warning
voice whispered that it was too soon, time was
moving too fast, and she ought to slow everything
down if for no other reason than to savor it. Delicate and yet richly flavorful, the ravioli slid down
her throat as smoothly as Chase's promises.

Suddenly she grew frightened. "Even using Carl
Drake's name, are you in any danger of being recognized here? Is this resort frequented by Alado
personnel who might know you're wanted?"

Her concern touched him, and Chase was quick
to reassure her. "I never flew any missions this
close to the frontier, so it's unlikely that I'd meet
any members of a former flight crew. Even if I
did run into someone, Alado doesn't publicize the
misdeeds of its employees, and so the fact I'm
wanted on criminal charges wouldn't be widely
known. You're sweet to worry about me, but you
needn't. I'm as safe here as you are."

Ivory needed a drink of wine before replying to
that assumption. "I've never moved among strangers as we do here, but it's never wise for anyone in our business to assume they are safe anywhere. My father doesn't travel without Stokes

and Vik, and of course I have you, but still—"
she glanced out over the crowded restaurant. The
other diners were all talking, laughing, dancing
to the primitive music, but she knew how easily
such a lively scene could be used to screen violence.

"My father killed a man on Mars years ago.
It was in a place like this—well, as popular as
this but certainly not as nice. He just walked up
behind him and cut him in half with a single
swipe of a laser pistol. The man was dead before
he fell to the floor in two gory pieces. The other
patrons were so horrified, no one saw my father's
face, and in the confusion he just strolled out
the door."

Chase needed a moment to catch his breath,
for the gruesome killing she had described was
one of the most celebrated in the Mars colony's
decidedly colorful history. "Spider's the one who
killed Sonny Duran? Sonny's death has always
been one of the biggest mysteries of the galaxy.
Not that anyone cared about Sonny, he was no
more than a—" he caught himself, and searched
for an appropriate word.

"He was a pirate," Ivory offered without any
hesitation, "just as we are, but one given to
double-crossing his partners, and in this business,
that is a fatal flaw."

"As well it should be," Chase replied convincingly. "I hadn't considered that remaining here at
the Paradise longer than we'd originally planned
might be making you nervous. Do you want to
leave tomorrow?"

Ivory rolled a succulent ravioli around on her

plate to soak up the sauce. "No, I don't want to ever leave. Everything will change once we get back to the Mine, and we may never spend another carefree day."

"Things don't have to change," Chase argued. "If we don't let other people come between us, they never will."

"By other people, you mean my father, don't you? He likes you, Chase, although I'm not sure why. But if you make even the slightest error in judgment, he'll change his mind in an instant."

"I can't believe Stokes is all that reliable."

"You're wrong. Stokes is thoroughly predictable and reliable. Unlike you, he isn't burdened by a need to think for himself. He follows my father's orders as explicitly as the silver boys follow mine. He's the perfect employee. It's only ambitious men like you who create a problem."

Chase waited to catch her eye. "I've always had a talent for machines. Would it pose less problems if I told your father I'd like to oversee the operation of the Mine's maintenance facilities, rather than become involved in any other facet of his business?"

A slow smile lit Ivory's face. "You don't understand how vital a part the maintenance facilities are, Chase. You run them, and you'll be right in the middle of things, not safely off to the side."

"What do you mean?"

It wasn't merely the lemon-scented wine that made Ivory more willing to confide in him now. She knew he loved her, and in her mind, love and betrayal did not mix. "When we made the run to the bank, you may have noticed the PJC

Tomahawks docked in our bays."

"I did, but so what? They're used for all kinds of commercial transport."

"They also make excellent mobile factories."

Stunned, Chase sat back in his chair. "Do you mean that Spider is building the Celestial Cannon and your pretty silver boys on board the Tomahawks I saw?"

He appeared to be so amazed by her father's cleverness, Ivory found it difficult not to laugh. "Those may have been part of our fleet, but perhaps not. Ours come in occasionally to refuel and pick up supplies, so they could very well have been ours, or they could have belonged to anyone who patronizes the Mine. The point was merely that you could not have chosen a location that would involve you any more directly in our operation, or nefarious deeds if you wish to regard them as such."

Ivory had just handed Chase such a critical piece of information that he could have gotten up from the table, contacted Control, and brought in a raid on The Diamond Mine without ever needing to return to her father's stronghold, or see her again. Nearly crushed under the weight of that knowledge, he had a difficult time catching his breath. A more detached operative would have had her arrested and put the raid into motion, but he wasn't nearly ready to complete his assignment at The Diamond Mine.

"That's brilliant," he complimented sincerely, "but can enough arms be manufactured on board to supply everyone who wants them?"

"Scarcity works in our favor, Chase. We want

to be able to sell all the cannons we build without glutting the market."

"That makes sense." They were interrupted as the waitress brought their salads, and when they were again alone, Chase promptly changed the subject. "We're here on a vacation. Let's talk business another time. Now what do you want to do tomorrow?"

"Just lie on the beach," Ivory decided in an instant, "and maybe, just maybe, you could give me another lesson in how to float."

"It will be my pleasure."

"Let's hope not the only one."

Chase's ready grin assured her she would have pleasure in abundance, but he could feel the net tightening around her, and his joy was overlaid with pain.

After dinner, Ivory wanted to visit a tavern or two to compare them with The Diamond Mine. Neither the Crystal Palace on the fantasy level nor the silk-draped Oasis in the desert park rivaled her father's establishment for elegance and beauty. At the Oasis, they ordered almond-scented liqueurs served over shaved ice, and for several minutes talked of nothing more serious than what really went on in a sheik's tent. Then Ivory again grew pensive.

"Life must be very hard in the colonies for people to want to lose themselves in illusion," Ivory said.

"A vacation is supposed to supply a change. After all, if people were satisfied at home, they wouldn't leave. The resorts have to offer something wildly different to attract the colonists in the first place."

Feeling a relaxed laziness, Ivory was content to remain curled atop a silk cushion and simply imagine the other wonders the resort might contain. "I prefer the real environments," she confided. "Not that they are any more real than this, but at least they offer the appearance of reality."

"Precisely, but there are people who want to escape from, not experience, reality on their vacations. If you worked in a mine, you'd surely want to visit a beach, or a desert, anywhere bright and sunny. Then again, if you were struggling to grow crops at a new colony and had had your fill of open spaces, the fantasy level might be your favorite. They hope to please everyone here. That's why they have so many options."

"I keep comparing everything to The Diamond Mine. Of course, we don't have families visiting us, but even with just a few amusements, our customers never get bored."

"That's because you have such fascinating amusements." Chase finished his drink and, after briefly debating having another, decided against it. He was already slightly drunk, but his mind kept churning Ivory's earlier revelations, whipping them into a damning shriek that kept echoing through his mind.

"Gambling and women?" Ivory scoffed. "They are certainly the oldest, aren't they? But if we could come up with something new, or a new approach to what we now offer, it might be a good idea to seriously consider incorporating it when we get home."

Ivory was obviously serious, but The Diamond

Mine was the last place Chase wanted to discuss. "You misunderstand our purpose in coming here." He paused, searching for an appropriate endearment, but nothing nearly pretty enough came to mind. "We are supposed to be getting away from the Mine, not trying to come up with ideas to remodel it."

Ivory ignored that comment. "Do they have a casino here?"

"No. Gambling isn't permitted on the frontier, or at least you won't find it in any of the legitimate resorts."

Ivory turned her glass to swirl the liqueur through the ice. "Life is a gamble though, isn't it? Especially on the frontier."

"Life is indeed a gamble," Chase assured her, but when their eyes met there was no trace of uncertainty in her glance. "Let's go back to the lagoon," he suggested.

Apparently enjoying tormenting him with desire, Ivory made no move to rise. "Are you always going to want me as badly as you do tonight?"

His answer came easily to Chase. "No, tomorrow I'll want you more, and the day after that . . ." He left the progression to her imagination.

"Then you'll soon be a very dangerous man." Obviously pleased rather than threatened by that possibility, Ivory rose in a slinky stretch. "I understand, and while I eagerly look forward to tomorrow, let's not waste another minute of tonight."

When they reached the resort, Chase started to again lead Ivory into his cottage, but she turned toward her own.

"I want you in my bed tonight," she coaxed with an enticing caress. "It's yet to be used."

"Is that the only reason?"

"No. It's several feet closer and I don't want to tax your strength any more than necessary."

"You certainly know how to treat a man right." Chase followed her in her door, then caught her hand to pull her down on the bed and began to pay the rest of his compliments in the way he had been longing to do all evening.

Ivory drank in his affection, but now confident of his love, she was no longer hesitant to show her own. She slid from his arms and kicked off her sandals. "Here, let me help you with your boots," she offered.

Chase propped himself on his elbows. "I've never had a woman undress me."

"At last, something new," Ivory exclaimed. She yanked off first one boot and then the other, tossed his socks aside, and tickled his foot. "Just lie still and I'll remove your clothes." She moved very slowly to help him out of his jacket, and then hung it over the back of a chair. She was equally deliberate with his shirt and took her time pulling it off over his head. She lay the soft gray garment atop his jacket and then leaned over the bed to unbuckle his belt.

"You need a whole new wardrobe," she said. "You're still wearing Alado's clothes, when you ought to be wearing ours. With your dark coloring, you'll be far more handsome in dark blue than gray."

Ivory was directing her attention solely to his clothes, but Chase found her gentle touch deeply stirring. Fully aroused, he stood to take off his pants. "I can do the rest myself," he insisted.

"No, you can't do anything for yourself, not tonight you can't."

Her comment was both a command and a promise, and delivered in the authoritative tone that came so easily to her. Chase briefly debated defying her and then decided it might be much more fun to be obedient that night. "Yes, Ms. Diamond, whatever you say."

Ivory ran her hands down his narrow hips as she eased off his pants. "You needn't be so formal with your fiancée." She folded the pants neatly and placed them across the seat of the chair that held his other garments. She turned back to him and hooked her thumbs in the waistband of his underwear. He sucked in a deep breath, and she paused to look up at him.

"I'm not rushing you, am I?" she asked.

"No, not at all."

"Good. We have all night to amuse ourselves in whatever way we choose, so there's no reason to hurry." She watched the pulse in his throat beat more rapidly and bent down to lick his nipple. He jerked in surprise, then tried to embrace her, but she brushed his hands away. "Please, I'm not finished," she scolded. She scraped a nail across his bare belly with one hand and peeled off the last of his clothes with the other. Then with a playful shove she pushed him down on the bed.

She turned her back toward him as she stepped out of the red dress with a teasing grace, but, leaving her scarlet lingerie in place, she crawled up over the end of the bed and knelt between his legs.

"There's always been a brothel at The Diamond Mine," she revealed in a husky whisper. "I might as well have been raised in a harem. I know what men like, and exactly how they like it."

Before Chase could argue with her boast, she drew the soft, smooth tip of his hardened shaft into her mouth, immediately silencing any comment he might have cared to make. She did not simply use her mouth and tongue to excite him, but her talented hands as well to fondle, caress, and finally withhold the ecstasy her exotic kisses inspired. Desperate for release from her tender torture, he arched up off the bed. Understanding his exquisite pain, she coaxed his climax from him in wave after wave of shuddering rapture.

When he had no more to give, she stretched out over him with her head pillowed on the flatness of his belly, and waited for him to regain the energy to speak. She knew she had probably shocked him, but doubted it mattered when the pleasure she had given had been so intense. Completely relaxed, she had nearly fallen asleep before he recovered his senses.

At first Chase was merely curious, and then he began to wonder how much time Ivory had spent with Summer Moon's girls and just what she had been doing. He also knew what a handsome sum men would be willing to pay for the incomparable thrill she had given him with such practiced ease. That thought made him angry. He plucked the pins from Ivory's hair and tossed them aside.

He tried to control his temper, but his voice still held a fierce edge. "How old were you when you starting doing that, Ivory? Ten, twelve, how old?"

Amazed by his question, Ivory rested her hands on his thighs and sat up slowly. "Didn't you tell me earlier this evening that I ought not to be jealous because there's a vast difference between playful affection and making love?"

Chase also sat up and leaned back against the headboard. "There's no way you can describe what you just did as playful affection. You've raised an ancient technique to an art form, and if your father's been making money off that talent, then so help me, I'll—"

Ivory eyed him coldly. "You'll what? Kill him? What is your real complaint, that you think I've been with other men, or that they might have paid me for it? From the depth of your reaction, it's plain that what I did is definitely worth a great deal."

Chase closed his eyes to focus his thoughts, but the erotic images that flooded his mind jarred him so badly he quickly gave up the attempt to shut her out. He felt sick, disgusted and sick, but he did not want Ivory to think he was angry with her. "I'm not jealous," he explained. "I'm horrified to think Summer Moon, or one of your father's other mistresses, might have taught you how to please a man that way in order to make money. I can't think of a worse crime than using a beautiful child in such a perverted fashion."

"Pornography pales by comparison, doesn't it?"

Chase reached out to grab her arms and yanked her up beside him. "That you might have been subjected to such horrendous abuse isn't funny, Ivory. Now tell me the truth, and all of it."

"Let go of me," Ivory demanded. As infuriated as he, her gaze was bitter, and as soon as he relaxed his grasp, she scrambled off the bed. She was now sorry they were in her room because it meant she couldn't walk out on him. She moved to the end of the bed to put more distance between them.

"It's possible to learn all manner of useful skills without ever having an opportunity to practice them. I've never done any of the things I've done with you with another man, and that you could even imagine that my father would pimp me is an accusation that's beneath contempt. Get out. I'm leaving at seven tomorrow, and I don't care in the slightest whether or not you're on board."

Chase had had a girlfriend or two with a temper, and his response had always been to walk out and not come back. But he loved Ivory, so walking out wasn't an option. "No," he stated firmly. He stood and started toward her, but she backed away, and he stopped rather than chase her around the room.

"I love you," he said, "and I'm not leaving until you understand that I meant to protect you if you'd been mistreated in the past. How can that insult you?"

"That you could believe my father pimps children is what insults me!"

Chase continued to stare at her, his dark eyes troubled. Red was definitely her color, but her lacy lingerie hid damn little of her gorgeous figure, and what it revealed was terribly distracting. "Your father is a murdering pirate who thinks nothing of selling arms to colonists who'll turn peaceful settlements into war zones. That he might also pimp children doesn't take a great leap of imagination.

"But he really isn't the issue here, Ivory. It's you. I want you always to be safe, and happy. There's a terrible sorrow in you at times that I can't seem to reach. If I leapt to the wrong conclusion as to its cause, then I'm sorry, but don't ask me to leave when my only crime is loving you."

It was Chase's mention of sorrow that kept Ivory from again demanding that he leave. She brushed her hair out of her eyes and sat down on the edge of the bed. "I'll readily admit to being sad at times, but isn't everyone? It doesn't have to mean I was subjected to some horrible abuse."

Chase knelt at her feet and took her hands. Perhaps it was only the painful memory of her mother's death that haunted her, and he did not want to remind her of that tragedy tonight, or any other night. "You're the most amazing woman I've ever met," he assured her, "bold one minute, shy the next. You fascinate me, and somehow I doubt you'll ever run out of surprises. Please forgive me for not simply thanking you for your generous affection by making love to you."

Ivory slipped her hand from his, and when she ran her fingers through his hair, he rested his cheek against her knee. "You're not really like us," she mused softly. "You're not truly a pirate at heart."

"You are my heart, Ivory, and I'll be whatever you want me to be."

"I want you to be Chase Duncan. Can you manage that?"

Chase looked up with a teasing grin. "I can manage a lot more if you'll let me." He joined her on the bed, and, their argument forgotten, he returned her gift of love with a delicious devotion, but he knew that in one important respect he had not fooled her. He was not really a pirate, and never would be.

PART TWO

Chapter Twelve

After an all too brief romantic interlude at the Paradise Retreat, Ivory convinced a reluctant Chase it was time to return home. Their newfound closeness made the return voyage far more enjoyable than the one to the Eagle's Nest, and after stopping off at Spider's private bank to leave the money Mordecai Black had paid for the Celestial Cannons, Chase landed the Blaster in its home bay at The Diamond Mine. He had no reason to celebrate their return, but clearly Spider did, for he met them as soon as their docking bay had been pressurized and they had left their ship.

Spider immediately took Ivory's arm and began to lead her away. "I'll speak with you later, Duncan," he called over his shoulder.

Chase waited for Ivory to stop at least long enough to mention their engagement, but she sent him only a regretful glance and left with her father without offering so much as a half-hearted protest at his being left behind. He had never had a woman treat him with such casual disregard for his feelings. Coming from her, such treatment was not only a huge disappointment, but hurt badly. Rather than curse her indifference until he had a chance to confront her over it, he looked for a productive way to fill his time, and went to check on his own ship as an excuse to take much more careful note of the PJC Tomahawks he passed along the way.

He had not had an opportunity to send Control another message after learning that Spider maintained mobile factories aboard the massive transport ships. The next time he communicated with his superior, it would be to call in a raid. Knowing his remaining days at the Mine would be few, Chase was determined to focus his energies on doing his job with the precision it required. The only problem was that he had never had a job where his heart as well as his life had been at risk, and none of the brilliant strategies he had mastered seemed to apply.

Spider took Ivory up to his office on the third level where he managed his numerous interests. Functional rather than elegant, its pale gray furnishings were streamlined and spare. He sat down behind the desk, and Ivory took the room's only other chair. Prepared for an interrogation rather than a fatherly chat, Spider dispensed with pleasantries and began without any pretense as to his true purpose.

"I have two questions for you. The first is

whether or not Chase Duncan proved useful with Mordecai Black, and the second is whether or not his services of a more personal nature merit keeping him alive."

Ivory knew that her father despised weakness of any kind, and, returning his level stare, she replied in an equally firm tone. "I raised the price on the cannons because Mordecai didn't have enough respect for me to adequately prepare a docking bay. He was outraged by the new amount, but Chase was a sufficiently forceful presence to ensure that I got my way. As for his 'services,' as you put it, he's asked me to marry him."

She raised her left hand to show off her diamond ring. "I said yes, but I'm in no hurry."

Impressed, Spider sat back in his chair but continued to regard her with a perceptive gaze. "Do you trust him?"

Ivory turned the elegant ring, and the perfect stone caught the light with a fiery sparkle. An ageless symbol of love, it meant a great deal to her and had not left her hand since Chase had put it there. "I trust his love. He's completely devoted to me, which is a bit overwhelming. As for our business interests, I know he would kill in an instant to protect me, but he doesn't have Stokes's perverse meanness and I doubt he would ever kill a man simply to make a point, as you sometimes do."

Spider considered her comments thoughtfully, and then stood. "Let's give him another little test. If he passes, fine; if he doesn't, then you can decide if you still want him for a husband."

Ivory followed him to the door. "I don't want him hurt," she cautioned.

Cinnamon Burke

Spider's grin was immediate. "I understand. Besides, I'm too pleased by the prospect of finally having a son-in-law to abuse him. Still, you ought to know exactly what kind of man you're marrying, so a test of his character is appropriate. Come with me. You may find this amusing as well as instructive."

Chase had just taken his flight bag up to his room when Spider sent Stokes to find him. He glanced toward the communications panel, but there were no messages waiting for him. Surprised by the personal summons, he couldn't resist taunting the burly blond.

"Doesn't Spider give you anything more significant to do than serve as an errand boy?"

Stokes stretched to his full height. He was not quite as tall as Chase, but he outweighed him and in his own mind was easily the better man. "You've been running errands too," he replied.

Chase started down the hall ahead of him. "That's true," he agreed, "but I had Ivory along for company and I haven't seen Spider giving her to you."

Had Spider not impressed Stokes with the need to bring Chase to him, he would have beaten Chase to death right then and there in front of André's desk, or at least tried to. "Ivory's her own woman," he argued instead. "She's not Spider's to give away."

As they entered the elevator, Chase had a difficult time keeping his smile from sliding into a satisfied smirk. Because Spider had ordered him to marry Ivory under penalty of death, he felt certain his future father-in-law would approve of their engagement, but as a courtesy to Ivory, he did not reveal their plans to Stokes. He just smiled slyly and hoped Spider would announce their engagement before the day was out.

The chill of the second level caught Chase by surprise, and he left the elevator positive that Spider would not have chosen the detention section for a private celebration. He didn't let Stokes fall behind him here, but instead walked along the corridor at his side. Returning to the Mine had been a gamble, but he prayed it was not one he had already lost. Spider and Ivory were waiting for them around the next corner, and her welcoming smile gave him courage.

"Well, Duncan," Spider greeted him, "Ivory tells me you proved to be of invaluable assistance. I wonder if you might take care of a troublesome matter for me now. It's the kind of thing Stokes usually handles, but you don't mind Duncan taking over some of your work, do you, Stokes?"

Deeply insulted, Stokes began to argue. "I sure as hell do, sir. I've never failed you, and Vik and I can take care of whatever needs to be done just like we always have."

Spider's eyes opened wide in pretended amazement. "You surprise me, Stokes. I had no idea you might object to sharing the fun with Duncan. No matter which way I decide the matter now, one of you will surely be insulted, so rather than relying on me to make a choice, why don't you two work it out between yourselves."

Stokes immediately began to peel off his jacket, making clear the manner in which he preferred to settle disputes. "Wait just a minute," Chase said. "If I'm going to have to fight for the privilege of handling a job, I'd like to know a little more about it."

"That's reasonable," Spider agreed. He frowned slightly, as if searching for an accurate way to describe his needs. He was clean-shaven that day, but as usual his hair looked windblown although there was never a breeze inside the Mine. "Stokes caught a visitor who appeared to be more keenly interested in us than in having a good time. That's such a rare occurrence, I want the man dealt with promptly. Whether he's spying for one of my more ambitious competitors, or for one of the corporations, he must have been sent to infiltrate our operation and close it down. I know Stokes could handle the matter efficiently, but I want you to have the chance to show me you can do the same."

Because Spider had just described Chase's own mission, he dared not arouse the man's suspicions. This was precisely the type of challenge Chase had expected to face, and, believing he would simply be putting an end to some hapless pirate who probably had a high price on his head anyway, he did not object. First he looked to Ivory, and while she appeared to be keenly interested in his response, she obviously had no objection to a calm discussion of murder. She had definitely been abused, Chase thought to himself, for she had been raised without any respect for right and wrong. Unfortunately, he was in no position to teach her the distinction now.

"I can not only do anything Stokes can do," Chase bragged, "I can do it a whole lot faster." Without stopping to take off his jacket, he turned and punched Stokes in the face so hard the man's head snapped back with an audible crack. Blood squirted from his broken nose and sprayed across the wall, but Chase had to hit him two more times to knock him off his feet. When Stokes lay in a dazed heap, Chase turned back to Spider.

"All right, where's your spy?"

Very favorably impressed, Spider slapped Chase on the shoulder. "Good man. He's back in the cage. Stokes and Vik have already had quite a bit of fun with him. He refused to admit who sent him, but I kept him alive until you returned." Spider started down the brightly lit corridor, and then almost as an afterthought stopped to speak with Ivory.

"I want you to go on up to your room and rest. I'll need you to deal in the casino tonight, and I don't want you to be too tired to work your whole shift."

Ivory hesitated. "You remember what I said?"

"Of course, although I do believe your lover just proved he can take care of himself."

"Just don't put him in another situation where he'll have to."

Chase was touched by Ivory's defense, but he was fully capable of speaking for himself. "I'll be fine," he swore. "Go take a nap and I'll see you later."

Ivory's glance swung between them, and while she still harbored reservations, with both men urging her to go, she gave in. She brushed Chase's arm with a light caress in passing, and when she reached Stokes, stepped over him without breaking her stride. Spider waited until he heard her board the elevator before continuing on his way.

"Ivory is very fond of you," he remarked. "Don't

ever give her a reason to change her mind."

"I don't intend to," Chase insisted. "We've not set a wedding date, but I'm hoping it will be soon."

Spider opened the last door in the corridor and led the way into the room containing the cage Chase had good reason to loathe. Vik had been standing guard over the captive, but with a diffident nod, he stepped back out of the way. A naked man was huddled in the far corner of the cage, desperately trying to hold in his own body's heat against the room's icy chill. His back was covered with long ugly bruises. Clearly he had been beaten with some evil instrument.

Chase didn't care who the poor devil was; he was touched by his plight. It didn't matter that he was probably no better a man than Stokes or Vik; he was human, and suffering. Still, this wouldn't be the first time Chase had killed a man during an assignment, and when compared to the lives of the colonists whom Spider's arms would endanger, one pirate wasn't much to sacrifice.

"How do you want me to do it?" Chase asked.

"What would you prefer?"

"I'm a pilot, not an assassin," Chase reminded him. "Don't make the mistake of believing I'll enjoy this."

"What a shame; Stokes certainly would. You would too, wouldn't you, Vik?"

"Yes, sir, Mr. Diamond." Vik's grin grew wide, but it didn't make his scarred face any more handsome. "It's the best part of this job."

"Unlock the cage, Vik, and bring him out," Spider ordered.

Chase stepped back slightly to give him room.

He knew a dozen different ways to kill a man with his bare hands, but he didn't want to show off his deadly expertise in front of Spider and make him suspicious as to how he had acquired such a unique set of skills. "A laser pistol would be quick," he finally announced.

"Haste isn't usually one of our priorities, but if it's what you want, fine. Vik, give him yours."

Vik was still struggling to bring the captive out of the cage and replied with a low grunt. The battered man staggered and fell against the bars, and Vik had to grab his hair to hold him upright and thrust him out through the door. It wasn't until then that Chase got a look at his face, and even though it was badly beaten he recognized Yale Lincoln.

"Oh, Jesus," Chase cried.

"You know this man?" Spider asked accusingly.

"Of course I know him. He's no spy; he's another of Alado's pilots, and a stupid one at that. He probably came here on a dare and was just looking around so he could brag about it." Chase reached out to grip Yale's chin and forced him to look up at him. Yale was barely conscious, but Chase hoped he was alert enough to play along.

"It's Chase Duncan," he enunciated clearly. "What are you doing here?"

Yale mumbled through badly swollen lips, "Cards, girls."

"That's all he's ever said," Vik confirmed. "Are you certain he's with Alado? His identification badge didn't say so."

"It was undoubtedly a fake. This was probably his idea of a swell place for a vacation, and now look at him. Poor bastard. Let me take him to the medical unit and then send him on his way. He won't tell anyone what happened here, but there have to be others who knew he was coming. If he doesn't return to his base, we'll have Alado swarming all over us, and I know you don't want them here any more than I do."

Chase reached out to get hold of Yale to take him from Vik, but Spider stopped him. "Wait," Spider cautioned. "You're forgetting something."

Chase had been hoping to hurry Yale out of there before Spider had time to consider the decision to let him go. Every second of delay worked against Yale, and yet he couldn't allow his impatience to show. "What?" he asked with a suitably puzzled frown.

"He's seen you, and you're a wanted man. He has to die."

Spider had him there, and Chase's first thought was that if he wavered in the slightest he would not only lose Yale but Ivory as well. It was the memory of how coolly she had stated her terms to Mordecai Black that inspired him to adopt a similar attitude. She had been trained by Spider to be cold, fearless, and never back down. Chase strove to use Spider's own techniques against him.

"He's not going to tell anyone where I am," Chase replied confidently, "because he would be admitting that he's been to The Diamond Mine, and that would cost him his job. He's not much of a pilot, you see, and he'd be unlikely to ever find a position with another firm that paid as well as Alado. No, my whereabouts are a secret he'll have to keep to save himself."

Without waiting for Spider's consent, Chase got a firm grip on Yale's waist and started out of the room. As he neared the door, he held his breath, but Spider made no move to stop him and he got Yale to the medical unit without any interference. He waited outside while a technician worked on the injured agent and found him some clothes.

Once dressed, Yale met Chase out in the hall. The superficial wounds to his body had been healed, but the haunted look hadn't left his eyes. He cast a fearful glance up and down the hall, clearly eager to be on his way.

"Do you have a ship?" Chase asked.

"I did."

"You've never been particularly bright," Chase chided, "but coming here when you had any other option proves you're brain-dead. Now I'm going to do what I can to get you back home, but no one is ever to know you saw me here, and under no circumstance are you ever to come back. Is that understood?"

Yale assumed that Chase's sarcastic speech had been for the benefit of whoever might be monitoring the Mine's security cameras, but it still sickened him to be treated like a disobedient child. "I never liked you, Duncan, and if we never meet again I won't grieve."

"Fine, I won't miss you either. Come on, let's go down to the docking bays, and if Spider hasn't already sold your ship, you can fly it out of here."

His features set in a stubborn pout, Yale walked along beside Chase but he didn't speak to him in the elevator, or even after they had reached the bay where his ship was moored. He requested permission to depart, and after a brief but agonizing delay, it was granted. Chase turned away as Yale boarded his ship, but remained in the corridor outside the bay to make certain his departure went smoothly.

For all he knew, Spider could have shot Yale down as soon as he cleared The Diamond Mine. Chase knew he had done all he could to rescue Yale Lincoln and send him back to Control. Now all he could do was pray that Yale got himself there.

Ivory showered, donned a flowing robe, and tried to rest, but she was far too anxious to sleep. She couldn't forget how casually her father had asked if Chase was worth keeping alive. The question ate away at her until she could no longer bear the torment. If she had ever had any doubts as to whether she loved Chase, she would have had her answer now, for she loved him with a passion that was frightening. Missing him terribly, she went to her communications panel and left a message asking him to come to her room as soon as he returned to his.

Unfortunately, Chase interpreted Ivory's request as a command, and after the way she had walked off and left him earlier in the day, he was not all that eager to do her bidding. Finally he decided they were definitely going to have to establish some ground rules, and wanting to get that chore out of the way, he went to her suite. Despite Spider's admonition to rest, he was surprised she wasn't working in her studio. When he found the spacious room empty, he went on through it to her private apartment, and knocked lightly at her door.

Ivory was dressed in one of the showy silver gowns she wore when she worked in the casino, and when she opened the door,

Chase was sufficiently dazzled to forget his anger for a moment. He kissed her soundly, then took her hand. "We've got to talk," he announced.

"Yes, I know. We've not been back even a day and already everything's changed. Just as I feared it would," Ivory complained. "I wanted to speak with my father privately when we arrived so that if he posed any objections to our engagement I could overcome them without your being insulted, but I saw the way you looked at me when I left you, and I know you couldn't have understood my motives."

"No, I didn't, but the next time you try to protect my feelings, you might alert me to the fact so I won't be hurt at being excluded."

Ivory pulled her hand from his and took a step away. It was difficult to think clearly when his nearness brought an indescribable longing for love, but she tried her best to be rational. "I hope it won't happen again, but at the same time, I'm almost positive it will. Perhaps we don't trust each other enough as yet to avoid feeling slighted now and then. Let's be on guard and try to prevent it from now on."

She faced him again, and asked what was for her a difficult question. "Did you actually kill the poor wretch my father had confined?"

She appeared badly upset by that possibility, and Chase was surprised. He described Yale Lincoln as Alado's least talented pilot and how he had set him free. "I can understand Spider's disgust with spies, but Yale isn't smart enough to keep track of himself, let alone spy on someone as clever as Spider."

Cinnamon Burke

He reached out for Ivory, wrapped his arms around her, and nuzzled her neck gently. "Hmm, you smell good."

Ivory slid her arms around his waist, but her pose wasn't truly relaxed. "Thank you, but I'm still worried. I've seen my father push too many men, taunting them until they make mistakes. I'm so afraid he's going to do the same to you."

"Why? From what he said to me, he approves of our being together."

"Yes," she assured him hesitantly, "that's what he says, but he respects strength. When he pushes you, push back, or he'll criticize you for being weak and make you pay dearly for that flaw."

"Yes, I've already caught on to him, but I thought it was a man's mother-in-law who caused all the problems. Are you warning me to be careful of Spider?"

Ivory stepped back so she could study his expression closely. Slipping her hands inside his jacket, she raised her arms to his shoulders. "Yes, be careful. Don't let him own you, but don't ever cross him. I've no idea what his given name was, and he won't tell me, but he earned the nickname Spider early in life, and it's well deserved. He can spin webs with the best of them. Don't let him catch you in one."

Chase lowered his hands to her hips and molded her supple body to his own. He was well aware of how dangerous a man Spider Diamond was, but, again deeply touched by her concern, he did not discount her warning. "He's had you all to himself for too long," he murmured against her cheek, "but he'll soon get used to me. Now, why must you work in

254

the casino? It can't be because you need the money."

Reassured by his calming presence, Ivory finally relaxed against him. "It's so I'll be a part of the Mine," she explained. "It's an extension of ourselves, and we have to live it fully to be able to run it well."

"That makes sense, but I haven't seen Spider dealing cards or tending bar."

Amused by that thought, Ivory began to smile, and the last of her apprehensions faded. "No, but he keeps a close watch on everything. Believe me, nothing escapes his notice, and too often I find myself daydreaming when I should be equally observant."

"Is that how you happened to deal off the bottom of the deck when I was at your table?"

He was teasing her now, and Ivory pulled away from him. "No. I was being a little too observant that evening, but it obviously wasn't a mistake. I do love you, Chase. Don't ever doubt that. Do you want to move in here with me? I can't bear the thought of sleeping alone now that I've been with you."

Chase took her hands, brought them to his lips, and kissed each fingertip. "I'll share your bed every chance I get, but I want to keep my room until we're married."

Disappointed, Ivory slipped from his grasp. "What's the matter? Are you afraid that if you live here I won't have any incentive to marry you?"

Backing away, Chase started for the door. "No, it's nothing so obvious as that. I'd just like to have a place to be by myself when I want to think about how lucky I am to have found you. I'll see you later."

As soon as he had gone, the warmth Ivory had felt in his arms was dampened by a mist of loneliness. She enjoyed her independence, and respected his. She certainly did not expect him to spend all his time with her, nor did she want him distracting her from her art. She did not want to have to go looking for him when she wanted his company, though. She supposed every couple had to come to an agreement as to when to be together and when apart, but she doubted that just having Chase in her bed at night would be nearly enough of his delightful company.

Chase had left Ivory's quarters without making plans for dinner, but the unexpected encounter with Yale Lincoln had sapped whatever appetite he might have had. He could not imagine why Yale had remained at the Mine after he had waved him off. Chase had been assigned to the investigation there, and by staying, Yale had not only put his own life in jeopardy, but Chase's mission as well.

The whole sorry incident had left him suffering from the same strange sensation of foreboding he had experienced on the flight to the Eagle's Nest. Nothing bad had happened there, though, and he tried to sweep away the perplexing anxiety. The only trouble was, he kept thinking of Ivory's mention of a web. If Spider had woven one around Yale, then Yale had escaped it, but Chase wondered whether he himself was in danger.

Not wanting to wait for Spider to assign him another nasty disposal job, he again considered asking to work on ship maintenance. Covered in grease, no one would suspect him of anything, but what would he learn that he did not already know? No, he decided, keeping track of security would be a far more valuable pastime.

Spider had already granted permission for him to gain access to the security floor above the casino, so Chase decided to begin there. There were viewing ports with cameras above each dealer, as well as a team of guards who monitored both the live action in the casino and the recorded tapes. It was a busy room, yet only the soft hum of the ventilation system broke the silence. This was spying at its most primitive level, but Chase felt strangely at home among the guards whose only duty was to observe.

His main interest was Ivory, and as he watched her deal a couple of hands of the peculiar poker game he still did not fully understand, he could not help but be impressed by the smoothness of her technique. She dealt the cards with a methodical precision, and brushed aside the players' lascivious suggestions with good humor, but Chase couldn't abide having her subjected to such verbal abuse.

Intending to make that point with Spider, he was halfway to the door before he realized it would be a grave mistake. He was supposed to be ingratiating himself with the pirate, not alienating him by demanding he change the way he treated his lovely daughter. *Patience,* he repeated silently. If only he could find the patience to conduct his mission as it had to be run. When it was over, Ivory's life would be irrevocably changed. Until then he would have to protect her from men who wanted to use her beauty as though it were another of the Mine's many exotic amusements.

He went down to the tavern, sipped a Martian ale, and then went up to Ivory's quarters to wait for her. He strolled around the studio, reviewed the sketches she had made on their trip, and then went to her room and stretched out across the bed. Unlike the navy blue of the guest quarters, her room was a sweetly seductive mauve. Several of her paintings were displayed on the walls. They were still lifes with the same odd juxtaposition of unlikely objects he had seen in her sketchbook, but none was as strikingly beautiful as the unfinished portrait of her mother.

He was convinced it must have been a budding love for art that had saved her when her mother had died. Perhaps once her father was arrested, it would be art that would save her again. Longing for her, he dozed off, and it seemed as though only seconds had elapsed before she joined him. She had already removed her silver boots and low-cut gown before stretching out beside him in her lavender lingerie.

"You didn't have to wait up for me," she whispered in his ear.

Awakened by her delicious scent as much as by her sultry voice, Chase wrapped her in his arms and rolled over to catch her beneath him. "So much for independence," he moaned. "I couldn't stay away from you, not even for tonight."

"Did you really want to?"

"Obviously not, but—"

"I don't regard you as a possession, Chase." She reached up to catch his lips in a kiss he deepened with passionate abandon. She stretched beneath him, gracefully aligning their bodies in a more pleasurable pose, then ran her fingers through his hair as he nuzzled her throat with eager kisses. "I know I'll never tire of you," she breathed against his ear.

Surprised by the question her comment implied, Chase leaned back slightly. "Nor I of you. I've never asked another woman to marry me, Ivory. I thought you understood that I mean to love you, as desperately as this, forever." He sealed his vow with a lingering kiss and then left her only long enough to cast off his clothes.

"You feel so good," he exclaimed as he pulled her back into his arms. "So right."

Crawling over him, Ivory traced Raven's wings with tender kisses, then lured Chase into another night of such remarkable bliss that neither got any sleep, nor cared.

Yale Lincoln's ship had communications equipment with the capability to transmit in code, but he waited until he was well out of range of The Diamond Mine before he contacted Control. First, he had to account for the days he had lost as Spider's prisoner, and explain how Drew Jordan had set him free. That was fact, and while embarrassing, not difficult to relate. It was only when he tried to describe how easily Drew had gotten his way with Spider that he had to exercise more caution.

Ever vigilant, Control responded with questions Yale tried to evade, but the Spymaster came at him again and again until he finally admitted what his instincts told him must be true. "I think he's turned," Yale stated reluctantly. "Drew Jordan is Spider Diamond's man now."

Cinnamon Burke

As he read the transcript, Control's expression betrayed no hint of his dismay, but if Drew Jordan had gone over to Spider Diamond's side, not only was the operation lost, but an extremely talented agent as well. Refusing to believe that Yale's impression could possibly be correct, he reached for his list of agents. He would send Ian St. Ives and, if need be, another man, but he was going to close The Diamond Mine, and if Drew Jordan couldn't do it, then he would find an agent of unquestioned loyalty who could.

Chapter Thirteen

Ivory's studio was lit with full-spectrum light to provide the same bright, clear illumination as the sun. Bathed in a warm golden glow, she stood at her easel, working on the painting of her mother and singing softly to herself. It was such an enchanting scene, Chase remained at the doorway drinking in the sight of the woman he adored, and reveling in the innocent beauty of the moment.

He did not immediately realize the lovely voice he heard was Ivory's. Then he remembered that Spider had remarked on her talent as a singer. Chase had forgotten to ask her to sing for him, but the words of the love song were so poignant he could not help but believe she sang them for him. He had never heard the song before, but it conveyed an aching longing for love that touched him deeply.

Cinnamon Burke

Sensing his presence, Ivory glanced toward the door and broke into a delighted smile. "Come in," she offered with a welcoming gesture. "I'm just putting in the last of the details. Come tell me what you think."

Chase did so as he walked toward her. "I think you're one of the most incredibly talented women who has ever lived." When Ivory looked somewhat less than pleased by his effusive compliment, he realized his mistake. "I should have said individuals, not women, for you outshine most men any day."

"You're prejudiced," Ivory protested, "and scarcely an impartial judge of my work. Look at it anyway though, please."

Chase found a spot on her cheek not smudged with paint and kissed her before turning his attention to the painting. "I thought this was exquisite the first time I saw it. It's even more marvelous now. Has your father seen it?"

Ivory took great care as she added a nuance of shadow to a fold near the angel's bare feet. "No. He loved her too much, Chase. This would only cause him pain."

Chase reached out to brush a stray curl out of her eyes. "Can a man ever love a woman too much?"

"Yes, but I think it only becomes an issue if he loses her."

That he might soon lose Ivory was too painful a consequence to imagine, and he quickly shoved the possibility from his mind. "Yes, I understand. Where are you going to hang this masterpiece when it's finished?"

"In my room. My father's unlikely to see it there,

but it will be a comfort to me."

"What was her name?"

"Willow. I know it seems an odd choice for a woman, but it's a lovely name."

Chase repeated the word softly. "Yes, it is. Willow, Spider, and Ivory. None of you has a common name, but that's not surprising when you're such extraordinary individuals. I liked the song you were singing. Do you ever sing for your dinner guests?"

Ivory stood back to judge the total effect of her final efforts. Pleased, she set her palette and brush aside. "I used to sit on my father's lap and sing when I was small, but now I usually try to bring out our guests' talents rather than showing off mine. I think we may have guests coming in again this week, but I've forgotten just who they are. That's your fault, you know. You're a terrible distraction."

"And so are you," Chase replied. "Spider sent me over to ask if you could join us for lunch, but when I saw you at your easel, I completely forgot why I was here."

"Is it time for lunch already?"

"It's one o'clock."

"Just let me clean up a bit and I'll be right there." Ivory started toward her apartment.

"I'll wait for you." Turning again to the magnificent painting, Chase was struck once again by its superb color harmonies, but the angel's pose still worried him. "Fleeing Angel," he titled it softly, and wondered if Ivory didn't recall more about her parents' marriage than she believed.

Ivory was back in an instant, clothed in a tunic and pants that matched her sapphire eyes.

Responding to her smile, Chase made no further reference to her mother, but he hoped one day to learn all there was to know about Willow Diamond. Ivory had inherited her beauty, but he was curious as to what sort of woman could have loved Spider Diamond, and inspired such a great love in return.

Spider welcomed them with an impatient wave. "Sit down. Let's have lunch first, and then make some plans."

"For a wedding?" Chase asked as he dropped into the chair opposite Ivory's.

Spider prefaced his answer with a rude laugh. "No, I've no interest in wedding plans. Handle those yourselves. I have a business decision in mind, but as I said, let's enjoy a meal together first."

"Why do I feel like a condemned man?" Chase joked.

Ivory gasped at what in her home was a tasteless remark. "That's really not funny."

"Sorry." Chase waited quietly while André brought in warm whole wheat rolls and bowls of corn chowder filled with bits of hot peppers. Chase finished three of the freshly baked rolls before André reappeared with a colorful platter of vegetables and pasta. Chase reached for another roll.

"Would you like something else?" Ivory inquired thoughtfully.

"No, this is fine, for lunch." Chase winked at André and made a mental note to tell him he wanted a steak for dinner. "Vegetables never hurt anyone." He speared a broccoli floret and tried to look as though he wanted to eat it.

Perfectly satisfied with the fare, Spider asked Ivory about her work. "It's progressing well," she replied, without revealing the subject. "I made quite a few sketches at the Paradise Retreat, and I may work up a couple for paintings. I don't want to neglect my ceramics, though. I'm not nearly finished with my iguana series."

"Can one ever finish such a fascinating subject?" Spider asked.

Although his remark had been made in jest, Ivory gave him a serious reply. "Any subject can be pursued endlessly. It's all in having the imagination to see the familiar with an exciting and creative perspective."

"As you do so well," Spider complimented.

Although their banter was light, Chase had the uncomfortable feeling that Spider was merely masking his true agenda for the day. Chase grew increasingly curious as to what Spider's ulterior motive might be. He hurried through his meal, or what he chose to eat of it, but Spider and Ivory ate at a leisurely pace that delayed any mention of business matters for more than an hour.

"The Celestial Cannons need to be delivered," Spider then announced. "I usually leave that chore to Stokes and Vik, but I'd like you to go along with them this time, Duncan."

"I think not," Ivory argued before Chase had a chance to speak. "Stokes is still sulking because Chase broke his nose, and he'd only use the trip to find a way to pay him back. Preoccupied with revenge, he can't be counted on to handle the delivery efficiently. I'll go along with Chase instead. We can drop off the weapons as easily as we collected the money."

Spider's cold gray eyes narrowed slightly. "I have already made the decision as to who makes the delivery, Ivory. Don't argue with me."

In a fiery burst of defiance, Ivory glanced toward Chase. "If you send Chase, he'll come back alone. Do you really want to sacrifice Stokes and Vik in a ridiculous contest over who is the strongest man? Chase has more brains than Stokes and Vik put together, and he'll surely win, but he won't stop with broken noses next time."

Though he was thrilled that Ivory believed so strongly in his abilities, Chase understood her father's reasoning. He chose his words with care so as not to insult her, and his tone was soft, conciliatory. "From what I understand, neither Spider nor you ever delivers weapons, and I agree with that policy. It's too dangerous, and there's no point in risking your life simply to keep me company. I can handle the job alone."

Highly amused by Chase's boast, Spider threw back his head and howled with laughter. "You cannot possibly imagine that I would be so stupid as to load a ship with Celestial Cannons, kiss you good-bye, and actually expect you to deliver them to Mordecai Black rather than sell them elsewhere."

Infuriated by Spider's suspicions, which were totally unjustified in this case, Chase lost his temper. "And you can't possibly imagine that I would be so stupid as to double-cross you," he replied. "I don't want to end up in two quivering hunks like Sonny Duran."

His grin gone, Spider immediately switched his

attention to his daughter. "You told him about Sonny?"

"I've heard you recount that story for as long as I can remember. There's no reason to keep it a secret from Chase," Ivory insisted. "I intend to marry him, Dad, and I trust him with the family secrets."

While obviously not pleased, Spider made no move to punish her. Instead, he regarded Chase with a determined stare. "I won't send you alone. That's completely out of the question, but I think you could handle the trip with Vik. I doubt he likes you any better than Stokes does, but he won't force the issue as Stokes surely would. An unmarked ship is being loaded with the merchandise now. Plan to leave first thing in the morning. I'll tell Vik to meet you at docking bay twelve."

"I want to go too," Ivory repeated. Disgusted with Chase for not taking her side, she concentrated on her father. "We've never had any trouble with a delivery."

"Because I know who to send," Spider cautioned. "Besides, we're having guests tomorrow evening and I'll need you here with me. The violinist you admire, Paul Godwyn, will be here, along with the renowned baritone Sergio Leonetti, and that wonderful poet Basil Danby. They'll all be looking forward to seeing you again, and I know you don't want to disappoint them."

Ivory had a colorfully obscene comment as to what he could do with his guests, and then added, "I'm going with Chase."

"Would you like to spend the night in the cage?" Spider asked. He was leaning forward now, his expression as menacing as his words.

"You wouldn't."

"Oh yes, I would, and we both know what a thrill Stokes would have putting you there."

Revolted by Spider's threats, Chase raised his hand. "That's enough, both of you. I'll make the delivery with Vik, and I'll be back before you've even noticed I've gone. I'll make you one promise though, Spider. Don't ever put Ivory in that ghastly cage of yours, or you'll have to answer to me. What I did to Stokes will look like a love pat compared to what I'll do to you."

Spider rose slowly from his chair but remained at his place, resting his palms on the tabletop. "If you really want to fight me, let's do it now. I've not the slightest doubt who'll win, but I'll at least give you a sporting chance to survive."

"Stop it!" Ivory cried. "I don't want you two fighting over anything, least of all me." Obviously in pain, she raised her hands to her temples, then slowly left her chair. "I'll see you when you get back, Chase, and don't bother to tell me good-bye."

Chase started to rise, but Spider waved him back down into his chair. "Let her go," he advised. "Don't ever try to reason with an angry woman. You'll simply be wasting your breath, and increasing her sense of indignation. This is my fault, of course. I've spoiled Ivory, and she expects to get her way. It's no wonder she feels so badly thwarted when I have to say no."

Chase nodded as though he agreed with his future father-in-law, but he was frightened by how close he had come to fighting the man. There would have been no way he could have refused the challenge and kept his respect, so he was grateful to Ivory for stopping the bout before it began. Of course, killing Spider would have put a decisive end to his investigation, but it wasn't something he would have wanted Ivory to see.

"She has enormous courage," Chase murmured.

"Yes, indeed, but there's no trace of cowardice in you either, is there, Duncan?"

"I hope not." Chase left his chair, but took Spider's advice and did not follow Ivory. Instead, he went down to docking bay twelve to make certain the ship he had been assigned had been fully prepared to fly.

Rather than return to her room, Ivory went up to the hydroponic gardens and strolled in the aisles between the tanks. She came there often, and the technicians greeted her with cheerful waves and went on with their work. It was the serenity of the chemical gardens that appealed to her, and she sat down in the orchid arbor to rest, and to think.

She did not want another scene like the one they had just had, but knowing that Chase Duncan was as strong-willed as her father, she feared the hostile encounters would occur frequently. She would boycott meals if the men in her life wished to use the dining table as a battleground, but when the atmosphere was so highly charged between them, she doubted they would notice she was gone. She wondered how often her father could demand a fight to the death before Chase finally took him up on it.

Positive that Spider knew more ways to kill a man than Chase could imagine, she feared the outcome of any such contest. "I should have fallen in love with a poet," she moaned softly. He would have been able to read his melancholy sonnets while she worked, and they could have had a life untouched by the violence her father craved like some exotic drug.

Too restless to remain alone with her thoughts, she plucked a stem of cymbidiums, carried them back to her apartment, and placed them in a crystal vase. There was the painting to complete, and she was scheduled for another shift in the casino that night. The routine she had known would overtake them weighed heavily on her, but as she added the last golden highlight to the angel's wings, her imagination took flight. When Chase came to apologize for upsetting her at lunch, she had a difficult time hiding her smile.

"We're three strong personalities," she reminded him. "We're bound to clash again and again, but you mustn't allow your arguments with my father to become physical. He's older than you, probably no longer as fast, but he wouldn't fight fair, and that will give him a tremendous advantage."

Chase had plenty of dirty tricks of his own, but he couldn't bear to see her worry so about him. "I'm not going to get into any kind of a fight with your father," he assured her. "I think he's just trying to hang on to you for as long as he can. At least I'm trying to view it that way, and it keeps me from getting so mad I can't think clearly. I'll miss you terribly while I'm gone, but I'll be back in a few days. Perhaps then you'll be ready to set a date for the wedding."

Ivory shrugged slightly. "Well, that all depends."

"On what?"

"On how good Basil Danby's poetry is. If it's truly as wonderful as my father says, then I may have eloped with him before you get back."

"I've never even heard of Basil Danby, but he sounds like a pompous old man you couldn't possibly love. What are you trying to do, make me jealous?"

"Certainly not, that would be childish."

"Yes, it would." Chase propped his fists on his hips. "Don't you know I'd much rather take you with me than Vik? I don't relish the prospect of having that brute's company, but I'm already wanted, so if I'm arrested for trafficking in arms, things can't go any worse for me than they already have. Your record's clean, Ivory, and it ought to stay that way."

The painting was at last complete, and Ivory bent down to sign her name. "I already have a father, Chase. I don't need another."

Chase's voice softened to a husky whisper. "Believe me, your father is the last person I want to be. I mean to be your husband, and soon."

"I don't want a husband who'll take my father's side against me."

Chase waited while Ivory dropped her brush into the turpentine to soak, set her palette on the table, and began to clean her hands. "You can't rub me out like a spot of paint," he insisted. "I'm here to stay, Ivory, and whenever your father moves to protect you, I'm going to agree with him. It's who's right that's important, not stubborn loyalty without regard for what's best."

Disgusted with his patronizing tone, Ivory

shook her head. "Do you remember what I told you before?"

Confused by what seemed a totally inappropriate question, Chase shrugged. "About what?"

Ivory began to unbutton her smock. "I told you not to bother telling me good-bye. I want to get to bed early tonight, so please sleep in your own room. When you get back, we can talk about the wedding, but I'll warn you now, if you continue to treat me in such a condescending fashion, I'll call off the engagement rather than set a date."

Chase opened his mouth to argue, and then thought better of it. Ivory was not only bright, beautiful, and talented, she was just plain stubborn. Recognizing a lost cause when he saw it, he turned and walked out. He missed her before he reached the door, and relying on her to miss him just as badly, he tried to believe they could work out their differences when he returned.

Ivory put her time alone that night to good use by preparing a plan of action. She rose early, dressed in a flight suit, packed her bag, and went to Vik's quarters. Still half asleep, he answered her knock dressed in baggy underwear. He yawned widely, and had to brush his hair out of his eyes before he could see well enough to recognize her. Even then he did not look all that alert.

"Ms. Diamond, I wasn't expecting you. Let me get dressed."

"There's no need, Vik." Ivory pushed past him and, once inside his room, took the Celestial Cannon from her flight bag. She motioned for him to return to his bunk. "There's been a change in plan. Lie down; you're going to sleep late today."

"Oh, Ms. Diamond, please—" His eyes were focused on the deadly laser pistol.

Ivory wanted cooperation, and Vik's pathetic whining didn't please her. "I'm not going to kill you, Vik, and no one is going to be mad at you when they find we've traded places. You're going to tell my father that I threatened to blast you with a cannon, tied you up, and stole your clothes. I've seen you practically tear men apart with your bare hands. I had no idea you had so little courage. Now lie down and be quick about it."

Ivory had brought along strips from the rags she used to clean her brushes, and she quickly lashed him to his bunk. "I hate to use a gag, but I can't have you screaming for help the minute I walk out the door."

"I won't yell, Ms. Diamond. I swear I won't."

Ivory wasn't even tempted to trust him. She surveyed his cluttered room. Food trays were piled up by the door, dirty clothes littered the floor, and "art" of the variety that Chase had sold covered the walls. "I really expected better of you, Vik. When I get home, I'm going to come back down here and run a quick inspection. If you're still living in such a filthy mess, you'll find yourself living elsewhere."

Ivory slipped a gag over his mouth before he could offer a pitiful promise to improve. She checked his closet, found a clean, dark blue flight suit, and put it on over her own. She donned his jacket and pulled the hood up over her head. A quick glance in the mirror didn't satisfy her that she would be mistaken for Vik, so she removed the jacket and rolled a couple of clean undershirts around her upper arms to add the missing bulk.

After again slipping on Vik's jacket, she thought the resemblance close enough to fool Chase if he caught only a glimpse of her, and she would make certain that was all he got.

On an impulse, she bent down and kissed Vik on the forehead. "That's a good boy. Someone will surely find you later in the day, but if not, I'll untie you as soon as I get back." She left his quarters with her head down. She did her best impression of Vik's rolling gait, and wasn't recognized on her way to docking bay twelve.

Chase debated stopping by Ivory's suite to say good-bye, but doubting she would be awake that early, or admit him even if she were, he had to be content with leaving a message. He wished he could think of something as tender as the haunting song he had heard her sing, but, lacking any talent for poetic expression, he could only say that he loved her and would miss her. Disappointed he had to leave with things so strained between them, he was grateful to find Vik crouched over the stacks of Celestial Cannons in the unmarked Blaster's hold.

"Close the hatch," he shouted as he passed by, "and we'll get under way."

Vik raised a gloved hand in response, and Chase went on up to the cockpit. As he slid into the pilot's seat, the prospect of spending the next few days with Vik surely didn't excite him, but he had had to put up with worse company on other assignments, and he was confident he would survive the voyage. As soon as the light came on to show the hatch was sealed, he requested permission to depart. It was promptly granted, and in a matter of minutes they were on their way.

Chase turned the voyage over to the navigational computer, but, preferring his own company to Vik's, he remained in the cockpit until it was time for lunch. When he found Vik curled up beneath a blanket napping, he did not wake him to offer to share the meal. Delighted to find the protein drinks he had missed on the voyage with Ivory, he drank one, and took another back to the cockpit. As he sipped it, he went over everything he had learned about Spider Diamond, and was positive he had enough to call in a raid on The Diamond Mine.

The only complication was Ivory. A sad smile played across his lips as he thought of her. She would probably spend the time while he was away giving form to her sketches for the iguana candelabra, and he would need all the tact he could muster to find compliments for that monstrosity. In the past, he had taken a great deal of satisfaction in apprehending criminals, but the only way he would ever be pleased with this operation was by separating Ivory from her father's crimes, and keeping her free.

Their marriage would protect her because he could then demand that Control grant her immunity from prosecution. Control had that power, and Drew was determined to extract the favor as payment for the many times he had risked his life for him. The challenge would be to convince Ivory that he was the husband of her dreams. Unfortunately, it looked as though that might be impossible after he brought Spider Diamond to justice. Sleepy, he finished the vampire float and closed his eyes for a nap.

When two hours later he was teased awake by a delectable aroma, he wondered what Vik might be cooking. He was surprised that the man could read well enough to follow the directions on the food packets. The savory smells floating into the cockpit were too marvelous to ignore. Hoping Vik had prepared enough for two, he went back to the galley, but what he found there shocked him to the marrow.

"Ivory! What are you doing on board? And where's Vik?"

Ivory checked her watch. Certain they had traveled far enough from The Diamond Mine to preclude his returning, she replied with a delighted smile, "Vik is probably still tied to his bunk back at the Mine. He may be a little stiff and sore by the time he's discovered, but he'll be no worse for the experience. As for you, I'll tell my father you weren't in on my ruse, so you've no reason to be afraid. I doubt I'll suffer any serious consequences, so let's just enjoy ourselves, shall we?"

It wasn't that Chase wasn't glad to see her; he was. But she had defied both her father and him to make the voyage. Even in a flight suit she looked appealingly feminine and sweet, but he now knew that that was as deceptive an image as her earlier masquerade as Vik.

"Headstrong doesn't even begin to describe you, does it?"

Ivory gestured with a fork. "When a man takes decisive action, he's complimented for being forceful and called a hero. When a woman takes charge of her life, she's criticized for being headstrong. I don't know about you, but that doesn't strike me as being fair."

"The decision to leave you at the Mine wasn't about being fair, Ivory, it was about keeping you safe."

"You said you wanted us to be partners," she reminded him. "You've a strange idea of what equality means if you're the only one who ever has to take any risks. What's my role? Am I just supposed to look good and paint pretty pictures?"

Chase shrugged helplessly. "Don't dismiss your talent as though it were nothing."

This time Ivory used the fork to poke him in the chest. "I'm my father's daughter, Chase Duncan, and I'll not be left out of the fun just because it's dangerous. I told you equality was important to me, and either we are equal partners in everything we do, or you're not the man I believed you to be, and you're certainly not the man I want to marry."

Chase knew he wasn't the man she believed him to be, but he was going to have to continue playing the part for a while longer. He raised his hands in a universal gesture of surrender. "Fine. You're here, and frankly I'm not a bit disappointed to find Vik isn't on board. I'd much rather spend my time making love to you than avoiding him. We should, however, make plans right now for how the cannons will be delivered. You convinced me you were a muscular man when I saw you this morning. I want you to look that way again when we drop off the cannons."

Ivory raised her brows slightly. "I do believe I've earned Mordecai's respect. Why should I hide who I am?"

"You're never going to make things easy for me, are you?"

"If you're looking for easy, try the girls at the Eagle's Nest." Ivory turned her attention to the stew she was heating. Chock-full of hunks of beef, it had been chosen with Chase in mind.

"Don't be flippant," Chase scolded. "Mordecai and his men will be so eager to get hold of the cannons I doubt they'll notice who's delivering them, but on the off chance he might try something foolish, I want you fully disguised."

"You've got it backward," Ivory exclaimed. "He'll be far more likely to cause trouble if he believes we're just a couple of men who mean nothing to Spider. He might shoot us, steal this Blaster, and then tell Spider the ship blew up shortly after we left the Eagle's Nest. There would be no way for my father to prove the story wasn't true, either. No, it's too great a gamble for me to go in wearing a disguise."

The way Ivory described the chance for disaster was so totally convincing, Chase chose not to argue with her. She thought like a pirate, after all, and despite all his training, he did not. He had met plenty of other women who had looked him right in the eye and stated their case more defiantly, but never one who had made so much sense.

"You're right," he offered with admiration. "You've considerable power not simply because you deserve it, but because you're Spider's daughter, and it would be foolish not to take advantage of it. Still, I want you to keep your own Celestial Cannon in your hand while the arms are being unloaded. Will you at least agree to that?"

Ivory speared a piece of beef and guided it to his mouth. "You don't have to advise the obvious,

Chase. I fully intend to not only defend myself, but to keep you covered as well."

Chase bit down on the beef. The Burgundy sauce was superb, and the meat so tender he barely needed to chew. "We're going to make an incredible team," he assured her, "and this is the best food I've ever eaten on a flight."

"The secret is in knowing how to use the oven. People generally go for hot and fast, when low and slow produces much better results."

Ivory's glance traveled over him as she provided that bit of advice, and suddenly Chase's appetite for her was all that mattered. "I had no idea that cooking had so much in common with making love." He reached out to take her hand and drew her into the main cabin. "I want you for an appetizer," he whispered as he unzipped her flight suit.

"Hmm." Ivory arched against him. "I could use a few nibbles of you too."

Chase tried to respond with something equally clever, but Ivory's lips beckoned with a succulent sweetness he couldn't resist. For a fleeting instant he thought of poor Vik, then Ivory slid her hands down over him, feeling how badly he wanted her, and he couldn't think at all.

Chapter Fourteen

As they neared the Eagle's Nest, Ivory donned the Rocketball suit and metallic wig she had worn on her previous visit. Even knowing she planned to wear it, Chase was stunned by the transformation in her appearance. As tight as her skin, the sheer silver garment hugged her figure as closely as a lover's lips, and Chase had a difficult time concentrating on the task at hand. "I swear that suit could deliver the cannons by itself," he swore softly.

"I'll take that as a compliment."

"Oh, yes, it definitely is." Chase requested permission to dock at the Eagle's Nest, and it was given, but he half expected another confrontation over the condition of the bays. When the one to which they were assigned proved to be brilliantly lit, he was relieved, but not so pleased as to drop his guard.

They waited in the cockpit for the bay to be pressurized and Mordecai Black to appear. Before leaving the co-pilot's seat, Ivory leaned over to kiss Chase. "I'm going to give him a time limit," she explained. "If we rush him, he won't be able to spring any nasty traps."

"Fine, the sooner we're out of here the better." Chase followed her through the main cabin to the hatch. In the captivating suit, she was a delight to trail, but he moved ahead of her to open the hatch himself. "If I were going to try anything, I'd do it now. Cover me while I swing open the hatch."

Ivory's fingers tightened on the cannon's grip, but she didn't wait for one of Mordecai's gray-suited minions to make a false move. Instead, as soon as she had a clear view of the bay, she fired, drawing a line across the floor with one deliberate burst. When the men scattered, she laughed and stepped out on the ramp. "You have five minutes to unload the hold, or I'll start firing again and next time I won't take such careful aim."

Chase moved behind her, went down the ramp, and opened the aft cargo hold. Wanting to make certain that Mordecai's men did not place anything in the hold that might cause them trouble later, he stood where he could observe them. He leaned back against the ship and adopted the most menacing expression he could affect.

Mordecai shoved his men back into place as he approached the Blaster. "There's no need for fireworks, Ms. Diamond. We can complete the transfer of goods in a few minutes, and then I want you and your companion to join me in the Eagle's Nest for a little celebration."

"You've already used up thirty precious seconds, Mordecai. Better get moving. As for the invitation, I'm sorry, but tonight we're pressed for time and can't possibly accept."

Mordecai signaled his men to begin unloading the cannons from the hold. "You're not making another delivery in the area, are you? Spider promised me I'd be the only one with the Celestial Cannon, and I expect him to keep his word."

"My father is generous to a fault," Ivory replied. "If he said you'd be the only one in your tiny corner of the universe with the cannon, then you can believe him—for the time being, at any rate. You can't honestly expect to have an exclusive right to the weapon forever. Nor can you expect to simply give your men the cannon and set them loose on any enemies you may have. The pistol requires intensive training before it can be used effectively."

"Yes," Mordecai agreed, "I've read the manual and I understand. I won't hand them out like chips in the casino."

"Good. I'd hate for any of your men to be injured needlessly." Ivory glanced at her watch. "You've only three minutes left to finish. I'd help out if I were you."

Insulted by that demeaning piece of advice, Mordecai shouted to his men to hurry. The cannons were packaged in individual crates, and cumbersome to carry rather than heavy. He watched anxiously, attempting to judge the time, and offered what urging he could to the workers. When the last of the crates was unloaded, he pulled a handkerchief from his pocket and wiped the perspiration from his brow.

"There," he called to Ivory. "The job's done."

"Better move the crates out of the bay before we launch."

Mordecai saw Ivory again check her watch and began to swear. "I'll have them removed this instant, Ms. Diamond. There's no need to time it."

"I disagree. You have farther to go now, so I'll give you ten minutes, and then we'll be on our way."

Mordecai frowned angrily but did not plead for more time. There were storage lockers along the sides of the bay, and he quickly directed his men to stack the crates inside. He clapped his hands to set a rhythm for their steps, and then waved his arms to direct their progress. The half-dozen men ran back and forth, often colliding with one another, but they again beat Ivory's deadline.

Ivory saluted Mordecai with a wave of her cannon. After Chase secured the hatch to the hold, she followed him up the ramp. He closed the main hatch and then they went up to the cockpit. "Get us out of here as quickly as you can," Ivory ordered.

Chase made an immediate request for departure, then sat back to wait for the bay doors to roll open. "How many of the Celestial Cannons would be needed to put a hole in this ship large enough to destroy it?"

Ivory pulled off her curly gold and copper wig and shook out her hair. "I could do it with mine, but Mordecai would have to uncrate a cannon, complete the assembly, which takes approximately one hour, and then master the art of using the weapon before he could cause us any real damage. We're not stupid, Chase. That's why the cannons aren't delivered ready to fire."

"Believe me, I'm well aware of your intelligence. It was just a thought."

"And obviously a good one, because we have already made an allowance for it. The Celestial Cannon is like a great many things. Men see it and want to own one, but firing it accurately takes more practice than most assume."

"Almost any weapon does," Chase argued before he remembered that weapons were not supposed to be one of his areas of expertise. He held his breath until he was positive that Ivory was unaware he had made a dangerous slip. She simply nodded, encouraging him to continue. "It stands to reason a weapon ought not to be given to a man who can't use it accurately, but do you really believe that Mordecai Black will take the time to train his men?"

"If he doesn't train them initially, he soon will, because there are sure to be fatal accidents if he doesn't."

The bay doors slid open, and, cleared for departure, Chase got the ship away from the Eagle's Nest in a graceful swoop. "Maybe you ought not to wave your cannon around like you do," he worried aloud.

Cradled in her lap, the pistol didn't look particularly dangerous to Ivory. "This was the first one we built, and I know it better than the engineer who designed it. You don't have to worry about me slicing off one of your ears by mistake."

"I could live without an ear," Chase replied. "Just don't aim any lower; better yet, don't aim at me at all."

"I can see this is making you nervous. I'll go put it away and change my clothes. This damn suit is so tight I don't understand how the Rocketball players stand them."

"Wait a minute," Chase called. "I want to peel it off you."

Delighted by his request, Ivory remained in her seat until he had passed control of the Blaster to the navigational computer. Unlike the one on Spider's ship, this computer responded in a normal tone without the sultry tones programmed into Rainbow. "Maybe that's why the Rocketball players like these suits: their fans all want to peel them off."

"If you don't hurry up and get back to the main cabin," Chase threatened, "you're going to have to peel me off!"

Ivory was out of her seat in an instant, but after stowing away the Celestial Cannon, she made certain he caught her. His kiss was hot, urgent, and her response joyous until the computer called Chase's name and warned of an approaching ship. Startled, she looked up at Chase. "If Mordecai has sent a ship after us, he'll not live out the day."

Chase moaned. "I don't know which is worse, being interrupted or having to contend with him." He followed Ivory to the cockpit, but instantly recognized the codes being transmitted by the approaching ship. "That's a Confederation security vessel. There's no reason for them to be after us unless Mordecai Black tipped them off." Other than Ivory's Celestial Cannon, there was nothing illegal on board, but that one cannon was enough to create a serious incident. He slid into the pilot's seat. "What do you want to do?"

Cinnamon Burke

Ivory took her place beside him. "We're broadcasting Peregrine's science mission codes, and that wouldn't have caught their notice. Change the course to wrap us around the asteroid, and when we're blocked from the Confederation's sensors, go to full power. We'll be gone before they can track us."

"Unless they know who we are and where we're going," Chase warned.

The darkness of his glance revealed his fear, but Ivory remained remarkably cool. "Just do it."

Chase took back control of the ship and followed her directions. When he went to full power, the Blaster responded with a surge that surprised him. "My God, you've boosted the engines on this ship, haven't you?"

"We've doubled its performance," Ivory replied, "but we save the extra power for emergencies. Unfortunately, this appears to be one."

Chase had to agree, but he was still angry. "Why didn't you tell me about this before? If I'd come with Vik, did Spider expect me to just discover this ship's potential on my own?"

Ivory continued to watch the navigational computer's screen, but the Confederation ship's codes were no longer shown. "They haven't followed us, so either our code threw them off or they weren't looking for us in the first place."

"Or they haven't the speed to catch us."

"We'd still see their codes if they were tracking us. They're not." Ivory unbuckled her seat belt and turned slightly to face him. "If you had done a complete inventory of the ship's capabilities prior to flight, you would have found it had extra

286

power. Maybe my father just assumed you were the cautious sort."

"I am!" Chase slammed his fist down on his armrest. "How about Spider's Blaster, has that been modified too?"

"Not as yet. It's never used for any illegal activity, so extra speed isn't required. Frankly, I'm amazed that you're so upset. For all we know, the Confederation security forces fly by the Eagle's Nest twice each day. They can't stop ships without a reason, though, nor search the Nest without a just cause. Now stop worrying. All they'll note in their log is a sighting of one of Peregrine's science missions, so we're in absolutely no danger from them."

Chase was as appalled by his own carelessness as he was with Ivory's cavalier dismissal of a potentially disastrous encounter. He had assumed this Blaster was identical to Spider's, and it was not. What other foolish mistakes had he made because he had relied on an assumption rather than fact? he agonized silently.

Ivory watched Chase's jaw tighten as he clenched his teeth, and she doubted that anything she said would make him feel better. She and her father had given the Confederation's security forces the slip so many times they no longer considered losing them a challenge, but clearly Chase was envisioning himself serving a long prison term. Her earlier misgivings as to the wisdom of involving him in her father's business returned, but failed to diminish her love for him in the slightest.

"Chase?" She reached out to touch him and felt him flinch. She left her fingertips resting lightly on his arm. "I should have told you this ship has extra power, and that we routinely use Peregrine's codes to confuse anyone who might come in range. It's nothing new to me, and I'm sorry I didn't think to share the information with you. That was my mistake, not yours. Please don't brood over it."

"I'm not brooding," Chase denied in a harsh rasp.

"Fine. You're merely scowling because you enjoy being in a foul mood. Excuse me, I've got much better things to do." Ivory left the cockpit, hoping Chase would follow. He didn't. To go from a passionate embrace to cold silence in such a short time was deeply disappointing, certainly not the way she had wanted the evening to end. When she finally realized she would have to change out of the provocative Rocketball suit on her own, she did, then showered and dressed in her own flight suit for what she feared would be a very lonely journey home.

By the time Chase calmed down enough to want to be with Ivory, she had already gone to sleep. He reclined another seat for himself and stretched out, but didn't fall asleep for nearly an hour. When he awoke the next morning, Ivory was drawing in her sketchbook and didn't even wave as he went back to the lavatory. When he finished his grooming, he knelt by her side.

"There's a great deal to your father's operation I don't know as yet, and like firing a Celestial Cannon, it's going to take me a while to learn. I wasn't mad at you last night but with myself for taking such poor care of you. Can you forgive me?"

Steeling herself against his masculine charm,

Ivory refused to look up from her work. "I'm used to taking care of myself. I'm not a child. I don't need a nanny."

"No one would mistake you for a child, Ivory." Chase remained at her side, confident she would glance his way soon, but when she did, her gaze was clouded with sorrow. "I didn't mean to hurt you. I'm sorry, truly I am. Have you had breakfast?"

"I didn't want anything."

"Come help me find something good." Chase rose and extended his hand. After a long hesitation Ivory finally took it, and he pulled her to her feet. She was so close he could not resist kissing her, but her lips were cool, her response almost too brief to measure. Hoping all she needed was time, he didn't complain, but they reached The Diamond Mine before her chilly mood had begun to thaw.

Spider met them with Stokes, Vik, and six other men Chase recognized as part of Spider's private security force. Rather than taking Ivory aside this time, Spider simply waved her out of his way. "You had your orders, Duncan, but chose to completely disregard them. I won't tolerate disobedience of any kind. You're finished here."

"He didn't disobey you," Ivory protested. "I did. If you have to be furious with someone, then I'm the logical target. Chase didn't even suspect I was on board the Blaster until we'd gone too far to turn back. He scolded me the whole time we were away, and I had such a miserable trip I'm sorry I bothered to tie up Vik and go."

Unmoved by Ivory's plea, Spider motioned to Stokes. "Get her out of here."

A demented grin split Stokes's face as he started toward Ivory, but she stepped back and Chase caught her hand. He pulled her against his side and wrapped his arm around her waist. The indifference she had shown him on the return flight was gone in an instant, and she clung to him with all the passion he had sorely missed.

He dropped his flight bag, but Ivory still had hers slung over her shoulder, and he wondered if she would go for her Celestial Cannon rather than watch him be beaten. He hoped it would not come to that, but the situation did not look good. For an experienced agent, he had made a regrettable series of blunders. He could imagine Control calmly ascribing his death while on a mission as due to agent error rather than any failure on Control's part to protect him. It was a horrifying mental image, and he immediately replaced it with one of himself receiving a commendation for the excellence of his work.

"I was no happier to find Ivory on board the Blaster than you must have been to discover she'd gone, but we delivered the arms and returned safely," Chase stated. "I'll give you my word that after we're married, I'll continue to put Ivory's welfare above my own, and this will definitely be the last time she'll ever make an unauthorized flight."

Poised for a savage fight, Spider glared at them both. "Neither of you is in a position to bargain with me."

"No, you're wrong," Ivory cried, stiffening into a defensive stance. "This is a family matter and ought not to be discussed here in front of others, but don't make the mistake of believing you can intimidate me with numbers. I won't let you harm Chase or send him away. You gave him to me, and I won't let you go back on your word. I want to marry him as soon as it can be arranged."

Holding her so tightly, Chase could feel Ivory trembling, but her voice rang with a stirring clarity that belied her fear. This wasn't the way he had wanted to plan their wedding, but it had been Spider who had forced her to take sides, not him. That she had chosen him thrilled Chase clear through. Stokes still looked much too keen to get into a fight, while Vik and the other young men hung back. Clearly Vik, who was looking down at his boots, was still embarrassed by the way Ivory had traded places with him.

Determined to project the confidence he knew would impress the pirate, Chase regarded Spider with a level stare. "Don't break your daughter's heart," he advised softly. "You ought to be pleased she's as daring as you and isn't afraid to go after whatever, or whomever, she wants. A woman of Ivory's courage is a rare prize. I won't give her up."

Barely containing his anger, Spider closed the distance between them. He clasped his hands behind his back and studied Chase with a gelid gaze before turning to Ivory. "Do you truly want this man for a husband?" he asked. "If you're merely worried about his safety, I'll see he flies his own ship out of here within the hour. You needn't marry him to save his life, so please don't make a needless sacrifice."

Without hesitating an instant, Ivory replied, "How long will it take for you to finally grasp the simple fact that I'm an adult, and fully capable of running my own life and making my own decisions, even in something so important as this?"

Ivory's words only served to inflame Spider's hostility. "You are never to take such a belligerent tone with me again," he ordered in a harsh whisper. "You have defied me for the last time. You're my daughter, but that doesn't give you the right to question my orders, or ignore them. Now is that simple fact finally understood?"

Ivory had known she had gone too far, but Chase was too important to her to do any less. "Yes, sir," she replied, but there was nothing docile about her expression or tone.

Deeply insulted, Spider made the only choice he could. "You're right," he said. "This is far too personal a matter to share with others. We'll go up to my suite and make the preparations for your marriage there." He nodded to his men. "You're no longer needed." Not one dared laugh or offer a rude joke as to how the confrontation had ended. To a man, they filed out in respectful silence.

Spider waited until they had gone before starting for the door himself. Chase gave Ivory an encouraging squeeze, and released his hold on her so that she could precede him. She gave him a shaky smile. "We'll be all right," he promised, but she still looked unconvinced.

Not a word was spoken in the elevator, but once they had entered the frescoed dining room, Spider exploded in a fit of temper. "You made a fool of Vik," he began, "and now none of the other men has any respect for him. He knows too much for me to let him go, but he's a liability now, and that's your fault rather than his. I can't have you undermining our operation, Ivory. I absolutely refuse to allow it. It will all be yours one day, but there will be nothing left to inherit if our enemies learn we're fighting among ourselves."

Chase listened as Spider characterized Ivory's behavior as an outright betrayal. Chase considered the pirate's complaint overdramatic, but he thought it wise to allow him to vent his anger before he offered any suggestions for the future. He had hoped that Spider would be pleased rather than outraged by Ivory's resourcefulness. Spider paced as he continued to rant about the danger Ivory's willful disobedience might bring down on them.

Ivory found herself giving only half her attention to her father, for somewhere in the dim reaches of her memory she recalled the same strident voice, though not any specific words. The time and place were lost in a murky blur, as was the person to whom he had directed the tirade, but the recollection was deeply disturbing all the same. She had witnessed or overheard a similar fiery rebuke which had frightened her, but she must have been small, and the details of the event refused to come clear. She stood by Chase's side, her hand in his, and waited with growing impatience for her father to exhaust his rage.

Finally noticing they were no longer defending themselves against his stinging criticism, Spider came to an abrupt halt and swung around to face them squarely. "I do hope I've impressed upon you the dire necessity for obedience. Anything less can only lead to disaster. Our guests were sorry to have missed you," he added almost as an afterthought. "It's a shame we've no one arriving soon, as it would make your wedding so much more memorable if we had famous guests."

"If you're there, and Chase, I'll be happy," Ivory replied, relieved he had finally adopted a more reasonable tone.

Spider summoned André, who brought fresh fruit, pastries, coffee, and tea. Spider sat down in his place and waited for them to take theirs. "As the owner of the Mine, I have the authority to perform weddings, but I'd rather not officiate at yours. Perhaps I can lure a missionary here for a day."

"I'm sure you could entice anyone fired with evangelical zeal to come here, but how would we get him to leave?" Ivory asked. She filled her iguana cup with cinnamon tea and took a long sip.

"Getting rid of visitors has never been a problem before," Spider boasted with a challenging glance toward Chase. "Give me a few days, and I'll find someone to serve as clergy. You'll need something new to wear. Ask Summer Moon to design an elegant gown. I know she'd be happy to do it."

Ivory glanced over her cup at Chase. "I'd rather be nude than wear anything your whore designed."

Spider shook his head. "After what you've put me through in the last hour, how can you still fail to understand the need to show me proper respect? I know you've never liked Summer, but I've no plans to send her away. I do wish you'd make more of an effort to appreciate her."

"Why? Half the men in the galaxy have already done that."

"Ivory!" Spider shoved his chair back as he stood. "I had hoped Duncan would have a calming effect on you, but obviously his influence has produced the exact opposite. If anything, you've become more willful since he arrived. I can't continually forgive either him or you. Don't push me again, Ivory, because the next time you defy me, I will most definitely punish you both, and severely."

Chase didn't speak until Spider had left the room. "I didn't realize how angry he'd be with you or I would have come back to get Vik and dropped you off."

Ivory rubbed her temple lightly. "I hate it when he gets angry; I absolutely hate it, but I can't allow him to run our lives."

Chase got up, circled the table to come up behind her, and began to give her shoulders a gentle massage. "Your muscles are so tense it's no wonder you have a headache."

Ivory leaned back against him. "That feels so good, but I don't have a headache. I was just trying to remember an argument my father once had with someone. It must have been a hellacious fight for me to recall it after all these years, but I can't remember who it was with or what it was about."

"Take a deep breath and try to relax. That sometimes helps to bring memories clear."

The warmth of Chase's hands was soothing, and Ivory's thoughts soon turned to him rather than fuzzy recollections from childhood. "Let's go to my room and celebrate."

"That's an intriguing invitation. Is this some special occasion?"

"We're together. Isn't that enough?"

Chase could still feel the tightness in her muscles and feared that his efforts to soothe away the lingering tension of their bitter homecoming wasn't having much effect. He bent down to kiss her cheek, and she turned her head to catch his mouth. He ran his fingers through her hair and pressed her close. "I'd stay here and use the table," he finally offered, "but I'd hate to shock André."

Ivory left her chair in an agile stretch and took his hand. "I doubt anything we could do would shock André, but I'd rather not give him another chance to flirt with you."

When André had brought in the refreshments, he had sent Chase a smile Chase had regarded as overly warm, but he had hoped Ivory hadn't noticed. "Apparently I'm his type, but he definitely isn't mine and I'll tell him again to look elsewhere for love."

"I don't believe it's love he's after." Ivory almost danced across the oak floor of her studio and into her apartment. As soon as she had shut the door, she locked it and stepped into Chase's arms. "Let's start in the shower," she suggested as she began to help him out of his flight suit. "After that argument with my father I don't feel clean."

Chase knew exactly how she felt, but hot soapy water wouldn't wash away the layer of lies covering him and they were what made him feel unclean. Love lit her beautiful blue eyes with a lively sparkle, but she saw only the man he wished her to see. Suddenly he longed to reveal much more. He cupped her face between his hands and kissed her very gently before pulling away. "I do love you so very much."

Puzzled by his seriousness, Ivory sought the best way she knew to lighten his mood. Her gestures weren't in the least subtle as she continued to strip off his clothes. Leading him to the bed, she satisfied him again with magical kisses that soon had him eagerly surrendering his very soul. Afterward, she curled up with him until he found the energy to join her in the shower.

The spacious enclosure allowed plenty of room for playful affection, and Chase was both teasing and generous with his. All wet, Ivory's lissome figure was slippery perfection, and he bent to kiss her breasts, then knelt to bestow some magical kisses of his own. In no danger of drowning in anything except desire, they prolonged their impromptu celebration for more than an hour. When they finally fell asleep in a damp heap on Ivory's bed, Spider's anger colored their dreams.

Ivory heard faint echoes of her father's voice. At one moment his arguments were absurd, and in the next he made blistering accusations that brought tears to her closed eyes. She clung to Chase, comforted by his presence even in her sleep. His dreams played out a dozen violent scenarios. Awakened by hideous images, he pulled Ivory close and nuzzled her damp curls. She had stood by him again, and no matter how dangerous things became, he would never abandon her.

Chapter Fifteen

Although it would need additional time to dry, Chase helped Ivory hang the angel portrait in her bedroom. As they stood back to admire it, he offered a suggestion. "There are many artists' colonies on Earth. Visiting one would provide you with an opportunity not merely to work, but to meet other artists. Although you already do exquisite work, I believe that discussing techniques and goals with other artists would be of enormous benefit to you."

Ivory studied the portrait with a far more critical eye than Chase, and while she was pleased with the dynamic pose and subtle color harmonies, she didn't share his exceedingly complimentary view. "We've never had an artist as a guest, but I doubt they're as talkative as poets and philosophers. Art is a very private means of expression, Chase. At least mine is, and I have no need to discuss it with others."

"Your work is superb," Chase insisted. "You owe it to the galaxy, if not to yourself, to share it."

Ivory moved to her bed, sat down, and with an unconsciously provocative motion leaned back on her elbows. "We're not even married, and you're already looking for ways to send me away on extended trips. That's not a good sign, Chase."

"I had no difficulty using Carl Drake's identification at the Paradise Retreat. Wouldn't it work equally well on Earth? After all, Alado's personnel don't frequent the artists' colonies, so I doubt I'd be recognized."

"You intend to come with me?"

"Of course!" Chase ached to join her on the bed, but, wanting to convince her to make the journey to Earth, he remained by the lovely painting. "It's taken me a lifetime to find you. I don't want us to be apart ever."

Ivory never tired of looking at Chase, and it wasn't merely because he was handsome. His feelings for her colored each of his expressions, constantly reassuring her that his love was real. She trusted him more completely than she had ever thought possible. "New clothes," she said absently. Her glance slowly traveled down his body as she remembered how good he looked without the uniform Alado had supplied. "We have to get you some new clothes today."

"I don't believe that's an appropriate response to a declaration of undying love." Unable to stay away from her now, Chase crossed to the bed, knelt between her legs, and nuzzled her tender inner thigh with playful nibbles. She was dressed in a silver flight suit, but that didn't spoil his fun. "I don't give a damn about clothes. In fact, you wear too many."

Ivory ran her fingers through his hair; dark and thick, it fell into place without needing to be recombed. She caressed his cheek, then leaned forward to kiss him. "Earth is so very far away," she mused softly, "but I know we'd have a marvelous time getting there."

"Where else would you like to go?" Chase asked. "We're entitled to an extended honeymoon, so let's take it." He held his breath, hoping to lure her into visiting every colony between there and Earth. It was time to call in a raid, and he didn't want her to be there to see it.

"After the way my father greeted us, I don't believe this is the time to ask for favors."

"A honeymoon trip is the groom's responsibility," Chase reminded her, "not the father's. It's not a favor either, it's a tradition."

"Like this pretty ring?" Ivory held out her hand to admire it, and its fiery sparkle was as bright as her smile.

"Yes, like your ring. We've been home two days, and if Spider doesn't find a minister soon, maybe we ought to consider paying a visit to a colony where there will at least be an administrator who can marry us."

Chase looked determined to marry her soon, but there was a flaw in his plan he hadn't seen. "If we leave here, I'll have to wed Carl Drake, and while we both might know that's you, it might be terribly confusing for our heirs."

Chase slid his hands up her shapely thighs. "You distract me so badly I'd forgotten that Chase

Duncan is a wanted man. I certainly don't want any confusion as to whose wife you are, so it looks as though I'll have to wait for a ceremony here, but it had better be soon."

"Why? What possible benefit of marriage don't we already enjoy?" Ivory slipped her hand inside his shirt. His golden bronze skin felt alive beneath her fingertips, almost as though it hummed their own private love song. "What difference will a formal ceremony make to us when everything is already so good?"

He dared not reveal his true objective: that once they were wed he could demand that Control grant her immunity from prosecution. "I like the idea of marriage," he said instead. "It's an ancient bond, and one that exists for a good reason. It's not merely a legal link, but a foundation for all that a couple builds together. I want everything possible with you."

Ivory could see her reflection in his dark eyes, and behind her image, a glow of love that warmed her clear through. She curled her lip in a playful snarl, and Chase responded with an eager growl of his own. He crawled up over her, forcing her down on the bed, and proved with every kiss what a devoted husband he intended to be.

"I've found a minister," Spider told them as they entered the dining room for lunch. "He's without a congregation at present, but he has the proper documentation to prove he has the right to perform weddings. Would you like to set a time?"

"Yes, this afternoon," Chase responded immediately. Taking his place opposite Ivory, he regarded her with an eager grin despite the fact they had spent the last hour making love.

"Is he someone I know?" Ivory asked, while her glance remained locked with her fiancé's.

"No, I don't believe so. This is his first trip here, and from what I've seen, you've not left your suite since your return."

Her father's observation was correct, but Ivory chose to ignore the barely veiled disapproval behind it. André served them avocado and alfalfa sprout sandwiches on thick slices of oatmeal bread. Suddenly hungry, Ivory took a large bite of hers. It was delicious. The bread was warm and soft, the avocado delicately seasoned, and the sprouts fresh and crisp. A long moment passed before she swallowed and was again able to speak.

"This afternoon is too soon," she announced calmly. A flash of anger crossed Chase's brow. "I would prefer this evening," she added.

Relieved, Chase let out an ecstatic whoop. "This evening it is then, and I guess you're right about my clothes. I will need something new to wear."

Spider waited a moment for the lovestruck pair to note his presence, then realized they never would. "After my last suggestion met with such disastrous results, I won't comment on whatever Ivory selects, but come with me after lunch, Duncan, and I'll see you're given the best suit my staff can produce on such short notice."

"This sandwich is so good," Ivory called as André came in to refill their water glasses. "Could you please bring me another?"

"Of course, Ms. Diamond. Would either of you

gentlemen care for another?"

Chase looked down at the sandwich and found he was as hungry as Ivory. "Yes, André, bring me two." He winked at Ivory, and finished his lunch in the best mood he could possibly enjoy when not making love to her.

Spider found the couple's rapt glances increasingly annoying and hurried Chase to the Mine's tailor at the earliest possible moment. The tailor was a tall red-haired man named Maxwell, who took his work so seriously he did not smile during the entire time he took Chase's measurements. He promised a splendid suit of clothes by five that afternoon. To be on the safe side, Spider set the wedding for seven.

"Not that you'll wear the suit long, but on this of all days you must look your best."

"I intend to," Chase assured him.

"A smirk won't be considered appropriate," Spider warned.

Chase knew his smile was too wide, but he just couldn't help it. "Yes, sir. I'll do my best to look dignified."

Doubting Chase's sincerity, Spider raised his brows, but then let the comment pass. "Come on down to the office. There's something we need to discuss."

"If it's a prenuptial agreement, I'll be happy to sign. I've told Ivory repeatedly that my interest is in her, not the Mine."

Spider waited until they had reached his office to respond. He closed the door, then leaned back against the front of his desk. He motioned to the chair in front of him, but Chase chose to remain standing too.

"Although your name is on the agreement, I didn't draw this up specifically for you. It was created for any man who became serious about Ivory. As you know, I'm a very wealthy man, but I regard Ivory as my most precious treasure." He paused, and the usual coldness of his gaze grew even more chilly.

"I'll do anything I must to protect her, and I want the same promise from you, Duncan."

Chase nodded thoughtfully. "You have it." Chase was reminded of their initial conversation when he had agreed to wed Ivory, or at least to try to win her consent to marriage. "Why didn't you show me the agreement earlier? After all, the only reason you kept me alive was to marry Ivory, so it would have made sense to get my signature on whatever agreement you wanted long before this."

Spider picked up the folder lying on his desk and handed it to Chase. "Let's just say I didn't want to confuse you. As you see, you'll be giving up all claim to Ivory's holdings. Should you have children, the Mine will go to them, not you, at Ivory's death. It is to your advantage to see that Ivory has a long and happy life, because you'll receive an allowance of ten million dollars on your anniversary, each year of your marriage. I don't want you to be impoverished this first year though, so I've placed five million in an account for you."

Chase had read a great many contracts, but this one was mercifully brief. After scanning it quickly, he reread it more carefully. There were no trick clauses, and no threats of sudden death should he and Ivory separate. "In the event of a divorce, I'm to be allowed to visit my children here twice a year. How generous of you."

"Yes, I thought you'd like that paragraph. I'm hoping custody arrangements will never be required. I want you to make Ivory so deliriously happy she'll never have any reason to think of divorce."

As an undercover agent, Chase was free to sign contracts if necessary. After all, they couldn't be enforced later because Chase Duncan didn't exist. In this case, Spider Diamond would soon have too many legal problems to worry over a prenuptial agreement anyway. Still, Chase wanted to look convincingly thoughtful. He read the agreement a third time, and then shrugged.

"I have just one request. Money's never been of much interest to me—not that ten million a year isn't generous, it certainly is—but I don't need to be paid to love Ivory."

"Think of it as a reward then."

"No, I don't need to be rewarded either. I regard her as a treasure too, and to take money every year just doesn't seem right."

Spider shook his head as though he could not believe what he was hearing. "You don't want the money? Is that what you're telling me?"

"Pay me a percentage for the work I do. That way I'll be earning the money honestly, or as honestly as money can be earned working for you. Where's a pen? Let's just cross out the section about a yearly allowance."

Spider had spent all his adult life in a world where enormous profits were the norm, and no one ever turned down the opportunity to earn money in as easy a manner as he was offering

Chase. It worried him. It was a simple matter to control a man whose primary motivation was greed, but clearly Chase Duncan wasn't such a man. That definitely posed a problem. Then again, he had never expected Ivory to fall in love with a man who could be easily intimidated. After all, he had raised her, and she would quite naturally seek a mate whose strength matched his own.

"You may have noticed," he counseled, "that Ivory tends to be rather wild. She has her mother's beauty, but unfortunately she wasn't with Willow long enough to develop her charm. I've raised her as a son, which in some ways was a mistake, but it has given her the strength to run the Mine when the time comes."

Hoping to encourage Spider to confide in him, Chase finally took the chair. He sat back, the prenuptial agreement still in his hand. "Ivory's a talented artist. I'd like her to devote her time to refining her craft. I understand why you have her work in the casino, but I ought to be the one working there to study the operation, not her. It might take me a while to understand how your version of poker is played, but when I master it, I'd like to take her place."

Spider considered Chase's request, but saw more pitfalls than advantages. "No. Ivory will eventually have control of the Mine, and I don't want her ignorant of how it runs. Perhaps you truly do wish she could devote herself to art, but the simple fact is, art can never be more to her than a hobby. When it comes to our business interests, I don't want her dependent on you in any way.

"Why do you think I've taken her with me when

I sell arms?" Spider went on. "It's not just to show off how gorgeous she is. It's because I want the people I deal with to know her, and fear her power as they do mine. I'll teach you what I must, Duncan, but you'll never replace Ivory, and I'm warning you now not to try."

Another dire threat, Chase thought with disgust. "You do plan to give me some work, don't you? I want to keep Ivory happy, but it won't be easy if I'm miserable, and I surely will be if I'm given nothing else to do."

Spider flicked a bit of lint off his sleeve. "Don't worry. I plan to work you hard. You'll be given more important assignments than any of my other men, and more of them as well. Ivory told me you were impressed with her silver boys. Perhaps you'd like to start with them."

Chase tried not to look too eager to become involved with the beautiful robots. "They appear to have enormous potential."

"And then some," Spider agreed. "The only problem is producing them in sufficient numbers." He straightened up and reached for the agreement. "Sign this, and we'll discuss the silver boys another time. After all, I do have a wedding to plan and I need to tell André to prepare a special dinner for us all."

Spider handed him a pen, and Chase stood to sign the agreement on the desk, after crossing out the yearly-allowance clause. "You're inviting Summer Moon?" he asked.

"Of course I'm inviting her. Do you dislike her too?"

"No. I haven't had the opportunity to become acquainted with her as yet."

Cinnamon Burke

"Then you'll have something else to look forward to tonight. I'll see you in the lounge at seven."

They walked to the elevator together but got off on different floors. Chase wanted to see Ivory, but thought perhaps he shouldn't. Then again, he didn't want her to feel neglected. Torn for a moment, he finally listened to his heart and went to her suite. She appeared at his first knock, peeking around her bedroom door.

"Is it customary for the bride and groom to spend the hours before the wedding together?" she asked.

"Probably not, but I missed you."

Ivory looked delighted by the sweetness of that confession. "Good. Did you and Dad set a time for the ceremony?"

"Seven, in the lounge."

Ivory started to close her door. "I'll see you then."

Chase shoved the toe of his boot in her way. "Wait a minute. I haven't had time to say I love you."

"You just did."

"I really do, Ivory. I really, really do."

Ivory kissed him lightly and then closed her door, leaving Chase with several hours to kill before taking her as his wife. He walked through her studio, stopped at the door, and looked back. This should have been the happiest day of his life, but it was tainted by the fact he was an agent who had come there to destroy everything Ivory loved. Would she still want to be his wife when she learned who, and what, he was?

The doubts that crushed him now had ended

308

the careers of more good agents than any laser pistol ever had, but he straightened his shoulders and, determined to play out his part, went to his room to unpack the wedding band he had bought at the Paradise Retreat. The circle was a symbol of endless love, and when he placed it on Ivory's finger, he would pray that their love would outlive his betrayal.

When Chase walked into the lounge at ten to seven, he found André arranging a huge bouquet of white orchids on a long table in the center of the room. "Brother Samuel insisted there be an altar," he explained to Chase. "He'll be the only religious person here, but Spider said we had to accommodate him."

André didn't look at all pleased. Chase assumed that Brother Samuel was the minister. "Is there anything else he needs?" Chase asked. "Some candles, perhaps? Incense? Altar boys?"

André rolled his eyes. "Do you really think we need candles?"

Chase nodded. "Definitely. If you have some, go and get them." It was a shame that Ivory's iguana candelabra wasn't ready yet, but just the thought of the scaly beasts decorating an altar made him laugh. André looked back over his shoulder, but Chase waved him on his way.

A navy blue uniform had been delivered to Chase's room, and like the general's uniform he had been given, it fit perfectly. It had come with a pair of navy blue boots such as Spider wore, and while the idea of dressing in Spider's favorite color made Chase's skin crawl, he had to admit he looked damn good. It was too bad Nelson wasn't there to take photographs.

Summer Moon glanced in the doorway. She was dressed in a spectacular ice blue gown heavily embroidered with silver. "I was afraid I was late," she called to Chase.

"No, you're early, but it looks as though we're running late."

Summer walked toward him with tiny, mincing steps. When she reached the makeshift altar, she began to rearrange the orchids. "André has no talent with flowers," she complained. She had a child's high-pitched and breathless voice. She gave each of the stems a quarter turn, then stepped back to judge the effect. "That's much better, don't you think?"

Chase couldn't see much difference but knew better than to insult Spider's woman. "They're lovely," he replied.

Summer smiled her most winsome smile. "You look very handsome tonight. It is a shame . . ."

When she hesitated, Chase leaned forward slightly. "What's a shame?"

"That you never visited my girls. They would have shown you a real good time. Now it is too late, of course." She lowered her voice to a conspiratorial whisper. "Spider would not merely frown on your forming a liaison with one of my girls now, it would cost you your life."

"Really? He must have forgotten to mention that to me, but I know you couldn't possibly have any girls more appealing than Ivory, so I won't feel deprived."

"Is her beauty the only reason you'll be faithful?" Clearly offering more than advice, Summer cocked her head and looked up at him through a thick sweep of artificial lashes.

"No," Chase assured her. "I'll be faithful because I love her."

Summer sent a hurried glance toward the door before stepping close to confide in him. "Until you arrived, I did not think Ivory liked men."

The Asian beauty appeared to want to hear a delicious detail or two about their relationship, but Chase would not share indiscreet comments with anyone, least of all her.

The woodwind trio that had played for Spider's dinner party came in, set up their music stands in a corner, and began to tune their instruments. Chase had not remembered that music was a part of every wedding, and was grateful that Spider or Ivory had. He smiled at the trio and they nodded.

André returned with a handful of white candles and a silver candelabra. He failed to notice the subtle changes Summer Moon had made to the arrangement of orchids, and, placing the ornate candelabra beside it, added the candles and lit them. "Charming, if I do say so myself," he murmured as he backed away. "Did you ask someone to serve as your best man, Mr. Duncan?"

A best man was another requisite Chase had forgotten. "Not yet. Are you busy for the next half hour, André?"

André positively beamed. "No, and I will consider it a great honor. I believe I'm supposed to hold the ring."

Chase reached into his pocket and handed the ring to André. He knew he would not have to warn the fastidious fellow not to lose it, and looked around to make certain they hadn't forgotten anything else. "It looks as though we have everything except the bride and Brother Samuel. Where is he?"

Summer Moon caressed Chase's sleeve. "He's with Spider. Apparently he had a book describing several ceremonies, and Spider is choosing one."

"Wonderful. Just what sort of a minister is this Brother Samuel?"

Summer looked perplexed for an instant, then her features relaxed into their former serene mask. "I did not hear him say. If it's important to you, I could go and ask."

"No, it really doesn't matter. I was just curious."

"It's past seven," André worried aloud. "I'll go see what's keeping them."

Chase stopped him. "No. If Ivory wants to primp for an hour, I don't mind. Besides, there's no reason to rush."

"You're remarkably calm for a bridegroom," Summer mused.

Chase was so superbly trained he could remain calm while walking through fire. A wedding was no challenge at all to him. "Do you really think so?" he asked. "I didn't realize you had had so much experience with weddings."

Stung by that taunt, Summer Moon abruptly turned away and walked over to the musicians, who were about to begin their first tune. She had several requests, and they promised to include her favorites in the evening's program. She knew them all, for they were frequent visitors at her brothel. The oboe and clarinet players were excruciatingly ordinary in their tastes, but the bassoonist had an astonishing array of perversions, and she favored

312

him with a lingering smile.

Spider entered the room and went straight to Chase. "The suit looks good. How does it feel?"

Chase didn't want to chat about clothes, but tried to be civil. "It's as comfortable as my own skin. Are we ready?"

"Yes, I think so. André, dim the lights a bit to create a more romantic atmosphere."

André, after several attempts which resulted in near darkness, finally found the perfect illumination. Brother Samuel entered wearing a hooded gray robe, looking positively medieval. With a series of imperious waves he took charge of the final preparations. He motioned for Chase and André to stand at the right of the altar, then stepped to the center. Summer Moon was a guest rather than Ivory's attendant, and she moved toward the wall, where in the dim light her presence would go unnoticed.

Satisfied they were ready, Brother Samuel cued the musicians, who responded with the opening strains of the traditional wedding march. Spider then escorted Ivory into the room. She was wearing the gold gown she had brought home from the Paradise Retreat, complete with the matching boots and exquisite shell earrings. Far from demure, she winked at Chase, and when he stepped forward to take her hand, her grasp was as firm as his.

"Dearly beloved," Brother Samuel began to intone.

Because the minister's hood was pulled forward, Chase hadn't caught a glimpse of his face, nor had he heard the man speak before then, but it took no more than those first two words for him to recognize Brother Samuel. Had he been struck by lightning he could not have felt a harsher jolt. It was all he could do to keep his panic from showing in his expression. He looked at the orchids, the shimmering candles, over at the musicians, who had paused in silence for the exchange of vows.

This ceremony was as phony as he was, for Brother Samuel was no more a minister than Spider was. He was Ian St. Ives, the agent Control had sent in as a last resort to save an operation that seemed in danger of being lost. With his heart pounding in his ears, Chase could barely hear Ian's words, but managed to provide the proper responses. He looked down at Ivory, his promises sincere, even if the ceremony wasn't the one he had expected.

He didn't know which was worse, that Control had sent Ian, or that the wedding wouldn't be legal. Both situations were disastrous. He tried to follow along with "Brother Samuel's" prayers at the same time he searched his mind for a way to signal Ian that he had no need of his expert services.

When the time came to slip the gold wedding band on Ivory's finger, he smiled as though this were truly the most joyous moment of his life, but he was ready to kill Ian St. Ives for making a mockery of what should have been sacred vows. True to his reputation, Ian was thoroughly convincing as he exhorted them to let God's love light the path of their marriage and bring them everlasting joy. Ready to kill Control for meddling in his assignment, Chase kissed Ivory, then lifted her clear off her feet in a boisterous hug.

After setting her down, he turned to Ian. "I don't know how to thank you, Brother Samuel, but believe me, I'll find a way before you leave."

"God bless you, son. May you have a long and fruitful marriage."

André adjusted the lighting, and served champagne, but Chase didn't hear a word of the toasts being offered. If he appeared distracted, no one commented, but he had seldom been so angry. He was determined to find a way to speak to Ian privately before he took Ivory to bed, because otherwise he would be in no mood to consummate their marriage.

Chapter Sixteen

After the toasts, André produced a camera and took photographs. Chase did his best to smile but feared he produced only an awkward grimace. Ivory was as radiant as a bride should be, and he prayed she would never learn they had just participated in a cruel hoax rather than a legal ceremony. When Ivory wanted a photograph including Brother Samuel, the monk stepped up to join them.

"Would you please lower your hood, Brother Samuel?" Ivory requested. "If you don't, I'm afraid you'll be no more than a formless shadow in our photographs, and I want to remember your being at the ceremony clearly."

"Whatever you wish, my dear," Brother Samuel responded. With a quick tug, his hood fell to his shoulders in relaxed folds, but his well-muscled build remained hidden beneath the voluminous gray robe. His very blond hair hadn't been trimmed in over a year, giving him a look of wild innocence. His eyes were amber, his features so finely sculpted they would have flattered a woman, but his manner was so thoroughly masculine that even with long hair he was never mistaken for one.

Somewhat startled by the cleric's good looks, Ivory stared at him a moment too long, and then caught herself and arranged another grouping. Then, certain they had more than enough photographs, she suggested they have dinner. The musicians had already left the lounge for the dining room, and André hurried off to see to the last of the meal's preparations.

"You will join us for dinner, won't you, Brother Samuel?" Ivory asked.

"Yes, I was very pleased to accept the invitation your father extended earlier."

"I'll just bet you were," Chase whispered under his breath.

Brother Samuel turned toward him. "I beg your pardon?"

Ian St. Ives had a chameleon's talent for changing the fine shadings of his personality, and while Chase knew him to be one of Control's more vicious agents, there was nothing threatening in his manner now. He looked as passive as a plaster saint, and Chase suddenly had the sickening thought that Control might have sent Ian rather than him to The Diamond Mine in the first place. Would Ivory have fallen in love with Ian? he wondered. He had seen how surprised she had been to find him attractive, and feared she would have been drawn to him too.

317

Cinnamon Burke

Ian's a snake! he wanted to shout, but he had sworn an oath that included a promise never to betray another agent. From somewhere deep inside, he came up with a deceptively pleasant smile. "I said we'd be delighted by your company. After all, we're indebted to you for performing our wedding ceremony."

Ian responded with an expansive gesture a bishop might have employed to bless an entire cathedralful of people. "It was a joy to be present at the beginning of your life together."

Another of the musicians' lilting tunes lured Spider toward the dining room, and he gestured for everyone to follow him across the hall. He took Summer Moon's hand and again seated her at his right. Ivory took her place at the end of the table, Chase was at her right, and the saintly Brother Samuel at her left. The meal began with one of André's delicate, delicious soups, but Chase found it difficult to hold his spoon steady enough to guide it to his lips.

"You've become surprisingly subdued, Duncan," Spider soon noted. "Not that I object to a taciturn son-in-law, but it isn't like you."

"It's not every day that a man marries," Brother Samuel reminded him. "It's only natural for him to reflect seriously upon his new responsibilities."

Directly opposite Ian, Chase seized the only opportunity he might have to speak with him. "I wonder if I might have a word with you privately after supper, Brother Samuel. Not that I have a great deal to confess, but I would like to begin my marriage with a clear conscience."

"An excellent goal," Brother Samuel replied.

"I had no idea you were religious," Ivory said with a puzzled frown.

"I'm not," Chase responded, "but I do believe in luck, and if Brother Samuel can bring me some, then I intend to take it."

"Oh, now I see." Ivory took another sip of the savory broth. "I have a different type of request, Brother Samuel. I hope you'll be able to accommodate me as well."

Brother Samuel's strange amber eyes brightened with a delighted sparkle. "Of course, my dear. What is it you wish?"

"I'm an artist. My husband refuses to pose for me, but I wonder if you'd mind if I made a few sketches of you. You radiate a tranquillity we don't often see here, and I hope I'll be able to capture it."

A look of sorrow creased Brother Samuel's brow. "I'm so sorry, but mechanical problems forced me to land here, and as you might suspect, this is not the type of place I ordinarily frequent. I'm hoping that the repairs will be complete by tonight, and then I'll be on my way. Unlike your new husband, were I staying longer, I would be happy to pose for you."

"You don't know the way she wanted me to pose," Chase complained.

Brother Samuel sent Ivory a questioning glance, and she reached out to touch his sleeve. The fabric of his robe was very soft, and stroking it was remarkably pleasant. Certain she ought not to be petting a monk, she quickly slid her hand into her lap. "I wanted to draw him for the beauty of his form, so quite naturally I asked him to pose nude. In your case, it's your spirituality that sets you apart, and your robe is the perfect garb."

"It's a shame there's no time," Brother Samuel replied regretfully. "Your drawings are undoubtedly superb."

Highly amused that a monk wished to flirt with Ivory at her wedding supper, Summer Moon observed Chase's discomfort with a sly smile. She looked up at Spider, found he was enjoying the scene too, and wished they were the ones who had been married that day. Spider was the most exciting man she had ever known, and the only one who hadn't been eager to make her his mistress. He had been a challenge, and she considered him one still.

André cleared away the soup bowls and returned with salads made from a lively assortment of mixed greens. Ruffled, crisp, deep green, bright red, clear yellow—each diner had a colorful garden of produce on his plate. The dressing was a piquant blend of herbs that contrasted sharply with the mellow flavor of the first course.

Chase tasted nothing as he tried to think of a place where he and Ian could talk without being overheard. With all the equipment on the security floor, he knew Spider had the capability to observe not merely the operation of the Mine's tavern, casino, and brothel, but what went on in every room on every floor. He doubted Spider's bedroom had hidden cameras, but there was no way he could speak with Ian there.

"Are you all right?" Ivory inquired.

Chase knew he had been too quiet, and the worry darkening Ivory's expression told him she did not understand his silence. He wanted to be happy for her, but for once couldn't fake the required mood. "I'm sorry if I seem preoccupied; I promise to make it up to you later."

While his gaze held no lascivious gleam, Ivory gave his comment the most obvious interpretation, and was shocked he would refer to how he planned for them to spend the night. Concerned that Brother Samuel would be insulted, she glanced toward him and was relieved to find he was giving his full attention to his salad. "We have wonderful gardens here," she exclaimed, hoping to send the conversation in a less personal direction. "We're entirely self-sufficient except for a few luxury items. The avocados in the salad, as an example. We can't grow them here."

Brother Samuel looked up only briefly. "It's like being in paradise to eat fresh food. It's what I miss most on my travels."

Chase was required to support whatever cover a fellow agent might adopt, but he couldn't help needling Ian. "Aren't there sufficient believers at any of the colonies to provide you with a permanent flock?" he asked.

Brother Samuel paused to allow a slice of avocado to slide down his throat. "I belong to an evangelical order that follows Christ's example and journeys extensively." His confident smile told Chase he had a ready answer for every question; at the same time it warned him to stop asking them.

"Alleluia," Chase replied. He ran his fork through his salad like a spear and brought a flavorful heap of greens to his mouth. He decided then to just keep eating. It would prevent him from goading Ian, and give him the strength to keep Ivory entertained all night. She didn't usually wear perfume, but tonight she had on an exotic fragrance that teased his senses even when he wasn't looking her way.

He heard Spider and Summer Moon talking softly at the other end of the table, and wished his parents had been there to celebrate a real wedding. When he had first begun working for Control, he had enjoyed assuming a new identity, and then adopting another as soon as an assignment was over. Now he had grown tired of fleshing out Control's fantasies. This adventure would be his last. It was a promise he made to himself.

Game birds filled with a delectable pecan stuffing were the main course, along with wild rice and asparagus. Chase made a better effort to enter the conversation, while Brother Samuel offered a steady steam of agreeable pleasantries. Chase glanced toward Spider and Summer Moon frequently to include them, but he could not help but think how quickly the meal would be over should Spider discover that two of Alado's most experienced intelligence operatives were seated at his table. It was an absurd situation really, for while Ivory, Spider, and Summer Moon were happily celebrating a marriage, he and Ian were silently plotting to send them all to prison.

Control had boasted that Alado never resorted to assassins, but Chase regarded his role as far more dangerous. After all, an assassin would end Spider's life in an instant, while his own investigation would surely lead to a life sentence in a maximum-security prison colony. Ivory had said her father would rather die than go to prison, and with each bite of their wedding supper, Chase felt more heavily burdened.

There had been very little time to bake, but somehow André produced a three-tiered wedding cake for dessert. The white frosting was decorated with clusters of sugar stars and flavored with a hint of almond. The cake itself was so light it melted as it touched the tongue. It was greeted with appreciative sighs and murmurs. Chase was the first to speak.

"Thank you, André. This cake is absolute perfection," he told him.

André beamed widely and made a promise on his way out. "I'll bake one each year on your anniversary."

"What a lovely thought," Ivory said. She reached for Chase's hand and laced her fingers in his. "We've not known each other long, but I know we'll be together forever."

Chase leaned over to kiss her, and when he sat back he found Ian observing him with an incredulous stare. The look passed before anyone else noticed, and Chase's responding smile was genuinely warm. He adored Ivory and didn't care who knew it.

"Where are you two going for your honeymoon?" Brother Samuel asked pointedly.

"I'd like to take Ivory to Earth," Chase replied.

"Unfortunately, that's completely out of the question," Spider quickly interjected.

Ivory paused between bites of cake. "It's our honeymoon," she reminded him. "We're the ones who'll decide where we'll go."

Spider's expression hardened, as did his tone. "Your disobedience is a regrettable habit I'll no longer tolerate. The trip to Earth is a lengthy journey. Your new husband has just begun working for me and certainly hasn't earned any time off for a vacation, let alone a voyage to Earth."

Astonished by the harshness of her father's attitude, Ivory continued to argue. "We're not talking about vacation time; we're talking about taking a honeymoon. Chase and I are entitled to some time away together."

Spider responded with a mocking grin. "Didn't you and Chase just return from a trip?"

Ivory glanced toward Chase, who just smiled and shook his head to warn her not to press that particular issue. "That was business, not a pleasure trip."

Spider was quick to disagree. "No, you're mistaken. Had Chase gone alone, it would have been a business trip, but when you sneaked on board, everything changed."

Ivory could not believe that her father was being so petty. "What are you doing, trying to punish me for going along with Chase?"

Spider took a sip of wine and glanced toward the ceiling as he mulled over her question. "Punish is too strong a word," he replied. "You're my only daughter, and I want you to have a splendid honeymoon. Eventually I'm sure you will. This just isn't the time."

Again Ivory waited for Chase to join in the argument, but he remained maddeningly silent. She did not want to pit the two men she loved against each other, but she would have welcomed Chase's support. "That's absurd. A honeymoon is supposed to be taken immediately after the wedding, not months or years later."

"That may very well be true," Spider agreed, "but generally couples give more thoughtful planning to the date of their wedding than you two did. You should have asked me about a honeymoon before now if it was so important to you."

Thoroughly disgusted, Ivory glared at her father. Clean-shaven and with his hair tamed in sleek waves, he looked his best, but no less imposing than usual. She had not had too much champagne to recognize exactly what he was doing and she wanted no part of it. "No one disputes the fact that you run the Mine," she told him, "but that doesn't give you the right to play with our lives."

"I wouldn't dream of it," Spider assured her. "When Duncan has been with us long enough to have earned time off, I'll be delighted to see him take you on a honeymoon. Until then, let's drop the subject. It's becoming tiresome."

Ivory was so angry she couldn't even see the last bites of the wedding cake on her plate. "Please excuse me. Take all the time you need to visit with Brother Samuel, Chase. After all, we have all of eternity to be together."

"I won't be long," Chase promised, but Ivory left the room so quickly he wasn't certain that she had heard him. Her spirited argument had forced him into an uncomfortable corner, and he was as anxious to leave the table as she was. "If you're finished, Brother Samuel, I'll walk you down to the docking bays."

"How thoughtful of you." Playing his part with gusto, Ian thanked Spider effusively for including him in the lovely dinner, and then bade him and Summer Moon good night. Once alone with Chase, he quickly dropped his benevolent role and made no pretense of approving of what he had seen. He relied upon the seriousness of his expression to convey his mood until they left the elevator; then with his hood drawn forward to muffle his words should the halls be wired for sound, he gave Chase his appraisal of the situation.

"It's obvious you've lost the objectivity Control requires. You've jeopardized your mission, perhaps irrevocably."

When they reached the doorway of the docking bay, Chase was certain no one would hear them above the clatter and clang of the mechanics' tools and the whir of the ventilation system. He still took the precaution of turning so only Ian could see him speak, and replied very softly. "You're wrong. I've won Spider's trust, and know enough to convict him, but the longer I stay, the more evidence I'll gather."

Everything Ian had seen that evening had confirmed Yale Lincoln's suspicions. Perhaps Chase had not gone over to Spider's side yet, but he was so close, Ian refused to allow him to risk compromising his loyalty any further. "It's over," he stated simply. "I can't say when, but expect a raid, and soon."

"That's Control's decision, not yours."

Folding his arms over his chest, Ian slid his hands inside his wide sleeves. "You're supposed to be pursuing your quest for forgiveness, not arguing. Try to look penitent if you possibly can."

"I've never liked you," Chase replied instead.

"Nor I you, but don't forget that when the raid

comes, if you fire a single laser blast at any of us, you'll be prosecuted along with Spider and his lovely daughter. They swim in the galaxy's cesspool. Don't risk drowning with them."

"I don't recall asking for your advice."

"Oh, but you did," Ian was quick to remind him. "You stated your wish to begin your marriage with a clear conscience, and I'll be happy to use whatever trivial powers I may possess to absolve you of all your sins."

Knowing that Chase couldn't fight him here, Ian was pushing him, and Chase was forced to respond with words rather than his fists. "I expected a real priest," he confided. "Since what we got was a flamboyant performance by a fraud, I intend to marry Ivory again. Tell Control I will make her my wife."

Ian's eyes narrowed slightly. "If Brother Samuel is a fraud, then what is Chase Duncan? Do you really believe Ivory Diamond will still want you when she learns who you are?" He shook his head as though the prospect were ridiculous. "You'll lose her, and if you aren't far more careful, your career will be over as well."

"I don't give a damn about my career."

"Obviously." Ian turned and walked over to speak with the bay's foreman. The work on his ship was complete, and he would soon be cleared for departure. He raised his hand to wave good-bye, but Chase left without bothering to bid him farewell.

Chase was as upset with the way their wedding supper had ended as Ivory, but when he reached her suite, he found the door to her bedroom half

Cinnamon Burke

open, the lights turned low to create a soft golden glow, and the haunting scent of a sea breeze on the air. It was incense, but rather than having a heavy, smoky fragrance, it conveyed the aromatic freshness of the sea. Music was playing softly, a rhythmic tune with the rolling pattern of ocean waves.

"Ivory?" he called, and she appeared dressed in a filmy white gown that floated from her shoulders to her feet with the wispy lightness of a cloud. "This is a very pleasant surprise. I was afraid you'd be angry with me. I want to take you away on a honeymoon as badly as you want to go, but I didn't want to get into a fight with your father on our wedding day."

Ivory raised her hand to caress his cheek. "I know you'll always be on my side even if expediency forces you not to say so aloud."

"Don't think me unprincipled. We're a team, remember? Let's give your father a chance to get used to us being together, and then I'll go up against him as loudly as you whenever he's wrong."

"He was wrong tonight."

"Yes, he was, but we'll still be together and that's all that truly matters." Chase paused to hug her tightly. "I want our honeymoon to begin tonight and never end."

"I didn't realize men could be so wonderfully romantic."

"I can speak only for myself, not other men." Chase vowed not to let anything spoil their wedding night. They were together as they were meant to be, and his kiss was flavored with love.

After a moment, Ivory slipped from his embrace

328

to pour some champagne, and then linked arms with him so each could drink from the other's crystal flute. "I was surprised you wished to speak with Brother Samuel; I got the impression you didn't like the man. I hope you weren't jealous because I asked him to pose for me."

She had just given Chase a reasonable explanation for his sullen behavior, and he promptly took it. "I'm ashamed to confess I was. He's a handsome man, even if his coloring is a bit strange."

"You mean his eyes? I haven't met many people with amber eyes, but they were the perfect color for a man of his pious nature. His gaze held an ethereal light I probably wouldn't have been able to capture anyway, but I'm sorry he wasn't able to pose for me. Please don't be jealous of other men. I'll never betray my wedding vows, nor give you any reason to doubt me."

That Chase could not make the same sweet promise tore his heart in two. "I'll never be unfaithful to you either, Ivory. You'll always have all my love." He waited until she had set her champagne flute aside and then, taking her hand, kissed her fingertips. "You look like an angel in that gown. All you need is wings."

"No, the feathers would tickle terribly when we make love."

Chase ran his fingers up her arms in a gentle caress. "I'd not thought of that, but it might be nice." He brushed her lips with a light kiss, then bent down slightly to nibble her earlobe. Taking his time, Chase kissed her throat, and then, brushing the gown's strap aside, slid his tongue across the hollow of her shoulder.

"I like your perfume."

It had been her mother's, but wanting him to associate the heavenly fragrance only with her, Ivory kept that secret to herself. "Thank you." She circled his waist and rested her cheek against his shoulder. "This is so nice. It's as though we had forever to make love."

"We do."

"I hope so."

She sounded so wistful that Chase caught her chin to tilt her head back and met her gaze. Her eyes were bright, but with love rather than tears. "I want so much for us," he confided softly. "Not .the things money can buy, but everything that truly matters: health, happiness, bright little children. I want it all with you."

Ivory kissed his palm. "And I with you.·We're going to have such a glorious life together. I know we will."

Chase crushed her against him in a fervent embrace, then wound his fingers in her soft, silken curls to bring her mouth to his for a lingering kiss that left them both breathless, but still eager for more. He cupped her breast, teasing the crest with his thumb, then slid his hands down her back to press her hips against his. He could feel her warmth through the sheer gown and grew uncomfortably hot.

"Help me out of this suit," he whispered between kisses.

Ivory responded with a delighted giggle. "I love removing your clothes. It's as much fun as unwrapping a present." She raked her nails lightly across his now bare belly. "You're so handsome."

"What if I weren't?" Chase sat down on the

end of her bed. "What if I were excruciatingly ordinary?"

"Hmm." Ivory pretended to give his question serious thought as she yanked off his boots. "I won't deny that it was your looks that first attracted my notice, so who knows? Would you love me if I were ugly?"

"I didn't say ugly, I said ordinary."

Ivory sat down beside him. "I'd like to think it's my charming personality that you love, rather than the pretty face or shapely body I inherited from my parents. To love me only for my looks would be unbearably shallow."

Chase rose and pulled her to her feet. "No one has ever accused me of being shallow." He slipped the narrow straps of her gown off her shoulders, and with a joyous shrug she sent it sliding to her feet. He bent to pick it up, tossed it on a chair, and then moving close, had her sit down on the end of the bed. Kneeling between her legs, he rubbed his cheek against her thigh. "No, if anything, people complain I'm too deep."

Tingling with anticipation, Ivory leaned back on her elbows. "People in general, or just women?"

Chase nuzzled the blond triangle of curls nestled between her thighs. "I can't remember any other women." He exhaled, his warm breath as wildly exciting as a caress. He moved very slowly, each motion chosen for its effect. He trailed his fingertips up her inner thighs, then playfully retraced their path with light kisses.

"Your skin is so soft," he murmured against her feminine folds.

Filled with an aching need, Ivory lost all interest in continuing their teasing banter and slid down on the bed, pressing against Chase's mouth in urgent invitation. She felt hot and wet, and so in love with him she wished there were a thousand different ways to make love. Her longing swelled as he made her wait several agonizing seconds, but when the tip of his tongue split her open, she reached for his hair, pulling him closer still, begging for more with soft, incoherent moans, and he did not disappoint her.

He found the sensitive nub at the top of her cleft and flicked it lightly. Ivory trembled all over, for being with Chase was more thrilling than a wild ride through the heavens. She gasped for breath as tiny sparks of ecstasy burst through her. Boldly teasing, he varied his kiss, barely touching her one moment, and then delving deep the next. He kept luring her on toward the richest of pleasures, and when the rapture he had created at last reached its peak, her whole body throbbed with joy. Her lovely fair skin flushed with a glowing blush. She felt too deeply satisfied to utter more than a breathless, "I love you."

Chase had meant only to please Ivory, but in teasing her he had also teased himself. Desperate for his own release, he crawled up over her, dragging her up on the bed where their bodies moved together in an ageless dance that sealed the bond between them as tightly as two lovers ever could. Husband and wife in their hearts, they were filled with a magical blend of excitement and peace that left them floating on wings of desire softer than any angel's.

Blissfully relaxed, Chase fought sleep, for he did not want to abandon Ivory even in his dreams. He longed to tell her of his childhood adventures along the verdant Northwest Coast and spin some of the marvelous Indian legends his grandfather had taught him. There was so much about him Ivory did not know, and though he could not reveal a word of it now, he hoped the time would come when he could share not only his body, but all of his life with her.

Ivory took a deep breath and sighed softly. "I didn't think making love with you could get any better, but it does every time."

They were snuggled together in a lazy tangle of arms and legs that felt completely natural to Chase. "That's quite a challenge, but I'll do my best not to disappoint you."

"You could never disappoint me, Chase. Not ever." Ivory raised her hand to cover a sleepy yawn, and then laid her head on his shoulder.

Unable to thank her for having such unshakable confidence in him, Chase let her drift off to sleep rather than torment her with the doubts that plagued him. Disappointment was too mild a word for her reaction to what he was going to do, but he hoped by the time the raid came, she would be too deeply in love with him to care.

The fragrance of her mother's perfume permeated Ivory's dreams, bringing haunting memories of Willow's smile and touch. She saw her from a child's-eye view as a regal beauty who danced with astonishing style and grace. Tall and slim, she wore red, purple, and green, the colors blending as she spun on her toes. Again a child of four, Ivory clapped her hands and danced too, until a dark shadow crossed the floor, putting an end to their game.

Overcome with a sudden burden of sorrow, she

awoke with tears streaming down her face. Cradled in Chase's arms, she knew she was safe, but the deeply disturbing dream continued to torment her. She had fallen asleep in a happy daze; to be awakened by evil shadows left her badly troubled. Was it a premonition, or a memory? she wondered. She clung to Chase and waited for the threatening dream to fade. But when he awoke hours later, she could not hide her anguish.

Chapter Seventeen

All warm, soft, and sweet, Ivory was every bit as alluring as she had been the night before, but as soon as Chase pulled her into his arms he sensed something was amiss. Alarmed by the rigidity of her pose, he leaned back to gauge her expression. "What's wrong? You look miserable, and I thought you'd be as happy as I am this morning."

Not wanting him to feel at fault, Ivory struggled to find the words to describe her despair. "I had an awful dream."

Chase smoothed the curls off her forehead and kissed her brow. "A nightmare? Why didn't you wake me?"

"No, it wasn't a nightmare."

Chase waited for her to say more, and when she didn't, he grew worried. "Well, whatever it was, it obviously upset you very badly, and I wish you'd awakened me."

He looked so deeply distressed, Ivory was sorry she had confided in him. "It was nothing. I shouldn't have mentioned it."

She started to sit up, but Chase tightened his hold on her to prevent her escape. "Ivory, tell me. Whenever anything upsets you, don't hide it. Even if it's something I can't remedy immediately, I still want you to share your problems with me."

Feeling exhausted after a mostly sleepless night, Ivory ceased trying to elude him and relaxed in his embrace. His bare shoulder made a comfortable pillow, and she rubbed her cheek against him, savoring the smoothness of his skin. "Perhaps it was the wedding, or the fact I wore my mother's perfume, but I dreamed of her last night. At least I think it was merely a vivid dream rather than a memory."

"I thought you didn't remember her."

"I don't, but the dream was so real, Chase. My mother and I were dancing in my studio. She was very beautiful, and danced with such grace while I was just a chubby child who bounced around with her. We were laughing, having such a wonderful time, when suddenly the music stopped and a shadow fell across the studio, fading the bright colors of my mother's gown to gray. It wasn't just that the fun was over either. It was as though my whole world had simply ceased to exist. I woke up crying and couldn't go back to sleep."

"I wish you'd awakened me."

"There was nothing you could do."

"I could have held you like this, and listened. If that didn't help, then I'm sure I could have found

336

a way to take your mind off the dream."

Ivory knew exactly what he would have done, but she was too sad to welcome his affection. "I don't think so. Oh, I know you would have tried your best, but you can't imagine how unhappy I feel. I don't remember my mother's death, but if we were as happy together as we were in my dream, then I must have been devastated when she died."

Chase kept her cradled in his arms and wished he knew what to say. His grandfather had been an elderly man when he died, and while his death had not been unexpected, Chase and his parents had grieved deeply. Now time had healed the sense of loss, and he recalled the times he had spent with his grandfather as some of the best of his youth. He thought it sad that Ivory had no such comforting memories of her mother.

"Didn't you tell me your mother died quite suddenly?"

"That's what I've been told. My father says her heart failed. One day we were a loving family, and the next she was gone."

Chase's first thought was that Willow might have died while playing with Ivory. They could have been dancing together, laughing happily, and then she might have collapsed and died. While it was rare, he had heard of people dying suddenly from undiagnosed heart ailments, and apparently that was what had happened to Willow Diamond. Children always blamed themselves for the tragedies that befell their families, and he did not want Ivory to feel responsible for her mother's death if it had occurred while they had been together.

"It's probably quite natural for you to think of your mother on your wedding day," he assured her. "Her death was undoubtedly such a terrible trauma for you that you sealed off your memories of her to spare yourself pain. Is there a psychiatrist or psychologist working in the medical clinic?"

Ivory sighed softly. "No. We have only technicians who provide the most basic health care. They treat injuries from fights mostly. They're very good, as you know, but they aren't trained to do counseling. Is that what you think I need, a psychiatrist?"

Chase kissed her before responding. Her lips were soft, but her response was so slight he scarcely felt it. "All I know is that people can suppress all manner of hideous experiences— deaths, accidents, abuse, whatever. Then sometimes years later they start having flashbacks. If that's what's happening to you, then you might very well need professional help to deal with unexpressed grief."

Ivory had confided all she could, and though Chase had been wonderfully sympathetic, she didn't feel a bit better. When the shadow had moved across her dream, all the joy she had found in his arms had dissolved in a mist of tears. She had just married a man she adored, and she didn't want anything, least of all troubling childhood memories, to ruin what should be an ecstatically happy time together.

She brushed the last hint of tears from her lashes and sat up. "Please don't mention this to my father. Let's just hope I'll feel better in an hour or so. We ought to make a run to the bank, and—"

Chase sat up beside her. "Business as usual? Is that what you want?"

He looked appalled, but Ivory couldn't think of anything else to do. "If I lose myself in routine, it ought to help me get my mind off that wretched dream. I don't know what else to try. Do you?"

Chase could see by the despair of her posture that making love was not a viable option. "If you didn't sleep well, perhaps what you really need is a nap. I can make the run to the bank alone."

"No, you can't. The silver boys are programmed to respond to my voice or my father's. They would just stand there and stare at you, and the crates are too heavy for you to unload by yourself."

Another valuable piece of information, Chase noted, then immediately felt like the traitor he was. "All right, we'll make the run together, but you can still nap on the trips there and back."

"I'll try."

Ivory gave Chase another kiss so light he barely felt it, and he was glad she couldn't see the hunger in his expression as she left the bed. Her figure was enticing, but her mood so forlorn he dared not follow her into the shower. Instead, he got up, pulled on his suit and boots, and went back to his own room to shower and dress.

Ivory was uncharacteristically quiet at breakfast, but Spider seemed to enjoy being able to talk to Chase without her interrupting to argue. She ate very little, and at their first opportunity, she and Chase excused themselves to make the trip to the bank. As soon as they were airborne, Chase encouraged her to take a nap, but she soon found she couldn't rest for more than a few seconds at a time.

"It's no use," Ivory complained. "The instant I close my eyes, I feel a fresh burst of despair. I'm so sorry, Chase. This is no way to begin a honeymoon."

Chase agreed but didn't voice his disappointment. "From what I know of dreams, the images are symbolic. Perhaps wearing your mother's perfume triggered childhood memories of happy times, as well as a time of terrible loss, and the images became intertwined in your dream."

"I understand symbols, but that wasn't what my dream was about. The images were in sharp focus, the colors bright, and the music delightful. It was all vivid, crisp, until the shadow appeared."

"Still, it was only a dream, and you mustn't allow it to ruin your whole day."

Ivory slid down lower in her seat. "Do you think I'm deliberately dwelling on something that upsets me? Why in God's name would I do that? Believe me, it's no fun feeling this depressed."

"I can see that." Hoping to distract her, he changed the subject. "You brought your Celestial Cannon along. When we get to the bank, will you show me how to use it? After all, if it takes practice, I ought to start using it now."

Ivory knew her father wouldn't like Chase using a cannon, but he wasn't there to object. After the silver boys had unloaded the cash, stowed it away, and returned to their closet, she showed Chase the prized weapon. "You've held it once, so you know how light it is. That's one of its advantages. It's also its major flaw, for if it's not aimed carefully, things can be disintegrated unintentionally."

Chase looked down the long corridor. The walls of the underground bunker looked thick enough to withstand a bit of target practice, but he did not want to take any chances with their lives. "Is there a firing range at the Mine, or will I have to practice in here?"

Ivory pressed the button to arm the pistol. "Set the beam on the low end of the scale and you can fire at the end wall without bringing the whole structure down on us. That's what I used at the Eagle's Nest. The laser blast will hit exactly where the target beam strikes, so take your time, aim, and then fire. You'll just singe the wall, not pierce it."

"You're sure?"

"Positive. I'll fire first if you like."

Chase had qualified as an expert marksman with every weapon in Alado's arsenal, but reined in the impulse to show off his skill. He took his time, focused the target beam on the center of the end wall, and then squeezed the trigger. He felt only a slight vibration as the Celestial Cannon fired precisely where he had wanted it to.

"What would happen if I put it on full power?" he asked.

"The walls of the bank are approximately six feet thick, but you'd crack the back wall and probably create a deep channel behind it that might reach all the way into the asteroid's core. That's why I warned Mordecai to be careful. The cannon's potential for destruction is immense, and it would be a pity if he blew the Eagle's Nest out of existence during target practice."

"I for one wouldn't miss the place, but I know you don't want to lose a valuable customer. Let's hope he takes your advice. Is knowing the cannon's power the only trick?"

Ivory took the pistol from him. "No. In addition to the power setting, there's also a lever to scatter the ray up to a 180-degree span. Using that mode, I could have killed Mordecai and all his men with one shot. We don't recommend using that wide a spray because it's too easy to shoot your own men should they get a step or two ahead of you."

Chase could easily imagine such a tragedy. He took the cannon back, but didn't adjust the ray. "One man could fight off a whole army with this, couldn't he?"

"Easily, unless the army had them too. Do you want to fire it again?"

"Not really." Chase pressed the button to disarm the pistol, and then carried it back to the shuttle. Ivory kept it stowed in a specially designed compartment, and he was relieved when it had been put away. "Spider isn't really going to let Mordecai have exclusive use of the Celestial Cannon, is he?"

Ivory laughed at the very thought. "Of course not. It's for sale to whomever can afford it."

Just as Chase had hoped, Ivory had been distracted while they discussed the cannon, but as they began the return flight to the Mine, the disturbing dream again invaded her thoughts. She closed her eyes and pretended to nap for Chase's benefit, but the whole time the dream replayed in her mind like a piece of film on an endless loop. It stopped each time in exactly the same place, but she knew instinctively that a secret lay beyond the shadow.

As soon as they had docked, she offered Chase a quick excuse. "I want to spend the rest of the day working with my ceramics. I won't stop for lunch, so I'll see you at dinner."

Hoping she would find comfort in her art, Chase didn't argue, but her unsettling dream had prompted a curiosity he was eager to satisfy. He found André at his desk and engaged him in a rambling conversation which he skillfully guided to Willow. When André sent an anxious glance up and down the corridor to make certain they were alone, Chase knew he was on to something.

"Did you know her?" he asked.

André gestured for Chase to come closer. "I didn't have that pleasure, and from what I've observed, Spider discourages any mention of her name. Despite your new status as part of the Diamond family, you ought not provoke him by asking questions about his late wife."

Chase leaned back against André's desk. "I can understand respect for the dead, but why all the secrecy? Ivory told me her mother had a weak heart. Have you heard anything different?"

André raised his hands in a helpless gesture made all the more pitiful by his fluttering fingers. "Please, Mr. Duncan, I know absolutely nothing about the dear woman."

Chase's glance narrowed slightly. "I'll bet you know all sorts of interesting things, André. Loosen up. You can trust me. I'm just trying to understand my wife, not unearth closely guarded family secrets. Ivory can't remember her mother, and I thought talking with someone who did would be a comfort to her."

"That's very thoughtful of you, but isn't Spider the most obvious choice?"

"Yes, he is, but apparently Ivory is reluctant to upset him by asking him to share his memories of Willow."

André straightened the menus he had been preparing, carefully aligning the corners as though his desk were to be inspected soon. "I'd like to help you, but I know only what I've heard," he whispered without looking up.

"Which is?"

André again scanned the hallway. "Willow was an extraordinary woman. She was as beautiful and talented as her daughter. Her death came as a terrible shock to everyone. Out of respect for Spider's grief, she simply isn't mentioned."

"You're not telling me anything I don't already know," Chase complained.

"That's all there is to tell," André again insisted.

What was plain in André's averted glance was that he was afraid to say more. Respect for Spider's feelings was one thing, but fear was something else entirely. Recognizing André's reaction for what it was, Chase shrugged as though the matter held little interest for him and moved on. Just because André hadn't known Willow didn't mean there wasn't someone else at the Mine who had, and as he toured the outpost he sought out the employees with the most seniority. It didn't take him long to discover that most hadn't been at the Mine more than five years.

Then he remembered Maxwell. The tailor appeared to be Spider's age, and seemed a likely source of information. Chase found him in his workroom cutting out a black lace gown. "Another costume?" he asked.

Maxwell made an adjustment in the pattern for a sleeve before looking up. "Yes. Spider complained I've been neglecting the clothes for our female guests. I'm re-creating one of Queen Victoria's gowns."

Chase picked up a scrap of the lace and drew it through his fingers. It was stiff rather than soft as he had expected. "She must have been an amazing woman."

"Indeed," Maxwell agreed. He added a final pin before reaching for his shears. "I doubt you came to chat about long-dead monarchs though. Do you have a request? I have your measurements now, so I can make anything you like. I would prefer several days' notice if possible, however."

"No, I've no requests for myself, but I did have an idea for a dress for my wife. I wonder if you recall which costumes were Willow's favorites?"

Maxwell paused for a fraction of a second and then continued to cut along the edge of his pattern. "I've been instructed to forget her, and I have."

The tailor's workroom was lined with bolts of fabric and big spools of ribbon, lace, and braid. Sketches of costumes Maxwell had made, or intended to make, were pinned to the far wall. "Really? That's a shame. I'm concerned about Ivory," Chase confided. "She can't remember Willow, and I thought she might enjoy wearing some of her mother's favorite costumes."

Maxwell laid his shears aside and turned to

face Chase. An intense individual, he was always annoyed whenever anyone interrupted his work. Now he frowned impatiently. "I love Ivory; we all do. But don't encourage her to chase after her mother's memory. Tell her to leave Willow to the angels where she belongs."

Maxwell's advice only served to pique Chase's interest, but seeing the same fear in the tailor's eyes that he had observed in André's, he did not push him to reveal more. "I want to thank you again for the suit you made for me for the wedding. I'll give some thought to costumes and let you know if there's one I'd like made."

Maxwell nodded slightly and continued cutting out the new gown. Chase tossed the scrap of lace he had been holding on the table as he went out the door, but he hadn't taken three steps down the corridor before he ran into Stokes and Vik. They had been waiting for him, and clearly had no intention of stepping out of his way.

"Good morning, boys," Chase greeted them. "Did Spider let you out to play?"

Stokes took a step toward him. "You might have married the boss's daughter, but that don't make you our boss."

Not intimidated by the lumbering pair, Chase leaned back against the wall and struck a relaxed pose. "Is that a fact? Well, I'm not disappointed, since I can't think of a single thing you two could possibly do for me that I couldn't do a hell of a lot better myself. Of course, if you'd like another demonstration, Stokes, I'll be glad to provide it."

"That was a lucky shot and you know it!"

Chase laughed. "You're about as tough to hit as this wall. There was no luck involved."

"Are you going to let him talk to you like that?" Vik asked.

"Come on, Vik," Chase scolded. "He has no more choice than you did when Ivory tied you to your bed."

Since the moment Stokes had found him bound and gagged, Vik had been teased unmercifully for letting himself fall prey to Ivory's pranks, and though he had silenced more than one man with his fists, Chase's remark infuriated him anew. He let out a wild howl and lunged for him, but Chase waited until the last moment to slide out of his way and Vik went careening into the wall.

Chase kept his eye on Stokes while he taunted Vik. "That was absolutely pathetic. Can you peel potatoes? Maybe André can put you to work in the private kitchen."

"I'm going to kill you!" Vik shrieked, and he withdrew the laser pistol from his belt.

"Worst mistake you could ever make," Chase warned. "Ivory's a lot more fond of me than she is of you, and if I show up for lunch with so much as a scratch, you won't live to see supper."

"Bastard!" Vik yelled.

Chase felt Stokes inching closer, and in a single move kicked the laser pistol out of Vik's grasp, breaking three of his fingers in the process, and then spun and slammed the heel of his hand into Stokes's nose, smashing it again. With both men screaming in pain, he bent down to grab the pistol, and looked up to find Maxwell watching him.

"You need some help?" the tailor called.

"No, but why don't you call the medical unit and tell them Stokes and Vik are on the way over again. Maybe you ought to make a standing appointment, boys." Chase shoved Vik's pistol under his own belt and walked on down the hall to the elevator. It was time for lunch, and he had worked up quite an appetite.

Spider was disappointed to learn that Ivory wouldn't be joining them, but waited until Chase had taken a bite of his sandwich to issue a stern reprimand. "I won't have you pestering the staff with questions about my late wife. If there's something you must know, ask me."

Chase wondered whether it had been André or Maxwell who had reported his interest, or perhaps a security guard monitoring his conversations. He had known that everyone was being watched there, and wasn't all that surprised. André had made him a roast beef sandwich, and, enjoying it thoroughly, he waited a moment to swallow.

"The wedding made Ivory think of her mother," he replied, taking care not to mention her puzzling dream. "Because she's very sensitive to your feelings, I didn't want to come to you and remind you of your loss. I asked around, looking for someone else who might have happy memories of Willow to share with her."

Accepting Chase's explanation, Spider relaxed visibly. "No matter how well intentioned, your efforts were misguided. Nothing can be gained by dwelling on the past. Ivory knows how dearly her mother loved us both, and that's really all she needs to know. Now, what's this I hear about another fight between you and Stokes and Vik?"

Because Maxwell had been the only witness to the row, Chase assumed he had also been the one who had repeated his questions to Spider. The tailor had appeared to be close-mouthed, but obviously he tipped Spider whenever anything interesting came his way. Chase made a mental note not to speak to him about anything other than costumes.

Chase pretended a greater interest in his sandwich than in how quickly Spider had steered away from the subject of his late wife. He had not merely avoided discussing her, he had soundly slammed the door of her tomb. It did not require a trained agent to sense there was a good deal more to the story of Willow Diamond's untimely death than Spider was willing to tell.

Struck by the sudden realization that Spider was missing from Ivory's dream, Chase wondered if the pirate might not be represented by the menacing shadow. He sat back slightly and took a deep breath. Spider wanted him to talk about his latest misadventure, however, and, knowing this wasn't the time for lengthy dream analysis, Chase readily indulged him.

"They're both more than a little in love with Ivory, and they're jealous," he replied. "Eventually they'll learn not to cross me."

"For their sakes I hope it's soon. Are all of Alado's pilots as accomplished with their fists?"

Chase forced a wry laugh, and wished he had not been so distracted when he had reviewed Chase Duncan's personal history that he could not now recall the details.

"I didn't always fly the best routes, and fights are frequent in a lot of the outpost taverns. I learned to defend myself, and while I'd rather not have to go up against Stokes and Vik, I doubt they'll try to provoke me again."

"Let's hope not. They're useful, and I'd hate to have to get rid of them, although Vik's value has diminished considerably since Ivory got the better of him. That was most unfortunate. I do hope you'll make an effort to exert a calming influence on her so she'll not be tempted to disobey me again."

Rather than calm, Ivory was downright depressed that day, but Chase couldn't take any credit for it, nor did he wish to. "I love her just the way she is," he said.

"Yes, I can see that you do. Our arrangement has worked out remarkably well, hasn't it?"

"Yes, sir, and it will get even better." Chase meant what he said, but when Ivory joined them for supper that evening in as somber a mood as she had been at breakfast, he felt he had to do something to help her, and quickly. When they returned to her room, he took her hand and pulled her down across the bed. He kissed her, but very tenderly rather than with the passion he dared not unleash.

Hoping she had found at least some solace in her art, he encouraged her to talk about it. "How did your work go today?"

Ivory looked away. "I spent most of the day pounding air bubbles out of the clay. Each time I stopped and tried to sculpt an iguana, I got a hideous blob rather than a lizard. I've never had any trouble making what I want. What if I've used up all my talent? What if it's gone?"

She looked as terrified by that possibility as she had been by the darkly threatening dream, and he wrapped her more tightly in his arms. "Talent is an endless well, my love. You can't use it up. You didn't sleep well last night, and you were probably too tired to think, let alone create. Let's take a shower together and then get some sleep. Tomorrow is sure to look better."

"Do you really think so?"

Chase responded with a reassuring kiss. "I know so." Reluctantly he got up and guided her into the bathroom. She fumbled with his clothes as he peeled away hers, and they stepped into the shower together. He had planned only to help her relax, but as her hands moved over him it became instantly clear she wanted something far more exciting. He turned so the spray hit his back and picked her up. Agilely she climbed on him, wound her legs around his waist, draped her arms around his neck, and clung to him.

Chase was eager to make love to her in any way she wished. Their motions were limited in the shower, but not sufficiently impaired to dim the glow of pleasure they always found together. She moved with a serpentine grace, rolling her hips in a slow, undulating curl that rocked him back on his heels. He had to use his arms to brace himself, but once he regained his balance, he held her waist, guiding her toward a rapturous bliss made all the more delicious by the warmth of the soapy spray that dripped over his shoulders and trickled down between her breasts.

Ivory was so content, she might have fallen asleep in his arms had Chase not eased their way out of the shower and wrapped her in a towel. She looked up at him with a lazy smile that made him want her all over again. "Good. I knew a shower would make you feel better."

Cinnamon Burke

"No, it's you," Ivory argued before covering a wide yawn. "Let's go to bed."

Chase dried her hair first and then his own before leading her back into the bedroom. The bed was wide and inviting, and, snuggled in his arms, Ivory was asleep in seconds. Filled with the same relaxed warmth, Chase closed his eyes and hoped they would never share another day as troubling as this one had been. Then he realized just how impossible such a hope was. They had more dangerous pitfalls than bad dreams ahead.

Unmindful of her husband's fears, Ivory dreamed of being a child again, dancing with her mother to the most glorious tune. Their laughter sparkled as bright as sunlight until the music stopped. Frightened, Ivory clung to her mother's skirt, but the shadow found her even there, and she awoke with a strangled scream in her throat.

While she had uttered no more than a whimper, Chase felt her distress and awakened with her. He reached for the light. "Did you have another bad dream?"

Ivory clutched his hand to her breast, but couldn't reply until she had caught her breath. "No, it was the very same dream. My mother and I were dancing, and then a shadow crossed the room, and I can't bear to see any more."

"No, wait, that's different," Chase pointed out. "Was there more, something you refused to watch?"

Her eyes wide with fright, Ivory shook her head. "I don't know, and I don't want to know."

Chase pulled her across his lap and held her

352

tight. "I don't suppose you have any material on dream interpretation in your science files?"

"It's more than a dream, Chase. It's real, and I don't need a psychiatrist to tell me the shadow is evil. Something horrible is going to happen. I just know it will."

Chase muffled a choked sigh against her curls, for if the frightening dream was indeed a premonition, then surely it foretold the coming raid. He could not stop it, but he could try again to take Ivory away. "I can't bear to see you like this. Even if your father refused to allow us to go away on a honeymoon, I'm going to try to convince him to let us go back to the Paradise Retreat for a few days."

"No, don't ask," Ivory begged. "You'll just infuriate him again and we mustn't do that."

That response was so unlike the defiant beauty he loved, Chase became all the more intent upon leaving. "I think you need to get away from here. If you told your father about your dreams, I'm sure he would let us go."

"No!" Ivory pressed her nails into his arm. "This has to be our secret, Chase. Promise me you won't tell anyone."

There was an hysterical gleam in her eyes that frightened Chase more than any bad dream ever could. Ivory was undeniably high-strung. Spider described her as wild; but what if it was more than that? What if the young woman he adored completely lost touch with reality? Refusing to accept such a possibility, he quickly gave her his word.

"All right. We'll stay here, and we won't tell anyone about your dream. Maybe you won't have it again, but if you do, the medical unit has sedatives, and I'm going to insist that you start taking one to help you sleep. I should probably go and get you something right now."

"No, don't leave me," Ivory implored. "Just stay here with me, and I'll be able to sleep."

Chase doubted that she could, but switched off the light and pulled her down beside him. He rubbed her back, humming softly, and she surprised him by again falling asleep, but now he couldn't relax. He didn't want to think about scary dreams, or premonitions, or even memories in which death might hide behind a shadow, but the images Ivory had described spun in his mind until he was as badly confused as she.

This would definitely be his last assignment, he promised himself, and somehow he was going to carry it off without losing his bride.

Chapter Eighteen

Ivory got more sleep than Chase that night, but in the morning he tried to appear well rested for her sake and greeted her warmly. In turn, she attempted to fool him with a brave smile, and hurriedly left the bed before he could ask the questions that would have revealed her true mood. Spider had already eaten breakfast, leaving the distracted pair with no one to deceive but each other while they ate, but he met them as they left the dining room.

"Still working on iguanas?" Spider asked his daughter.

Ivory sent an apprehensive glance toward Chase, warning him not to contradict her, then smiled at her father. "Yesterday I prepared the clay, but I hope to turn out an iguana or two today. If you'll excuse me, I'm anxious to get started."

"Good luck!" Chase called, and she turned to wave.

Spider took Chase's arm. "Come with me," he said. "I've something to show you that I believe you'll find interesting."

Chase lingered for a final glimpse of Ivory before following his father-in-law. He doubted the raid would come during the day, but hated to be away from Ivory for a minute. Control preferred to stage raids in the early hours of the morning, after all the drunks had passed out and before the sober people were up for the day. Four was his favorite hour to strike, but he never followed the same plan twice. Ian St. Ives had warned the raid would come soon, but other than that, Chase didn't know what to expect.

Preoccupied, he made no effort to converse with Spider as they took the elevator down to the docking bays on the first level. There were three PJC Tomahawks in the main maintenance bay, and Spider led him on board the center ship. Reluctant to reveal that Ivory had already told him of the ship's real function, Chase feigned surprise when they entered the main cargo hold and were surrounded by shelves stacked with neat rows of parts, and benches lined with equipment used in the manufacture of Spider's magnificent silver robots.

"A mobile factory," Chase murmured with an admiring whistle. "Very clever."

Pleased by Chase's praise, Spider broke into a wide grin, but as usual the show of mirth failed to brighten his cold gray eyes. "I like to think so. I'd send you out on the next voyage so you could observe the whole process, but I know Ivory would never forgive me for separating you two."

"Send her along with me," Chase suggested in another attempt to spare her from having to witness the coming raid.

"I think not," Spider refused. He gestured for Chase to precede him and continued the tour. "We operate on a random schedule: four to six weeks out, two or three days here to resupply. The ship is registered to a legitimate salvage corporation. It cruises along the usual transport routes and draws no attention whatsoever."

"Where are the completed units stored?" Chase watched the subtle changes in Spider's expression as he weighed the wisdom of revealing that information. He hesitated for a long moment, clearly wavering, then gave in. "They're in one of the vaults at the bank. You've seen the first set, but there are others."

As they strolled along an aisle crowded with the gleaming robots' intricate components, Chase listened carefully to Spider's ambitious plans for the silver soldiers. He had no difficulty admiring their superb engineering, but he was determined to prevent them from ever fulfilling their evil purpose. They spent the whole morning on board the Tomahawk, and Spider made it clear that Chase would be involved in the next phase of his plan.

"I want to have a hundred silver boys ready to march before I advertise their capabilities, but when they go on sale, I'll expect you to play a major role. You asked for a percentage on the work you do for me, so the better the price you get, the more you'll earn."

"That's fine with me, but I probably should

have negotiated the percentage before I married Ivory."

Amused, Spider responded with a rumbling chuckle. "I'm glad to see you're learning how to look out for yourself so quickly. You needn't worry, however. You'll receive a generous commission." The ship was deserted as the crew and workers relaxed in the Mine, and, knowing they would not be overheard, Spider broached a more personal subject.

"I've not seen much of Ivory since your wedding, but I've seen enough to know she's not happy. How can something have gone wrong between you already?"

Unable to supply an easy answer, Chase revealed only part of the truth. "Ivory and I are getting along just fine. She misses her mother, though. Now, as I see it, our agreement ended with the wedding. If you want personal information on your daughter, ask her yourself."

Spider was used to getting his way, and there was no trace of a smile on his face now. "No. As a married woman, she ought to be confiding in her husband, not her father. If she's brooding over her mother's death, distract her."

"I'm doing my best."

"See that you do, because our agreement will never end, Duncan. Your job is to make Ivory happy forever."

Chase returned his father-in-law's steel-eyed stare with a level gaze. Counting down the final hours of his mission, he had no reason to fear him. "Your plan worked a little too well, didn't it?" he asked. "Ivory really does love me, and if anything ever happened to me it would break her heart. You needn't worry I won't be a good husband to her. I'll do it without any need for threats."

Having made his point, Chase walked down the Tomahawk's ramp. Hoping Ivory's work was going so well she would not mind his interrupting her, he went straight to her studio. He found her poring over her sketches, but if she had done any work that morning, it was out of sight. He kissed her and took the stool next to hers. "How's it going?"

Ivory closed her sketchbook and swept a stray curl out of her eyes. "Poorly, but I'm endeavoring to regard it as a slight dip in my creative output rather than an abyss. What have you been up to?"

Chase told her he had toured the silver boys' factory ship. "Your father's noticed you're not the happiest of brides, and strongly suggested I do something about it."

Ivory laced her fingers in his. "It's not your fault, Chase, it's mine. Just lousy timing, I guess."

Because he wanted so desperately to separate Ivory from her father after the raid, he shared his latest thoughts on her baffling dream. "If your dream is an amalgam of childhood memories, and not some strange premonition, has it occurred to you that someone important is missing from it? Except perhaps as a symbol?"

Ivory's gaze was wary but not guarded. "My father, you mean? Yes, it's occurred to me, but he adored my mother and has always spoiled me, so why would he cast such a threatening shadow over us?"

Chase pressed her to find an interpretation.

"Couples, even those who love each other, sometimes argue. A small child would naturally be frightened if she overheard angry voices."

Ivory mulled over that possibility. "That's logical, but I thought we were looking for symbols."

"What I want you to find is peace of mind. If you have the dream again, don't fight it. Perhaps all you'll see behind the shadow is some ridiculous argument your parents had and quickly forgot, while your fear remained with you all these years."

Ivory straightened up, grabbed the front of his jacket to draw him near, and gave him an enthusiastic kiss. "I hope you're right," she told him, but in her heart she feared that the foreboding shadow hid something far worse than a lovers' quarrel.

Ivory worked in the casino that night, and Chase wandered in and out keeping an eye on her as well as looking for patrons who might get out of line. The Mine was more crowded than usual, and he watched closely, trying to pick out the men who assembled silver boys for a living from the pirates. He had no way to judge the accuracy of his guesses except to inquire, which he didn't care to do, but it was an amusing pastime, until he saw Nelson snaking his way through the casino crowd toward Ivory's table.

The wiry Corkscrew dropped a handful of chips on her table and joined the next game. Despite his clanking belt and frizzled hair, Chase knew that Nelson must be as resourceful as Control's other operatives. Still, Chase doubted Nelson would be privy to the plans for the raid. There was the possibility he had come to bring a message, but even when Chase ambled past the table to give him the opportunity to pass it, Nelson ignored him.

Chase was tired, and he yawned as he and Ivory rode the elevator up to her quarters. "Sorry," he mumbled. "I should have taken a nap."

Ivory relaxed against him. "You needn't apologize. I could hardly keep my eyes open the last hour of my shift. Can we please just go to bed?"

Chase slipped his arm around her waist as they walked to her suite. "That's where we're going, isn't it?"

Ivory waited to reply until he had helped her out of her gown. She turned toward him and draped the slinky silver garment over her arm. "What I meant was, can we just go to sleep?"

Chase clucked his tongue, then trailed his fingertips down her throat. "We've only been married two days and you're bored with me already?"

The teasing light in his eyes dispelled her fear that she might have offended him. Relieved, she moved close and nibbled his earlobe. "No, I'll never grow bored with you. I'm just too tired to do anything more than lie in your arms and fall asleep. Do you mind?"

Chase gave her a hug, then sat on the side of her bed and yanked off his boots. "No, I'm not insulted. I'm worn out too."

"Good. I'd hate for either of us to feel pressured to make love when we're not in the mood."

Chase winked at her. "I didn't say I wasn't in the mood."

Ivory ruffled his hair. "You're an awful tease, Chase Duncan."

Chase grabbed her hand and brought it to his lips. "I'm not teasing either. Take a shower if you like. I'm going to sleep."

He stood to remove his jacket. Other than the suit he had worn for their wedding, he still hadn't gotten any new clothes. He had forgotten to ask Maxwell to duplicate his Alado wardrobe in navy blue. Of course, the tailor probably wouldn't have time to complete much before the raid, but Chase ought not to put off asking for new clothes as it showed a distinct lack of commitment to the Mine, and he did not want anyone to suspect he didn't plan to stay. Fortunately, he didn't need to wear anything to sleep.

He had a difficult time staying awake until Ivory joined him in bed. He slipped his arm around her waist and fit the curves of his body to hers. "This is nice," he whispered.

"I love you, Chase."

"Hmm." Chase knew he ought to say more, but he was too tired to make his lips move.

The Diamond Mine was open twenty-four hours to accommodate visitors, no matter what their arrival time, but business slacked off after three a.m. There were only two tables of poker operating in the casino, and no more than half a dozen men in the tavern sipping volcanoes and swapping outrageous tales they swore were true. At the brothel, most of the girls were either sleeping alone or with men who had paid an exorbitant sum to enjoy their favors for the whole night. The others were playing cards and waiting for the last of the winners in the casino to appear. As for

Summer Moon, she was coiled around Spider in his bed.

A small crew of controllers was on duty to clear ships for landing and departure, but the only activity at that hour was the arrival of the routine flight bringing liquor for the tavern and delicacies for Spider's table. Assigned to bay five, the pilot joked with the controllers and brought his ship in for a perfect landing. The guards on watch at the security cameras noted the arrival of the supply ship in their log, but as the unloading began, their interest quickly strayed.

With a growing stack of barrels blocking their view, they failed to see two men park a dolly carrying camouflaged canisters of Sweet Dreams, an odorless, tasteless, colorless gas, next to one of the ventilation ducts. When the gas began seeping into the Mine's ventilation system, the guards became blissfully relaxed. They stretched, yawned, and like the rest of the personnel at the Mine, fell sound asleep where they sat, or stood. Those already asleep sank deeper into their dreams.

Control had timed the operation down to the last second, and he was enormously pleased with how well the initial phase had gone. He waited another five minutes to be absolutely certain there wasn't a single soul awake at the Mine, and then gave the signal for the troops hidden in the supply ship's hold to move out. Heavily armed and wearing gas masks, they moved through the facility one level at a time, disarming and handcuffing everyone they found, and leaving each slumbering group under guard.

At four a.m. three more ships bearing members

of Alado's security forces docked with the aid of Control's team. Designed for the transport of prisoners, they disgorged their troops and then waited for their cargo of captives to be brought on board. It was the first time ships from the mighty Alado corporation had visited The Diamond Mine, but in the hours while the Mine's original owner slept through drugged dreams, the outpost was silently transformed from a pirate's den to Alado's latest colony.

Chase heard someone calling his name, but the sound was muffled and failed to pierce his dreams until it grew more insistent. Even then, he came awake slowly. At first he was elated that their sleep hadn't been disturbed by a repetition of Ivory's unnerving dream, and he snuggled closer to enjoy her luscious warmth. Then a harsh command jarred him out of his complacency.

"Damn it, Drew, wake up," Ian St. Ives ordered. He waited until Drew turned to look at him and then tossed him a pair of handcuffs. "Put those on your bride. Control wants to see you as soon as your head's clear enough to talk."

Drew had seen an hourglass in a museum, and as he struggled to focus his eyes on Ian, the ancient timepiece instantly came to mind. He felt himself disintegrating; it was as though every particle of his being were slipping away, but unlike the bottom half of an hourglass, there was nothing to catch the part of him that had turned to sand. He yawned and struggled to shake off the thick blanket of sleep that had turned his limbs to lead.

"Sweet Dreams," he mumbled through lips that

felt swollen to twice their size.

"That's right, Sweet Dreams it was. Best sleeping potion ever devised, but it ought to have worn off by now." Ian walked around to Ivory's side of the bed and shook her shoulder. "Wake up, princess, the party's over."

"Leave her alone." Drew swung his arm in a wide arc in a totally ineffective effort to push Ian away. He had heard about Sweet Dreams, but had never fallen prey to it. Now, though he wanted desperately to protect his wife, his motions were so slow he felt he could be overrun by marauding snails.

Ian shook Ivory again, and when that failed to wake her, he drew back his hand and slapped her across the face. She cried out, and her eyes at last fluttered open, but her expression remained as blank as a mannequin's. Ian pulled back the sheet and found her nude. He smiled appreciatively and didn't bother to recover her. He scooped up the handcuffs resting between Chase's knees and quickly locked them around her wrists.

"You're under arrest, Ms. Diamond," Ian announced, "for violating the Confederation weapons ban and trafficking in stolen goods. There are sure to be other charges, but those were the first to be filed."

Ivory could barely keep her eyes open. She could make out the fuzzy outline of a man's form, but she couldn't understand his words. She tried to sit up, but her hands wouldn't go where she wanted them to. She tugged, but couldn't pull them apart.

"Drew!" Ian shouted, but his fellow operative just watched him with a befuddled stare. Ian walked to the door, called for another agent to bring him a small tank of oxygen, and carried it to the bed. "Try breathing this," he ordered, and held the mask up to Drew's face.

It took several deep breaths, but Drew finally overcame the lingering effects of the gas which had put the whole complex to sleep. He could tell at a glance that Ivory was still lost in a dreamy haze. Embarrassed by her nudity, he quickly pulled the sheet up over her bare breasts. "You know better than to treat her like that," he growled.

"Like what?" Ian countered. "Like the lawless pirate she is?"

Drew had known the raid was going to be bad, but he had expected to be fully alert, not so weary from the effects of Sweet Dreams that he would be ill equipped to handle the situation. Pulling himself together, he left the bed and dressed. He had avoided thinking about how he would reveal his identity to Ivory, but now that the time had come, he wished he had rehearsed something, anything.

He knelt beside the bed to give her enough oxygen to sweep the last wisps of Sweet Dreams from her brain. When her gaze cleared, he told her as little as possible. "Alado's raided the Mine. Please don't worry, I'll take care of you."

The earnestness of her husband's expression convinced Ivory he would try, but she was shocked to discover Brother Samuel standing behind him. He was dressed in the same gray uniform Chase wore, and, sickened by his taunting smirk, she realized they had been duped. "You bastard," she screamed. "You're no priest."

Lady Rogue

Ian was happy to concede that point. "Smart girl. I'm not a priest, so Chase Duncan isn't your husband, but then he isn't Chase Duncan either. His name's Drew Jordan and he's been working for Alado the whole time he's been here."

Shocked to her soul, Ivory waited for Chase to deny the awful accusation, but the truth was plain in his anguished expression. Suffering the worst kind of betrayal, she let out a feral howl and, despite being handcuffed, went for his throat with a savage lunge that knocked him off balance. He caught her wrists as he fell, pulling her down with him. As his head hit the floor, she clawed his face with her nails. Rising up, he rolled over her in a desperate effort to pin her beneath him, but she fought him so fiercely he couldn't suppress her tortured writhings.

Ian leapt out of the way as they slammed into the bed. Highly amused by the sight of Drew Jordan grappling with the naked beauty he claimed as his wife, he made no move to help him restrain her. He knew that Drew had the strength to eventually subdue her, but he was enjoying their spectacular brawl too much to see it end quickly. Ivory Diamond was one of the most beautiful women he had ever seen, and when she was enraged, and stark naked, she was a breathtaking sight.

She also possessed one of the most colorful vocabularies Ian had encountered and was calling Drew such vile names, he didn't understand why Drew didn't slam his fist into her chin to knock her out. Shrieking epithets, she fought like a demon from hell, biting, scratching, and kicking. Handcuffs didn't hinder her attack; she just laced

367

her fingers and used her joined fists as a club to clobber Drew with repeated blows to the temple.

Growing impatient, Control opened the bedroom door and glanced in. Appalled, he entered the room, withdrew a small drug canister from his pocket, and aiming carefully, slammed it against Ivory's upper arm. She went limp and unconscious, rolling away from Drew.

Drew looked up at Control and shook his head. "Sorry. I thought I could handle her."

"I'm deeply disappointed in you," Control replied. "Ian told me your plans, but you cannot possibly still want to marry this . . . well, this woman."

Not about to allow the woman he loved to lie sprawled across the floor, Drew scooped her up in his arms and sat down on the side of the bed. Out of breath, he needed a moment to compose himself. "It's only natural that Ivory was disappointed to discover who I really am."

"Disappointed?" Ian scoffed. "She was outraged and made it perfectly plain that she despises you. You're lucky there's anything left of your face."

Blood dripped from the slash in Drew's cheek and splashed on Ivory's bare breast. Feeling sick, he hugged her more tightly. "Give me the keys to the handcuffs and leave us alone so I can get her dressed," he begged.

Control nodded, and Ian slipped past him and closed the door on his way out. Not ready to leave Drew alone with Ivory, Control pulled up a chair and sat down. "I assume you have a great deal to tell me."

"Later, when I know Ivory's safe."

"She's in no danger, Drew. Spider's an arrogant

bastard, but we had far less trouble with him than you had with her. Of course, he doesn't know about you yet, and she does." Control crimped the crease in his pant leg with a nervous pinch. "Will she testify against her father?"

Drew watched the blood trickle down between Ivory's breasts, a crimson river of despair. "Never," he swore, but then he recalled her dream. "Can you find out what happened to Spider's wife? Ivory was told her mother had a weak heart, but that might have been a convenient lie."

"I'll see what we can discover, but I can't make any promises." He rose and tossed a key for the handcuffs on the bed. "Get her dressed. I'll wait outside, but don't keep me waiting long."

Drew nodded, but couldn't bring himself to move for several minutes. Then, leaving Ivory on the bed, he went into the bathroom, wet the end of a towel, and tried to stem the flow of blood from his cheek. Ivory had gone for his left eye, but caught the cheekbone and gouged three bloody trails. Control would have brought medical technicians with him who could undo the damage in a few minutes with their miracle lights, but as he gazed into the mirror he decided against seeking their attention.

He redampened the towel and wiped his blood off Ivory's fair skin. They hadn't shared her room long enough for him to know where she kept her lingerie, and he had to hunt through several drawers for it. He removed her handcuffs, then dressed her in pale blue lingerie and one of the silver flight suits she usually wore. It wasn't easy, but he finally managed to get her dressed. He washed her face, brushed her hair, and bent down to kiss her. He carried the handcuffs with him to the door and handed them to Control.

"I won't need these. Where do you want me to take her?"

"You needn't do it yourself."

"I want to," Drew insisted.

Control took Drew's unfortunate attachment to Ivory as a personal insult. After all, he was Drew's supervisor, and any deviation from procedure reflected poorly on him as well. "You should never have allowed yourself to become personally involved with Ivory Diamond. It's our cardinal rule. How could you have been so careless?"

Drew propped his hand against the door. "Save the lectures for later. I want to make certain my wife's comfortable, and then we'll talk."

"There's no longer any need for that ridiculous pretense," Control argued smugly.

Drew wondered if love had ever touched Control's heart. Deciding it was doubtful, he avoided any mention of the joys of romance. "We're not as unlikely a pair as you think. She's an extraordinary woman, and a talented artist. I intend to stay with her."

Control rolled his eyes. "Such misplaced devotion is absurd, but I imagine you'll soon tire of visiting her in prison. Women will wait years for a man to serve out his term, but men never display the same loyalty. We're wasting time. If you don't trust anyone else to transport her to a ship, then just heft her over your shoulder and bring her along now."

Rather than follow Control's order, Drew lifted Ivory off the bed and carried her in his arms as tenderly as a sleeping child. He paused at the door and glanced around her room. "I want to pack some of her things," he told Control.

"Do it later."

Drew turned sideways to ease Ivory out the door without bumping against the jamb. "Where are you taking her?"

"A prison ship for now, then she's to be held at Confederation headquarters. This will be the trial of the century, Drew, and you're going to be the star witness."

Rather than pride, Drew felt only an immense sorrow. He knew that Spider's arms operation had threatened the existence of every peaceful colony, but Ivory was an artist who wasn't a threat to anyone. He shifted her weight in his arms as they entered the elevator. "You'll have plenty of evidence," he promised. "There won't be any need for me to testify."

"This has been a very difficult assignment," Control offered in a conciliatory tone. "You'll feel differently in a few days."

Drew brushed Ivory's curls with a kiss. "Never," he swore.

Ivory awoke in a brightly lit cell, lying on a narrow bunk. She raised herself up and looked over the toes of her boots to see a sink and toilet against the back wall. Glancing over her shoulder, she saw a metal door that completely sealed off the outside world. The cell was so narrow that when she rolled off the bunk, she could only pace alongside it.

A camera above the door slowly tracked her as she walked up and down the cell. It was barely ten feet long, and no more than five feet wide.

The walls, ceiling, and floor were painted white, and the overhead light reflected off them with a painful glare.

Pausing, Ivory rested her hands against the wall opposite the bunk. She closed her eyes and held her breath, trying to get some sense of place. The fan above her head had a bent blade and made a soft thumping sound with each revolution, but that was the only sound. She waited, but detecting no motion, decided she must still be at the Mine.

She had heard about prison ships, and thought that must be where she was confined. Restless, she resumed pacing until a small opening appeared in the door, and a tray slid forward holding a container of water and an apple. It was a bright red apple that had been polished until it glowed.

Thinking they might be her entire rations for the day, she quickly picked them up. "Where's the bread?" she called, but no one answered, and the tray disappeared into the cold metal door with a sharp clang.

Ivory sat down on the bunk and took a sip of water. It was cold and sweet, and suddenly she was desperately thirsty. She gulped down half the container, then forced herself to save the rest for later. She was hungry too, and saw no reason to save the apple. It was crisp and juicy, but she didn't enjoy eating alone in a room no bigger than a closet.

Once she had finished, she tossed the apple core in the toilet, lay back down on the bunk, and tried to remember what had happened to land her in such a wretched predicament. Her father had never regarded the Mine as impregnable, but it had excellent security, and guards who knew their lives depended upon how seriously they took their work. Yet here she was in a cramped cell, so something must have gone dreadfully wrong.

Oh yes, she finally remembered. They had been betrayed by a man who had sworn that he loved her. Blurred first by Sweet Dreams, and then by the drug Control had injected, her memories weren't all that clear, but gradually she recalled that Chase wasn't Chase at all, but one of Alado's spies. Tears welled up in her eyes, but she forced them away. She refused to weep for the love she had lost, when it had all been clever lies.

She had not really known Chase Duncan, but before he died, he would discover just how badly he had underestimated Ivory Diamond and how painful it was to be betrayed.

Chapter Nineteen

Unable to take his eyes off the monitor, Drew folded his arms over his chest and planted his feet wide. "How long has Ivory been pacing her cell?"

The guard shrugged. Seated in front of a bank of monitors, he was trained to watch for self-destructive behavior, nothing more. "An hour, maybe two. I don't keep detailed records."

Annoyed by the guard's sarcasm, Drew turned to Control. "Now that all the prisoners have been loaded on to prison ships, I want her released in my custody. You have my word we'll both appear at the trial."

Control shoved his hands into his coat pockets. "That is undoubtedly the most bizarre offer anyone has ever made me. The answer is an unequivocal no. Both Ivory and Spider are being held without bail. They'll not be released before the trial for any reason, and with convictions virtually assured, they won't be doing any sight-seeing afterward either."

Drew had not really expected Control to agree to his first request, so he went on to the next. "I want her transferred to a larger cell. That one is much too small for extended confinement."

"It will not be an extended stay," Control argued. "Our investigations here should be complete within a week. Of course, a lot depends on you."

Drew was already painfully aware of that fact. "That cell is no larger than a doghouse!" he complained.

"It conforms to Confederation standards."

"Well, it doesn't meet mine, and I want Ivory moved. There's no reason for her to be kept in solitary confinement. It's cruel."

Control had gone without sleep for nearly two days and was in no mood to debate Ivory Diamond's comfort. "She stays where she is. I'm going to rest for a couple of hours, and then we'll continue your debriefing."

Ivory was still pacing the tiny cell, and every step made Drew's heart ache for her. He would let Control sleep for as long as he wished, but he was not going to tell him one more thing until he had done all he could for Ivory. He might not have a Celestial Cannon to wave around, but he could drive just as hard a bargain as Ivory any day.

"I want to see my wife."

Control sighed unhappily. "First, you must stop referring to her as your wife, and second, you must cease all contact with her. From what I saw, she'd much rather see you dead than at her door."

"Frankly, I can't blame her."

"Get a grip on yourself, man!"

Drew glanced down at his superior. "You raided the Mine too soon. I may not have known Ivory long, but I know enough to be certain that I didn't inspire that furious anger you saw this morning. It was already a part of her when I arrived, and I think it's been with her since her mother died. A little more time, and I could have blown Spider Diamond's operation wide open from inside."

"You can't be certain of that," Control insisted. "Does it really surprise you that Spider might have some dark family secrets, or that he hasn't raised a well-adjusted daughter? It really doesn't matter if his wife died under mysterious circumstances. He'll get life in prison for the illegal manufacture and sale of Celestial Cannons.

"As for his robot soldiers, it was an amazing piece of luck that we found his factory ship moored in one of the bays. Their design is Alado's, by the way, although they were intended for peaceful not military use, and no one had even suspected that Spider had gotten detailed plans for them. The man had an incredible talent for knowing precisely what to steal."

Before Drew could respond, Ian St. Ives joined them. He was wearing a cocky smirk that raised Drew's temper another couple of degrees. Drew could not imagine that the agent would have anything to contribute to his conversation with Control. He moved to block Ian's view of the monitor covering Ivory's cell to give her what privacy he could.

"Spider won't cooperate," Ian told them, "but

he did have one interesting bit of information to report."

Intrigued, Control postponed his nap. "Yes, what was it?"

Ian spoke to Drew rather than Control. "He says his daughter has to be treated as a juvenile. He claims she's only sixteen years old."

Control gasped. "Nonsense. How old is she, Drew?"

Drew's stomach lurched, and he had to swallow hard. Ivory had always presented a mass of contradictions. She could don a Rocketball suit and be the toughest bitch in the galaxy, but he hadn't forgotten the wonder in her eyes the night he'd kissed her amid a forest of orchids. It wasn't her brash confidence that had appealed to him, but her touching vulnerability. He remembered her delight in building the sand castle at the Paradise Retreat and knew she might indeed be only sixteen. She could not receive a life sentence if she were tried as a juvenile, and he made no effort to contradict Spider.

"I've no idea how old she is," he told them. "I never asked."

"Do the words statutory rape mean anything to you?" Ian asked.

Control waved him off. "That was uncalled for. You know you agents have immunity from prosecution for your actions while on assignment."

"Sure we do," Ian agreed.

"Go find a pirate to wrestle!" Control snapped. "Drew and I have better things to do than listen to your jibes."

"Yes, sir," Ian responded, and after giving Control a lazy salute, he executed a sharp turn on his heel and left the guard station.

Control closed his eyes and breathed deeply. When he looked up at Drew, he already had a plan. "This provides an added incentive for a search of Spider's records, so you can rest assured that I'll have Ivory's birthdate, and details of her mother's demise before the day is out." He checked his watch and made some hasty mental calculations. "Meet me at one in Spider's office."

"I'll be there," Drew replied. He waited until Control was gone and turned back toward the monitor. "What time will the prisoners be served lunch?"

"The trays will come up from the kitchen at 11:30," the guard replied. He checked the day's menu. "Cheese sandwiches, mixed vegetables, and chocolate pudding. Yummy. Our food isn't half bad. Want to order a tray for yourself?"

"No, thanks." Drew hadn't eaten breakfast, but he hadn't missed it, nor would he miss lunch. "I want to see my wife."

"Man, have you ever got a one-track mind. None of the prisoners we took into custody today is allowed to have visitors. You're just torturing yourself watching her. Why don't you go catalog evidence with the rest of the agents?"

"Where's the key?"

"What?"

"You heard me. I want the key to her cell. I'll just open the outer door and talk with her for five minutes. You can time me if you like."

The guard knew who Drew Jordan was, and regarded him with fear and respect. "I don't want to lose my job."

"Who'll know?"

The guard glanced toward the alarm button.

"Don't even think about it," Drew warned. "Just give me the key."

As the guard saw it, he didn't have much choice. He didn't dare risk making Drew force the issue when he could easily end up crippled, or worse. He thought of his wife and children, and became downright cooperative. "There isn't one. The cell doors operate with electronic codes." He typed in the proper sequence for Ivory's cell and looked up at her monitor. The outer door slid open, and Ivory walked toward it.

"Five minutes," the guard announced with more courage than he felt. "Then I'm shutting her door."

Drew sprinted down the corridor. His boots hit the perforated metal flooring with a force that made the whole walkway vibrate, but he reached Ivory's cell in a matter of seconds. When she saw him, the same cold fury he'd seen that morning filled her eyes, but before she could shriek another filthy name, he reached through the bars, grabbed her hair to yank her against the bars, and covered her mouth with his other hand. She struggled to break free, but he refused to release her.

"Calm down and listen," he implored in a harsh whisper. "Spider says you're sixteen. I don't care whether that's true or not, but you're going to swear that it is because it will save you a life sentence. You understand? You may be the wildest kid in the galaxy, but that's all you are. Now, I'll do my damnedest to see you're not tried at all, but you've got to help me, Ivory. Don't tell anyone, not even the attorney they assign you, a damn thing."

Ivory could do no more than scowl in his grip, but she couldn't imagine why Chase . . . oh damn, what was this man's name? Well, whoever he was, why would he want to help her? Another trick, she feared, but he was so intent upon impressing her that she was almost tempted to believe him. She was surprised he still wore the slashes she'd put in his cheek. Why hadn't he had the damage repaired? she wondered. If he wanted her to feel sorry for him, he had failed, but she relaxed slightly, and when he slackened his hold, she nodded.

"Good. Now I'm trying to get you out of here. You've got to trust me, Ivory. When I came here to stop Spider from selling Celestial Cannons, I never expected to fall in love with you. I still want you for my wife, and please, please, think of me as your husband. I'm not supposed to be here, so I can't stay, but I'll come back as often as I can." Fearing his time was nearly up, Drew released her and stepped back. "I love you."

Ivory shook her head. "You rotten two-faced sonofabitch," she screamed. She grabbed the bars and continued to yell. "I wouldn't trust you any farther than I can spit! Get the hell out of here and don't come back!"

The door slid shut, silencing her tirade, but Drew had heard enough to know she hadn't believed him. All he could do was pray that she would go along with her father's ruse, if it was a ruse, and swear she was only sixteen. He walked back to the guard station. "Thanks. Have you got a piece of paper?"

The guard had heard what Ivory thought of him and doubted that Drew would be a frequent visitor. Relieved, he tore off the bottom half of the menu and handed it to him. Without waiting to be asked, he also provided a pen.

Drew wrote a quick note and folded it into a neat square. "I want you to put this on Ivory's lunch tray. Will you do that for me?"

"Do I have a choice?"

"Not really, no."

"Then I'll do it." The guard took the note, and when Drew had left he started to unfold it. Then thinking it was probably some mushy love note he would be embarrassed to read, he placed it on Ivory's tray as directed.

When an unseen guard slid her lunch tray through her door, Ivory sat down on her bunk and just looked at it. Then it occurred to her that if she didn't pick it up, it might soon disappear, and she reached over to take it. Seeing Chase had upset her too badly to have any appetite, but she was used to having her meals whenever she wanted them, and didn't like the idea of going hungry later while she waited for supper.

She took a bite of the sandwich, and had to wash it down with a long swig of water. The vegetables were overcooked, and the pudding had a watery film on it that revolted her. Thinking she would keep only the sandwich for later, she picked up the napkin to wrap it, and saw the note. Her name was printed across it in block letters. She had never seen Chase's writing, but knew it had to be his.

She wouldn't have read it, but with nothing else to do, decided she might as well. She unfolded it slowly, smoothed out the creases, and read it. The message was brief: *Trust me. We'll find Paradise again. Drew.*

"Drew," she said softly. So that was the bastard's name, or one of his numerous aliases. She tore the note into tiny bits and put them under her pillow. If he bothered her again, she'd throw them in his face.

At one o'clock Drew met Control in Spider's office. Control didn't look happy, but then he seldom did. "What did you find?" Drew asked.

Control slapped a stack of computer printouts on the desk and sat down. "There's no record of Ivory Diamond ever being born. We've both met her, so there's no question that she exists, but Spider never bothered to register her birth with the Confederation. That in itself isn't surprising. Most criminals don't keep the Confederation Records Bureau informed of additions to their families, but it makes it difficult to judge her age. Perhaps we could X-ray her bones and teeth."

"Not without her consent," Drew reminded him. "And I know you're a stickler for following the proper procedures."

"True," Control agreed with a weary frown. "I did find her mother, however. Willow Bennett Diamond was born at the original Mars colony in 2217, which would make her forty-three if she were alive today, which you tell me she isn't. She and Spider were married on Mars in 2240 by a magistrate named Joshua Mitchell, who had no idea Spider was a wanted man. She had been employed by a design firm, but simply disappeared after her marriage.

"Let's say Ivory was born the year after their

marriage, in 2241. That would make her eighteen, possibly nineteen now. Either would qualify her for trial as an adult."

"That's merely conjecture," Drew mused, "not proof of her age."

Control sat back in his chair and stared at Drew until an idea finally occurred to him. "Spider hasn't spoken with his daughter since the raid. There's always the chance they had this scheme planned, but if not, she might not be clever enough to think to lie herself. You stay here. I'm going over to the ship to ask her."

Not trusting himself to speak, Drew nodded. When Control left, he wiped his forehead on his sleeve and concentrated with all his might, hoping to send Ivory a mental signal to repeat exactly what he had told her. She might despise him, but he had explained why it was to her advantage to be sixteen, and he prayed she would either say that or nothing when Control questioned her.

He had gained a newfound respect for Spider, and wished he had been smart enough to plan how to protect Ivory from prosecution when he had first realized their marriage wouldn't be legal. He waited, more frightened for Ivory than he had ever been for himself. Now he wished he had just taken her and left in his ship the night Ian had appeared. The certain knowledge that Spider wouldn't have let them go didn't ease his pain.

"I should have tried," he swore under his breath. "I should have at least tried."

The guard did not argue with Control's request to see Ivory Diamond, but he did not reveal that he had let Drew Jordan see her either. Thinking that Control was in for a very nasty surprise, he leaned back in his chair and watched her monitor.

When her door slid open, Ivory was ready for Drew with a handful of scraps, but didn't throw them when she saw instead a little man in a black suit. He raked her with a piercing gaze, and then gestured for her to come closer. She backed away.

"I mean you no harm," Control assured her. "Tell me when you were born."

Ivory regarded him with an innocent gaze. "June 11, 2243."

Control started to swear, then caught himself. "Thank you." He had no other questions and returned to Drew still scowling angrily. "She'll be seventeen in June," he informed him as he came through the door. "I'll petition to have her tried as an adult."

Drew waited until Control had taken his seat behind Spider's desk. "No, you'll do nothing of the kind," he told him. "You're going to see she's treated as a juvenile, given probation, and assigned to me, or I won't say another thing about Spider Diamond. Believe me, there's a great deal more to tell."

Control pursed his lips thoughtfully. He detested threats, and found this one particularly offensive. "I should have known that morning in Vancouver when you were so reluctant to board the shuttle that your days as a useful operative were over. Because I regard this whole regrettable incident as an error in judgment on my part rather than yours, I'm going to do what I can to see that your child bride goes free. But you're finished with our branch, Drew. Alado will always have work for you as a pilot, of course, but your days with the intelligence unit are over."

Drew had already made that decision on his own, but felt he had to argue. "That's rather harsh," he complained. "I didn't fail in this mission. I found out where Spider is building arms and to whom he's sold them. That's all that was required."

"Fine. I'll see that another commendation is placed in your file, but clearly you think more of Ivory Diamond than you do of Alado, and I can't have an agent of questionable loyalty. That's final. Now, you have my assurance I'll do whatever I can for your foul-mouthed bride. Let's continue the debriefing."

"I want it in writing."

Control was shocked. "You don't trust me?"

"I trust you to do your job with unwavering integrity, Control, but Ivory's future is at stake, and I want your promise in writing that she'll be tried as a juvenile."

Control shook his head as though this were a very sad day indeed. He searched through Spider's desk, found a sheet of paper, and quickly penned the promise Drew required. "Would you like witnesses while I sign?"

"That won't be necessary." When Control handed him the sheet, he folded it and slipped it into his jacket pocket.

"Oh yes," Control added absently. "I have something else for you." He opened the top drawer and withdrew Ivory's engagement and wedding rings. "Here, these are yours. Prisoners aren't allowed to keep any jewelry other than religious items."

The rings lay on the desk, discarded symbols of

a love and marriage that Drew was determined weren't over. He scooped them up and held them in a reverent grasp. "I'll save them for her."

"Drew," Control cajoled in a soft, fatherly tone. "Put yourself in Ivory's place. Would you forgive her if she had betrayed your trust and destroyed your family?"

"My parents aren't pirates."

"But if they were, would you forgive her because she had a righteous cause?"

If he were the one locked up in a cell barely big enough to turn around, would he forgive her? He didn't even want to think about it. "I realize this is a preposterous situation."

"Thank God you still have a partial grasp of reality. There's hope for you after all. We've digressed," Control announced suddenly, and squaring his narrow shoulders, he tapped impatiently on the desk. "Let's get back to our discussion of Spider's activities."

Convinced he had a written guaranty for Ivory's future, Drew sat back and described the private bank where he was positive that all manner of contraband could be found. He promised to take Control there in the morning.

"The Celestial Cannon factory is on board another PJC Tomahawk, probably registered to the same salvage firm that owns the silver boys' ship docked here now. It shouldn't be hard to locate."

"The search will begin immediately," Control assured him. "Spider must have a record of his business transactions on computer files somewhere, but so far we've not found anything other than an accounting of the Mine's profits. Do you know where his private records are?"

Drew thought for a minute, and then nodded. "Let's try Spider's Blaster." They went down to the bay where it was moored and Drew activated Rainbow. "Rainbow, it's Chase Duncan. How are you?"

The computer responded with a delighted purr. "I'm ever so much better now that you're here, Chase."

Drew laughed at Control's astonished expression. "I have a friend with me. Call him Control, and give him access to your files. Say something to her," Drew urged.

Nonplussed, Control stuttered a moment and coughed to clear his throat. "I'm pleased to meet you, ah, madame. I trust we'll enjoy working together."

Rainbow's tone grew even more seductive. "I enjoy everything I do, Control. Your voice print is complete."

Drew requested a listing of Rainbow's files, and they scrolled down the navigational computer's screen for more than five minutes. It had been a lucky guess on Drew's part, but he took full credit for it. "As you can see, I haven't been wasting my time here."

Control conceded the point grudgingly. "Well, perhaps not all of it. Print out the first file for me, Rainbow."

"Love to, sweetheart."

"I've got some other things to check," Drew said, and he left the cockpit while Control was engrossed in reading the records Spider had never intended anyone to see.

Drew went up to Ivory's room and was relieved

to find that no one had searched it yet. The bed was still unmade, and he hurriedly smoothed out the covers. While looking for her lingerie that morning he had come across a jewelry box filled with an astonishing amount of diamonds and had quickly slipped it inside his jacket. He knew the jewels were either stolen, or bought with money Spider had earned any way but honestly. But Ivory no longer had the inheritance she had expected, and Drew wanted her to have some way to provide for herself if she refused to stay with him.

He wasn't stopped as he left the private quarters and went down to his ship, which sat exactly where it had landed. He entered the cockpit, opened the compartment behind the pilot's seat containing emergency supplies, and shoved Ivory's jewelry box under the last of the packaged rations. He knew that what he'd done would be regarded as theft of evidence, which would land him in even more serious trouble than he was in already, but it seemed a small risk compared to the terrible mess Ivory was in.

He sat down for a minute and reviewed the material he had yet to divulge. The fact that Spider bragged about killing Sonny Duran was worth a great deal, but he decided to keep it to himself a while longer. There were also the respectable poets, philosophers, and musicians who frequented the Mine. Control would go into ecstasy over that, but those names would also keep.

The next time the tray in Ivory's door slid open, it contained her sketchbook, half a dozen pencils, and three changes of lingerie. Even knowing who had sent them, she was grateful to have clean underwear and something to occupy her time. If the snake slithered by again, she would tell him to send some books.

She sat down on her bunk and flipped through the sketchbook. Just as she had expected, there was another note written across the corner of the first blank page: *I'm still in the mood. Love you, Drew.*

Ivory's immediate reaction was anger that became a fierce, seething rage welling up from deep inside her. The sonofabitch had used her, and now he was pretending to stand by her like the most faithful of husbands! She wouldn't even be in trouble if it weren't for him. He must think her the most gullible girl in the galaxy, but she wouldn't be taken in again. She folded down the corner of the page and made a crease with her thumbnail. She then ripped off a neat triangle and tore it into more little bits, which she stuffed under her pillow.

Picking up a pencil, she began to create an abstract pattern that swirled and dipped across the page in tortured lines that soon began to take on a life of their own. They writhed like serpents in an ancient snake pit and flowed over the page and onto the next. The drawing grew, pulsating, a living work of art, and lost in it, Ivory failed to notice when her dinner tray arrived until the baked apple's spicy aroma teased her senses.

"More apples?" Thinking Alado must have gotten a bargain price, she picked up the bowl and ate her dessert first. The split pea soup went untouched as did the vegetable salad. She stood up to stretch, then sat back down, made herself comfortable, and concentrated on giving the abstract pattern the freedom she now lacked.

Rather than ask Control's permission and be refused, Drew had simply slept in the bed he and Ivory had shared. He awoke at two, so worried about Ivory he got dressed and went down to the ship where she was being held. There was a new guard on duty, and he quickly introduced himself as her husband.

One look at Ivory's monitor told him she wasn't doing any better than he was. The light in her cell was turned down low, but he could still see her clearly. She was pacing again, and slamming her fist into the door each time she reached it. He couldn't bear to watch.

"Hasn't she slept at all?" he asked.

The guard rocked back in his chair. The other prisoners in his cell block were all asleep, so he had had no one to watch but Ivory Diamond for the last hour. "She might have slept an hour or two, but then she left her bunk."

Drew felt certain it was because of the dream. "Open her outer door," he said.

"You know I can't do that."

Drew kicked the guard's chair so hard he went careening into the far wall. "Open her door," he repeated. "Or I'm going to start kicking you."

Like his counterpart on the day shift, the guard knew better than to argue with Drew Jordan. "Yes, sir." He scooted his chair back to the control panel and typed in her code. When Drew started down the corridor, the guard eyed the alarm button, but was far too frightened to punch it.

Lost in thoughts darker than the dimly lit room, Ivory didn't notice that the door had opened until she reached the end of her cell and saw Drew standing there. She quickly slipped her hand under her pillow and threw all that remained of his notes in his face. "That's what I think of you," she called, but her voice was too hoarse for her to yell as loudly as on his earlier visit.

"You're trash. Nothing." She turned her back on him and went to the opposite end of her cell.

Drew ignored her outburst. "You had the dream again, didn't you? I'll ask for sedatives for you. You've got to sleep. Take care of yourself, Ivory. I'll have you released as soon as I can."

His solicitous concern nauseated her, and she walked back to the door. "Liar," she snapped. "I wouldn't be here if it weren't for you."

"I know." Drew tried to reach through the bars to touch her, but she quickly stepped back to elude him. "This isn't the way I wanted it to end," he swore. "I was sent to get Spider, not you."

That he had still not done anything about his cheek puzzled her. Then she understood. "You must hate yourself for what you've done," she declared. "Judas killed himself, but you don't have that much courage, do you? We may be pirates, but you're cowardly vermin."

He stared at her, unable to counter her loathing with the words of love that no longer meant anything to her.

"I don't need to commit suicide," he said. "If

I've lost you, I'm already dead." He turned away before she could taunt him again, but her laughter echoed down the corridor. He hurried past the guard to hide his tears.

Chapter Twenty

The base of operations of the Confederation of Populated Worlds was a huge rotating space station resembling a domed wheel. It was maintained by the five Earth corporations chartered for the exploration of space, and the installation was a magnificent monument to their combined success. The only criminals brought here for trial were those whose activities threatened the orderly, peaceful exploration and colonization of space. The crimes of which Spider and Ivory Diamond were accused fit well within that category.

As a witness, Drew was given plush quarters, but he was again distressed by what he regarded as the inhumane way Ivory was treated. Drew wasn't permitted to see her, but Control assured him her cell was twice the size of the one on board the prison ship, though she was still completely isolated. A matron escorted her to a shower stall at the end of the cell block each morning, and after a precisely timed three-minute shower, the woman handed her another set of the bright orange coveralls all detainees wore. Once Ivory was dressed, she was marched back to her cell for the remainder of the day. She was allowed only one visitor, the attorney assigned to her defense, Gail Bolyn.

A petite woman with dark eyes and thick auburn curls, Ms. Bolyn refused to meet with Drew, so he resorted to waiting outside the detention wing, where he tried to speak with her whenever she appeared. "I'm going to report you," she threatened. "You're stalking me, and that's a punishable offense."

Drew was aware that Ivory's low opinion of him was the source of Gail's exasperating hostility, but he refused to give up his efforts to win back Ivory's trust. "I brought all my wife's ceramics and paintings with me from the Mine. Will you tell her that, please? I don't want her to worry that her work's been lost."

Gail stared at Drew as though he were some strange curiosity displayed under glass. "Ivory Diamond is not, nor will she ever be, your wife, Mr. Jordan. Now, I'll give her your message on the one condition that you promise not to bother me again."

Since he had arrived at the Confederation base, everyone had conspired to keep him away from Ivory. There was a higher level of security in the detention wing than on the prison ship, so he had not been able to force his way past the guards. "I can't give you that promise, and I won't lie and say I will," he replied. "But if you have the slightest concern for Ivory, you'll tell her her work is safe."

Gail Bolyn had never inspired in any man the devotion Ivory received from Drew, and she mistook his unwavering love for a dark obsession. "Make an appointment to see one of the psychologists," she advised. "Maybe with some help you'll be able to overcome your perverse attachment to Ivory and salvage your career."

Drew backed away rather than continue their conversation, but he was completely disheartened by it. If that weren't bad enough, he went up to his room and found Control waiting for him. One glance at his expression warned Drew his news wasn't good. Rather than ask his supervisor how he had gotten into his room, he just closed the door and inquired about the only subject that existed for him: Ivory Diamond.

"I'm afraid things haven't gone as you'd hoped," Control replied. "As you know, the responsibility of our branch is limited to the gathering of evidence and the apprehension of criminals. The prosecution is handled by Confederation staff, and the prosecutor assigned to the Diamond case insists upon trying Ivory as an adult." Seeing that Drew was about to interrupt, Control gestured for patience with hands as small and soft as a woman's.

"Mordecai Black has been arrested with one hundred Celestial Cannons in his possession, and he's named Ivory as the person who negotiated and delivered the weapons. Unlike Spider, he's talking to anyone who will listen in hopes of gaining clemency. I want you to know I kept my part of our bargain. I described Ivory as an artistically talented adolescent, but Mordecai painted such a vicious picture of her, I wasn't believed. Here, I brought you a copy of my statement."

Drew sat down on the side of his bed and held his head in his hands. "Thanks, I'll read it later." He knew it would be a masterpiece, but doubted that Control had presented it with any real conviction.

Control laid it on the bed. "Someone gave the prosecutor a copy of Nelson's photograph of Ivory holding a cannon. There was nothing childish about her pose or expression, if you'll recall, and I still doubt that she's underage." He paused, and when Drew didn't speak, he shuffled his feet nervously. "Will you be all right?" he asked.

"Not until Ivory's free."

Embarrassed by any show of emotion, and especially by one he considered inappropriate, Control moved to the door. "I don't doubt that you sincerely believe you love her, Drew, but you'll get over her. Believe me, once you put this regrettable interlude behind you, everything will work out for the best."

Drew did not dignify that patronizing remark with a response, and Control left without offering any more trite advice. Drew stretched out on the bed and, accepting the horror of a trial, searched his mind for a way to influence its outcome. Criminal cases at the Confederation base were decided by a panel of judges rather than a jury he might possibly sway with an impassioned plea on Ivory's behalf.

As a prosecution witness, however, everything he said would be used against her, and although he would word his answers carefully, he feared the prosecutor would twist each of his remarks into a condemnation. He couldn't simply refuse to testify without being cited for contempt, and then he would end up in the detention wing himself. He could see no possible benefit to Ivory in that. Fortunately, the judges were known to be fair, but with the amount of evidence that had been gathered at the Mine, Drew couldn't imagine Ivory and her father receiving anything less than life sentences.

The Confederation did not regard prostitution as a crime, and Summer Moon and her girls had all been released and transported to various colonies. He had heard that André, Maxwell, and several others whose only mistake was working for Spider had not been charged either. They too were gone. Stokes and Vik would go on trial though, as would a great many others involved in Spider's operation.

The pirates who had been caught at the Mine were awaiting prosecution. The trials would probably last months, if not years. Ivory and Spider were to be tried first. Drew took a deep breath and exhaled slowly. He had been counting on Ivory being treated as an obstreperous teenager, but that wasn't going to happen. She would have to stand trial, and there was no hope of an acquittal.

He hated the thought of her having to endure the monotony of the detention wing. The prospect of her spending the rest of her life in a prison colony was too great a tragedy to accept. While he trusted Gail Bolyn to do her best for Ivory, he couldn't leave the fate of the woman he loved in the attorney's hands. Sitting up, he knew it was time he took control of the situation.

With that decision came a sense of peace that had eluded him since Ivory's arrest. He left his room intent upon devising a plan to save her. First, he was going to find out if Nelson, who had been arrested with the other Corkscrews at the Mine to protect his cover, had been released. He would need an accomplice, and from the way Nelson had eyed Ivory at the Eagle's Nest, he was certain the little man would volunteer.

Just after one a.m., the sleepy guard on duty at the main gate of the detention wing was startled awake by a loud rattle as two members of the base's emergency medical team came running toward him pushing a gurney. They were a mismatched pair in size, one quite tall, the other not even medium height. They were dressed in the emergency team's baggy sky blue coveralls complete with hair-covering caps and surgical facemasks.

The guard hurriedly checked the report left by the day shift. "I don't have any notations of anyone being sick," he said. "Who called you?"

Drew slid a clipboard with what looked like an official transfer form through the narrow opening in the gate. "Ms. Bolyn says her client, a Ms. Diamond, has been coughing up blood. We should have been here hours ago, but someone misplaced the request for a transfer to the hospital. I sure hope she hasn't expired."

The guard went pale and immediately keyed in the code to slide open the gate. "Anything happens to her while she's in our custody and we'll never hear the end of it," he moaned. "She's in the women's wing. That's to your right at the end of this corridor." He scrawled his name at the bottom of the transfer order and handed it back to Drew.

Drew and Nelson nodded their thanks, and looking as though they were on a true emergency, rolled the gurney down the hall at a near run. They cleared the next checkpoint at the entrance of the women's wing with equal ease, but here there were two guards, and one walked with them down to Ivory's cell and stationed himself outside before the other typed in the code to open her door. Sweat dampened the edge of Nelson's cap, and he looked sick himself, but Drew projected the confident air of a seasoned medic.

He knew getting by the guards had been the easy part compared with winning Ivory's cooperation, but he hoped the element of surprise would work in his favor. The lights in the corridor only partially brightened the cell's dim interior, and the lack of illumination worked to his advantage as well.

"I know we're unforgivably late," he greeted her, "but Ms. Bolyn's request for medical treatment was mislaid."

Unable to sleep, Ivory had been pacing her cell in a bored stupor. She didn't recognize Drew until he grabbed her shoulders and forced her to sit down on her bunk. Amazed by his charade, she was too intrigued by where it might lead to protest. Instead, she leaned over to pick up her sketchbook in the hope that she would be leaving.

Drew knelt in front of her and grabbed her wrist. "I can barely find a pulse," he called over his shoulder, and Nelson began maneuvering the gurney to block the guard's view of the open cell.

"This is the only way I can save you," Drew whispered. "Don't fight me." Before Ivory could respond, he reached into his pocket and pulled out a vial of what looked like blood and splashed it on the front of her coveralls. "Oh my God," he shouted. "She's hemorrhaging!"

He scooped her up in his arms and carried her and her precious sketchbook out to the gurney. Nelson quickly affixed the straps to keep her from rolling off, and then they sprinted down the corridor, shoving their patient along at a frantic pace. The guard who'd accompanied them dashed along behind them until they reached his post, but then, winded, he remained in the women's wing.

The guard at the entrance of the detention center heard them coming and had the gate open for them. One glimpse of Ivory's bloody coveralls and he was terrified they had arrived too late. "Good luck!" he shouted as they ran by, then collapsed in his chair and prayed that Ivory Diamond hadn't died on his watch.

Drew and Nelson guided the gurney into the service elevator, but bypassed the hospital level and went on down to the docking bays. While Nelson kept the doors closed, Drew ripped off his disguise. He helped Ivory off the gurney, and then pulled an iridescent flight suit belonging to Alado's Expeditionary Force out from under the padded top.

"Here, put this on. I've already requested a launch time and we don't dare be late."

Ivory ripped the orange coveralls down the front in her haste to remove them. She shoved one leg into the flight suit and hopped up and down to pull it on. She had only the detention wing's soft slippers to wear rather than boots, but thought it a poor time to complain that her outfit wasn't complete.

"I still hate you," she gasped between hops.

"I know, but at least this way you'll be free to do it. Come on." Drew took her hand the instant she was dressed. They dashed out of the elevator, leaving behind a trembling Nelson, who was nearly an emergency case himself after what they had done.

Nelson's job was to return the gurney to the hospital level and throw their borrowed clothes and Ivory's coveralls down the chute for soiled linens. Nelson accomplished his mission in less than a minute, and then strolled into the base's main cafeteria, where he ordered a large dish of chocolate ice cream. As he ate it, he joked with the woman wiping off the tables, and went to bed confident he had a witness as to his whereabouts at that late hour should anyone ask.

Even after they had reached his ship, Drew didn't draw a deep breath until the bay doors began to roll open. Until then, he had been straining to hear the alarm sirens screaming throughout the base. "Come on, come on," he urged, and the instant the doors were fully withdrawn he eased his ship out, followed the prescribed route for departure, and successfully completed the only escape ever attempted from the heavily guarded detention center at the Confederation base.

Then he looked over at Ivory's sullen frown and knew this was when the real challenge began. "They won't know you're gone until tomorrow morning, and maybe not even then if no one from the detention center is conscientious enough to check with the hospital on your condition."

"You can't count on that," Ivory warned. "You mentioned Gail. Was she in on this?"

"No. She wouldn't have anything to do with me, and even if she had, I wouldn't have risked involving her."

"Then if the escape isn't discovered before tomorrow morning, it will be when she goes to visit me and I'm nowhere to be found."

Drew had overlooked that aspect. "That still gives us a good head start."

Ivory gripped her armrests. She was shaking all over and couldn't seem to stop. "Where are we going?"

"Earth, eventually."

"That's the first place they'll look for you."

"Don't you mean for us?"

Ivory closed her eyes and recalled in vivid detail what it had been like to wake up in a groggy haze with the phony Brother Samuel at the foot of her bed. She recalled with fresh pain the instant that she realized Chase Duncan had betrayed her. As she glanced toward him, she despised him with a virulent hatred that accented each of her words.

"You're forgetting that I know what you are, Drew, or whatever your name is. You're one of Alado's master spies, and your honey-sweet lies won't work on me ever again. I know why you arranged my escape. You must feel you've missed something, some vital bit of evidence that's more damning than what you already have. Well, the effort's bound to fail, because if I live to be one hundred, which is extremely doubtful, I'll never trust you again."

Drew could understand her anger, but he had to try to plow through it. "You're right about one thing. I was one of Alado's best agents, but not anymore. I just threw away my career, my reputation, and very possibly my life for you, and you think it's merely a trick to get a conviction? The Confederation has enough evidence to convict you ten times over. I'm as far from Alado as you are, Ivory, and if it takes me a lifetime to prove it, I will."

Ivory responded with a disgusted sneer. "Do you honestly expect me to believe you planned an escape on your own?"

"You know Nelson helped me."

"Why is he free, and why would he help you?"

Drew hated to admit the truth, but wouldn't tell her another lie. "He works for Alado. Being a Corkscrew is a useful cover."

Ivory swore under her breath. "The Mine was swarming with Alado's spies, wasn't it?"

"And pirates."

"At least pirates are honest about who they are!"

Drew knew he deserved that, but he was too tired to take any more abuse, earned or not. "Look, this isn't getting us anywhere. I've got your artwork in the hold, and some of your clothes in the main cabin. I didn't have time to forge any identification, but I know people who will supply it. I got you out of the detention center because it was either that or plan an escape from a prison colony. There was no way you were going to be acquitted. I had only one motive, and that was for us to be together."

"You should have saved yourself the trouble. I'd rather be in prison than with you. Chart a course for the frontier, any colony will do. We have contacts in all of them who'll hide me until the Confederation stops looking."

"I won't abandon you, Ivory. Haven't I already proved that?"

"All you've proved is that you're lower than an iguana's belly. Did you manage to get away with my cannon?"

Drew had handed over the evil weapon without a single regret. "No. It was designed to stop an alien invasion. It was never meant for use on men."

"How noble. God, this discussion is making me sick. I'm going to get some sleep." She left the cockpit and went back to the main cabin, but the last thing on her mind was rest. She searched the ship, looking for something, anything, to use to disable Drew. In the lavatory she found a compartment marked medical supplies and there among the antiseptics and antibiotics were several injection canisters of a powerful sedative meant to relieve an accident victim's pain.

Hoping two would be enough, she carried them back to the cockpit. She slid into her seat and smiled apologetically. "Whatever your reasons, I appreciate your helping me escape."

Inordinately pleased by that grudging bit of praise, Drew grinned. When Ivory leaned toward him, he was so eager to kiss her he did not stop to question the sudden change in her mood. Then when she slammed the injection canisters into his arm, it was too late. He stared at her wide-eyed, his last conscious thought one of bewildered rage.

"Now you know how it feels," Ivory taunted, "to be betrayed."

He was too heavy to move, so she had to leave him in the pilot's seat. She wasn't surprised that he had underestimated her. Knowing that the Confederation would misjudge her too, she sat back, thought of what her father would do, and then gave the navigational computer a change in course. Unlike Drew, she did not want to flee to Earth, but to remain close enough to the detention center to set her father free.

Control was awakened at 5:00 a.m. by Ian St. Ives with news of the escape. Incredulous at first, then sick clear through, he had a difficult time accepting the fact that Drew Jordan had turned outlaw and escaped with his pirate bride. "Yale warned me, you warned me," he mumbled as he rubbed the sleep from his eyes. "I saw for myself how depressed he was yesterday, but it never occurred to me that he would take matters into his own hands."

Ian leaned back against Control's door. "Somebody helped him, but the guards didn't get a good look at him."

"Was it you?"

"Hell, no, although I do admire him for pulling it off. If the guards hadn't been so worried about Ivory and called the hospital, we wouldn't have learned about the escape for hours. We've tracked Drew's ship. It appears he's heading back toward the Mine."

"That makes no sense."

"I know it doesn't, unless he knows there's something there we didn't find."

Still in his pajamas, Control sat down on the side of his bed. Miserable, he didn't relish what lay ahead. "I've never had to go after one of our own. Drew has to know where this will end."

"Well, apparently he'd rather die with Ivory Diamond than live with us."

"This was all my fault. He was tired, and I should have sent him on vacation rather than to The Diamond Mine."

"And who would you have sent after Spider? Me?"

Control looked up at the ruthless, amber-eyed agent and nodded. "Tell me. You've met Ivory Diamond. Would this case have ended the same way?"

Ian could not imagine throwing away his life for love. "No, sir. Give me the chance to bring Drew in, and I won't disappoint you."

Control wanted to get back in bed and pull the covers up over his head. Instead, he rose and gathered the resolve that had deserted him for a moment. "We will get him," he promised, "but I doubt he will be alive."

Drew awoke in a cage identical to the one in which he had spent his first night at the Mine, but this one was underground, in a vault like those in Spider's private bank. He tried to sit up, but his hands and feet were firmly secured to the metal bars, and he couldn't move. He still had on his clothes, but that was small consolation.

"Ivory!" he called, and his voice echoed off the

stone walls in an eerie wail. Fearing she had left him to die, he yelled her name again, and this time he heard a thudding footstep that only served to increase his dread.

It was a silver boy, holding a Celestial Cannon. Drew looked up at him and tried to smile. "Hello there. Untie me, and find me something to eat," he ordered in hopes the beautiful machine would respond, but it just looked at him. The fact that it resembled Spider made its glowing stare all the more ominous.

"Well, do you play word games or offer any amusements to help us pass the time?"

Again the robot remained silent.

Drew raised his head as best he could and looked around. All he saw were crates of the size used to hold Celestial Cannons. He had no doubt that was precisely what they contained. How many secret arsenals did Spider have? he wondered. Not that it mattered if he had been left to die in this one. Blinded by love, he hadn't considered Ivory a threat, but she had quickly proved how dangerous she was. He had not expected to live forever, but he had never envisioned a death as cruel as this.

Drew had been awake for perhaps an hour when Ivory appeared. She was still wearing the iridescent flight suit he had given her, but now had on a pair of her own silver boots. "You look uncomfortable," she said. "I apologize for the primitive conditions, but I wanted you to suffer as badly as I have."

"You've succeeded," Drew assured her. He knew better than to tease her, or try to make her laugh. He was too proud to beg to be set free. "I knew you might not want to stay with me, so I brought your diamonds. I didn't want you to have to worry about money. I love you, Ivory, though I can understand why you refuse to believe that."

"Can you really? I'm amazed."

"Where are we?"

"I don't see how our location is of any relevance to you."

"All right, then. What's for dinner?"

Ivory knelt beside him. "Don't worry, I'll keep you well fed. I intend to swap you for my father, so you're worth more to me alive and well than dead."

Drew had been frightened for himself when he had awakened, but now he was terrified for her. "The Confederation will never agree."

"They already have," Ivory informed him. "You've been asleep for two days. We've yet to work out the details, but I expect to reach an agreement soon."

Drew didn't see any way Ivory could survive a prisoner exchange. "It won't work," he told her. "They might agree to your demands, but it will be a trick. They'll have snipers, or an agent disguised to look like Spider, but they'll never let you and your father go free."

He wasn't telling her anything she did not know. "I've got nothing to lose, not one blasted thing. I can't see myself painting murals on prison walls for fifty years, and it doesn't seem fair to leave my father to stand trial alone now that you've set me free."

Flat on his back, Drew had to fight to remain calm enough to argue. "Why weren't you asleep when we came for you? Are you still having the same frightening dream? You thought it was a warning, but it wasn't about me, Ivory. It was about Spider. Push it to the end and you'll see."

Ivory rose to her feet. "The thought of cutting out your tongue is tempting, but I promised to return you in reasonably good condition. I'm going to untie you and let you out to use the lavatory, but Conrad here goes with you. You were right about our silver boys. They can do a lot more than lug crates and count money. Don't try to outsmart him. He has orders to aim for your knees, and even with his cannon set on low, you'd never walk again."

"Conrad," Drew called after her. "That's as bad as Rex!" But neither of them was laughing.

"Where did you get fresh food?" Drew took the plate Ivory slipped beneath the door of his cage and inhaled the luscious aromas. There was a thick slice of roast beef, boiled potatoes dusted with cheese, and a heap of bright green peas. Rather than give him a knife as well as a fork, she had cut the meat into bite-size pieces. It tasted every bit as good as it looked.

Ivory sat down on the floor cross-legged outside the cage. "We're on Fleur-de-lys. It's home to an agrarian colony that frequently needed loans for expansion. My father was extremely generous, and they were so grateful they did not question his constructing a small storage facility here."

Drew tried to remember where Fleur-de-lys was. As he recalled, the small planet was on the edge of the frontier. "We're close to the Mine, aren't we?"

"Perilously close, you might say, but that's the beauty of it. It's always been regarded as wholly innocent, while the Mine . . . well, you know what everyone thought of The Diamond Mine."

Drew felt as though he had not eaten in days, which was the truth. "Can you get more of this?" he asked before popping a hunk of potato into his mouth.

"You can't still be growing."

"No, I'm just hungry. Aren't you? You've lost weight, and that's not surprising when all you've had is jail food."

Ivory watched him eat, unable to remember when she had last been hungry. She knew what he was doing: behaving as though they were still lovers in an effort to lull her into a complacency he would swiftly use against her. Again. "Yes, I can get you seconds, but it will cost you something."

Drew surveyed the close confines of the cage. "It doesn't look as though I'm in a position to deny you anything."

"Good. I'm glad we finally understand each other."

Drew had been trained to handle all manner of desperate situations, but he'd not had one lesson on how to talk the woman he adored out of a suicide mission. He continued with an oblique approach. "My name's Andrew Jordan, but I've always gone by Drew. I'm from Vancouver. I'm a quarter Haida Indian, and I'm as at home in a forest as I am in a spaceship. I graduated from Alado's Flight Academy when I was twenty-one, flew until I got bored, and then joined the intelligence unit.

"I believe in peace, justice, freedom, and definitely equality. I believe in us too." He set his plate aside, reached into his shirt, and pulled out a gold chain. Dangling from it were her rings. "I want to marry you again. I'd expected a legal ceremony the first time, and I'm going to insist upon it when you marry me again."

Ivory picked a piece of straw off the bottom of her boot, and twirled it in her fingers. "You're absolutely amazing. You're so damn smooth the lies just gush out of you like bubbles from champagne. You've undoubtedly seduced women from one end of the galaxy to the other, but you ought to give me enough credit to know I won't fall for your line a second time."

Drew picked up his plate to finish his meal. "It was never a line with you."

"Why does that sound like an epitaph?"

"All right, so I've ruined everything between us," Drew finally admitted. "It hurts me as well as you, but I can't let you throw your life away in a hostage exchange that will only get you killed. Leave me here on Fleur-de-lys and save yourself, Ivory. Leave here now, while you still have a chance to get away. Your diamonds are behind the packaged rations in the emergency supplies. You can go a long way on what they'll bring."

Tossing away the straw, Ivory grabbed hold of the side of the cage to pull herself up. "Why did you rescue me?"

Drew set aside his now empty plate and stood to face her. "Because I had to!"

Ivory studied his expression, marveling again at how persuasive he was when she knew he could not possibly be sincere. "And I have to rescue my

411

father. Don't go away, I'll get you more food, but then you're going to do something for me."

She turned away, but Drew called after her. "Wait, what is it you want?"

Ivory came back and leaned against the cage. "We were too tired to do more than sleep the last night we were together, and I don't want to waste what may very well be my last chance to make love."

That she understood the tremendous risk she was taking broke Drew's heart. He wrapped his hands over hers. "Forget the food. Just let me out."

Ivory slipped out of his grasp. "Later. I still have a few more things to do. Conrad will keep you company until I get back."

Drew heard the robot move closer but kept his eyes on Ivory as she walked away. The iridescent flight suit flattered her slender figure beautifully, but her looks had never been the sole fascination for him. He was positive they had been born to be together, and if all he had was one night to convince her they ought never to part, then he must not fail.

Chapter Twenty-one

The underground compound was furnished as though Spider had never expected to use it. The cage was in the last of three rectangular rooms. The lavatory, a bed, table and chairs, and a rudimentary kitchen occupied the middle room, and the first was outfitted as a maintenance bay for emergency repairs for spacecraft. No attempt had been made to decorate the small apartment with the taste and style of the Mine. Drew had seen army barracks with more charm, but he doubted that Ivory had noticed, and the lack of ambience certainly didn't faze him.

The lavatory was small, and with Conrad blocking the door, Drew could scarcely turn around. He showered, shaved, and pulled on his pants, but didn't bother with anything more. "Let me by, Conrad. I need to speak with your mistress."

The robot stepped aside, but followed Drew as he approached the table where Ivory was seated. She was drawing in her sketchbook, and when Drew glanced over her shoulder he was surprised by the strange design filling the page. She had always had a flair for unusual combinations, but she had preferred representations of reality to the grim abstraction he saw now. The lines were jagged, dark, and to him deeply disturbing.

He took the chair beside hers and tapped the page. "Is this what the arrest did to you?"

Ivory dropped her pencil. She looked at him, her expression unbearably sad. "No, this is what you did to me."

Spider had deserved every bit of grief Drew had caused him, but to have extinguished the joyous flame of artistic talent that had burned so brightly within Ivory was a criminal act in itself. He left his chair and, taking her hands, drew her to her feet. He wrapped her in his arms and pressed her cheek against his bare shoulder.

Conrad raised his Celestial Cannon.

"I think you'd better tell your silver boy that what I'm doing isn't dangerous. He's getting nervous."

Ivory glanced over her shoulder. "I want you to guard the door, Conrad. I'll watch Drew; you just keep him from leaving."

Drew waited until Conrad had positioned himself in front of the door to the maintenance bay before he caressed Ivory's cheek. "Do you really think I'd leave you?"

Ivory slid her arms around his waist and laid her hands against his bare back. His skin held the same delicious allure it always had, but she had not forgotten how badly he had wronged her. "I've no idea what you might do, but I need you for the exchange, so I can't let you go."

Drew cupped her dear face between his hands. "Is that the only reason you need me?" He watched the tears well up in her eyes, and then dried her lashes with tender kisses. He pushed all thought of her desperate scheme from his mind and gloried in the joy of holding her in his arms. He could not bear to think she might not be with him forever. She had told him once that all the great love stories were tragedies, but he refused to let theirs have a tragic ending.

He led her to the bed and removed her flight suit with graceful tugs. She had on lavender lingerie, and that came off much more easily. He ran his thumbs down her ribs, sorry to find her so much thinner. She was lovely still, but now possessed an almost ethereal glow that reminded him of the angel portrait of her mother. Who would paint Ivory? he wondered, and knew that if he did not find a way to save her, no one would.

He ran his hands up her arms, touching her so lightly the pads of his fingers whispered against her skin like a gentle breeze. He traced the curve of her throat, the hollow of her shoulder, then ran his hands down her back and over her hips. He wanted to memorize every delectable inch of the woman he loved as though this were the first time they were ever together, rather than the last.

She leaned against him, silently encouraging his lazy exploration until her need for him became too great for touch alone to satisfy. She raised her lips to his, drawing him into a kiss so filled with desire that neither could bear to bring it to an end. Hungry for the taste of her, Drew yanked off his pants without breaking away, and then lifted her onto the bed where they continued to savor the lingering kiss as though it were all they would ever share.

At last he moved over her, caressing her with his whole body, teasing her gently with the tip of his manhood, separating the tender lips that veiled her feminine core. He did not enter her yet, but instead slid over her, slowly coaxing forth the first flutterings of rapture. She called his name in a breathless whisper, and he was thrilled she had used the right one.

Even knowing how badly she wanted him, he entered her with only a shallow thrust and then quickly withdrew. He repeated the pattern, seeking a brief burst of her warmth and then retreating until he ached to pierce her more fully. She clung to him, drawing him down ever deeper, making their erotic dance hers as well as his. Lost in her fiery embrace, Drew knew that the madness of loving her was his destiny, and he gladly surrendered his very soul.

Ivory doubted that Drew's lovemaking was motivated by anything more than a desire for pleasure, but she closed her eyes, wanting him to again be the man she had loved. He had once been so precious to her, and she wanted the love they had shared so briefly to live again now and remain in her heart forever. She welcomed his fevered kisses, and slid her fingers through the inky blackness of his hair, likening him again to Raven who flew across his back.

She soared aloft with him, fighting to make the ecstasy last until she drew her final breath, but all too soon the glorious sensation reached its crest and began to subside, leaving her adrift in passion's wake, lost and alone. Her love had been real, even if his never had, but she said the words in the silence of her mind, not to him.

Drew shifted his position to spare her his weight, then kept her cradled in his arms. "Go to sleep," he whispered, "and this time, finish the dream."

Too relaxed to argue, Ivory closed her eyes. When the dream came, it unfolded with brilliant clarity. She and her mother were dancing, their arms raised, their steps light, the music an enchanting tune. She stirred slightly in her sleep as the shadow appeared, darkening the room. It spread over them with an evil chill, and she hid behind her mother's brightly colored skirt.

This was the point where fear had always intervened, but she had survived too much of late to give in to shadows now. She peered around her mother to see who had ruined their game, and found her father, his face contorted with rage. "You'll never leave me," he screamed, "nor take my beautiful daughter away."

He struck Willow, then grabbed her throat, and, terrified, Ivory ran to the door. She darted through it and, muffling her cries with her hands, turned to watch. There, right in front of her, her father choked the last breath of life from her mother. He cast her limp body aside and strode from the room without ever looking Ivory's way. She ran to hide, desperate to forget the horror she had witnessed.

Cinnamon Burke

When Drew awakened, Ivory was gone. Disappointed, he sat up slowly. He would never forget last night, but obviously it had not been enough to distract her from her disastrous course of action. He looked around for Conrad, but the robot wasn't in the room.

Suddenly terrified that Ivory might have left him, he scrambled out of bed and pulled on his pants. She had said she needed him for the exchange, but what if all he had done last night was to convince her to leave him behind? "Ivory!" he yelled, and he ran to the door to the maintenance bay. It was unlocked, and after making another quick check to be certain Conrad wasn't standing guard, he sprinted through the bay to the outer doors. They were partially open, allowing the light of a new day to stream across the floor.

"Ivory!" he screamed as he barreled through the door, but blinded by the bright sunlight, he couldn't see a thing once he got outside.

"I'm right here." Ivory touched his arm. "It's early yet. The exchange isn't set for another hour."

Drew looked down at the ground until his eyes adjusted to the brightness of the day. Then he found that the compound was built into the side of a gently sloping hill, and they were surrounded by miles of newly plowed fields. The soil here on Fleur-de-lys was a strange grayish green. There was a house in the distance, a low, domed structure, and he supposed that whoever lived there had provided his dinner. His ship was no more than twenty feet away, and ready for launch, facing out toward the barren fields. Conrad was standing by the open hatch.

"An hour's enough time to get away," he urged. "Let's go."

"No. I've got to stay. Don't worry, I'm going to have Conrad serve as your guard. He'll remain with you until my father and I get away. I'm sorry about your ship. I'll try to leave it somewhere for you."

Drew rested his hands on his hips. "I don't give a damn about losing the ship. You're all I care about. Must you go through with this?"

Ivory looked away. "Yes. This is how it has to end, Drew. Don't try to stop me."

She looked different this morning. The sadness that had filled her eyes last night had been replaced with a determined glow. Dressed in one of her favorite silver flight suits, rather than the figure-hugging Rocketball suit she had worn to enhance her power, she still looked tough enough to take on any opponent and win.

"Do you know what *kamikazes* are?"

A slight smile played across Ivory's lips. "Yes, they were Japanese pilots who flew suicide missions in World War II back in the twentieth century. Is that what you think I'm about to do?"

"Yes, but I don't want to stand around and watch with Conrad. If you're actually going to try to go through with an exchange, then let me help you, because neither Alado nor the Confederation will follow through on any promise they've made. Oh, they'll go far enough to make it look as though they will, but the instant they get a clear shot, they'll kill both you and your father."

Ivory couldn't help but laugh. "Are you saying they have no honor?"

Drew looked down at his feet. It had been a long time since he had gone barefoot in dirt, and despite its peculiar shade, its gritty warmth felt good. "No. Honor is important to them, but when dealing with pirates they'll do whatever they must to seize the advantage. They won't have me on their side today though; you will."

"You've just warned me Alado will do whatever they must to win, so I'd be a fool not to assume that anything you tell me will be another clever lie."

Drew swore a bitter oath. "I left Alado when I rescued you. Actually, I'd already decided to resign. After falling in love with you, I couldn't work undercover again."

Ivory again found it impossible to meet his intense gaze. "You sound just the same as you always have," she said. "You were lying before, and I can't trust you now. Just do as I say and you'll come out alive."

"It's not me I'm worried about!"

"I'm touched, but it's too late for any show of devotion. You'd better get dressed. The exchange is scheduled to take place here, and I want you to be ready."

A look at the determined set of her chin convinced Drew he was wasting his breath and he ceased arguing with her. "Can Conrad walk on the dirt without jamming all his gears?"

"Come here please, Conrad," Ivory called to him, and the gleaming silver robot walked over to her with as smooth a stride as he had used indoors. "You see? He can dance in snow if he has to. There will be no problems with him."

"Well, he'll be the only thing you can count on. I don't like being here by this hill. They can send snipers up behind us here."

"That's unlikely. The hillside is covered with the indigenous equivalent of cactus. Conrad could walk through it, but the Confederation doesn't have anything like him yet, do they?"

Drew's scowl darkened. "Not yet they don't." Still anxious to protect her, he went back inside and dressed hurriedly. As he walked back through the maintenance bay, he considered picking up a handy tool and knocking Ivory out with it, but he doubted he could make Conrad understand he had done it for her own good before the robot fired his Celestial Cannon. His knees ached just thinking about it.

Rejoining Ivory, he made another attempt to encourage her to confide in him. "What did you demand?"

"Nothing complicated, just that a single pilot fly my father here in a shuttle. There's to be no one else. As soon as my father is comfortably seated in your ship, I'll set you free. We'll depart, and you can do as you please."

"There are sure to be snipers hidden in the shuttle."

"If anyone other than my father appears, Conrad will start firing. I don't want a bloody massacre, just a simple, peaceful exchange."

"Right."

It was plain he wasn't pleased with her plan, but Ivory didn't care. She walked over to his ship and withdrew one of the Celestial Cannons she had assembled while he had been in the cage.

There was another on board the ship, but she wouldn't need it unless something went wrong.

"The first time I saw you, I knew there was definitely something special about you," she told him as she walked back toward him. "It wasn't just your looks. It was your smile, the way you moved, your confidence, I suppose. I was pathetically easy prey for you, wasn't I?"

"I don't think this is a conversation we ought to have with you holding a cannon," Drew replied. "I've told you before, and I'll swear it again, my feelings for you are real and they always have been. I'm not like Conrad here. I can't be sent out on jobs and not have what I do affect my emotions."

Ivory knew that everything would be so much easier if she could believe him, but she didn't. She looked up, scanning the sky, and saw a tiny dark speck against the clouds. "Here comes the shuttle. I suppose I ought to have some parting words prepared, but I'll have to settle for good-bye."

"I won't. I hope you manage to pull this off and get away clean. As for me, I'll probably go to prison for arranging your escape. I shouldn't have to serve more than five years or so, and then I'll do my best to find you. I'll bring the rings."

More lies, Ivory told herself. "You're breaking my heart," she said sarcastically.

"You've already broken mine."

Ivory pointed her Celestial Cannon at his chest. "Stand over there by Conrad. If there is going to be any shooting, I don't want you in the line of fire."

Drew couldn't stifle a grin as he started to back away. "Why is that? Is it possible you still have feelings for me?"

"Does revulsion count?"

"No!" Drew walked over to Conrad. "We're on the same team now, buddy. Try to remember that." As usual, Conrad was unimpressed. They were standing to the left of the open bay, perhaps fifty feet from his ship. He watched, his apprehension mounting, as the shuttle settled in for a perfect landing on the freshly tilled soil, and he had to fight off the wave of dread curling through his insides.

The hatch opened, and the pilot came down the steps first. He was wearing a helmet with the visor down, and Drew doubted that Ivory would recognize him, but he did. It was Ian St. Ives.

"Are you all right?" Ian called in a voice disguised by a thick accent.

"I've been better," Drew shouted back. "It's a trap," he whispered loudly enough for only Conrad and Ivory to hear.

"Yes, I know," she assured him in an equally hushed voice. She called to the pilot, "Send my father over, and then you can have Drew."

Ian waved and reentered the shuttle. In a moment, he brought Spider down the ramp, and then removed the pirate's handcuffs. He tapped him on the shoulder, and Spider started walking toward Ivory.

"Keep your eye on the pilot!" Drew called to her.

Ivory took a step forward. Her father was smiling, clearly relieved to be free. She waited until he was only twenty feet away. "Stop there," she ordered, "and tell me what really happened to Mama."

Spider kept on walking. "I'll tell you as soon as we're in the air."

Ivory fired a short burst across the dirt where he would have placed his next step. "No! Tell me now."

A look of horrified disbelief filled Spider's eyes. "You know what happened. She had a weak heart, and hid it from us. Her death came as a terrible shock to me, to us both."

Ivory took another step toward him. "You're lying. She wanted to take me and leave you. Isn't that what really happened?"

Drew had no idea what Ivory was getting at, but he gestured for Ian to back off. He was positive there were others in the shuttle about to leap out and start firing, and he couldn't just stand there and watch. He started moving toward Ivory; Conrad, trampling the dirt, came too.

Also suspecting a trick, Spider glanced back over his shoulder to make certain the pilot hadn't moved. "All couples have arguments, baby, and your mother and I had more than most, but I loved her, and I would never have let her go. Now come on, it's not safe for us here."

"It wasn't safe for my mother at the Mine, was it?"

"She's dead, and we will be too if we don't get out of here!" Spider tried to take another step toward her, but again Ivory fired across his path.

"I saw you kill her," she revealed. "I was too little to do anything more than run and hide, but I'm not too little now."

With sudden terrible insight, Drew understood what Ivory was doing. She didn't care if the Confederation had laid a trap for her; she had already laid one for her father. "Ivory!" he screamed. "Shoot him and leave!"

She turned toward Drew, aiming at his chest just as he had once imagined. Their eyes met, and in a split second he saw her confusion, but he knew she would never fire at him. Out of the corner of his eye, he saw Ian drop to one knee and reach for the laser pistol hidden under the back of his jacket.

"Get down!" Drew yelled, and he started running toward Ivory. He raced toward her, his boots digging into the gray-green soil, but he knew he would never reach her in time.

Conrad started firing, but at Ian, rather than Drew. Ivory turned back toward her father, ready to carry out the grim revenge she had been plotting since dawn, but seeing the fury in her eyes, Spider made a dash for the open hatch of Drew's ship. Hearing Conrad fire, three men came tumbling out the back of Ian's shuttle and, kneeling behind him, joined in the battle. All four aimed for Spider, and as they fired, the fleeing pirate's blood sprayed across Ivory. Knowing she would be next, Drew went for her with a wild, flying leap and knocked her to the ground.

Shielding her with his body, Drew wrenched the Celestial Cannon from her hand and tossed it away, but the firing continued as Conrad fought on. He wounded one of the agents and then another, and since Ivory had reprogrammed him to guard Drew, he kept moving closer. Every step increased the danger to the pair huddled on the ground by drawing fire toward them.

Drew was wrapped so tightly around Ivory that she felt each ragged breath he took. Her face pressed against his chest, she could feel his heart pounding against her cheek. He had sworn that he loved her, and proved it in many ways, but she had been too badly hurt to believe he was sincere. Now with laser fire scorching the air all around them, and choking on coarse green dust, she finally saw him clearly and knew that only a man who loved her would risk his life to save hers. That it was too late to matter broke all that was left of her heart.

She placed her hands over his and, expecting them both to die in a matter of seconds, wished she had thanked him for loving her. A laser blast tore the heel off her boot. She felt Drew flinch, and feared he had been hit with more than a glancing shot. He had promised a return to paradise, but she knew he had not meant in the here-after.

Using the shuttle ramp as a shield, Ian took careful aim, fired, and finally succeeded in ripping apart the Celestial Cannon and knocking it from Conrad's grasp. Not programmed for hand-to-hand combat, the robot dropped its arms to its sides and stood at attention awaiting Ivory's next command.

Ian waited to make certain the robot wasn't going to produce another weapon before he came out from behind the ramp. He knelt beside Yale Lincoln, who had been hit in the leg, as had the other injured agent. He left the casualties to the other uninjured agent and then, leaving his laser pistol primed to fire, started toward the pair in the dirt.

"Drew? Are you hit?" he called.

"Play dead," Drew whispered to Ivory. "I don't care if you don't trust me, just do it!" When she went limp, he staggered to his feet, but remained where he would block Ian's view of her. Only Spider's blood, not hers, stained her flight suit, but he prayed Ian wouldn't realize that.

Covered with dirt, and hoping to look distraught, Drew ran his hands through his hair, tangling it with his fingers. "You killed her!" he screamed. "You rotten bastards killed her!"

Not about to fight Drew when he was crazed with grief, Ian halted ten feet away. "Control, we need you out here!" he yelled.

Hiding in the rear of the shuttle, Control peeked out the hatch. After he had satisfied himself that the battle was over and that his side had won, he came down the ramp. He stopped to speak with the injured men, was relieved to find their wounds minor, and then walked up to Ian. One look at Drew's anguished expression was enough to make him halt.

"You were a fine agent," he told him. "With Spider and his daughter dead, I can see no purpose in prosecuting you for her escape, and I'll use my influence to make the authorities drop all charges. I'm placing you on permanent leave. Go home and rest. In time today's bloody horror will all be a merciful blur, and you'll find a new life for yourself. We all wish you good luck."

Disconsolate, Drew shook his head. "I'll have no life without my wife." He bent down and scooped Ivory into his arms. His tears spashed on her face, and her head rolled off his shoulder, dropped back, and dangled at a lifeless angle. "It was Spider she meant to kill, not any of you. I'm going to bury her at home, where she belongs. You owe me that much, Control. You owe me my wife's body."

Without waiting for permission, Drew carried Ivory to his ship and up the ramp. Once inside, he quickly laid her in a seat and shut the hatch. As he glanced around the cockpit, he saw a silver boy waiting just out of sight of Control and his men, holding a Celestial Cannon. "Oh my God," he cried. "Call off that thing before he starts firing!"

"I'm dead," Ivory reminded him. "I can't do anything."

"Oh, hell." Drew sat down at the controls and fired his ship's engines. He looked out and saw Control and Ian staring up at them, but he didn't wave. He eased the ship off the ground and guided it away from the shuttle before launching it on a course he set for Earth. He watched Fleur-de-lys fade into a gray haze before he went back to the main cabin. Ivory had removed the Celestial Cannon from the silver boy's hand, for which he was extremely grateful.

He sank down into the seat beside hers. They were both covered with green dust, but neither cared. "I realized when I fell in love with you that we'd never have what is generally considered a 'normal' life, but I don't know how many times I can keep on rescuing you and survive."

Ivory was a disheveled mess, but her smile lit her whole face. "I love you, Drew Jordan, and I don't want to risk losing you ever again. May I have my rings back, please? Surely what we just survived makes us husband and wife."

Drew produced the rings before she could change her mind. His hand shook as he placed them on her finger, but there was nothing tentative about his kiss. There would be time later to ask her if she had seen Spider kill her mother in her dream, but for now he wanted to concentrate on their future. He nodded toward the silver boy. "What's his name?"

"Orpheus, and he's so well mannered he'll make a perfect pet, or bodyguard in case Alado comes after us."

"They won't. I'll bury an empty coffin in Vancouver and put your name on the headstone. We'll create a new identity for you. Who would you like to be?"

"Other than Mrs. Jordan?"

"Yes. I can't very well introduce you to my parents with no first name."

"Hmm." Ivory closed her eyes and thought a moment. "Dawn, that's good for a new beginning."

"Yes, Dawn Jordan sounds perfect. Now, I want to build us a house in the woods where you can paint and I can hunt and fish. Our most exciting adventures will take place in our bedroom. I've retired, Dawn." He brought her dusty palm to his lips, then winked as he looked up at her. "But I promise you'll never get bored."

Ivory reached out to caress his cheek. "I won't live that long."

"Please. I want you to live forever. Say, how old are you?"

Ivory laughed. "Does it matter?"

Cinnamon Burke

"Yeah, it matters. I don't want any secrets between us ever again."

Ivory took a deep breath and savored that delicious thought. "Yes, I agree with you. I'll be nineteen on June eleventh, but I feel about ninety. Do you think that's too old for motherhood?"

Drew stared at her, and when she started to laugh, he knew she wasn't teasing. He was appalled. "What was your real plan this morning? Did you expect to blast your father to hell and then fly off to raise our child alone?"

Ivory twisted her rings. She had missed seeing them on her hand. "I'm sorry, but I'd misjudged you, and I didn't think we had any hope for a future."

"But now you do?"

Ivory began her answer with a lingering kiss. "Yes. When you knocked me into the dirt I finally understood there wasn't any limit to your love. I just hope I won't have to make such a dramatic demonstration of mine."

"Come here," Drew breathed against her cheek, and Ivory relaxed in his arms. They were trembling with excitement now, each so grateful the other was alive that nothing else mattered. It was a very long way to Earth, but as Ivory had once predicted, they had a marvelous time getting there.

Epilogue

Spring, 2261

Ivory glanced from her easel out toward the roiling waters of the Pacific Ocean. She'd not had an opportunity to paint seascapes until Drew had brought her to the Queen Charlotte Islands to live, but she found portraying the sunlight and shadow skipping over the waves an endlessly fascinating challenge. She had painted the view from their living room window at every hour between the silvery dawn and violet-hued dusk, and had yet to feel she had successfully captured the incomparable beauty of the sea.

There were many subtle color variations in the greens, blues, and grays, and at that hour of the afternoon the water shimmered with a bright golden glow. Concentrating on a spray of lacy foam, Ivory frowned slightly and again looked out

431

to study her obstreperous subject, who would not for a second hold still. What she saw this time frightened her so badly she dropped her brush.

"There's a hovercraft landing on the beach," she cried.

Drew shifted their sleeping daughter in his arms and crossed to the windows spanning the front of the stone house. The glass provided not only a magnificent view, but a ready means to assess the danger should an uninvited visitor approach. "It's Control. Do you suppose he's come to offer me an assignment?"

Ivory knelt to retrieve her brush and wiped the paint smear off the oak floor. "This is no time for humor." She rose, laid the rag and brush aside, and went to him. "Here, give me the baby."

Drew kissed them both as they made the exchange. With his black hair and Ivory's blue eyes and peach-toned skin, Star was an adorable infant. She was the only baby Drew had ever held, but he never tired of looking after her while her mother pursued her art.

"I'll go down and meet him," he said. "You needn't worry; I'll not invite him in."

Ivory pressed her daughter to her breast. "Isn't it worry enough that he's here?"

Drew brushed her lips again with a silent promise that she need have no fears while he was alive to protect her. Since leaving Fleur-de-lys, they had spent so few moments apart that even a brief walk down to the beach struck him as a deprivation. He waved to Control as he hurried down the long flight of stairs leading to the shore.

Relieved not to have to climb the stairs, his former boss sat down on a bench built into a curve and waited for him.

Drew was dressed in the gray clothes he had worn as one of Alado's top pilots, but he'd not cut his hair and it brushed his shoulders in thick, black waves. "I must say you're looking relaxed and fit," Control greeted him.

As always, Control was wearing a severely tailored black suit. In the years Drew had known him, he had not aged, nor mellowed, and Drew knew this could not possibly be a social call. "Thank you. I wish I could say the same for you."

Control let the comment slide. "I admire you enormously, Drew. It takes great flair to hide in plain sight, and you've carried it off with a verve few men would even attempt."

Drew rested his elbows on the stone wall bordering the steps and stared out at the sea. "I'm not trying to hide."

"No, of course not," Control scoffed. "I was very moved when you left Fleur-de-lys with Ivory Diamond's body in your arms. I can imagine no greater tragedy than watching the woman you love die such a violent death. I would have been deeply saddened, although not surprised, had you taken your own life. But when you married almost immediately, and then you and your bride produced a daughter in only seven months, I was absolutely astonished."

"Love is a powerful tonic for grief," Drew advised.

"Oh yes, if you're an example, it certainly is. But as you may suspect, I'm the curious sort, and I was especially curious about your bride. I want to compliment you again, Drew. You used our own techniques to embed her history in our files, but being a tenacious individual, I conducted such a diligent search I eventually found the truth."

Drew refused to admit a thing. Instead, he inhaled the salty breeze. "I can't tell you how much I enjoy air you can feel and taste, rather than the anonymous vapor Alado pipes through its ships. This is a glorious day. Now, why don't you stop wasting it and tell me why you're really here."

A sea gull swooping low over the waves caught Control's attention for a moment, but then he gave Drew an honest reply. "My wife and I weren't blessed with children, and while this will undoubtedly surprise you, I like to think of my agents as the offspring we didn't have. I'm fond of them all, but I always had a special fondness for you."

Amazed by the completely unexpected revelation, Drew turned back toward Control. "I'm honored, but what is it you want?"

Control responded with an innocent shrug. "I can understand why you suspect I have an ulterior motive, but my visit today is of an entirely personal nature."

Drew regarded the spymaster with a skeptical gaze. Did anyone ever get the truth out of a spy? he wondered. "Well, if you came simply to find out how I was doing, as you can see, I'm doing quite well, so I won't keep you."

"Actually, I do have a couple of questions."

"Finally. What are they?"

"First, let me assure you that I've not shared

my suspicions as to your bride's background with anyone. As far as I'm concerned, Ivory Diamond was killed along with Spider when her attempt to force us to release him in exchange for you ended in a regrettable slaughter. I would like to know, however, how she discovered that Spider had killed her mother. I was unable to find a single witness who could corroborate the story, but clearly she was prepared to execute him for the crime."

"Ivory's dead," Drew stubbornly maintained.

"Yes, of course, she is."

"So naturally this is a painful subject."

"I apologize for that."

Positive that if Control had wanted Ivory, he would have come after her with another canister of Sweet Dreams, Drew decided to trust him. "When we tried to plan a honeymoon, Spider refused to allow us to leave the Mine. Apparently that triggered long-suppressed memories that seeped into Ivory's dreams. It wasn't until the morning of the exchange that she finally remembered the murder, but when she did, well, she felt compelled to avenge her mother's death.

"She and her father had always been close, but once she recalled the circumstances of her mother's death, she finally saw him for the heartless pirate he was, and the bond between them was broken. Ian killed him, but only because they beat her to it. Had she survived," he added, "she would not have grieved for him."

"I visited her grave, and I was particularly impressed by the magnificent marble angel. It reminded me of the painting I'd seen in Ivory's bedroom."

"Yes. It was carved with the painting as a guide. I thought it a fitting tribute."

"Indeed." Control stood and reached into his coat pocket. "I took the liberty of having a new birth certificate and passport made for Dawn. While I was positive the documents you'd secured for her were of excellent quality, these are authentic."

Drew took the package Control handed him, but didn't open it. "You're a better man than I'd realized. Thank you."

Control gave a self-conscious nod. "I'll have to retire one day. May I suggest you as my successor? Frankly, I can't imagine anyone being more adept at working both sides of the law, and that's precisely what the job requires. Too many fail to realize that."

"I'm flattered, but no. With what Alado paid me, I'll never have to work again, and I'm content as I am."

Frowning with disappointment, Control extended his hand. "This is good-bye then." He shook hands with Drew, took a step away, and then turned back. "Oh yes, there is just one other thing."

Fearing that Control was about to force him to perform one last assignment in exchange for guarding Ivory's identity, Drew held his breath. "Yes, what is it?"

"Spider's technicians built silver boys in groups of five. Counting the one we recovered on Fleur-de-lys, we have eighty-four. That means one is still missing. Do you know where it is?"

Drew broke into a wicked grin. "I might, but you don't really expect me to tell you, do you?"

Control pursed his lips thoughtfully. "I suppose wherever he is, he's been programmed to do routine household chores rather than military assaults?"

"I imagine so."

"Good. Well, you know where I'll be should you ever need me."

Drew could not imagine such a circumstance. "Yes, sir, I appreciate your concern, but we'll all be fine." He waited on the steps until Control's hovercraft had moved out over the waves before returning to the house.

Star was awake and, unlike her mother, was giggling happily. "What did he want?" Ivory asked.

Drew dropped the documents in Ivory's lap and sat down beside her on the comfortable sofa in front of the massive stone fireplace where the three of them frequently cuddled together. "He wanted several things, actually. He definitely wanted me to know how clever he is. He traced the trail we created for you, but promised to keep our secret."

"Can we trust him?"

"Yes. It seems he thinks of me as a son, and he's rather proud that I've used what he taught me to our advantage. He did offer me a job, as his successor, but I told him I wasn't interested."

Expecting a threat to their blissful existence, Ivory was very pleasantly surprised. "Are you sure? Running Alado's intelligence unit would never be dull."

Drew took Star from Ivory's arms and held her aloft. The baby laughed and waved her arms in an attempt to touch his hair. "It wouldn't be nearly as much fun as this. Besides, there are too many places we want to go, scenes you want to paint, artists we've yet to meet. No, we're much too busy for me to wrangle spies."

"I don't know," Ivory argued. "There's a certain beauty to the thought of your seeking out master criminals with me at your side."

"Yes, it does have a diabolical appeal, but you've retired. Oh yes, Control says there's a missing silver boy, and I do believe he strongly suspects we have it."

"He didn't ask about the cannon?"

"No, why?"

Ivory snuggled down against him and placed a kiss in Star's hand. "They aren't that difficult to manufacture, and we know there's a ready market for them in the colonies."

"Ivory Diamond, you stop that this instant!"

"I'm Dawn Jordan, remember?" Ivory loved teasing him and erased his frown with an enthusiastic kiss. "I know. I'm strictly an artist now. You've taught me that honesty is best, but please forgive me if I slip occasionally. After all, the pirate's life is in my blood."

"And you're in mine," Drew swore. "Isn't it time for Star's nap?"

"No, she just woke up." Ivory rested her head on his shoulder. "What are we going to tell her, Drew? Are we going to repeat the same fable we put in Alado's files to explain my heritage?"

Drew laid Star on his lap and the little girl yawned widely. "She's going to be a very beautiful woman, and if she's anything like you, she'll discover her own truth about the past."

Ivory gazed into the blue eyes that matched her own. "It's only the future that counts now."

"No, it's the present, and we already have the best of all possible lives."

"Almost," Ivory replied in a sultry purr. She leaned back to look up at him. At her insistence, he had finally had the scars that her nails had left removed from his cheek, and she thought him more handsome every day.

"What you do mean, 'almost'?"

"I still wish you'd pose for me."

Drew shook his head, and then considered her request more seriously. Really, he had nothing to lose. After all, the worst that could happen when he stripped off his clothes was that they would end up making love. He could envision his portrait, and the reason it was never completed, being discussed by art historians for generations to come.

"All right, tomorrow when Star takes her nap, let's give it a try."

"Do you mean it?"

"Of course. Would I lie?"

"Yes!" Ivory exclaimed, but they both knew that only the truth existed between them now, and a love beyond their wildest dreams.

Futuristic Romance

Love in another time, another place.

New York *Times* Bestselling Author
Phoebe Conn writing as Cinnamon Burke!

Dedicated to preserving the old ways, Tynan Thorn has led the austere life of a recluse. He has never even laid eyes on a woman until the ravishing Amara sweeps into his spartan bedroom to change his life forever. Master of self-denial and mistress of sensual delight, Tynan and Amara are a study in contrasts. But as their bodies unite in explosive ecstasy they discover a whole new world, where together they can soar among the stars.

_3470-0 $5.99 US/$6.99 CAN

LOVE SPELL

THE MAGIC OF ROMANCE
PAST, PRESENT, AND FUTURE....

Dorchester Publishing Co., Inc., the leader in romantic fiction, is pleased to unveil its newest line—Love Spell. Every month, beginning in August 1993, Love Spell will publish one book in each of four categories:

1) *Timeswept Romance*—Modern-day heroines travel to the past to find the men who fulfill their hearts' desires.

2) *Futuristic Romance*—Love on distant worlds where passion is the lifeblood of every man and woman.

3) *Historical Romance*—Full of desire, adventure and intrigue, these stories will thrill readers everywhere.

4) *Contemporary Romance*—With novels by Lori Copeland, Heather Graham, and Jayne Ann Krentz, Love Spell's line of contemporary romance is first-rate.

Exploding with soaring passion and fiery sensuality, Love Spell romances are destined to take you to dazzling new heights of ecstasy.